Braided Dimensions

Book 1

A Novel

Marie Judson

Braided Dimensions: A Novel
© First edition 2018 by Marie Judson
© Second edition 2024 by Marie Judson

Contact the author for information:
www.mariejudson.com

ISBN: 978-1-64456-693-0 (Paperback)
ISBN: 978-1-64456-694-7 (Mobi)
ISBN: 978-1-64456-695-4 (ePub)
ISBN: 978-1-64456-696-1 (Audiobook)

Library of Congress Control Number: 2023952029

Printed in the United States of America

Cover design by Tatiana Viva
Formatted by The Book Khaleesi

INDIES UNITED PUBLISHING HOUSE, LLC
P.O. BOX 3071
QUINCY, IL 62305-3071
www.indiesunited.net

Books by Marie Judson

Braided Dimensions Series

Braided Dimensions: Book 1
Stretched Across Time: Book 2
Strange Alliances: Book 3
Pasts Undone: Book 4

Lost Xentu Series

Elf Stone of the Neyna: Book 1
A Far Cry; Book 2

Acknowledgements

With gratitude to the following for inspiration, valuable insights, and writerly camaraderie: A special appreciation to my earliest inception of this first book in the series, my earliest writing groups: Katy Pye, Fran Schwartz, Norma Watkins, Molly Dwyer, Laurel DawnFalcon Gates. To the next iteration: Skye Blaine, Patrice Garrett, Laura McHale Holland, Robbi Bryant.

A special thanks to my daughter, Piper Rosier, whose close reading and unrelenting demands were indispensable.

And to my son, Soren Rosier, for believing in me.

Chapter 1

I t was dark when Kay locked her front door and stepped onto the walkway. Trick-or-treaters filled the street. A twinge of guilt flitted through her for not sticking around to provide goodies to the Spider-Men and princesses as she scuffed down the block in the oversized footwear of her monk costume.

Franklin Street Café had a lively crowd bathed in the lurid orange glow of gauze-covered lights. A projector flashed images of old Celtic stones onto the wall. A fabric forest hung across the entrance to the next room, the air permeated by yeasty aromas of pizza crust and ale. Shouts of conversations battled to be heard over haunting music and the clatter of dishes.

Where were the nyads and faeries? In place of the figures of enchantment in the email invitation, Kay saw a faux belly dancer who never should have revealed her midriff, and men dressed in bathrobes and tennis shoes attempting, she supposed, to convey Druidic high priests. With absurd disappointment at seeing no apparent magic, she thought she wouldn't stay long. Then her attention was drawn by a hand-printed sign offering homemade organic mead, and pressed through to the bar. A young waitress, her peachy complexion disturbingly pierced with lead posts, asked for her order.

"Could I taste the Moonlight Mead?" she requested.

"Certainly." The young woman behind the bar handed over a sample.

Pushing aside glued-on mustache hairs, Kay sipped the tasty brew, then ordered a twelve-ounce, and again surveyed the crowd. She considered making the glass of mead a solo act when she noticed a birdlike creature, tall and hunched like a heron, tattered feathers splaying from head and neck. It stalked, with wild-bird grace, across the projection of ancient stones, through the cloth trees, into the next room. Kay's drink arrived, and she followed the strange apparition.

Trying not to jostle her glass, she squeezed through the throng and entered the connecting room where a wolf-man and his compatriots played a noisy dice-and-cup game amid appetizing pizza smells. Masked and painted faces, magnified by skull lights on tables, could have made a surreal scene from a video game. But no gangling heron.

In the third and final room, a band played a haunting old Celtic melody. The tall flautist swayed as if in a soft wind. The harpist plucked an ethereal chord, appearing lost in beautiful visions. Kay searched around and spotted an empty seat in a corner. Struggling to it, she lowered her pillowed bulk into place, apologizing to the Grim Reaper on one side and, on the other, an apparent medicine man dressed in fur pouches revealing most of his golden skin.

"Did a tall waterfowl stalk through here?" she asked,

as a conversation starter. The mead was already warming her with friendly relaxation.

They said they hadn't seen one and introduced themselves. The Reaper was Jarl, from Norway, and the Shaman was Joaquin, of Mayan origin.

To her delight, they slid into conversation on old writing. "Did you notice the Pictish cuneiform in the slideshow out front?" she asked.

"The swirly markings?" Jarl responded.

"Yes!" she answered with enthusiasm. "From the British Isles. Found on ancient stones."

Joaquin compared it to letters on Yucatan tombs. It felt good to be discussing ancient forms of language again. She missed that part of teaching at UC Berkeley. Jarl mentioned runes in the stones of his country of origin, and she expounded on one of her journeys there, after Finland. As he listened, he pushed back his Grim Reaper mask and wiped away sweat, revealing an attractive olive complexion. His dark hair curled to his shoulders, a touch of gray at his temples. Maybe we're around the same age, she thought, admiring him, then realizing he and Joaquin might be a couple. *That'd be just my luck.*

The time passed swiftly as they shared artisan pizza, and Kay ordered more mead. The music took her back to pubs in Dublin and Cork where she'd studied at archaeological dig sites. For a professor of ancient languages, these always held important evidence.

Midnight arrived all too soon. They exited the café with the other guests.

"By the way, a monk at a pagan party?" Jarl asked, as they stood on the sidewalk.

"A bit of irony," she answered. "Actually, it was all I had." Normally she would have explained that she'd used it in lessons about the monastaries and their role in copying rare texts, but it seemed time to part ways.

They said goodbye, and she headed down the street, lifting her oversized sandals carefully so as not to embarrass herself by falling on her face. *Plump Franciscan makes her exit.*

"You need a ride?" Joaquin called.

She turned, tempted. "No, thanks. I live close." She gave a sigh, regretting never having revealed her face. After all, this was the first real connection she'd made since leaving her teaching position and moving to the rural northern coast of California, taking possession of the small home left to her by her recently deceased parents.

She trudged past dark houses in slumbering neighborhoods; trick-or-treating had long since ended, leaving the streets deserted. Halfway down Partridge Street, moonlight filtered through the lofty branches of old oak tree, revealing a man in a long dark cape leaning against its trunk. Half in shadow, he studied her.

She considered crossing, unnerved by his sudden appearance. But she stopped and took in what appeared to be his costume: under the open cape, he wore an archaic tunic over breeches and worn slouching boots of a bygone era. A light breeze ruffled his long, dark hair streaked with silver. Dim half-moon rays etched his lightly bearded face.

They stared at each other, the only sound a breeze rustling in dry oak leaves above. The smell of wood fires wafted on the wind.

Fluidly, he pushed himself from the tree trunk and closed the distance between them. She thought she should run. Yet, something emanated from him—almost…a familiarity.

He looked down at her, eyes warm and intense. He

smelled of the woods and wild winds. She breathed in deep.

"Why d' ye dress yerself so, sister?" His voice, deep and sonorous, sent shivers through her. Something from the past hovered out of reach, a chaos of elusive images. A cottage. Herbs hanging from rafters. Faint voices. A smell—was it peat smoke?

Deep longing filled her. "It's just..." Her voice came out a squeak. She tried again. "It's my Halloween costume. You know." She indicated her monk's robe, bulging with pillows.

There was a somber deliberateness about his every breath as he waited, seemingly for a different answer.

She went for lighthearted, but her laugh sounded forced to her. "Hey, you called me 'sister'. My beard's not convincing?" She stroked the glued-on hairs, acutely aware of the ridiculous puffed rubber cheeks and round-rimmed glasses.

"I fathom yer spirit, Dove. No paunchy, baldin' monk," he said, teeth flashing in the moonlight.

A sweet frisson moved through her. *He fathoms my spirit.* She struggled to identify his accent. Was he an actor, with those arcane clothes, and the unusual speech? "Well, no, I'm not," she said. "But it *is* the time for masquerading and whatnot." She again gestured toward her long robe.

He placed his hand on her head. The bald pate slipped off.

Freed from the confining rubber piece, the night breeze felt cool on her scalp.

For a long moment, he studied her face, now exposed. Then he turned his attention to the costume pate with its circle of stringy yellowing hair. He turned it this way and that, peered inside. At last he chuckled and, reaching up, hooked it on a branch, leaving it to dangle and swing in the breeze.

She considered jumping to retrieve it, but decided she could return for it later.

He turned to scan the street, then faced her and murmured, "I, too, have viewed my share of dissembling raiment tonight." He held out his hand. "Would ye care to see a far different procession than ye've most-like observed before?"

She held back, perceiving a momentous decision was required.

His chin dropped, as if in disappointment. Again, he reached out. This time, curiosity overtook her. They walked down the street. The warmth of his hand holding hers kept her heart at a steady drumming.

He stopped between two homes.

She knew this block well. Where fence should have stretched seamlessly, a path now lay, leading toward hills. They walked between quiet, dark houses and climbed. At the crest of the first hill, she turned back and saw only treetops where there should have been a town. At the distinct paucity of rooftops, queasiness slushed in her belly, roiling with fading mead. Pomo Bluff was nowhere in sight. Terror crept, quiet as cats' feet, along her spine.

Chapter 2

The stranger tugged at her hand. "Come," his voice rich and melodic, carrying on a rising wind.

She let herself be pulled onward as they descended into a fold in the land.

The man of the oak let go and easily leaped over a creek, then turned to her. She squatted by the stream and dipped her hands into icy water to rub the hairs from her face. *I'll have to get more facial hair for my outfit*, she thought, as if she'd soon be teaching the history of writing course again.

Hands aching with cold, she rubbed them down her voluminous robe, bunched it, and jumped. Her sandals stuck in thick mud. She glanced back, then shrugged, leaving them behind.

The man reclaimed her hand and glanced briefly at her feet, sock toes hanging off with soggy weight. The barest smile lifted his lips before he aimed onward.

Soon, she abandoned her pillow paunch under a tree. Another flicker of a smile tugged at his mouth, but he appeared anxious, scanning the hillsides around them. She looked as well, wondering what he was searching for as she struggled to keep up with his long strides. Tall grasses and brambles grabbed at her hem, tangling her robe and tripping her. Each time she stumbled, the man caught her, checked her face with concern, then kept on. Sticks poked her feet, and she yelped. He tugged her along.

At the crest of the next treeless hill, they entered a cluster of huge stones forming a rough circle. Some fallen shards lay half-buried in tall grasses. Winded, she dropped onto a flat rock and picked stickers from her wet socks. The man remained standing, silently surveying the land. The moon slipped behind a cloud and the night darkened. She shivered. He sat beside her. Clouds moved and the half-moon appeared again, casting a wide path across the sea far below.

She searched for the lights of her coastal town. Only dark trees stretched before them. Slowly, she discerned golden flickerings ruffled by the breeze. Torches? She made out the shapes of crude huts, stone and wood structures with thatched roofs. Boats bobbed in an inlet; others were humped bottom-up on the shore.

This was not her town. It was a tiny hamlet nestled in the crook of a river feeding into the sea, like the Noyo, but this couldn't be Pomo Bluffs down there.

Shock played havoc with the remaining pizza and mead in her stomach. She scrambled from the rock, searching for anything familiar. Where was the lighthouse? There should have been a beam of light circling south of town, hitting shore, then water, then shore again.

My town is gone. Where am I?

The man took her arm gently as she stood, rigidly taking in the altered scene. "Come. Sit with me."

Frightened, the mead no longer carried her on this adventure. "Where's my town?" she asked, scrunching her robe to face him cross-legged on the stone bench. Their knees touched.

The man smiled with sad eyes. "We need t' call th' Otherworld bein's I promised ye."

She had no interest in his keeping his word on that. She wanted answers and wondered why she'd trusted him so implicitly. But she found it hard to resist the expectation in his expression.

He closed his eyes. He squeezed her hands, beckoning her to do the same. After a moment's hesitation, she complied. He chanted softly.

What was it he spoke? No living language, she was certain. The "n" was slightly nasal, as in French, with a soft fricative that reminded her of...what? She couldn't quite identify it. She peeked at him. He shook his head, his eyes still closed. She closed hers again. She heard his breathing slow and slowed her own.

He resumed the chant. The sound reverberated deep within her. *I should understand him.* This thought made no sense. Why should she?

A rustling came from lower on the hill. Something was headed toward them. Kay's skin tingled with apprehension. Her escort spoke. A deep booming male voice answered. She opened her eyes. The cloud cover had opened, and bright moonlight shone on a burly man. His copper-red hair, chopped with wild bangs, hung long at the back. She stood.

The newcomer threw his arms wide and grabbed her in a bear hug, swinging her from side to side, barrel chest rumbling as he chuckled. "Kyna. Kyna." He spoke the name with soft relish, then set her on her feet and pushed her back to check her over as though familiar with her, again chuckling in a delighted baritone.

He's mistaken me for someone named Kyna, she thought, *someone of whom he's clearly very fond. Friend? Relative?*

He was a huge man. Maybe she should have been afraid. Yet gentle affection radiated from him.

He peered into her eyes, reached for her hand, and stopped. "Ha! What is this ye're wearin', Kyna? Somethin's not right about ye." He frowned. "What is it?" He turned to the man who'd drawn her there. "Baird, there's somethin' different. Her spirit be wrong." He rolled the "r's" in a soft burr.

So that was her guide's name. Baird. She mulled it over, liking it.

Changing the subject, Baird asked, "Have th' players been yet, Duff?"

"Nay. But they're no' far off. Ye can hear 'em."

She noticed, then, a high flute and drumming drifted up from the base of the hill. Through trees, she spied a bonfire glowing on a circle of people. Muffled voices of men and women, children shouting, and a baby crying registered on the night air.

"I ken wha' 'tis." Duff had returned to studying her. "Ye've been and gone t' th' others." Besides the anger in his voice, she sensed fear. She realized he was staring at the cross dangling from her belt. "Not you, Kyna."

"It be dress-up, Duff. She's not gone from our ways."

"It be ill-omened," Duff growled and reached for her side.

Startled, she jumped away.

"Leave it, Duff." Baird stepped between them.

Pushing past him, Duff grasped the cord hanging from her waist. Again, she pulled away, but then stopped, fascinated. He loosened the knot holding the cross. Baird hovered, ready to intercede. The wood cross dropped to the ground and lay half-submerged in the dry grass. The man pulled a cord from around his neck and tied something to the end of her rope belt, braiding in deft knotwork. Baird waited, arms crossed, but with indulgent resignation.

Duff straightened, looking satisfied. As he dropped the object, letting it hang at her side, Kay caught a glint of silver. Before she could examine it, both men took her hands, and the three descended the hill toward darkly silhouetted figures around a blazing fire.

"On the night o' Samhain, the veils be thin. Look close fer yer dead kin…" Duff sang loudly.

Baird joined in, his voice vibrant, resonant.

Kay's hand in Duff's was a finch in a baseball glove, though his grasp was gentle.

The folk by the bonfire turned and pulled them into the circle. Several repeated the name "Kyna" when they saw Kay.

"She's back then?"

"You're back?"

"Where were ye?"

Baird broke in, telling of his travels. Kay realized if she didn't think too hard about it, she could understand what he said, that he'd been to the French alpes—les Hautes Alpes—and further travels.

A tiny woman with a wizened face moved to her side and patted her hand. "Are ye hungry?" She coaxed her to sit on a rough wool blanket.

Eager for news, the folk put all their attention toward Baird, and Kay sighed with relief. The old woman handed her a wooden bowl of steaming stew, thick, spiced with unfamiliar herbs. She brought a spoonful close to her nose and breathed in. Barley, maybe turnip, definitely leeks.

These people, from children to elderly, wore outfits straight out of a storybook. Their coarse fabric caps had animals painted on them. Linen and woolen cloaks, trimmed in brocade, were held together at the neck with simple clasps. Dresses were thickened by layers of undergarments. The men wore crude pantaloons and rough-woven leggings. Many had painted their faces with swirls and symbols.

She warmed her hands on the bowl for comfort, then took a tentative bite, savoring the unfamiliar flavors as she ingested meat for the first time since her late teens. The thought made her slightly queasy, but she turned her focus to the group's animated conversation. In some chasm of her mind, she knew their tongue. If she suspended conscious thought, she even understood some of what was said. She *recognized* the smell of the clothing and blankets, pungent yet not altogether unpleasant. The slight muskiness carried a comfortable familiarity, as though she'd known them her entire life. Which was absurd.

Looking at a young woman with a baby nestled to her chest, Kay *knew* she'd barely survived the birthing. Turning back toward the old woman who'd given her the stew, she recognized her as well. *I should know their names.* Kay sighed with frustration. Her head ached with the effort to remember things just out of reach, worried that she'd need to speak but would say the wrong things. A few more bites of stew helped settle her nerves. She set the bowl aside, leaned back, hands behind her on the blanket, and just listened to the merry chatter.

The more she concentrated, the less she understood. Deciding to stop thinking, she let herself become engulfed, breathing in the smell of the fire and aromatic spices drifting from pots bubbling near the flames, the wind through the trees, voices strange and familiar. A thick pan nestled in the coals sent up an aroma of roasting nuts.

Baird settled next to her, nudged and pointed. Far

below, a procession of minstrels emerged from the forest carrying torches and bright streamers. They played mandolins, flutes, and drums. Their festive music drifted up in the wind as they hopped and leaped, lit briefly by a distant bonfire. Folk rose to dance, whirling in circles, spreading out onto the hillside.

The players wended their way along to the various bonfires sprinkling the landscape. Their music—at times jubilant, at other times, haunting—danced on the air as they climbed. At last, they came close. There were greetings before they struck up a lively dance tune. Baird, Duff, and the others scattered into the nearby field and sprang into spinning, whirling action. Content where she was, Kay remained seated on the blanket and studied the rustic instruments, carved and painted with designs. The sounds bounced off trees next to the mountain meadow and wove back through the air.

Suddenly, hands reached for Kay, invading her calm contemplation. Strangers pulled her to her feet. She held back, reluctant to leave her comfortable position as spectator. She hadn't folk-danced since her earliest college days.

"Come, join us, Kyna." A man dragged her by the elbow toward the rest. "Ye canna' deny us yer marvelous dancin'." He was middle-aged and lacking a few strategic teeth but charming for all that, his warm face full of character, hat tilted rakishly to one side.

She gamely tried to move her arms and legs to match the steps of the traditional country dance she saw the others doing, but she was all left feet. Her damp socks caught in the grasses. She pulled away, shaking her head and laughing as she tried to return to the blanket. If Kyna was known for great dancing, she'd foul up her reputation, she thought. But with friendly insistence, others drew her back in, taking her arms, spinning her.

After another minute of floundering, something shifted. The music spoke to her as if it existed in long-lost memory. Delight crept into her spirit as her cold, stockinged feet took command and hopped over the grassy slope. She knew the steps as if she'd learned them as a child. Her mood soared as her mental churning dropped away, lost to the moment, to the spinning, to the grace and beauty of dances that were part of her cells, not a matter of thought at all.

A few dances in, unused to such cavorting, she stumbled away toward the blankets. Searching for Baird, she spotted him at the edge of the trees, surrounded by misty figures. She stared, blinked. Slowly, she made out illusory people everywhere, between the dancers, in the shadows surrounding them. They leaned in, peering hungrily at the revelry, following every move. So, this was what he'd meant by otherworldly beings. *"The veils be thin tonight."*

Baird bent in deep conversation with a phantom figure. If she looked to the side, she could make out rich, velvety fabric, breeches, and buckle boots. If she looked directly, the shadowy man disappeared. He faded away, and Baird strode forward to rejoin the dancers, smiling at Kay, joining the dance steps with the same grace and fluidity with which he'd stepped from the oak.

After a time, the minstrels turned from their fire and moved on. Their sounds faded, leaving them in silence. Someone called out, "A song, Baird."

He grinned, found his travel-worn bag, and dropped to a blanket next to Kay. He drew out a lyre or harp—Kay wasn't sure which—tenderly cared for, its yellow wood burnished to a glow and inlaid with mother-of-pearl though some was rubbed away. Its surface picked up the firelight with lustrous gleams as he strummed and sang. His voice rang out pure, sending a pang of confusing sorrow through her.

Duff, who'd been dancing nonstop, threw himself onto the blanket next to Baird. He lay with an enormous grin, eyes closed, chest forming a mountain that crested up and down with his breath.

Fondness as old as the worn hills flooded Kay. Far older than she could have developed in a mere evening. *What was going on inside her*?

Breathing in the pungent scents of fire, wild grasses, and spiced cider steaming over coals, she lay back to take in myriad stars. As she listened to Baird, a thin thread of light touched the hills. Her gaze moved sleepily toward the first rosy tones of dawn on the trees.

There she saw something luminous moving among the trees. An ephemeral avian creature—shaggy, heronlike—stalked in slow, high steps at the edge of the forest, then disappeared into denser woods.

She pushed up on one elbow trying to find the figure. It reminded her of the one in the café. *Could the creature have followed me*? She wanted to ask if anyone else had seen it but, exhausted, she lay back. The notes Baird played fell like honey and melted butter, enchanting, lulling. Her eyelids drifted shut.

Chapter 3

Sunrays warmed Kay's face as she struggled to wake. Through a miasma of too much mead and not enough sleep, memories of the night on the hillside seeped back, followed swiftly by awareness of where she lay—no longer on a scratchy wool blanket but snuggled into smooth sheets in a soft bed.

She sat up, checked under the covers, and found her long T-shirt nightgown twisted around her, per usual. *How did it get there*?

Where was the monk's robe? Curled at her feet, Oz cat watched.

"Did you see how I got here, fella?" she asked him. He gave a slow blink. "Is that a yes or a no?" She climbed from the bed and padded through the house, looking in the shadowed corners for visitors from ancient times. Oz stayed tight at her heels as far as the kitchen, then stopped, waiting for her to come to her senses and feed him.

It had been a dream. Of course. The mead, the unusual late-night hour... Sadness dropped over her. *Did I imagine it all? Even Baird*?

Finishing the circuit of her small house, she ended up where she started, by her bed. The edge of the monk's robe stuck partway from underneath. Kneeling, she pulled it out and searched for the rope belt. There at the end was the silver piece Duff had tied on. It had an intricate Celtic knot pattern. As she took it between her fingers, an odd sensation ran along her arms. She sat back, heart racing, and squeezed her eyes shut. So, it *had* happened, hadn't it? Wasn't this proof?

She studied the silver piece. About an inch across, she recognized the knot of delicate intertwining strands. She'd seen designs like it in the UK. She ran a fingertip over the beguiling design and grew dizzy. Images swirled. Words, half-formed, maddeningly elusive, drifted through her mind. She'd heard music and smelled a peat fire. She was inside a crude hut. The visions turned her queasy and she let go. All turned to normal, her bedroom surrounding her. Oz meowed for food from the kitchen.

Setting the robe aside, Kay fed the cat and made a hangover-mending smoothie, then ran a shower. Pleasure and regret mingled as the scent of an ancient peat fire washed from her shoulder-length hair and her skin.

After, in her robe, she knelt again by her bed and attached Duff's elaborate silver knotwork to a ribbon which she hung around her neck. As it settled on her chest, a zing of energy enlivened her heart. She took slow breaths until the rhythm settled, then rolled up the costume robe. Before shoving it in its bag, she pressed it to her nose and breathed in the scent of bonfire and wild grasses still clinging to the thick brown fabric. She stuffed in the belt and sealed the bag, then dressed in sensible slacks, button-down shirt, and cardigan sweater, and left the house.

Halfway to work, she diverted, drawn toward Partridge Street and the huge old oak where she'd found Baird. She circled the tree, hunting for signs of their late-night encounter, then knelt and examined the ground as though she might detect their footprints in the hard-packed dirt of the unloved lawn. She sat back against the broad tree trunk where Baird had stood leaning, in the vain hope of catching his scent lingering on the air.

For several minutes, she drifted in memories of the previous night: the warmth of Baird's hand as they climbed the hill, Duff's deep chuckle as he swung her around in dances she inexplicably knew.

When she opened her eyes, she noticed her bald pate dangling from the branch where Baird had hung it. The stringy fringe of hair fluttered in the morning breeze.

I was here last night. I really was. Sighing, she left the skullcap where it hung and walked up the block to where they'd crossed into the hills. No path led between houses. Fences solidly connected the yards, keeping her out. Viewed through side yards was only another 1950s working class neighborhood, with some gentrification sprinkled in, nothing more.

But the landscape *had* been different the night before. Baird had taken her hand and led her out of one world, into another. A sense of loss overwhelmed Kay.

This is ridiculous. I lived just fine without that path yesterday. But she could not deny she was forlorn, as if she'd been shut out from something—or someone—indispensable.

She'd never missed a day, or even been late, in the eight months she'd worked at Luminous Life, entering data into the raw food chef school's student database. But that day, after her return to the tree seeking vivid memories with

Baird, she arrived two hours late.

Esther, the wiry, middle-aged receptionist, looked her over with a crooked smile and asked, in her raspy voice, "Did you have a nice Halloween?" Her short-cropped, bleach-tipped hair framed a weathered face. Combining dry wit with motherly tenderness, she was, to Kay, the best part of the office.

She reminds me of that old spindle tree out back. The thought came to her unbidden. *Spindle tree? I've never even heard of one.* She stood in front of Esther's desk and fiddled with her plastic frog display, disoriented by the inexplicable memory. Coming back to the present, she tried to recall what Esther had asked her. Oh, yes, her Halloween. "It was...interesting."

"Reeeally?" Esther held out messages. "Did you meet someone?" she asked with a wink.

Kay thought of Baird. How could she tell of that? Then she remembered Jarl and Joaquin. "Yes. I did meet a couple of jolly fellows at Franklin Street Café."

Esther's eyes widened, inviting more, which Kay did not provide. "How was yours?" she asked.

"Oh, I tweezed my brows, clipped my—"

"Enough." Kay laughed, waving the slips of paper in the air as she headed for her cubicle. "I get the picture. Another exciting evening at Casa Esther." She heard the older woman's husky smoker's chuckle before answering a ringing phone.

Nola leaned around her desk's barrier, close to the picture windows that gave onto the historic Company Store's carpeted mezzanine, surrounded by shops. "Are you okay?" Nola asked solicitously, trying to draw gossip.

Kay was a fish out of water, working for a company that convinced hapless students to spend their hard-earned savings on a hypocrisy of owners strutting through like royalty while underpaid staff worked through the night to prepare for overpriced classes, after decades teaching at a university. Not that Kay minded the premise—raw and slow foods, vegan, it was right down her alley. But to claim the food was made with love when in truth, greed and hierarchy permeated the place? Her ambivalence probably pushed her to sequester herself in the familiar territory of databases with which she was familiar, having helped design UC Berkeley's extensive online bank of ancient language texts. She'd never counted the hours she spent on that.

Squeezing in at her desk, she thought back to recent Living Food Expo they'd hosted, where one attendee announced, "This wasn't made with love, it was made with sleeplessness and has negative energy," as she returned her exorbitantly priced salad. Kay had had to side with the customer. *Wow, she really is psychic,* she'd thought.

"I'm fine," she answered Nola. "Had a bit of a stomach ache this morning. Thanks for asking." That was true enough though it didn't include her return to the oak. She settled back in her rolling chair and stared blindly at the stack of messages in her hand.

Invisible behind her partition, Nola prattled on about her evening decorating with her husband.

"Lovely," Kay sang out.

Nola's phone jangled and she grabbed it, ready to ensnare another innocent raw food chef idolatrice.

Kay finally read her messages, then pawed through the stack of enrollments on her desk, wondering if she envied Nola decorating with a husband. It was not as though she'd never married, but most of the time she tried not to think about the suppressive Egyptian professor of biotech engineering who had fathered her two children.

She pushed papers and pens around on her desk and stretched her legs as far as they could go before bumping against the cubicle wall. She had to admit she was having difficulty adjusting to the office job after the thrill of the night before.

She opened Filemaker and stared blankly at a student's record. Restless, Kay stood and prowled over to the mail cubbies. In a fog, she gathered new enrollments from her slot and returned to her seat.

It took two times through the stack before she shook her head to bring herself back to the work at hand and began processing students, adding them to the database. She created a Raw Food Chef certificate and uploaded photos from a recent graduating class onto the company website. Over it all, Nola sold enrollments with exaggerated cheer, her voice buzzing in Kay's head like bees stuck in a jar.

Doris, the company bookkeeper, appeared suddenly at her elbow. "Why can't you write clear comments?" She thrust a wad of student records at Kay, quivering with indignation, then scrutinized her chest. By the expression on her face, you'd have thought she'd come to work in her bedclothes. Kay glanced down. Duff's silver piece, with its beguiling Celtic knot, glowed in the cleavage below her top button. The sight startled her; she'd thought her shirt covered it. And it hadn't glowed before.

The accountant's eyes remained pinned on it, mouth in a sour pucker. "A bit ostentatious for the office, don't you think?"

Why's she so disturbed by it? Kay wondered, *as though it's causing me to write unacceptable remarks on enrollment forms.* She took the papers shoved at her and skimmed over the notes Doris found offensive. They seemed comprehensible to Kay. She searched her mind for a non-combative reply. Meanwhile, her fingers strayed absently to the pendant that lay just north of her heart.

Doris' hair ruffled slightly, as if in a breeze—*unlikely in this airless tomb*. Her eyes widened as the accountant's features mutated into a bird-like visage, replacing her flushed, angry face. She threw back her avian head, opened a long, garish beak, and released a great cry. Wings arced high above her shoulders.

Startled, Kay whipped around to see if office mates had heard. No heads popped out of cubicles. She dropped the pendant as if it burned and closed her shirt over it.

Doris returned to her usual irritated form, arms crossed, fingers drumming, waiting for a response.

Kay, having no idea what the grumpy bookkeeper wanted to hear, pondered the beaked apparition that had appeared in her place.

Doris muttered, "I'll just see what our supervisor has to say," and stomped off.

"Good idea," Kay mumbled. She resisted the temptation to touch the pendant and see what else might happen. Why had Doris turned into a bird? Was it related to the heron-like creature she'd seen in the café, and at the edge of the woods on the hillside?

The phone ringing jolted her out of her musings. Natalia, the office manager, wanted her to come to the café in the mezzanine. Kay found Natalia at one of the round tables sucking at a towering green smoothie. Old blues drifted from hidden speakers. Kay took the chair opposite, and Natalia proceeded to alternately cajole and scold her, with many wink-winks about keeping everyone happy.

After a while, Kay ventured, "Doris appears to be better with numbers than comprehending written words strung together."

"I hear you, Kay," Natalia purred in her breathy, '40s actress style, her eyes bulging with sincerity. "I'll speak with her. Good, good. I'm sure we'll all be better for these understandings." She'd morphed her New-Age, Montessori-teacher past into her new role as owners' mouthpiece with a mix of "peace and love" and party line that never quite meshed for Kay.

"I'm sure, too," Kay said, mystified as to what those understandings were. Would the miffed accountant stop coming to her quivering like an angry bull terrier when she'd written quite coherent comments on her enrollment records?

But she reciprocated Natalia's "best friend" hug that left a nagging residue of moral compromise, and returned to her linen-walled cell. The minutes ticked by, made longer by her constant glances at the clock. When five p.m. arrived, she hurried out into open air, and breathed deeply. Salty ocean scents mixed with Main Street/Highway 1 fumes.

She walked to work and saved her car for long trips. Joining others at the light on the corner, she waited for the light to change, then trotted the seven blocks to Partridge Street.

The massive oak stood silent, rosy in sunset glow. She lingered at the edge of the neglected yard and studied the house at the back of the long, narrow lot. Its paint was faded and peeling. Cobwebs coated the windows and hammocked dried leaves from the eaves. A breeze rustled overhead, the sound reminding her of her encounter there with Baird. Near a dilapidated shed, vines pinned crumpled yard chairs into the weeds.

Why had Baird appeared here? She glanced around. Seeing no one, Kay stepped onto the dry lawn and approached the tree. Tall grasses caught at her pant legs, giving off a pungent memory of summer ended. She circled the gnarled trunk, looking up into the stark winter limbs over-head, some brown leaves rattling. The pate still hung, its fringe hairs fluttering, attesting to the encounter. She touched the craggy bark and willed Baird to appear. Her hand strayed to the silver pendant. Nothing happened. She heard no voices, saw no swirling images, detected no an-cient fragrances. Maybe this place had its own magic, something the pendant couldn't trump. Unsure where that thought came from, she leaned against the ridged bark and slid to crossed legs at the base. Eyes closed, she breathed in the oak and reminisced about Baird's wild forest scent.

Slowly, she attuned to the subtle scents of grass and tree and slipped into a meditative trance. When she opened her eyes, nothing had changed.

She returned to where they'd passed between houses into the hills. Now she faced an unbroken line of fences, pathless yards, and tract homes. This time, a woman stood at her front window, blonde hair immaculately coiffed in a French twist, arms crossed, scowling at Kay.

She moved down the block. What was happening? She used to be a perfectly respectable professor. Well, not per-fect. Somewhat respectable. Now, here she was, mooning over trees and nonexistent paths. Her feet dragged as she walked home in the darkening gloom.

Chapter 4

N ext day, as she sat at her dressing table preparing for work, she tugged at her hair, trying to braid it, which was difficult since it was only shoulder length. She asked Oz, "Why am I doing this?" He watched her as if she'd lost any semblance of sanity. Giving up, she pinned back a lock of hair with the most Celtic-looking clip she owned.

At work, she sat at her desk, more out of place than ever after her trip to the past.

Lunch came and she walked up the block to the fabric store with a sense of urgent purpose, though when she entered the shop, she had no idea why she was there. She sidled down aisles, pawing through cottons and wools with increasing intensity. Nothing satisfied her inexplicable need.

A saleswoman hurried over, shoving her body between Kay and the products neatly folded on the tables. "Can I help you?" she puffed, nostrils flaring. She was tall and rail-thin, her face papery, hair pinned into a severe bun.

"Probably not." Kay heaved a sigh.

The store clerk glanced toward the counter, most likely

considering calling the local shelters to see if any deranged individuals had gone missing.

Defeated in her unknown quest, Kay picked out a few spools of thread and a new hair clasp with a somewhat Celtic triadic design, paid for them, and made her desultory way back to the office.

Somehow, she got through the day. After work, she resisted returning to the oak. Instead, she walked home and sat in the darkening living room, sipping wine and staring out the glass French doors. The sky turned from crimson to rust on the western horizon. Like the sea, which stretched unseen from the edge of town, fenced off for the logging company, so Baird's world hovered, invisible and inaccessible.

When night turned as black as her mood, Kay crawled into bed and slept.

At three a.m., she awoke, stomach rumbling, and made a bowl of granola. Apparently, her new phase of adjustment to life-after-ancient-Samhain-celebration was to avoid thinking, and try to disappear into an oblivion of hunger. Meanwhile, her hands tried perplexing things like braiding her too-short hair and combing the local fabric store for unfindable cloth. She had a silver piece that turned the company accountant into a strange bird and, at times, seemed to hold answers. But answers refused to reveal themselves in any clear way.

She had discovered something at Samhain that held more meaning than anything else in her life at the moment, yet she had no way of reconnecting with it. Baird had ignited something deep in her soul. A longing welled from her depths. When she touched the silver pendant and heard snatches of their language, the core of her being lay elsewhere, in that other place.

As soon as Saturday dawned, Kay jumped into her old Volvo and drove east on the winding road that twisted away from the coast, through dense forest, to the highway running north-south between Eureka and San Francisco. Reaching the highway, she had no idea of her destination but turned south. An hour and a half from leaving home, seeming to follow a homing beacon, she veered off the highway into the nondescript town of Yakota and pulled up in front of a fabric shop. There she repeated, nearly move for move, her baffling behavior of the previous day. She needed something, but didn't know what. She wandered about, touching fabric, until a sales clerk appeared at her side.

This woman's head, covered in tiny white curls, barely reached her medium-height, 5'7" shoulder. The clerk surreptitiously tucked fabrics back in line, then peered up at Kay with watery eyes magnified behind thick glasses. "What can I do for you?" She looked intent on helping.

Kay fought the urge to touch her silver pendant and see what the woman might turn into—perhaps a magical being who could tell her what she sought there? Instead, she made to leave, mumbling something about looking for a zebra print they had last year.

The store employee, whose tag said "Madeleine", stared after her.

Kay returned to her car and took the next right toward the highway. She came upon a bright purple store, "Dragon's Lair" in swirling letters on a giant mural all across the street side of the building. A fanciful dragon scene covered painted-over bricks.

She swung out of traffic to the curb, drawn by the notable frivolity, so unexpected in this town of unrelenting '50s architecture.

A cowbell attached to the doorknob clanked as she pushed through into an enchanted world of dragons, fae creatures, twinkling lights, and frankincense. Kay meandered a labyrinth of shelves and cases, past fantasy realms of curios, puppets, and crystals. Pulled to the back, she grew dizzy as she neared a raw unadorned brick sidewall. She caught herself on a wood counter jammed with elves climbing on mushrooms. The sturdy-looking wall rippled, and the air crackled as if charged. She blinked, then touched the silver pendant and waited. Nothing. "Pfff," she remarked to herself as the wall turned solid again.

Picking out a string of leaf lights—gauze petals of delicate rainbow colors—she brought it to a willowy young woman in a tie-dye dress behind the counter, her hair worn in dozens of tiny braids pinned in elaborate chaos.

"This is a wondrous world," Kay said, as she paid.

"Isn't it?" answered the worker named "Swan" according to the tag pinned to her dress.

Kay thought maybe Swan's almond-shaped eyes conveyed a message. She shook herself, chagrined by the absurd notion, and started for the door. On a notice board, a pinned paper caught her eye. *Loom for sale. In perfect condition. Best offer. Irene.* Kay took out her phone and, bewildered as to why, punched in the number.

She stepped out of the shop as a woman's rich-timbred voice answered, "Hello."

"Hi." Kay started toward her car. "Irene?"

"Yes?"

"You have a loom for sale."

"I do. You weave?"

28

"I...I do. I think," Kay answered.

Irene, silent a moment, perhaps flummoxed by the cryptic response, said, "Okay. Well. Do you want to see it?"

This was all happening fast. Kay followed directions to a home in the hills backing the town. A rounded picket gate gave onto a sloping yard packed with mature fruit trees and honeysuckle vines. A golden retriever, muzzle graying, lay flopped across the porch like a doormat. He raised eyebrows at her and blew air as Kay stepped over him to knock. "Hey, Buddy," she said down to him. "Don't get up for me." He conceded willingly, eyes already shut again.

A tall, sturdy woman, maybe in her sixties, opened the door. Her reddish hair, dusted with gray, formed a halo around her stolid face. She wore wide-ribbed corduroy pants, a flannel shirt, and a craftsman smock with roomy pockets.

Kay liked her immediately.

She appraised Kay briefly with deep-set, discerning eyes, then held the door open. "You must be Kay."

"I am. Nice to meet you, Irene."

"Likewise." She led the way into a homey front room, sunny with rich, warm colors, oval throw rugs, and sturdy, comfortable furniture. The windows looked onto the yard and beyond, over the town set in its valley of vineyards. The room had the smell of wood, cut flowers, and...what else? Ah, yes, fibers, textiles. Between the windows, a loom held center stage. Baskets of dyed and raw wool, racks of yarns, and a spinning wheel filled the rest of the wall area.

Kay strode across to the loom, compelled by an overpowering longing, inexplicable to anything in her conscious memory. Kneeling, she ran her hands over the cloth forming, pressing for tension and evenness, examining the frame and treadle.

"You are a weaver then." It was a statement, not a question. Irene watched, arms crossed, expression bemused.

"Yes. I suppose so," Kay mumbled absently, hungry to get the apparatus home. She stood. "Why are you selling it?" It was so integral to the place.

"Hands." Irene held them out—strong but gnarled, with swollen, red joints.

A deep longing to mix her an herbal salve arose in Kay. The urge was not hers. Not exactly. She had no idea how to mix herbs for healing. She shook her head, willing her mind toward concrete matters. "How much would you like for it, then?"

"What seems fair?"

"I don't know the pricing on looms. I'm sorry. This was...a spur of the moment thing."

They settled on an amount and, together, loosened the strands to collapse the frame for travel. Kay hesitated before they detached the yarns, and glanced at Irene, but the woman shook her head. "This project has been sitting here for ages. Time it came off. I won't be finishing it."

Kay took in a deep breath, past a knot in her throat. The loom was leaving the place where it clearly belonged. She would be the cause of something coming to an end, or at least part of it. Sadness came over her. She blinked away a sting of tears.

Irene took up one end of the loom. She urged Kay to get on with it, by look and gesture. They trundled the bulky frame down the garden path and through the front gate. Heaving it up, they lashed it to the roof of Kay's station wagon with rope Irene dug out of her garage nearby.

Before leaving, Kay turned back, strangely reluctant to

part from this place. They hugged. Irene's strong brown eyes held Kay's. They nodded, as if some understanding had passed between them, and she left.

By the time she entered the downtown, night was falling. She found herself aiming toward the Dragon's Lair. Arriving, she pulled up in front just as the lights inside went off. She jumped from the car and hurried to the door. A young man turned the Open sign to Closed. She stood looking at him until he opened the front door.

"Yeh want next door." He pointed to his right. What was that accent? Scottish, she thought.

"What next door?" Looking where he pointed, she saw no other shop.

"That one. That's the one yeh want." He shut the door with a jangle and winked through an etched pattern on the glass. There was something strange about him, aside from his magenta hair greased up to a peak. Then he was gone. She tried the knob. It was locked. She knocked—he did not return.

She walked along the side of the building. No other door. No other shop. What was he talking about? She stood, frustrated. Her fingers strayed to her throat and fiddled with the silver pendant. A thread of light appeared on the wall. She let go of the pendant, and the line of light disappeared. She grabbed it again and stepped to the wall. The faint line reappeared. Tentatively she slid her finger along it, glancing back at the street as traffic passed by with the change of the signal. The street darkened again.

Slow and steady, a door opened inward into blackness. Residual light from the street showed a short way into a narrow hallway of old stone walls. A dank smell, like an old cellar, emanated. No, older: like ancient catacombs in Europe. At the far end, an archway shed flickering, golden light in. Undecided, she stood, one foot still on the sidewalk of the mostly deserted street.

Go in? Stay out? It was hardly a question because what she wanted was in there. She glanced back at her car, loom strapped on top. *No one will take that*. Her pendant warmed against her chest like an echo of some soul desire. She stepped in further and let the door go, hoping it would remain open, but it shut of its own accord, leaving her in blackness.

She took a tentative step toward the light at the other end. The air, sharp and thick with antiquity, seemed to vibrate. The hallway was barely wide enough for her shoulders. Kay slid her hands along the walls, her shoes crunching on gritty earth floor.

At last, she reached the low arch and peered into a medieval room of wattle-n-daub and round-edged walls. Flames crackled in a fireplace built into one corner as though carved there. A shriveled old woman sat rocking and knitting. Her head swivelled toward Kay. A name, half-formed in memory, hovered at the edge of Kay's mind, but it wouldn't take shape. With the familiar frustration of recollections that were not hers—the sense that she could weave when clearly she could not, the almost-understood language—she took in the half-lit chamber, noticing a salty, earthy scent.

Heavy, dark beams held a low ceiling. Warm natural textures wavered in the golden light of the fire and a lantern on a low table. The air, redolent with the slightly acrid fragrance, triggered a mixture of comfort and mystery. Burning peat—she knew this from trips to Ireland. Something else. As her eyes adjusted to the dim lighting, she took in rows upon rows of yarn balls and skeins filling built-in shelves. They were of natural tones—olive, cranberry, golden ochre, robin's-egg blue. She moved toward the shelving and breathed in the scents of plant dyes, salty from the brine used to set the colors, so familiar to one part of her, yet foreign to the rest.

The tiny woman grinned at her, exposing at least one missing tooth, as her hands continued to knit. Her booted feet were neatly aligned on a braided rug where an orange-striped cat curled, warming at the fire. Sensing encouragement, Kay touched the fibers, pressed her nose to them. *This is it. These are what I've been searching for.* A buzz of energy surged through her.

She glanced again at the woman, pulling away apologetically, but she nodded and indicated a stack of waist-high baskets behind her, then returned to knitting. Hesitating, Kay detached a basket from the stack and began selecting skeins of yarn, her hands sure now. Pursing her lips, she had definite plans. She set colors next to each other and dropped them into the basket, moved along the shelves, adding burnt umber and sienna, midnight blue and sunrise orange. Merely touching the yarn caused her heart to race. She held a green shade to her nose, breathed deep, assessing that leek was used in the dye.

When she'd filled one basket, she took another, assuming she had the woman's approval. When the second basket was full, she turned, heart still palpitating—not in fear but alive with pleasure. The woman smiled and nodded, never saying a word. As if in a trance, Kay lifted the baskets, then set them down and reached for her wallet. The elderly woman, wearing antique clothing, dress hem draping to the floor, frowned and shook her head. Waving Kay away, she bent back to her knitting.

Heaving the filled baskets into her arms, Kay stepped through the low archway to retrace her steps back from the phantom shop through darkness. There seemed no choice but to stumble her way to the street, and hope it was still there.

Chapter 5

Arriving home past midnight, she brought in the yarns but left the loom on the car roof for morning. When Sunday dawned, she threw on old sweats and jostled the loom into the living room. This was no mean feat, as Oz did figure eights around her ankles, doing his best to trip her the whole way. Leaning the structure against the wall, she patted it. "This'll never be Irene's house, but hopefully you'll adjust," she said.

Oz stopped preening to stare at her.

"Yes, I'm talking to the loom. Not a word, fur-face."

He pursued further coat maintenance, leg cocked in the air.

Tentatively, she reached out and touched the fibers in the baskets, afraid she might have imagined their potent energy. As before, a sensation passed through her. The magic had stayed with them.

Since it was Sunday, she had the luxury of spending all day setting up the loom. She'd never woven before, but her hands went to work. Swift and sure, she lined up the spindles and stretched the warp threads.

By evening, she had the yarns on, ready to start, colors selected according to the same mysterious knowing—

for she had no picture of what she would create.

She made salmon and a salad, and ate next to the fire. Wondering what it would be like to weave, and why she'd had so much confidence she could do so, she kept glancing at the loom.

The next day, she dragged herself to the Luminous Life offices. Throughout the morning, she carried out rote tasks while her mind wandered to the loom. It was hard to imagine herself weaving, though on some level she was sure she could do it. At lunch, she rushed out the front doors of the blocky Company Store—so called from the earliest days of the town, in the 1800s, when the logging company was sole proprietor in town. Increasingly anxious to escape the windowless maze of cramped cubicles and breathe in fresh ocean air, albeit blended with Route One traffic fumes, she mingled with the group waiting for the light.

Crossing the street, she headed north up Main Street. In front of Windsong, a fantasy esoteric shop, she nearly tripped over a man seated against the wall. Expecting a homeless person, she was surprised when a tidy, well-shaven man leapt up with elegant grace and bowed as though he'd been waiting for her. His clothes were reminiscent of a street performer: bright vest, full sleeves, fitted pants tucked into high boots, kerchief round his neck. His face, olive-complexioned, was bold and lively, his coal-black hair tied back in a ponytail. A gold hoop earring adorned one ear. A perfect beard etched his cheeks under fathomless black eyes.

Kay stood transfixed, unsure whether to wait or go. He

brought a pair of boots from behind his back and offered them to her. A tiny red jewel set in a front tooth caught the sun as he flashed a smile.

She held back. Strangers don't jump up and offer you boots. It's just not done. Then again, magical yarn shops smelling of ancient catacombs don't appear out of nowhere either. His smile wavered. He moved closer and sang softly, "Strong boots for the bonnie one," a slight burr to his r's. Again, he extended the boots.

Deep in her psyche, Kay realized he was not speaking English, yet she understood him. "Eyes of sapphire, chestnut hair, a smile like dawn," he sang with a wink, his voice ringing out.

She had to smile then. Self-conscious, she glanced around at people passing by, busier than usual at lunchtime. No one seemed to notice them. Could only she see and hear this captivating man offering her boots while serenading her with compliments?

He gave a slight bow and extended his gift again. "For you," he said, a bit more anxiously.

Still, she hesitated.

With a decorous bow, he set them at her feet. "If ye please, ye mun bring a length o' yer finest woven cloth." Turning, he gathered a carpetbag that rested under the store window and made to leave.

"Wait." She spoke at last, glancing at the boots, then back at him. "Who are you? What cloth?"

But he'd turned and strode down the block, blending into the lunch crowd.

She stared at the boots. *Bring cloth? My finest? I don't even know if I can weave.* "Wait!" she called out, craning to search for his retreating figure. He was gone.

Although the whole experience had been unreal, there

were the boots. What did they mean? Was she under some obligation? Why had the phantom shop appeared to her, and now, this mysterious, charming man? Perhaps she should not have taken the yarns in the first place.

She squatted to examine the boots. They had the coarse cut of medieval footwear, leather crossing over, fastened with a wood peg, reminding her of Baird's. She slipped her hand into one. The instant her fingertips touched crosshatched stitches along the inside seam, the street shifted. She looked upon caravan wagons in a forest grotto, smelled moss and bracken, heard a splatter of water, such as a splashing stream.

She yanked out her hand. The street returned to normal. The lunch crowd passed. Cars moved along the road. She considered leaving the boots and walking away. But her arms pulled them into a hug. Shaky, she stood and made her way to the corner where she waited for the light, acutely conscious of the boots, as if others might detect their magic. A woman smiled at her quite naturally. Maybe she worried for nothing.

Back in the office, she slipped the boots under her desk. Their energy sizzled against her ankle when she sat. Kay glanced with a sigh at the piled-up papers to be gone through.

At five p.m., she walked home, boots under one arm. At first, she couldn't decide where they belonged. The closet with her everyday shoes didn't seem right. She set them by the yarn baskets.

After feeding Oz, she grabbed hummus and carrots for herself, then sat at the loom. Taking up the shuttle, with only a moment's hesitation, she began expertly tossing it through the shed space, interweaving the fibers, warp and weft. The part of her mind that accessed someone else's memories knew how to weave. That other mind at first missed hanging weights to press down the pattern, but soon adjusted to working the modern treadle.

She hummed an old traditional tune—it, too, was from another's memory—glancing occasionally through the French doors at the layering colors of dusk settling over the ocean side of town. Everything was changed now. *She* was changed. Who was this person who could weave? What thoughts were hers?

Mid-evening, Kay knelt by the loom and touched the narrow strip of cloth she'd woven. At first, she saw only a delicate shift of color and pattern running through the threads. But as she slid her fingers over the few inches of fabric, she saw a delicately twisting design of the rune, *Wunjo*—a pointed "P" shape meaning "joy".

She sat back on her heels, amazed. For the second time in a few days, she hauled the ladder from the backyard shed to the front hall and climbed to the attic. In near dark, she found the string to the single bulb and pulled. It cast raw light over the low, slant-ceilinged space. She pushed past boxes to the farthest corner where her research grew dusty. She'd avoided the notes and artifacts since leaving her university post, not wanting to stumble across reminders of the controversy that had chased her from the work she loved.

Brushing dust off labels, she found the one on runes. Under the bare light bulb, she dug down to an Italian-bound notebook. It contained observations from her journey into Scandinavia when she'd studied with shamans.

She drew out the thick book, covered the box, and climbed back down.

By the fire, she flipped through pages filled with notes and drawings, located Wunjo, and read, "one of the most powerful of all the runes, Wunjo helps to focus and realize true will".

She pondered why she'd woven that symbol into the cloth. A strong will had driven her ever since she'd encountered Baird. Now she was at last digging back into her research materials. Someone else's memories knew songs, and dances, and how to weave. It was frightening to think a will other than her own might be directing her actions. Duff had mistaken her for someone named Kyna. Kay had a notion she was connected to all this. Beyond her uneasiness lay a thread of abiding trust, and even passion for her new knowledge.

She returned to the loom, fearing she'd be unable to continue the design, but her hands easily picked up where they'd left off.

She didn't want to give this cloth away—which was ungenerous since the yarn had come to her for free. But she dared not disappoint the Boot Man, certain he and the boots were linked to Baird. Or was that a forlorn hope?

Unable to stop, she worked through the night. By dawn, mind muddled from lack of sleep, she called in sick, threw a dark sheet over the window, and dropped into a deep sleep.

Knowing it was slow season and Nola could easily keep up with the enrollments, she wove nonstop for a week, obsessed with the idea of forming a wardrobe out of the magical threads. As she wove, she wondered if the mysterious Traveler waited for her on the street outside her work.

Unwilling to give up the first cloth she made, she spent an entire day duplicating it. Then she wove two more lengths of cloth.

It was difficult to make the first cut, but once she began, she was able to shape clothing. In a surreal state, knowing how to make the clothes, her hands stitched swiftly, using needle and thread rather than a sewing machine.

After a week, she donned her first woven outfit, fashioned by her hands, including underclothes and stockings. Woodland scenes, faint until you turned the cloth to a particular angle, covered the tunic. As she ran her hands over the garments, a sense of balance poured through her. Sitting on the edge of the bed, she shoved her foot into a boot for the first time, wondering if the caravan in the woods would appear. Nothing changed. Kay pulled on the other and stood.

She placed the duplicate fabric into the base of one of the baskets from the phantom shop, which was now empty, sure it was important to return the cloth that way; no other container seemed right.

Fifteen minutes later, she strode into work, dressed head to toe in shades of speckled green, brown, and gold: leggings, belted tunic, long over-vest, and antiquated boots. These clothes made her different—as if she might run and leap in forests or ride horseback with bow and arrow.

She tried to enter inconspicuously, clutching the waist-high basket, but Esther called out a greeting in her raspy voice, "Well, hello, Kay. Back from the dead, are we?"

"Hello, Esther." She quirked a smile. "Yes, I think I am." She made her way to her cubicle. Coworkers' heads popped out as she pushed the tall basket under her desk with a screeeeak.

Doris arrived at her side. "Funny. You don't look like you're wasting away from some dread disease. In fact, you're glowing." She scrutinized Kay with gimlet eyes, as though glowing were a crime. "We almost hired someone in your place." She looked her over. "Are we pretending we're at a Renaissance Faire?"

"I think she looks lovely," Natalia purred, coming up behind Doris and stroking Kay's soft sleeve. "We were worried about you." Her bubble eyes expressed concern and calculation.

"I'm much better, thank you," Kay said.

"Good. Then we'd better get you caught up on what's been happening." Natalia turned to go.

Nola bounded out of her cubicle. "Yes, good idea." She loved an opportunity to talk rather than do paperwork.

Doris marched away, back to her separate office in the bowels of the building, immense key ring clanging with each step.

"Right now? Oh, okay. That's best." Natalia, who had little real work to do, led the way.

"Sure." Kay followed them to a table in the lobby.

"We're trying to fill up the next Associate Chef series. And the Expo orders are starting to come in," Natalia began. "We really want to sell this idea of the inn being a full spa experience, as well."

Even though it wasn't.

Nola launched into a detailed monologue on her recent enrollment coups.

Unfortunately, Kay's seat faced glass doors giving onto the street, with a perfect view of Windsong. She tried to follow the conversation but kept glancing out. Then she saw her Boot Man lounging elegantly against the used bookstore. His gaze moved directly to her. She sat up straight with a quick intake of breath.

"Should I take the early lunch?" Kay fished her cell phone from a pocket and checked the time.

The two women stared at her, incredulous.

Perhaps I appear rude. But she couldn't help herself. She was in the thrall of something enormous.

"Okay," Nola agreed with a shrug, glancing at their boss, Natalia.

Kay hardly waited for the conversation to finish before hurrying back into the office. There she wiggled the three-foot basket out from under her desk with another loud scraping screech and marched through the historic Company Store lobby with it. Nola and Natalia had not moved. They watched her, still looking speechless. She gave them a quick smile—unable or unwilling to explain her odd behavior. Her priorities were across the street where a potential thread to Baird's world awaited.

The crossing light seemed to take forever. The boot maker—for she knew somehow it was he who'd made them—stood alert, facing her direction. When the signal changed, she hurried to him, heart thudding in her chest.

His eyes took her in solemnly from head to boots. "Ah," he said, and looked pleased, seeing the boots, her leggings tucked into them. His attention returned to her face. "Greetings, m'lady." He gave her a beautiful smile and a low bow.

Kay wondered if the women still watched from the two-story Company Store's mezzanine.

She held out the basket. He moved forward, reached into its depths and brought up the pale green-gold cloth, holding the soft, supple square like a nest of fragile eggs.

He barely breathed as he ran his fingers over the cloth, turning it to the light. Then his eyes met hers. "The Wunjo design," he whispered, as though in prayer.

A name tapped in a deep recess of her mind. "Boldo," Kay said. Suddenly he was familiar to her. She leaned forward and kissed his shadowed cheek. He smelled of wood fires and something muskier, like incense.

His eyes shone with a glimmer of tears.

She sucked in her breath, confused. She'd just kissed him. It had been easy, familiar. But also insane.

He took her hand and pressed his lips to it. Then he straightened and, basket under one arm, cloth held tightly to his chest, disappeared.

She stared at the space where he'd stood seconds before. The lunch crowd had dissipated. Still, no one glanced their way.

To have produced something with her hands that caused such reverence stirred her in ways she could not fathom. She put a hand to the brick wall, seeking equilibrium. What now?

Chapter 6

That night, Kay dreamed of a shimmering glade of green-gold leaves. A snake of the same colors, nearly camouflaged, glided on a branch next to her head, but she had no fear. She peered across the marsh where a woman sat spinning. The woman was not average. She appeared luminous. Glancing up, she etched the Wunjo rune in the air with her hand. The image lingered for an instant then disappeared, leaving a faint, smoky trail.

Kay glanced at the clock: four a.m. Filled with wonder from her dream, she climbed out of bed and padded to the living room. Just as she flipped on the light, a scratching came at the front door, startling her.

"Oz? Did I leave you outside?" She flicked on the porch light and opened the door a crack. There sat Oz staring up at her. Next to him stood a basket filled with yarns.

They know where I live as well as where I work. Her stomach churned with a multiplicity of emotions. She longed for reconnection with Baird but her life was destabilized. Oz rubbed her leg, softening the chaos, but the hairs stood out on his back. She petted him. "What were you doing outside, pal?" Her eyes darted around, searching for phantom visitors.

With one last glance into the shadows of the yard, she

pulled the wicker container into the house, wondering what the neighbors would think if they saw the delivery.

Placing the new yarns next to the remaining basket, she skimmed her fingers over them, then dug down to see all the colors. Mixed in was raw fiber, airy as corn silk. It tingled to her touch with the same potent energy as the yarns. She would need a spinning wheel, she thought. She heaped the yarns on the rug—a variety of tones, weights, and textures—and found a folded piece of cloth nestled into the yarns. She shook out the silvery length of fabric. Across its surface, slate-hued herons stood with wild grace in their natural habitat of swirling marsh waters, long beaks poised to stab what lay beneath the surface.

She stroked the cloth, glancing out the window into the night. Who made this cloth? She asked out to no one, then got up and closed the curtains.

A great yawn engulfed her, and she crawled back into bed, hugging the silk to her cheek.

For a while, she listened for more visitors. As she slipped back to sleep, she tried to remember if there had been herons in her dream. Then she remembered the bird-creature at the café, and in the woods, at Samhain.

All too soon, Kay jabbed the alarm off with a scowl. Although she longed to stay home and make a nightgown from the silk, she laid the cloth reverently on her bed and left for work.

At lunch, she wandered east on Redwood Avenue to the library. In the foyer, a flyer announced plots available at the community garden. "Plant your winter crop!

Workshop this weekend." Having her own yard, she didn't need community garden space, but she thought she might do well to learn what grew in this area through the winter. Noting the time of the event, Kay went to the shelves to find another Anne Rice vampire chronicle, checked out *The Body Thief*, and ambled back to work.

That evening, Kay studied the beautiful heron cloth, loath to cut into it. At last, she forced herself to snip enough for a neck hole between birds. She tucked and stitched, forming a serape-like nightgown with as few cuts as possible. That night, she descended into a silken slumber. She wore it every night that week. No more rune dreams graced her untroubled sleep.

On Saturday, she tucked garden tools and gloves into her backpack and walked to the community gardens, several blocks away. She'd never been inside the fence, had only admired the cheery faces of tall sunflowers visible from the street. She followed a wide path to the center, enjoying how each plot conveyed a gardener's unique stamp. Some had random, comic touches: vegetables planted in toilet bowls and in old boots, plastic toys glued to fences. Drying strands of snow peas climbed on brass bedsteads. In many, the soil was being mulched for the winter months with a pile of cardboard, manure, and straw, but a few flourished with greens, artichokes, asparagus, and other plants fond of damp, gray weather.

Halfway through the gardens, Kay came to a group seated on logs around a barbecue pit. In the back row, a bearded man in overalls grinned and made room for her.

She sat by him, mouthing *thank you*. At the front, a woman with blonde dreadlocks showed them how to prepare winter beds and suggested plants for the season.

Kay regarded the group and stopped on two men, one taller, both tanned, with dark hair. It took her a moment to identify them, then it hit her: the Grim Reaper and the Shaman from the All Hallows party—Jarl and Joaquin. They noticed her smiling and gave friendly nods, but clearly didn't recognize her. Well, of course not. She'd been wearing the rubber monk pate and mask. She tried to pay attention to the speaker, but her eyes kept traveling back to the two men, the memory of that night alive in her mind.

The workshop ended, and Kay made her way to one of the garden coordinators, a freckly young woman wearing overalls, hair in two long braids. "Are there still plots?" she asked.

"Just one," she responded happily. "Come, I'll show you." She introduced herself as Tracy.

Kay offered her own name in return and put out her hand.

"Oh, you don't want to do that." Tracy shook her head, laughing, and showed grubby fingers that had just demonstrated layering compost for winter beds.

"Mine'll match yours soon," Kay assured her, eager to join a community with a purpose that could hold her in the here and now.

Tracy led her to a tangled mat of dried plants covering hard-packed ground. A tiny bench adorned one side, and a gnarled apple tree struggled in a corner. A wonky fence, composed of a variety of materials patched together, attested to a once much-loved space.

"I'll take it," Kay said.

"It'll need TLC, but it's a nice size." Tracy nodded, then

explained the yearly fees and gave her a quick rundown of the basic rules of the community. "Be considerate. Don't pick other people's stuff. And so on."

After she left, Kay perched on the weathered, patched-together bench and scanned the plot. This *was* going to be a lot of work.

"Need some plants?" Jarl and Joaquin stood in the opening to her garden. "We've got extras. Chard and mixed lettuce greens." Joaquin held out a couple of six-packs of plant starts to her.

"Thanks. That's awfully nice of you," Kay said, standing.

"I'm Joaquin, and this is Jarl." They held out their hands.

"I know." She grinned as she shook their hands. "I'm Kay."

They glanced at each other blankly.

"We met at the Samhain party. Franklin Street Café."

They still wore puzzled frowns.

She gave up on them guessing. "I was the monk."

They examined her. She'd worn old jeans and sweat-shirt for the garden. She'd managed to get part of her henna-highlighted hair into a couple of braids just that day, clipped to the back, leaving the front a neat bob that framed her cheeks. Not much like a pudgy, bearded monk.

Realization dawned on their faces.

"No way," Jarl said, shaking his head.

For good measure, she repeated a smattering of their conversation about runes and early Mayan writing.

"You're the professor," Jarl confirmed.

"Of ancient languages," Joaquin remembered.

"Well, I used to be." It was not easy for Kay to say the past tense when it came to her university position.

"Our professors sure didn't look like you." Jarl waggled

his eyebrows.

Kay laughed at the flirtation. "In Norway, was that?"

"Yes!" He smiled, clearly pleased she'd remembered.

She swept her arm toward the overgrown soil at their feet. "Welcome to my plot."

They entered, and Joaquin dropped onto a stump. Jarl flipped a bucket, dumping slimy water onto the packed ground, and sat. She settled again on the bench.

"It needs a lot of work." She cast a baleful look over the brown, lifeless bit of land.

They laughed and nodded. "You should have seen ours when we got it," Joaquin offered.

"Maybe you can advise me then?" she said.

They discussed the pros and cons of raised beds and soil preparation. Eventually, though, the conversation circled back to their encounter at the café. Looking at their warm, friendly faces, she found herself blurting, "You know, something wild happened to me after I left you guys that night." She immediately wanted to take back the words. Even so, a surge of relief swept through her. She hadn't realized what a strain it had been to be the only one who knew about the other world. She no longer could bear being alone with that truth.

They looked expectant.

She told them about meeting Baird and their climb into the hills. When she got to the part where others surrounded them, speaking another language, they stopped her.

"But this guy, Baird, spoke English?"

"Well." She stopped. "He must have. I understood him." She'd never figured out that part. "Either that or I read his mind." She laughed as if she were joking. How could she convince them she had time-traveled or stepped through into another dimension? Suddenly, she wanted very much for them to believe her. Pulling down her sweatshirt neck, she showed them the silver piece hanging there. They leaned forward to get a closer look.

"Duff, the red-haired man Baird called my brother, tied this to my belt. In the morning, it was all that was left as proof that any of it happened. My wood cross was gone."

They sat back, waiting perhaps for more evidence.

"I suppose someone could have given it to me in this time as well," she admitted. It never occurred to her to doubt that it came from another dimension. She *knew* it had.

She needed to give them more. She took a deep breath. "When I sat on the hilltop with Baird, everything below had changed. Pomo Bluffs was no longer there. I saw only an old fishing village with thatched roofs. No electric lights, only torches."

Their eyes grew round.

She'd gone this far. She might as well tell the most bizarre aspects of her experience. "Some of the time, there were these faint people at the edges of the clearing. Like ghosts, really. It was like they say—the veils between the worlds are thinner on Samhain."

"We believe the same in Latin American culture," Joaquin offered.

A wave of relief washed through her. They weren't mocking her; they were, in fact, listening eagerly. But were they humoring her? After all, who could believe such a story? She wasn't entirely sure *she* did. "Day of the Dead. Día de los Muertos," she said.

"*Correcto.*" He nodded approval.

"Well, I think I saw…the dead," she said.

"Maybe it *was* an ancestor thing for you," Joaquin suggested.

She nodded slowly, glancing at Jarl. He was serious, with no mockery. "For sure, we have that too, in our old Norse traditions. We have great respect for the spirits of the dead, and the sacredness of the land. So, what happened next?"

"Well, after dancing to the minstrels' music, Baird played and sang, and then I fell asleep. In the morning, I was in my bed at home. I don't know how I got there."

"In your own bed?" Jarl asked, brow creased.

"Have you been back to that place in the hills?" Joaquin asked, eyes sparkling.

"I can't find the path," she grumbled, chin on fist.

"You mean..." Jarl started, then waited for further explanation.

"I mean it's gone. It's not there."

"Are you sure you went to the right place?" Joaquin leaned in, taut with excitement.

"Positive."

Joaquin jumped up, ready to go trudging into the hills that very moment. "We have to find it!"

"It's gone," she muttered. "There's a fence across the spot where I know we walked. There are streets and yards where the hills were. That's how I know we stepped into...I don't know...another world? Another time? Another dimension?" She laughed.

"Let's look for it tomorrow," Joaquin said.

Her hesitation about sharing the story slipped away as the men proved eager to investigate. While part of her grasped at the secrets protectively, light and warmth flooded in. It was good sharing it. "Okay. Sure. I don't know how—"

"We'll find it." Joaquin was confident. He stood at the garden entrance. She and Jarl followed.

"Hey, do you remember the band, Harper in the Glade, that played on Samhain?" Jarl asked.

"The Celtic music? Yeah. They were great."

"They're playing tonight at the Duck 'n Hen. Want to come?"

Another layer of warmth came into her at the thought of going out with friends in her new town. "I'd love to."

They named a time and the two men left. Kay sat back on the bench of her new community plot and enjoyed a sense of bliss emerging.

Chapter 7

In honor of her first social excursion as herself since moving from Berkeley, Kay decided a skirt was in order. Perhaps this, too, was the other woman being channeled. Regardless, an image was in her mind. She set about designing a calf-length garment for an evening of Celtic music.

At eight, she arrived at the Duck 'n' Hen in skirt and boots, with a lace bodice over her full-sleeved blouse. A poster in the window advertised the band: a brooding minstrel plucking his harp in an autumn glade, yellow leaves drifting to the ground.

Other patrons arrived and swept past her through the front door. She followed into a warm, loud, semi-darkness, scanning the crowd for familiar faces.

Joaquin came up behind her. "You made it." He pointed at Jarl who waved from the kitchen.

"Jarl's working tonight?" she asked. What was it like, she wondered, to be a chef after training as a scientist in Norway. "Too bad he can't join us."

"He said he'll come out when he can," Joaquin replied. "You look very nice."

"That you do." Jarl came up beside Joaquin.

Kay curtsied. "What do you recommend, chef?" she asked, studying swirly writing on a board behind the counter. Handwritten in colored chalk, the menu included East Indian, Southwest, and healthy Northern Californian options.

Jarl suggested the eggplant and roasted pepper pizza and returned to the kitchen.

"What can I get you?" asked the young man behind the bar who rubbed the counter with a cloth. A tattoo was visible under a shaven patch on one side of his head.

Kay asked for the pizza Jarl had recommended. She and Joaquin decided to share. He ordered extra garlic on it, and a pitcher of dark beer. They made their way through the thick throng in the main room to find a table. Joaquin waved to a handsome woman, her dark hair pinned up in a curly cloud with hints of silver at the brow.

He aimed that way. Shelley had apparently saved them a table.

"Shelley, meet Kay," Joaquin said. "Shelley's a midwife." He set down the pitcher and pulled out chairs.

"Good to meet you," Shelley said, holding her hand out to Kay. She had a down-to-earth charm Kay immediately liked. Her husky voice had a slight Appalachian twang.

"So how do you know each other?" Kay asked, sitting.

"We met at the gardens," Shelley answered.

"Oh, you have a plot, too?" Kay asked.

"I do. Mostly herbs. We started hanging out, coming here for music."

Strains of traditional Celtic music drew their attention to a rough-planked stage where the musicians from the Samhain party were striking up a song. The music brought Kay memories of that night on the hillside. She poured stout. Taking a first gulp, she sat back to enjoy the sounds.

At the break, the musicians pulled chairs over to their table. Three were from the British Isles, one from Canada. From England was Ian—lanky, slightly wolfish looking. He had the charisma of a lead singer, with light hair shagging past his shoulders, and charmingly imperfect teeth which Kay saw when he graced her with a smile. Shane, the fiddler, had curly red hair and a friendly, open grin. Kay remembered Sara, the harpist, from Franklin Street Café, with her dreamy, ethereal look, and the Canadian flautist, Candace, who had swayed as if in a soft wind.

They shared a second round of beer and finished off another pizza.

Joaquin startled her by saying, "Kay crossed the veils at Samhain! That night of the Samhain gig at Franklin Street. I think she time traveled." He looked around for a reaction. When he saw Kay's face, he stopped, expression worried. "Right, Kay?"

"I don't know what happened, exactly," she stammered, sick at heart. It had been her secret, her treasure. Had she ruined everything by speaking of her travel to ancient time? Might it chase away the memories?

"Where was it you saw him?" asked Shelley.

Kay wanted desperately to change the subject.

Shane checked his watch and nodded to the band. They pushed back their chairs. Break was over. She sighed with relief.

Back on stage, they sang a Gaelic song. A tingle, like deciphering an old language, ran through her. She got up to use the restroom, just to have a moment to herself.

As she passed the stage, Ian's deep grey eyes moved

to her like a spider to a fly. Her breaths came fast and shallow. She scurried down the hall. What was the hunger he conveyed?

The band joined them at the end of the evening, and the group chatted as the crowd dwindled. Kay thought the topic was safely forgotten until Joaquin tried to convince everyone to come on a picnic the next day. "Let's see if we can uncover the mysterious path and the stone circle." Excitement shone in his eyes.

No one took his suggestion seriously—which was fine with Kay. They gathered their things to leave.

Late the next morning, there was a knock at her door. She opened to find all the members of Harper in the Glen, plus Shelley, Joaquin, and Jarl on her porch. Arms loaded with bags and baskets, they greeted her cheerily.

She couldn't deny the pleasure of seeing these new acquaintances gathered on her porch. She'd missed the camaraderie tied with music in the multi-cultural life she'd led in Berkeley. An outing with new friends—why not?

The sun peeked through for the first time that day. "Come in. I'll get ready," she said.

It struck her that no visitors had been in her home since she added the loom. She imagined them pawing through her magical yarns, asking about the fibers, tainting them.

"We'll wait out here," Joaquin offered. "No sense for us to tromp dirt in."

A golden retriever bounded next to Jarl and nipped at his sleeve. "That'd be better," he said and commanded, "Down, Trouble."

"Trouble?" she laughed. "That's asking for it. I'll just be a mo'."

She stashed olives and other appealing delectables from the cupboard into a backpack, then joined the group out front as they headed down the block.

"We should retrace your steps of that night," Joaquin suggested. Being the one who initiated the expedition, he appeared eager to have a plan, probably hoping it wouldn't fall flat.

She had no such hope. "I guess that's the best way." She agreeably led them to Partridge Street and the old oak where she'd first seen Baird.

"Does anyone live here?" Candace asked, peering toward the shadowy house at the back.

"Spooky," Sara said in her Irish accent.

"It always appears abandoned," she responded.

"Okay. Where was Baird?" Jarl asked, tilting his head to one side with a somber expression. Maybe he sensed her anxiety over this whole endeavor.

She stepped onto the weedy, leaf-matted lawn and walked to the wide, craggy tree trunk. When she turned, seven pairs of eyes watched her.

"He stood right here," she said.

"Where were you? Show us," Joaquin urged.

The others watched, their expressions hopeful. But Ian had a different look. He walked to the tree where she'd first seen Baird, and pressed his hand to the bark, almost glowering, his gray eyes seeming to want to pierce the surface of the tree.

She returned to the sidewalk. "I was walking along when I saw him leaning against the tree." She described his clothes, the scent of wind and campfires on him as he stepped from the oak and came toward her.

The women were riveted; the men, too, though Jarl appeared slightly irritated. Ian rolled his eyes but then gave her his wild, enigmatic, stage smile. Did the two men envy her description of a mystical bard who could appear from the shadows and elicit awed expressions from the crowd?

Like a tour guide, she moved under the tree again and pointed up at the rubber pate that hung from a branch, fringe hairs dangling. There was a hushed silence, as of reverence, and she almost laughed. It would have been a giddy sound. She suppressed it.

Joaquin broke the silence. "Let's see where the path started."

They moved down the street, clustered in a group. They were having the time of their lives now. Kay thought the pate in the tree did it. A few cars passed them. Residents out gardening might have wondered about their procession.

Where the path had run between homes into the woods, she stopped. There was, of course, no trail, no forest, no hills, only more homes and yards.

"That night, the path was here," Kay said, holding up her palms and shrugging. "Now, as you see, it's all closed off by fences. Sorry. This is where the trail ends."

"Are you sure it was right here?" Shane asked.

She wanted to curl up around her memories and protect them.

Joaquin stepped forward. "Okay, this is what we're going to do. Let's work our way around, take whatever roads get us into the closest hills, and see what we find."

Curiosity ignited the group as they left Partridge Street and headed east of town. After a while, the neat grid of streets ended. A single road climbed toward open countryside and steepened. A crescent of mismatched trees capped the ridge to one side: shaggy bull pines, California bay laurels, and redwoods. Yards gave way to farms and orchards.

"Does any of this look like your hills?" Joaquin asked.

"Not in the least," she said. "I'm sorry, you guys. This is probably a wild goose chase."

They shrugged, appearing happy to stride into the country on a sunny Sunday. They continued upward, chatting cheerfully. The companionship buoyed her spirits.

After a while, Joaquin stepped over a chain crossing a dirt road. The rest followed. A short scramble later, down an overgrown path, they stood at the edge of a shelf high above the Noyo River estuary where derelict fishing boats listed on their sides, restaurants, hotels and fishing businesses out of sight.

They settled for lunch: olives, bread, fruits, cheeses, and wine. The musicians pulled out fiddle, flute, and mandolin. Shelley had brought a *bodhran*, a handheld Irish drum. Traditional airs sounded perfect out in nature. She imagined the notes drifting into the river valley as they harmonized. Some of their songs included words from obscure dialects; she listened hard to identify them.

During one particular melody, a powerful sensation ran through her. Her hand slipped to the silver pendant, and the words took on rightness, as if they might be akin to the language she sought: Baird's. She strained to understand, but a dark presence shadowed her thoughts. She turned to find Ian staring, that perplexing gleam in his eyes—too eager, too hungry. As though she needed to shield the pendant from an icy threat, she pulled her hand away.

"That's a beautiful silver piece y' have there," Ian remarked in his English accent. "You say it was given to you in the other realm?"

"Yes," she answered reluctantly, and shrugged. "I think so. You know that song you just played reminded me of the language the people spoke in that other place."

"My Irish gran taught it to me." Ian watched her intently. "She said it came down from the Bright Ones. That was the legend in our family."

"Like the Tuatha Dé Danann?" she asked, her heart skipping a beat at the mention of the sacred ancient people.

Maybe he had a passion for this kind of thing. Perhaps the look of hunger was nothing sinister.

"I learned this from my gran." Shane had a mischievous look as he struck up a song in Irish Gaelic. "*Dhá mbeinn trí léig—*"

"Not that one!" Sara protested. She threw a clump of grass at him, but he ignored her and continued.

"Is it dirty?" Kay asked.

"No, it just goes on forever," Sara said, and in an angelic voice, sang, "while I was talking to my fair Taimín, I would not think the night long."

Drops fell from a darkening sky. "Ah, Pomo Bluffs weather," Kay said, laughing. She gathered the remains of their repast.

"A lot like my homeland," Shane said.

They started back toward town. Along the way, the band members sang Irish and English ballads. The others made up words to sing along with the tunes.

Joaquin contributed a Mayan Warrior Dance song, which all gamely tried to pronounce: "*Conex, conex palanxen, xicubin, xicubin yocolquin . . ."*

Jarl chimed in next with a Norwegian lullaby, *"Byssan lulle barnet..."*

Shelley sang an Appalachian ballad in a rich, low timbre.

The chorus was familiar and, once Kay picked it up, she joined in with harmony.

Shelley turned to her at the end. "You harmonize beautifully."

"That song was haunting," Kay said. "Do you play any instruments?"

"I learned a bit of fiddle from my pa when I was young." She grinned, then added, "but not verra well," giving the word a mountain twang.

"That's not all he taught her," Ian said, clapping her on the shoulder. "Like how to make moonshine up in them hills?"

"Nah, that was my grandpappy," she protested with a wink.

Kay checked to see if there was any tension between them, but Shelley appeared to enjoy the banter. With a laugh, she elbowed him in the side.

A fine drizzle made pixie halos of their hair, but no heavy downpour followed those first drops. Back on the flatlands, Kay reconsidered inviting them into her home, and called out, "I have a pot of veggie stew. Won't take long to heat up if you'd like to join me for dinner." She had to break down and become social again at some point.

No one needed convincing.

"Let's stop by the gardens," Joaquin suggested. "We have chard, beets, the last of the carrots, and potatoes that need harvesting."

At Kay's house, they crammed into the tiny kitchen. Some helped cut veggies for salad while others brought in wood and made a fire. Kay cleared her table of sewing projects and they set places, getting out her mom's old china that had never been used since she'd lived there. Then she opened Anderson Valley wine and toasted their new fellowship. The room glowed with conviviality. Chatter moved naturally from one topic to another. She worried about her yarns as the band shared tales of being on the road—drunken mishaps, strange hangers-on. She talked a bit about her professor days.

"Research with shamans?" Shane was impressed.

Late in the evening, they rose, thanked her for a fine day and packed to leave.

After goodbyes on the front porch, Kay closed the door and headed straight to her yarns. They hadn't found any clues leading to the magical realm, but nothing had been lost either. She stroked her fibers. They were okay. *I can live in this world and try to hold onto the other one, come what may.* Oz sidled up against her ankle, and she squatted to stroke his soft coat.

"You made yourself scarce," she said. "We have to get used to visitors. We need to get grounded, buddy."

He stared at her.

Kay amended, "Maybe *I* need to get just a bit more grounded. You're a very grounded dude."

Chapter 8

Winter holidays approached with still no sign of the bard, and no more clarity about the magical yarns or the language Kay heard when she touched the silver piece. No further visitations occurred from Travelers or old women in archaic textile shops. At times, she thought she might be going mad.

One day in early December, Kay's daughter, Sophie, called from France to say she would spend a few days with her before a conference in San Francisco. As they spoke, Kay scanned the room. She considered putting away the heaps of yarns and woven fabrics. Quite a switch from the floor-to-ceiling bookshelves that had surrounded her kids in their early lives. Her volumes from the university remained boxed.

As she listened to her daughter enthuse over her plans, she wondered what she would think of her life now.

"Can you stay for the holidays?" she asked her.

"No. It's lousy timing, but I'm afraid this is the closest I'm going to get to spending Winter Solstice with you."

They had long used pagan terms for the seasonal holidays but homespun clothing was a new manifestation.

Three days later, Kay awaited the CC Rider, the only

daily transport between their rural coastal town and inland airport shuttles. Sophie's svelte, long-legged figure stepped confidently off the bus, wearing a ballerina skirt with lace edge and tailored jacket—the latest Paris street fashion, she was sure. At 5'9", Sophie stood two inches taller than her mom, her hair in a dark, curly wedge cut. Her Egyptian father had bestowed height, curls, and exotically shaped brown eyes on both of her kids.

"Mom." Her eyes traveled over Kay in a quick sweep before she wrapped her in a warm embrace. "You look beautiful."

"And you. As always." Kay held her tight.

That evening, they settled by the fire with glasses of wine, and Sophie scrutinized her further. "So, when do you return to university teaching?"

"Well," Kay stalled, "things have taken some interesting turns here."

"I see that." Sophie's eyes combed the piles of fabric, looped yarns, loom stretched with cloth radiating a wave of color that moved from burnt orange to tangerine. "Looks like you've gone in for handcrafts in a big way." Sophie grinned at Kay, a slight furrow between her perfect arched brows. "Your clothes would be a hit in some parts of Paris. It's like you stepped off the side of a tree."

Kay laughed in mock horror.

"No, but that's good," Sophie hurried to reassure her. "Kind of a Druid-wood nymph look."

Kay gauged her daughter's reaction to her garb.

Finally, Sophie asked cautiously, "What brought all this on?"

Kay searched for an answer.

Sophie turned to face her. "Mom, come back with me. To France. I think it'd be good for you."

Kay took a deep breath and sighed. "I might just do that one of these days, sweetheart. I would love to."

"Why not now? There's so much there for you. Remember?"

They'd lived in Paris when Kay served as visiting professor at the Collège de France. "You're right. I'm just...taking a break."

"Are you going to throw your years of graduate study and teaching to the wind? The book projects, your research? And what? Weave?"

Kay knew the changes in her hurt Sophie deeply. Her daughter was also weighing the value of graduate school. Kay didn't want to discourage her. She tried, nevertheless, to speak the truth. "I have to rethink things. Academia had been rendered sterile. The research I was driven to do could not be part of the establishment, it seemed. Everyone isolated the symbols from the spiritual and the mysterious, stripped them of the numinosity that defined their ancient beginnings." She paused. "You know what I mean?"

Sophie listened, her luminous eyes peering over the rim of her glass.

Kay went on, "No one in the upper echelons of our department wanted me to publish what was becoming most important to me. And that got sticky, as you know." Kay had shared much of the turmoil of her last year at the university with her children. She hated to tarnish their image of her or make them suffer on her behalf as she explored this new road. They had always championed her.

"So, it's better to work enrolling people in an overpriced raw food chef school?"

Kay made a face. "I don't think I'll do that much longer."

"Thank heavens." Sophie reached out to touch a strand

of gray-blue yarn. A strange look came over her face as she ran the strand between her fingers.

It hit Kay like a thunderbolt how much she didn't want her children drawn into her obsession. If she had stepped out of their time into another dimension, she hated the thought of either of her kids doing the same and perhaps not returning, just as she might not have.

Kay gently tugged the yarn from her daughter's hand, then tucked it back into its ball, pushing it in with the others. "This has become such a clutter. I need to have a better way of storing these. Maybe drawers." She fiddled with the skeins and tucked the fabric into neater piles.

Sophie's face lost its far-away look, and she focused intently on her mom. "What was that? When I touched the yarn."

"What do you mean?" Kay suppressed guilt.

Sophie's eyes narrowed. "Is this some research you're doing?" She swept her arm, indicating the array of woven goods.

"I guess you could call it that," Kay said, slightly hopeful that it made sense.

"But what about your teaching? The rave reviews by your students? Isn't that what counts? Don't you want to return to the university?" She added wine to their glasses and waited for Kay's reply.

"On one level, yes," Kay said. "But the hierarchies of the university don't care much about students' rave reviews, as far as tenure goes."

"Your research was strong and significant," Sophie defended.

Her loyalty touched Kay. "My research questions did not always meet their approval, and I wasn't sure I wanted to make the compromises satisfying them would entail.

Also, it got uncomfortable. I'm taking a break and thinking things through." It wouldn't hurt for her daughter to know the paradoxes one faces in holding to one's ethics and truth above ambition.

After that conversation, the topic got set aside and they spent the next two days rambling through charming coastal towns with water towers and rose-vine-covered sheds, or hiking in the redwoods.

All too soon, Sophie was packing for her return trip.

As they wound through redwoods and pastoral scenes, shafts of sunlight pierced through the redwood canopy onto the fern-covered forest floor, and mist rose from the wide green river that met the sea. Sophie slept, leaving Kay to her thoughts. By the time they crossed the Golden Gate Bridge into San Francisco, she awoke and took in the familiar sights of Nineteenth Avenue.

"Nothing's changed." Sophie's voice was pensive. She'd always loved San Francisco. "Nothing changes, and everything does," she finally said.

"So true." Kay glanced at her twenty-seven-year-old daughter. She was becoming a woman of the world. Kay wondered what lay under her words. She lived the life she'd prepared for. Starting in her early teens, she'd begun studying world politics and film. She was fluent in four languages. Now she worked in investigative journalism as a Parisian. Kay admired her with heart-stopping fervor. "You sound wistful. Is there something on your mind?"

"Oh, no. Just being here. It's hard. I love my life in Europe. But you're far from me. And things do change while I'm away. I just wonder what I'll come home to next."

"Sweetie, things do change, yes, but the most important changes are in us. We grow. We learn. We have to embrace that and what it might bring."

"Yeah, I agree, Mom. Just…be safe, and be happy, okay?"

Tears started up in Kay's eyes. "I will. And you, too."

They passed Stonestown Mall. Their time together was growing short. Kay pulled to the curb next to the lawns of San Francisco State University. Festooning the entrance were banners for the media conference Sophie had flown halfway around the world to attend.

"I could come back down to see you off at the airport," Kay offered.

"There's no need. It'd be silly."

"You'll be traveling back with people you work with?"

"Yeah. And…partings from you are not fun. I don't want to do it twice." Sophie's eyes glistened. "You're sure you won't come live in France for a while? Or London? That'd be close."

"I'll think about it, my sweetest."

They said a short goodbye, and Kay watched her daughter's receding figure as she rolled her suitcase away, turning once to wave.

Kay waved back and pulled into traffic. In the midst of sadness to leave her daughter, her heart soon sped up as she turned west, following an urge. She crossed San Francisco toward the Bay Bridge.

University Avenue teemed with the usual diverse crowd, in cars and on foot. Kay had dreaded returning to the Berkeley campus, but now the familiar thrum of a research chase returned. A deep longing welled up and nearly overtook her, to be on a mission, surrounded by ancient texts, immersed in a culture's past, laboring to ascertain a symbol's original meaning...

Like a homing bird, she headed for the hills north of campus, knowing exactly where to find parking in the neighborhoods full of steep slopes and shade trees.

As she trundled down sharp-angled sidewalks, she breathed in the familiar woody scents of wet foliage and fireplace fires. It was cloudy; early afternoon looked more like evening. Yellow leaves were pasted in patterns on dark streets, wet from recent rain. The unique atmosphere of those hills—houses with forest green trim, ivy on stone, signs of old money and the new intelligentsia's successes— made her nostalgic for her past life there, though not without conflicting emotions.

A huge squirrel bounded from tree to tree. He watched Kay; each time she stopped, he stopped, sat up on his hind feet, lush tail twitching. She started again—so did he.

"Are you following me?" she asked him. He jerked up his head as if listening.

I'm talking to squirrels now. She chuckled to herself and kept on.

At the bottom of the hill, she crossed Hearst Avenue onto campus, leaving Squirrel behind. A bittersweet pang hit her as her feet sank into the lush, green lawn leading toward the Grecian splendor of the main library. Once inside, she headed for Doe, with its massive collection of world languages.

At Doe Hall's entrance, a familiar grad student stared at her through thick lenses from behind the polished wood counter. "Dr. Halefin. How nice to see you!"

"Thank you, Lindsay. Good to see you, too." Kay knew she should stop and ask about progress on her dissertation, but the pull of the books was too much. She made her way deep into the labyrinth of the library, each level low-ceilinged and packed with heavy tomes. Old manuscripts, beautifully illuminated, protected in glass cases, stood at the ends of aisles. The smell of antiquated pages and bindings permeated the air. She loved it.

An hour later, Kay knelt on the floor between stacks, three volumes spread all around, one open across her lap.

"Kay?"

A prickle ran down her spine at the sound of Robert Sontag's voice. Spawn of generations of scholars, he was one of the old guard who wished the hallowed halls of the university would stay firmly in the hands of the elite—unquestioned, unchanging. Unlucky timing for her. He was one of the loudest in denouncing her research.

"Into a new project?" His red-rimmed eyes scanned the stacks in front of her. "*Languages of the British Isles*. What were you working on the last time we saw you? Women's role in the history of the ancient Futhark runes of Northern Europe?" He snickered as he peered down at her, his arms crossed smugly. "Weren't you asking shamans about it while in drug-induced trances? A bit of rattle-shaking and dancing 'round fires, I don't doubt?"

She found it disagreeable to kneel at Sontag's feet, peering up at him like a supplicant. But weighted down by the volume on her lap, she held her ground and stayed where she was. "What are you up to these days, Robert?"

"Didn't you see the recent piece in the New York Times? I'm countering the Sapir-Whorf hypothesis."

BRAIDED DIMENSIONS

Of course, he'd be unwilling to take wisdom from the Hopi regarding how we're shaped by the language we speak.

A fetching, bespectacled undergrad approached, arms piled with manuscripts. "Dr. Sontag? Here are the journals you wanted."

His face transformed at the sight of the young, malleable student. Kay breathed a sigh of relief at the reprieve from further discussion with the odious man. Without another word, he turned and followed her, head craned over her shoulder as he, no doubt, enlightened her with his formidable intellect.

Grateful, Kay watched their retreating backs and returned her attention to the document spread before her. It was an early copy of *The Táin and the Sacred Texts of the Dawntime*, about a *zoat* or centaurish creature. This sacred being told the leader of the *Tuatha Dé Danann*—what the early folk of the Isles called the Bright Ones, the immortals who came to the isles before them—to cross from the Grey Mountains of Northern Europe to their spiritual home, *Bretonia Nuada*. She leaned back and thought about Baird's ability to span dimensions. Maybe he was one of those immortals, beyond human ken—his presence, his voice. Perhaps she was building him up in her memory. She grimaced with self-mocking, closed the old volume, and slid it reverently back into place.

She had a growing pile of copied language texts beside her. She intended to amass samplings of all the early tongues of the Isles—twelve languages from six groups across four branches of the Indo-European family. She would be missing lesser-known Traveler dialects, but that would require research in other libraries, mostly in Europe. Glancing over one transcription after another, she mumbled the sounds, using pronunciation keys to see if any resonated with her memories of that night.

Near closing time, she came to the end of the British Isles collection. Her back hurt from getting up and down, carrying massive volumes to the copy machines. She laid the last legend gently on the glass, dropped in a coin, and pressed Start. Tucking the sheet that emerged in with the rest, she hefted her enormous canvas bag and left.

Outside, the campus had grown dark. She made her way back to her car and drove down the hill to University Avenue, now slick with reflected lights. As Kay crossed the San Rafael Bridge, San Francisco was a jeweled cityscape across the black waters of the bay. A deep well of sadness, knowing Sophie was there, yet would soon be thousands of miles away, weighed on her heart.

At the same time, she itched to reach home and work on the languages she'd copied. She would sound them all out until one resonated as the true one. In the meantime, she had a four-hour drive ahead of her. She pushed in a CD audio book of Anne Rice's *Blood and Gold*—a story where art, history and the supernatural collided. Perhaps it was no stranger than the story currently taking over her life.

As the dark countryside passed, Roger Rees's voice wove the tale of Marius, the scholarly vampire who traveled through ancient Italy. Cocooned between headlighted trees, she was two thousand years away, hanging out with the oldest vampires.

Chapter 9

Kay arrived home at two a.m. and hauled the sack of copied texts into the house. Tired as she was, it was hard to resist digging in right away. But her eyes prickled from the long drive and late hour. She dragged herself to bed.

In pre-dawn dark, she woke, too excited to sleep. She put on coffee and settled in the kitchen alcove, ready to sort the languages.

Was it time to quit ber job? she asked herself. She had enough savings to tide her for a while. How long could this tangent continue?

At eight a.m., she picked up the phone and punched in her work number. She started leaving a message explaining that she might not be able to continue to work for Luminous Life. To her surprise, the owner, Olivia Rivera, came on the line; she seldom deigned to come near phones until calls were filtered.

"Kay, take the holidays off," Olivia said. "In January, we can revisit the situation."

Kay thanked her, knowing classes were full for the season and work in enrollment would be light. In fact, Luminous Life could do very well without her; Nola would just have to resign herself to doing paperwork.

By noon, Kay had twelve neatly labeled stacks and was fairly sure the language she sought was an ancient form of Irish, Manx, Scottish Gaelic, Cornish, Welsh, or Breton.

When she came to the Welsh word for "dove"—*colomen*—a flash lit in her like an explosion. She sat back hard against the kitchen bench. Hadn't Baird said that to her? Wasn't it that exact sound? She said it aloud again, trying for the intonation, softly, eyes fluttering with the effort of imagining him speaking the word to her.

I'm trying too hard. She couldn't be absolutely sure, but the more she worked with Middle Welsh, the more signals shot up. In her mind? In her body? Somewhere. Yet what now? How would knowing that help her get back to Baird's time?

It seemed her only hope, her only connection. Each time she uttered words and phrases in Middle Welsh, using the pronunciation key, a juttering of unconscious knowledge awakened. There was not much Middle Welsh, solely religious manuscripts. Yet she dropped into unswerving focus on studying the language documents late into the night until she could no longer keep her eyes open.

Two days into a dialectal abyss, Sophie called. It was like climbing out of a tidal sink to work her way to surface consciousness and answer the phone. Her daughter was boarding the plane to return to France.

"Come when you can, Mom. I'll show you ruins with runes carved into them."

Kay could tell Sophie had given thought to further inducements. Her throat tightened. "I will definitely come. I'd love nothing better."

"Okay. They're calling my flight. Give Rousseau a Solstice hug for me. Tell him to visit."

"I will. You take care. And enjoy this time, honey. Make the most of it."

"I will. Love you."

Kay paced the house, reciting the lines of the ancient tongue. At times, she found herself crouched on the kitchen bench, hanging onto her silver pendant as she read the words. Sometimes sounds and scenes surrounded her. Then she thought she was drawing closer.

She barely ate, hardly took time for sleep.

Wanting more material, she went online and downloaded the manuscript of Taliesin's songs, *The Book of Taliesin*, from the National Library of Wales. These were the oldest recorded Welsh poems, published in the tenth century, though he was from the sixth.

"It would have been composed in the Cumbric dialect of the north," she murmured, consulting the map of Wales that she now had tacked to the wall. She ran a finger along the shoreline to see if anything drew her attention—a sensation or sign—but nothing happened. She studied and recited the poems again and again.

On December 20th, Jarl called to ask if he could come

by with a gift for her. She had not seen much of the clan since Sophie's visit, but had picked up gifts for Jarl, Joaquin, and Shelley earlier in the month. She quickly wrapped Jarl's present, a batik hanging depicting the ice bridge to Jotunheim, one of the Nine Worlds in the Nordic Tree of Life. Then she sat back down at the kitchen table to continue copying one of Taliesin's poems, the old-fashioned kinesthetic way of committing to memory.

A wave of urgency gripped her. She stared at the pen in her hand, confused, then placed the tip to the paper. "Very shoddy quality, this," she grumbled. Kay started to write and scowled at the ink coming out. The pen worked, but not to her satisfaction.

The doorbell rang.

"*Dewch i mewn*," Kay called. She rose as Jarl appeared in the kitchen doorway. "*Roeddwn i'n ysgrifennu nodyn atoch chi, ofn y byddwn i'n gweld eich eisiau.*"

Jarl stared at her, uncomprehending.

She repeated herself, pointing at the paper.

"Kay...you're not—you're not speaking English." His smile wavered. He lifted the paper she indicated. "I don't get it. Is this code?"

I stared at him, then down at the note and read, translating, "I mun hurry to fetch..." She glanced up.

"Fetch?" he asked. "That's quaint."

She continued reading, slower, "Centaury, hellebore, mandrake and mugwort from Aelfwyn." As Kay said the last word, the room whirled and she stumbled.

Jarl caught her. "Whoa!"

The room kept spinning. Kay saw not Jarl but a different scene altogether: the inside of a rustic cottage. She smelled peat smoke, that distinctive earthy aroma like aged whisky.

"Kay? Are you still with me?"

She nodded, trying to look into his eyes but not really seeing him. His voice seemed far away, his face blurred.

He took her by the shoulders.

Her vision cleared. She saw his worried expression.

"Kay," he said, struggling, "I care about you. I...get worried that you might be in a bit of an ... I hope you don't take this the wrong way but—a bit of an obsession."

She knew her clothes and hair must be in disarray, and now she appeared to be talking in tongues and swooning. She put out a hand to him, to convey apology. Had he been confessing affection for her? He was a good-looking guy, and an appealing romantic prospect. But she was only half present in that room.

"I'd better go," Jarl mumbled, obviously stung by her weird behavior, "and let you *fetch your herbs from yon village*," he tried to joke, then exited down the hall.

"Jarl. Let me fix you hot egg nog." She mustered graciousness. Her urgent errand with the languages, with the note she'd been writing, seemed distant and bizarre now, while Jarl was warm, real. What was wrong with her? She did need to ground herself on *terra ferma*.

She rushed out of the kitchen, only to hear the front door close. "Shit." She pulled the door open and looked out. He was gone.

She returned to the kitchen and picked up the note. A strange script was scrawled across the page—lines of varying lengths crosshatched along horizontal grids. She stared, uncomprehending. This was not her handwriting. It dawned on her that it was the ogham, oldest writing system of the British Isles. She had not studied it enough to have written in it spontaneously.

She sat and, with her finger, traced what must be a name

at the end. She'd said, "Aelfwyn." It sounded it like "ale-VEEN." Dizziness swept over her. She squeezed her eyes shut, gripping the table.

After a moment, she opened them a crack, stomach queasy. The room had darkened. No, it had not darkened. It was not the same room.

She sat at a table in a wattle-and-daub cottage, hay poking here and there on the walls from uneven plaster. Heavy drapes allowed in only dim light through deep window alcoves where she caught glimpses of a slate-gray sky.

Snuffling drew her attention to her feet. Two tan, slender hounds lay on coarse wood flooring, noses on forepaws. They watched her with adoring eyes, brows twisting expressively. One's head lay on the hem of her long dress.

Long dress? She wondered if she could be hallucinating from lack of nourishment. But it was too real: the textures, the woven seat of the chair that held her, the unfamiliar smells. Panic settled in her stomach as the implications of the ancient surroundings and floor-length dress gripped her.

Air, chilled and penetrating, slipped through the garments to her skin. She pulled a wool shawl close around her shoulders and noticed the sound of a fire. She turned to see a blaze crackling merrily in a fireplace molded into the wall. A candle, stuck into a clay figure of a bird, flickered on the table, disturbed by gusts of wind that eddied from the narrow windows.

Kay's arm rested near a sheet of thin, nearly translucent paper and a bottle of ink next to it. She held a quill pen. Her gaze rested on the note, written in the same long-lined scrawl she'd been penning moments before.

"I mun fetch centaury, hellebore, mandrake, and mugwort from Aelfwyn," she read silently. Her breathing came quick and shallow. She concentrated on the scents of burning wood and peat, lantern oil, and herbs hanging from rafters. She knew these scents, this cottage. She'd seen it dimly when she'd touched the silver piece.

A knock came at the door. Her heart raced full speed. An old quavering voice called, "Kyna? Mistress Healer, are y' in?"

Kyna. The woman she'd been mistaken for on the hillside at Samhain. Was she dreaming now? Had she been dreaming then? Was it the same dream?

Her body rose and walked to the door without her willing it. Her hand reached for the leather thong looped over a peg. But it was not her hand. The turquoise-and-onyx ring she always wore on her left middle finger was gone. Other rings adorned several fingers on both hands. As her palm turned, pulling the door open, she saw a deep scar at the base of the thumb pad. That was not hers either.

A worn-seeming woman leaned on a gnarled cane.

Kay's vocal cords vibrated with a rich-timbered voice, coming from her throat. "Efa. Do come in." The voice was like hers but also different. It was both familiar and foreign. As she reached to help the woman over the threshold, she glanced out at an icy landscape and several primitive homes with thatched roofs. A sparse line of trees, stark in winter, bordered a dirt road higher than the level of the house, shored up by stones. A tiny creek burbled alongside.

Efa hobbled past. Kyna closed the door. She slipped a hand under the bundled clothing of the woman's arm and guided her to a chair.

"What be troublin' ye?" Kay heard herself ask as she leaned, pressed fingertips to Efa's forehead, then peered into her eyes.

"I be weary th' past days. Can't sleep much at all."

Kay detected the presence of the other woman, Kyna, although not clearly discernible from her own thoughts. She wondered if Kyna noticed her presence as well. She hadn't said, "Oh my god, what's happening inside me!" Kay hoped her panic did not come through to the other woman. Shallow breathing, a racing heart, these they shared. How could Kyna not notice? Kay's thoughts circled, wondering how she'd gotten here, and how she might return home.

She forced herself away from the thoughts so as not to set off an anxiety attack for them both.

Kyna asked the woman about her diet and bodily functions. Kay tried to back off and let the healer work, bringing Efa water from a jug in a kitchen area.

Kyna left the room through a curtained doorway at the back. Turning right, she walked down a short hall, entered an apothecary, and stared at shelves that filled the four walls. Three were jammed with containers of every size and sort, carefully labeled in the sweeping lines of the ogham. Herbs hung and vines twined at the tops of shelves. There were tall, narrow windows on two sides letting in wan light. On the fourth wall, books and scrolls of varied textures and sizes were packed, tied in dyed leather cords, or stitched in heavy twine—a great number of texts for that era, some adorned with braids and tassels. The lettering was not just the ogham, but also runic, Latinate, and Greco.

A high table stretched through the center, cluttered with scales, bottles, tools, and bowls. Swift and sure, she selected herbs from the shelves, mixed, chopped, crushed, and folded them into neat cloth packets. Mesmerized, Kay watched her hands do trained work with which she was utterly unfamiliar.

She returned to the patient, handed her the herbal

remedies and helped tuck them into her basket. Then she instructed her on how to prepare the tonic "for yer blood".

Efa smiled, gap-toothed, and patted her cheek, then pulled a cloth sack from her basket. Kyna opened it, peered in, and touched the soft down she was being offered in payment. Kyna thanked her. Kay felt herself speaking medieval Welsh with the other woman's voice.

Efa hobbled out the door. Kay watched her make her way over the narrow bridge to the road. As she turned to the right, Kay noticed thatched homes snuggled closer together in that direction. She heard the ocean's low, steady rumbling. To her left, the road rose into a forest.

The hounds pressed into Kyna's legs, wheezing as their eyes circled to her face, brows twisting eloquently. She fondled their ears and cooed to them. They stayed with her as she turned back to the house.

Kay wanted to explore. She approached the weaving area and touched the cloth, self-conscious. Did her wants control the other woman's actions? Part of her knew the history of every object. She was full of curiosity about the rest. The loom was surrounded by a spinning wheel and yarns. It had the hanging weights she'd missed when she first started weaving. She now knew it was Kyna in her that had done the missing. She reached out and touched the cloth being woven. It bore the same energy as hers.

She wished she could talk to Kyna, ask her questions, but didn't know how. When had she acquired the other woman's skills and memories? Even her fluency in the language? Was she in a time preceding the Samhain when she thought she first met Baird? But then why had the memories just begun arising? They seemed to have started that night, with her Samhain trip to the hillside.

Kay continued exploring. In the back hall, opposite the

apothecary, a heavy curtain opened onto a bedroom dominated by a tall wooden bedstead, carved and stained dark. More drapes covered shelves of clothing. Rugs and tapestries warmed the floors and walls.

At a dresser, she picked up a hand mirror made of copper, one side shiny, enameled, and polished to a gleam; the other, of raised silver, depicted a heron in a marsh scene.

In the reflecting side, the woman stared back at her. Her face was uncannily similar. Kay understood, immediately, why on that moonlit Samhain, she'd been mistaken for Kyna. Her hair was a similar shade of chestnut. Kay wondered what might be used, a thousand years ago, to give it a bright henna-like sheen. Its intricate braiding, caught up with bone combs, was what she'd been trying to achieve.

Nervous, facing Kyna's intelligent eyes, she studied her. As she dwelt in her mind, she shared more and more of the other woman's knowledge. With sudden understanding, she knew that the pattern she'd plaited into her hair meant, "I will encounter something unusual and significant today". It could be used to signal others with a message, or perhaps express a prediction. It was a code of the Travelers by whom Kyna had been raised. She now understood more about her urge to plait her hair in designs.

As she held the mirror, she caught memories of when Kyna first acquired it, from a traveling salesman along the road, using some of her first earnings as a healer. She had gathered other items that made the home plush—velvet cloths, polished instruments with various purposes, stained glass insets. Kyna's pride, and more, came through to her. A determination to have a set dwelling. Kay saw other images—a dirty-faced child, always on the move with the Traveler caravan. There was a distant longing for parents lost. Only Duff, Kyna's brother, remained from her earliest life.

Kyna shook herself, as from an uninvited revery, and went methodically through the house, closing heavy drapes at every window. She took a chamberpot out the back door, down steps, and across the yard to empty. The hounds frisked past her, noses to the ground, sniffing. At the end of a row of sheds Kay emptied it in a crude out-house, through a gap in planking. The pit below ran be-hind, into a field. She pressed her tongue to the roof of her mouth to keep out the smell. The hounds leapt away and took care of their business as she took care of hers.

"Rhyn, Ffin," she sang out, climbing the back steps again.

In the main room, she fed the hounds scraps, then warmed stew at the fire. When it bubbled, she scooped some into a wood bowl and sat by the hearth, eating it with warmed flat bread.

Kay savored the unfamiliar flavors. The stew was de-licious and thick, with potatoes and root vegetables. The hounds settled on the rug and gnawed bones. Kay thought of Oz. Who would feed him? For that matter, what was happening to her body while she was there?

Kyna finished the stew and set down the bowl for the dogs to lick.

Kay longed for a novel. It would help settle her mind. She thought of the volumes in the apothecary. How fasci-nating it would be to see the texts of an ancient time. Very likely, few had survived, if this was as far back as she sus-pected—perhaps a thousand years.

Getting up, Kyna banked the fire. Kay marveled at the deftness with which her hands did these unfamiliar tasks while she rode along. She took the lantern from the table and willed Kyna to venture back to the apothecary. Not one to force others, she sought consensus: "Want to go look at those books again?" but she could not speak to Kyna directly from within her mind. Kay wondered if she'd ever learn how.

To Kay's surprise, Kyna headed back into the high-ceilinged work room full of the smell of herbs, sharp, earthy, complex, and held the lantern up to the books. *She understood my desire*, Kay thought. She set the lamp on the table, and pulled out a volume, then another, settling on one full of intriguing diagrams and sketches. She tucked the hide-bound book under her arm, and sent Kyna a thought: "Thank you very much," unsure if it came across to the other woman.

In the bedroom, Kyna's fingers made short work of the many fastenings on her dress. Underneath, clever under-clothing was surprisingly comfortable and unrestrictive. Before she pulled on a nightgown, Kay glanced down. The woman's build was similar to hers, strong with soft curves. Even a faint birthmark above her left breast resembled Kay's. She wondered how old Kyna was. She could pick up some, but not all, knowledge from the other's mind. There were touches of silver in her hair, as there were in Kay's, yet every aspect of Kyna appeared well preserved. If she was in her forties, she'd normally look far older a millennium ago. Perhaps her extensive knowledge of salves and balms made the difference.

Kyna pulled on a well-worn flannel nightgown. At the dressing table, she loosened her plaits and ran fingers through her hair. The smell of lavender, and perhaps rosemary, wafted up. Kay imagined she rubbed oils into her skin, just enough to moisten and soften. She pressed a sweet fennel stick to her teeth and scrubbed, then swished into a wooden bowl.

The bed smelled of lemongrass, mint, and sweet violet, overlaid by the gentle musk of humans. The mattress rustled like straw, softened by a thick layer of batting. The hounds settled on the braided rug with contented huffs and curled into each other. Kay pulled the book forward into the pool of lantern light and lay propped on an elbow, turning the pages. She avidly studied the notes and drawings until her eyelids drooped, then blew out the lamp. She lay listening to night sounds: gulls crying, the low rush of sea upon shore, and an underlying roar rising and falling as the tide moved. Dropping into a fitful sleep at last, her final thoughts were of her children. How would she communicate with them? Would she ever return to their time? What had she gotten herself into? A lump in her throat ached and she wondered if Kyna felt it, too. If she knew what it was about. If she read any of Kay's thoughts as Kay read some of hers.

Chapter 10

When she woke, wan light revealed the contours of Kyna's bedroom, reminding Kay that she was in another time. Thoughts of Oz starving gnawed at her. At least he had a cat door and could forage. Or hunt.

Bodily urges coaxed Kyna out of the warm covers. Her bare feet slid into fur-lined boots and she threw on a thick cloak. The hounds danced around her with playful crouches and leaps, jostled her down the short hall to the back door, and dashed past as she opened to icy wind. She decided in favor of the chamberpot, obscured behind a curtain in a tiny hall alcove.

Her desire for tea differed from Kay's preference for a strong cup of freshly ground coffee first thing. In the main room, she stirred up the fire, then scooped curled leaves from a tin into heating water. Pale light edged the drapes covering the windows.

She heard distant singing and her heart leapt.

Kay recognized the voice. Their shared heart raced for her as well.

Kyna rushed onto the porch as a figure emerged from the woods and strode along the lane in their direction, gliding with supple grace and vigor from light to shadow as the rising sun sent pink fingers between trees.

Kay knew that walk.

The man's breath plumed white in the frosty morning. His singing grew louder. The hounds whined, their tails banging against Kyna's legs and the railing.

Excitement cascaded through, along with confusion. Kay was about to see that enigmatic man, Baird, of whom she'd thought often the past seven weeks, who called her "Dove", and "fathomed her spirit".

Who was Kyna to him? The thought came to Kay then. *He won't even know I'm here.*

Baird's tall form bounded across the stream and, running the last strides up the steps to the porch, caught Kyna in a whirling hug. The hounds leapt and bayed around them. Kyna's heart thundered against his chest. Kay thought she must be adding to the thunder.

Baird drew back and looked into her eyes with delight and warmth. Kay knew it was not for her. She was a voyeur, lurking inside the other woman. After all this time, she was with Baird again, yet she wasn't. Panic rose. She was caged inside this other woman.

She made herself concentrate on enjoying his wild woodland scents.

"Kyna. Ye look fine this mornin'," he said, a huskiness of emotion deepening the tone.

Kay had tried to replay the sound of his voice so often that it zinged through her now to hear it.

His eyes, suddenly tentative, searched Kyna's face.

He looked different from when Kay had seen him at Samhain. Younger maybe, more carefree. There had been shadows under his eyes. Was there less silver in his hair now? This had to be a time years earlier. That meant that, at Samhain, she had already been here! She realized that was why she already had Kyna's knowledge of weaving. Her urge to set up a loom and plait patterns in her hair were memories she had already acquired. But had they been suppressed? She knew she hadn't thought about this for several years. There was no way.

At last Baird brought his mouth to Kyna's. A swirl of sensations pushed every other thought out except the pleasure. Kay melted into the heat of intimacy with this man who so entranced her. Morose thoughts flitted through her mind: he's Kyna's, not mine. Yet she let herself experience the passion as hers, for the moment. After all, she was stuck there.

They pulled apart.

"How long will ye stay this time?" Kyna snapped.

Was it Kay's imagination or was Kyna surprised at her own words, her tone? She gave a half-laugh and busied herself looking for ticks on Ffyn.

"Gi' a man a breath." Baird winked, but there was tension in his voice as he stomped his boots on the doormat. "We'll be off together t' the solstice faire on the morrow. Ye know that quite well, don' ye?" A slight question lifted the end.

"I do know that, my fine man." Kyna took his arm.

Solstice faire? A thrill ran through Kay. But how long would that take? How long could she stay out of her body?

Baird stepped into the house and dropped his dusty travel pack to the side. Next to it, he gently placed an angular harp bag, worn yet beautiful, with embroidery that must have once been bright. He hooked his cape on a peg and strode to the fire. His restless amble told her that four walls constrained him.

The hounds loped after him.

"Hungry?" Kyna asked.

"I'm caked wi' road dirt, m' lady." Baird made even that simple statement sound poetic. "No' fit for house nor vittles."

"Want a hot bath then?"

"Aye. But it'll wait. We need supplies from town. I can grab a bite there." Baird stepped to the table and peered down at the note. "I mun hurry to fetch centaury, hellebore, mandrake, and mugwort from Aelfwyn." He glanced up, quizzical. "This be fer me?"

Kyna appeared uncomfortable, as though a confusion of her own attached itself to the letter. "I was goin' yesterday, and then…" She shrugged.

He frowned. "These herbs be fer protection. Is that no' right?"

"I just wanted…clearer sight is all. No need to fuss," she said. briskly. "Let's get t' the market." She gathered bags and, after a quick inventory of the shelves, headed toward the back door.

"What be ye' seekin' sight on?" he asked.

Kyna turned, and her fists went to her hips. "I thought y' were in a hurry for the sellers, man."

Baird chuckled, dropped the note, and went past her down the hall, muttering, "That be fer protection, an amulet. I know it." At the back door, he called, "I don't like it. There be somethin' ye're not sayin'."

At the curtain to the apothecary, Kyna turned to him sharply. "Half the year I do jest fine without ye broodin' over me."

"Mayhap," said Baird. "But again, mayhap we sh'd ride t' Borth today. Yer kennin's never been wrong, my beautiful witch."

Kyna sniffed, but her pleasure at his remark was apparent. She softened. "I had a passin' fear. Let's get ourselves t' town."

Baird stepped out the back door.

In the apothecary, Kyna put a few items in her bags.

Moments later Baird returned, wet hair tied neatly back in a leather thong.

As they met in the hall Kyna said, laughing, "Well, that be a bit better. Ye've removed enough road dirt, I c'n see yer face."

Baird touched his lips to her cheek. "I need t' get a new harp string from Finch. Don' let me forget."

Kyna nodded. At the front door, they pulled on warm capes. Baird's was of fine hide, with embroidery around the lapel and hem, which brushed his calves. He looked dramatic, the free bard in his stance, an attractive blend of refined and wild. For the first time, Kay could imagine him at court. He drew the strap of his harp bag over his shoulder and they left. Unaware of the secret passenger, they crossed the bridge and started down the road in matching strides, hand in hand, arms swinging.

"Through the mist and dawning light," Kyna sang with a sturdy, full voice, into the bright, crisp morning air, "the song of warblers mellow." She cocked her head upward a tree as a tiny bird, as if inspired, let out a fine string of notes.

Baird whistled a replica of the bird's call. Then he joined Kyna's song, "Came floatin' o'er the meadow bright, where grew the wheat so yellow."

They harmonized, gliding and fitting into each other as they strode toward town.

Elation burbled in her. This was life as it should be, she thought.

A stout woman straightened from her work in a yard and called out, "Mornin' Kyna, Baird." Maredydd, Kyna's aunt. Kay knew this from Kyna's store of knowledge, surely. "How long ha' ye been back, Baird?"

"Just this morn'," he responded, waving.

Further along, a thin woman around Kyna's age eyed them from her porch.

"Mornin', Angharad," Kyna offered.

"Mornin', Baird." The woman ignored Kyna, her tone clipped. After a pause, she added, as if unwilling, "Kyna," then turned and entered her house, slamming the door.

"She always did resent me takin' ye from her." Kyna turned her face up to Baird.

"Ye never took me. I were never hers." Baird shrugged.

They came to where two roads met, at the sea and converging with a river estuary. A scattering of houses, a tavern, and market stalls lined the coastal road. To Kyna, this place was *Llanbadarn Fawr*. In modern time, Kay knew it as Aberystwyth; she'd visited the university there. She explored further into Kyna's thoughts and found out *Llanbadarn Fawr* was a Celtic monastery, down the road past her home. That was the only real name for the place. Beyond the stall, the road and sea wall ended in a hill.

Fishing boats dotted the beach and bobbed in the bay that formed at the mouth of the river. Kay thought of the sight from the hilltop at Samhain. Surely this was the same town. She imagined torches wavering in the night. Yes, this could well be it.

They stopped at the first booth.

"A fine lookin' cheese," Kyna remarked upon a round of cheese cut in slices on a board. Waxed balls hung from the stall's brim.

The woman behind the board was bundled in layers of warm woolen clothing. She slapped her thigh and gave a great guffaw. "Fine lookin' cheese it is, Mistress Kyna. And you two are a fine lookin' sight yerselves. Come in from the woods, have ye, Baird?" She cocked her head, her crinkling eyes giving the man a once over. "Fine lookin' cheese, indeed." Her voice bore a suggestive tone.

"Hands off, Gwladus," Kyna said, with no rancor.

Baird glanced up from sniffing a cheese round, one brow raised in mock alarm.

"Ye c'n do nothin' boot m' eyes though, c'n ye?" Gwladus shot back saucily.

"Oh, c'n I not?" Kyna's smile was wicked.

"If ye let 'im run all over the country and beyond, half the year and more, how c'n ye think you're keepin' 'im, love?" Gwladus replied, obviously ready to stir up whatever she could.

Holding out coins, Kyna stared back confidently, slipping her hand under Baird's arm. He was already moving toward the next booth.

Gwladus pushed away the coins. "I'll be by for treating an ailment o' mine one day soon."

"Nay, Gwladus, I'll pay," Kyna insisted.

"No sense tradin' money back and forth." Gwladus turned away with finality and began sorting merchandise.

"Ye'll come see me then?" Kyna said.

"And don't go askin' what 'tis, Master Bard. Or ye'll be singin' 'bout it cross the country." Gwladus tossed the words, teasing, over her substantial shoulder.

"That interestin' is it, this ailment?" he shot back as he headed down the row.

The woman howled with laughter. "Wouldn't ye like to know?"

"No, I wouldn't," Baird whispered, with a grin.

The couple moved to another booth. They greeted

townsfolk and vendors who obviously knew them well. All had fond comments, some bordering on reverent. Kyna and Baird exchanged relaxed banter with them.

Kay wavered between nervous tension and enjoying the prestige, trying to keep herself in the background, hoping not to confuse Kyna with her thoughts, which she now knew could affect the other woman.

They parted, Baird to climb a low hill to the fiddle maker, Kyna to tend to an injured fisherman. Hywel lived in a tiny hovel on the shore side, pressed between a smithy and storage sheds. He was laid up from an infected wound taken at sea. Kyna ducked under the low lintel and entered the dark gloom of the shack. Strong smells were nearly overpowering in the closeness. Hywel, deep under rough blankets in a bed by the wall, could barely be seen.

Kay mustered her defenses against the odors.

Kyna lifted a lantern and approached the bed. "Hywel, how ye be farin'?" she asked the shape under the covers. She set the lantern on a table close by and, taking his injured hand, examined the wound.

"Oh, it's lookin' much better," Kyna said, with strength that surprised Kay. It looked gruesome to her. She cleaned it, applied fresh liniment, and covered it with new bandages from her basket.

"Ye be an angel, Kyna," he croaked, looking miserable but clearly trying to muster good spirits.

Though his face had an unhealthy cast, Kay could see he was a robust man—probably not even middle-aged. The mound of tattered covers had made him appear more shrunken than he was. "I'm goin' t' give blessin's to Brigid fer ye when I'm back at sea."

"I accept that with honor, Master Hywel," Kyna said, rising and taking the lantern to the kitchen area where she scrubbed everything in sight. Then her eyes landed on a fresh meat pie, partially eaten. "I notice Widow Madwen's been by," she said, casting a smile toward the bed. "Ha' she been lookin' after ye'?"

"Oh, aye. She be by most days. She be a good woman, is Maddy."

"That she be," Kyna agreed as she put water on for tea.

By the time Baird poked his head through the doorway, Kyna had built up the fire and straightened the blankets around the fisherman. Baird crossed to the bed and greeted the injured man.

"Now you be gettin' yerself mended." He patted the man's shoulder, showing no sign of the smells that pervaded the place.

As they left Hywel's cabin, Kyna shoved the dirty bandages deep into her basket. The afternoon had darkened. Raindrops pounded on roofs. They pulled up their hoods and ran for the overhang of the only tavern, "The Kestrel" sign swinging and creaking in a rising wind. Baird opened the heavy door and they pushed through with others into a warm inn that glowed golden and hummed with happy noise. Half the town had had the same idea.

They squeezed in at a long table, among pungent steamy clothing. A spotty lad arrived with platters of baked fish and parsnips. Pitchers of frothy beer went around the table.

Once they'd eaten, patrons called to Baird for a song. He was more than happy to move to a stool by the wall and pull out his harp, with its new strings.

Several songs later, they said their goodbyes and pushed out the door with much of the crowd. The rain had lightened to mist.

Kyna climbed into bed next to Baird, her back to him.

He snuggled up and said drowsily, "I know ye were expectin' me a sun-turn ago, but Einion kept me at court t' sing th' end o' the hunt."

"A pox on Einion," she mumbled.

"Never say it, witch. That's me bread 'n butter."

She slipped her feet between his legs.

"Those be cold, woman." Baird circled her with his arms. "What have we got these on for?" He tugged at their nightclothes, then nuzzled her ear.

Trepidation rose in Kay.

Next thing, he was snoring quietly.

A great relief washed over Kay. Lower regions of Kyna's body, however, registered disappointment. Kay listened a long time to Baird's breaths before sleep consumed her.

Chapter 11

Kay woke several times in the dark. Baird slept soundly. She marveled to be pressed against his warm form, albeit in Kyna's body, her arm flung lightly across his waist. Not wanting to wake him, she took soft breaths, until sleep returned for both of them.

At last, she came fully awake to grey dawn light. No one lay next to her.

Kyna sat up and listened for sounds in the house or yard.

Kay heard jangling and shouting out on the road.

Throwing back the covers, she scrambled from the bed and layered on thick leggings, warm wool socks, skirts, shirts, and sweaters.

Emptying the chamberpot in the icy back of the house was an adventure of stiff blue fingers and frozen snot. Morning business done, she clumped through the house in thick boots and looked out the front door.

As far as she could see, wagons filled the road. Dark figures bustled about, carrying torches and lanterns in the predawn, checking loads, and chatting.

Kyna collected bulging bags and full baskets. Making three trips, she created a heap next to a wagon that stood across from the house. All the while, Ffyn and Rhyn leapt and jumped along. With the last load, Baird appeared and helped lift the bundles into the back. Kyna shoved a heap of blankets over the rim just as a young man approached.

For just a second, in the dim light, Kay thought she saw her son, Rousseau, with his dark curly hair and tall, slender build, and her heart stuttered.

"Mornin', Owain." Kyna gave the young man a peck on the cheek. Close up, Kay saw differences. A scar on one side of his face. His eyes were not the same, nor the mouth. He was not her Rousseau, but the reminder gave her situation stark new contours. He was due to arrive at her house in a few days. What would he do if no one answered the phone? If no one came to the door? Her spirits descended into a low-panicked simmer. She couldn't go to the faire. She had to get home.

The boy's response interrupted her troubled thoughts. "Mornin', Mistress Kyna." His smile revealed teeth that crossed slightly at the front. Not Rousseau's teeth. The less he looked like her son, the more her heart relaxed.

Others came to greet Kyna and enfold her in hugs in an atmosphere of jubilation. A crackled, dried-apple face appeared at the back of the wagon, over the bundles, and a gnarled hand held out a mug of warm cider.

"Ta, Beota," Kyna thanked the aged woman, accepting the hot drink in mittened hands.

She turned back to Owain. "How be yer family?"

"Mum's doin' well," he responded. "She stayed home with the li'llest. I've got two o' the eldest sleepin' inside with Gran. Han't seen Pa these three months."

"He's off fightin' with Thorold's men, nay?"

"Aye."

Baird approached. "How are things down in Dinbych-y-Pysgod, lad?"

Leave it to a bard to use the village's long name rather than the usual "down Din way", she caught Kyna's amused thought. What storyteller could resist saying, in full, "little town of the fishes"?

A chortle rose and Kay suddenly missed letting out a laugh of her own, even hearing her own voice. She hadn't spoken in a day and a half.

The men offered Kyna a hand up into the wagon. She gathered the thick layers of her skirt for the climb and settled, legs dangling over the backboard. Baird clapped Owain on the shoulder and jumped up next to Kyna. In a near frenzy, Ffyn and Rhyn ran up and down, anxious to get going.

The long caravan inched forward. Baird and Kyna stuffed blankets around themselves to cushion the bumping of the road. The hounds loped alongside, clearly filled with glee. Kay heard other dogs bark, howl, yip, and whine. They all seemed to stay near their designated wagons.

Glancing out the back at the receding houses, uneasiness welled. They were leaving the place that connected her to her time. With the rounded hill in sight, its standing stones bristling starkly against the faintly rosy edge of sky, the only anchor to everything Kay knew, her past. Would she lose the ability to return home? Even if she could separate herself from Kyna, what could she run to? She had no idea how to send herself back into the 21st Century.

The wagons entered dark woods. Looking back, she saw for the first time a stone tower half-covered in ivy at the back of Kyna's house. She ran through her memories of the hallway, trying to imagine where an entrance to a tower might be.

As they passed through dark woods, Baird sang, "T'was on the way to market I traveled, when on the road fair Kyna I saw." He squeezed Kyna's hand in the dark and leaned in for a kiss. Her heart raced and thoughts of the tower dissolved. They had clearly been together a long time. Would her heart still race for such a kiss, or did it beat harder because of me?

The family in the wagon behind joined the song. It carried on down the line and Kay let her worries drift into the back of her mind.

The forest lasted only a short while. The caravan emerged into fields and rolling hills, then onto a wider road along a river. The light of day grew swiftly. Beota, from where she lay snuggled into blankets toward the front of the wagon, called out over the grinding of the wheels, "I hear yer son'll be at Machynlleth this year wi' th'other fledglin' bards."

For a brief moment, she thought Kyna was talking about her own son. But Baird answered, "It be true. Hamelyn'll be there."

Hamelyn. They had a son? Or was it Baird's son?

"And when were ye gonna tell me he was goin' t' be there?" Kyna responded with some heat.

"I jest heard it at one o' the wagons, my fair one," Baird defended. "I was gettin' to it."

"Ye were gettin' to it." Kyna pinched him.

"Ow! Gods take ye, woman." Baird held his side and grabbed Kyna's waist for a tickle. She playfully pushed him away, pressed her hands together, and stared out the back of the wagon. Kyna contemplated seeing her son. Sweet tingles played in her stomach and shimmied to her heart. Baird and Kyna shared a son. Kay caught images in her mind. A handsome lad, in his late teens or early twenties.

Rousseau welled up in Kay's mind, and she added her own turmoil of emotions to the hand-wringing as the wagon wheels crunched on through the icy countryside. What if she couldn't get back to him? She was involved in things she had no idea how to control. She'd found her way back to Baird's world at last, but she had no idea how to get herself out. If Rousseau arrived at her house, and she was nowhere to be found, there'd be no clues to where she'd gone. In fact, he'd probably find her sitting in the kitchen, her mind not in her body.

Tears welled.

Kyna wiped her eyes.

Baird turned to her, curiosity puckering his brow. He started a new song, "Fiddler's Cat." Kyna and Beota joined in. Kyna's mouth formed the lyrics and Kay knew them, too, as others down the line of wagons sang along. She let Kyna's joy in singing drum out Kay's apprehension. She thought Kyna shared it, based on the tears. Could Kyna read any of her thoughts? How puzzling that would be for her. At least Kay knew the situation, knew who Kyna was and who she was. Did Kyna know about Kay at all?

Baird and Kyna turned to each other with laughing eyes, giving certain words extra punch. Kay heard a girl's voice pipe up from the mounds of blankets in the wagon, one of Owain's siblings, but she soon drifted back into sleep with the rocking and swaying of the wagon.

They crested a hill and descended into a long valley with its clusters of stone houses. Snow lightly dusted the ground and coated distant mountains. Soon they came upon a broad, ice-frosted estuary and marshlands where the River Dywi—"Dovey"—moved toward the sea. Heading toward what Kay thought was northeast, they angled through endless sheep land. The river, mostly frozen, zig-zagged alongside.

At midday, amid shouts and whistles, the caravan

came to a halt by a grove of leafless ash and oak trees. All climbed out and stretched stiff limbs. Their breaths puffed in clouds. Kyna's hounds circled the area, sniffing, then returned to her. Groups gathered along the roadside, arms loaded with lunch bundles. With thick quilts thrown over boulders surrounded by frost-rimed bilberry bushes, they formed a colorful scene on the riverside. The weak sun barely penetrated overcast skies. As they ate, laughter rang out and echoed on close hillsides. Baird perched next to Kyna. Kay would be cold in this environment, but Kyna, acclimated, relaxed comfortably and enjoyed the surroundings.

A red fox darted across a nearby hill, slipping beneath oaks and through brush. Owain and other young men ran after it, bows cocked, perhaps to see if they could chase down the fox's prey first. They returned empty-handed.

"Outfoxed by the fox?" one of the older men shouted. Other choice jabs followed.

A red squirrel, packing some last bit of food before the true freezes, scurried up a rowan tree. Kyna kept quiet, winking at Mother Squirrel.

Here I am, Kay thought, living within a woman who speaks an ancient tongue, writes the symbols I teach, uses herbs for healing in the oldest ways, and winks at squirrels, a thousand years ago. Has anyone ever had such an opportunity?

A falcon swept overhead, and wild geese honked their way across the sky.

Kyna slipped down from the boulder to pick late-growing wild leeks that survived in cracks and crevices of the rocks. "*I'll put it in stew,*" she thought. "*It'll add protection.*" The last came with a sense of foreboding.

Protection? Was her presence producing this concern in her?

Barley, oats, potatoes—Kyna made a mental checklist, easing her tension she helpd gather the lunch remains.

This time she and Baird climbed onto the front of the wagon, joining Owain on the buckboard for the last stretch.

It was colder up there in the full blast of the winter wind. The number of dwellings increased and Machynlleth came into view—Kay knew the town, pronounced "Ma-hunt-leth", was a center for alternative energies in her modern time. Nearing the town, the caravan crossed a stone bridge of the same gray slate as the buildings, and turned off on a rough dirt road. Encampments spread, bustling with movement: tents going up, animals being herded into makeshift corrals, loads dragged off wagons and carried on shoulders. In the distance, colorful streamers waved amidst groves of rowans, oaks, and hazels. Kay caught the blue glint of river water, where it was unfrozen. The valley climbed toward mountains. In the distance, fortress towers rose.

The wagon came to a stop where the rutted road veered into pasture lands. Baird jumped down and helped Kyna to the ground. Owain accompanied them to the back of the wagon and they piled bundles by the roadside. Then the caravan moved off toward other camps with shouts of, "See y' at the faire."

A group emerged from the trees, calling fond greetings, helping to shoulder bedding and bundles up a hill through light forest. The hounds found others to run with as Kyna and Baird walked between various hide structures—lean-tos and teepee forms—some still being erected. An elaborate mansion of a tent sat at the center. Its high cupola peaks shot up into the trees. People gathered around a campfire in the clearing by its entrance.

The area saved for Kyna and Baird was the last, higher

up the stream in a tiny glade of its own. A spacious tent had already been erected there. They entered and Kay heard the stream close by. Someone had piled sweet grasses, fresh heather, and clean batting to make a bed. Apprehension rose again as Kyna spread quilts over the top.

"Baird! Kyna!" someone called. "Come have stew."

Kyna rummaged in one of her baskets for the leeks, carrots, and potatoes to offer to the shared meal. As they arrived by the crackling communal fire, someone asked Baird, "Give us th' news."

Baird hugged adults and patted children on the head before he settled on a log by the fire. "Iago took his brother Ieuaf prisoner. He sits on the throne of Gwynedd and continues raiding."

Folks shook their heads. "What's to be done?" one man asked.

Baird shrugged, then pulled out his harp. "There be a song in the north 'bout that," he said as he tuned his strings and sang. *"Gasglu holl chi bobl a gwrando ar yr hyn a ddywedaf."* The words spoke of the reconciling of lands back to the Welsh, of a time of fair, just leadership, with some humorous barbs about royal princes thrown in.

Spirits rose. Kyna kissed her friends and dropped into low conversation. Ffyn and Rhyn sniffed the other hounds, then settled with a couple of choice bones. Their gnawing sounds combined with the medley of camp noises. Stew was passed around and conversation rose and fell comfortably as old friends caught up. Laughter rang out. The mood fell in memory of people who'd passed on since the group had last been together, but rose again with happier news, of births and weddings. Babes cried and were comforted. Children played chase games nearby.

Kyna gulped hot spiced cider. Kay enjoyed the warmth

that spread through her.

Several in the group pulled out instruments and Baird joined them for songs. Then, as if in silent understanding, he and Kyna rose. A protest went around the circle, begging Baird to stay and play. Baird grinned an apology and picked up a lantern that sent long shadows in among the trees. They made their way up the hill.

In the tent, Baird pulled Kyna into his arms.

Every cell ignited.

Kyna pushed him gently away. Her swift fingers undid her fastenings. She quickly folded her heavy winter clothing, stacking it over her travel bags, and pulled on her thick nightgown. She put out the light.

"Hey," Baird protested.

"Sorry. Did ye need that?"

"Guess not," he said. Kay heard him slipping off his clothes.

Kyna slid between the layers of bedding and a mix of scents of the hills—sweet grasses and green heather. The hounds circled several times before dropping by the entrance to the tent with gusty sighs. Baird's warm body pressed against Kyna's and his arms enfolded her. They lay listening to the sounds of camp settling for the night.

"D' ye miss seein' the stars?" Kyna asked, noticing Baird's eyes aimed at the tent roof.

"A bit, but I've got yer eyes t' keep me happy." He turned on one elbow, tucking her in close.

"You and yer honey tongue," Kyna responded, smiling.

Baird brought his mouth to hers. With a dizzying burst of elation, Kay let herself imagine him making love to her. His hand slid under the nightgown and over Kyna's breast. She gasped, moaned softly. Was it Kyna's moan or hers? Baird made no sound as his kisses built into a passionate storm. He worked off her nightgown. Skin rubbed together and, as he entered, she took in a long breath, the satisfaction deep and enthralling.

He stopped, drew back, and peered down in the dark.

What was wrong? Was she affecting how Kyna made love?

He brought his mouth back and slowly moved inside. Kay was surprised to find how well he pleasured her, bringing his hand down as he slid back and forth until she softly moaned, pleasure peaking. He came soon after, then lay still on top of her as they breathed in unison—his breath, her breath, as one. This was her favorite part—a unity words could not describe.

After a while, he moved to the side. Kyna turned into his chest. His hand softly stroked her lower back, his breath slow and satisfied. He again stared upward. "So, what is it?" he whispered, sending new shivers through her.

"What is what?" Kyna whispered into his neck.

"Th' other spirit in ye."

Kyna's breath stopped. She was silent a moment, then said, "A deer mayhap. She be needin' shelter, protection. Mayhap."

"A doe spirit, eh?" He lifted his head, angling his attention toward Kyna in the dark.

I could tell his expression from the way he spoke—a half-smile with a creased brow.

Kyna pushed up on one elbow. "D' ye sense her?"

"I think so. She do seem a gentle enough spirit. Still, worries me." His hands tightened on her, then loosened. His breathing softened and grew steady as he drifted into sleep.

Kyna slept better than Kay did that night. A tingling heat stayed in her belly a long while, giving her slow, soft, mental smiles, shared at first with a woman who was more and more a sister, until Kyna slipped into dreamland. Though the lovemaking had not been Kay's, she felt pleasure that he had detected her spirit.

Even if he thought she was a deer.

Chapter 12

Camp noises sifted into Kay's consciousness. Rosy pre-dawn light covered the entwined Baird and Kyna. He gave her neck a quick nuzzle, then bounded out of bed.

Reluctant to draw out of the warmth of the bed, Kay was relieved when Kyna stayed wrapped in the blankets.

Baird swiftly donned a handsome tunic with billowing sleeves, a vest, and trousers of soft, dyed leather. The outfit was more formal than his road wear, though Kay found it all entrancing. He tied back his hair, set a feathered hat in place, and, cape donned, leaned down for a kiss. "See ye at the faire," he said, then strode from the tent, whistling.

Once he was gone, Kyna ventured out of the cozy covers and gathered water from the stream for morning ablutions. Back in the tent, she washed, then pulled on a long, forest-green skirt. She laced a fitted bodice over a luxuriant muslin blouse. Intricate matching embroidery ran down the panels of the skirt and edged the bodice in blues and pale green shades. She fitted a wide belt around her waist, the weight of coins within it. Next, she tugged a red band, marked with the twining snakes of the healer, up her sleeve. All the while, she ran through her mind what booths she would visit.

Sitting on the bed, she carefully plaited her hair, mumbling with intensity as she concentrated, as though she were putting meanings into the design. She mumbled a different language. Kay had trouble picking up the drift but she seemed to be creating protection. She wondered what she feared. Then she checked in her hand mirror, touching here and there with lavender-scented oil. The wispy hennaed hairs at the edges of her forehead complemented her dusky peach complexion. She lined her eyes delicately with a charcoal stick and touched burgundy salve to her lips and cheeks. She finished by pulling on splendid, soft, dress boots and lifted a crimson cape to her shoulders.

"All right, all right," Kyna murmured to the hounds as they pressed tight, wheezing with excitement. She squatted to sort goods into baskets, then slipped their leather straps over her shoulders, and stepped out into the early dawn light. As she descended the hill, pride rose in Kay to be walking within a woman who moved with such dignity and confidence, who had such a profound sense of her own place and purpose in the world. Her world, Kay thought. Not mine, though she was growing more into her identity every moment.

Her boot heels struck the ground with a satisfying impact, giving her strides an extra swagger. Kay wanted to see the whole effect and longed to pass her reflection in a plate-glass window. Not likely in this time. They would need a glass-like surface on a lake.

Arriving next to the voluminous center tent, Kyna joined others around the blazing campfire. She squeezed onto the log and gaily accepted a hot mug and a warm bun filled with dried fruit bits. She smiled at a woman who cuddled a young child, next to a man dressed jauntily in his Sunday best, with a bright two-toned vest.

"We're off to see the sheep, and mayhap purchase a new ewe," the woman said, quietly.

"Best of luck finding the very best of ewes then," Kyna answered.

Baird gulped down the last of his drink, appearing poised toward the rising sounds of the faire. He slipped his harp over his shoulder, gave Kyna a wink, and strode off, waving his fruity bun as a farewell. All around the fire, folk were dressed in ornate clothing. Girls wore garlands of dried flowers, probably kept in cellars from springtime just for this purpose. Boys and men had stuck feathers into jaunty hats. Of the women, Kyna's outfit was by far the most attractive, but Kay was biased; after all, the beautiful fabrics Kyna wore shimmered with magical energy.

She finished her drink and took her leave, part of the bun still in her hand to finish along the road. Her hounds trotted alongside as she emerged from the woods and crossed a squat stone bridge to join others on the road. Sun-touched icicles, glowing pink and bright, hung from eaves along the edge of roofs in the town of Machynllyth.

She rounded a corner and a cacophony of noises rose up to meet her. She stood looking down over the faire that stretched into fields at the edge of the market town. Music, animal sounds, and laughter intermingled with babies crying, children's shouts and sellers calling their wares. Streamers and banners snapped in the cool morning wind.

Passing among the first stalls, Kay was assailed by a medley of smells—some enticing, some less so. The crowd was already a sea of color in eddies of activity, pushing, jostling, bartering or being entertained, consuming hot cider and chestnuts from booths. Faire-goers hunched by hot braziers at intervals, and the crowd swerved around them.

Kyna scanned the tops of the tents. Evidently, she spotted what she was looking for over the peaks and canvas turrets: a gold banner with a red boar indicating the artisan booths. The textile vendors and herbalists would be in the next aisle over. She made her way toward the center of the faire. Throngs thickened as she pushed past jugglers and puppeteers. Ffyn and Rhyn stayed close, occasionally humming in their throats, just short of a growl. Kyna mumbled soothing words in that tongue Kay did not recognize, as she stroked their wiry necks, delicately fingering soft under-hairs.

Shouts announced jousting and other contests of daring that would take place midday in the far fields. She passed a booth where birds of prey perched, tethered to poles. A grizzled, middle-aged man held up a falcon on a leather-gauntleted arm. Children peered wide-eyed.

A fiddling minstrel with painted face strolled toward us, giving Kay a jolt of recognition. She was sure it was the same Traveler who'd brought her boots. He wore a crimson vest, fitted black pants tucked into high boots, a scarf at his neck, dark hair tied back, and a gold hoop in one ear. Boldo. As he grinned, the jewel in his tooth flashed, and she was certain. Thoughts swirled as the time dimensions collided.

Kyna nodded toward Boldo and returned his smile. He winked and shifted tune, singing, "Healer woman, mend my heart". Stopping, he flicked his eyes toward a narrow gap between the tents. Kyna stepped forward and looked through the opening he indicated: A woman in bright skirts and shawls sat by a painted wagon in the next aisle, bending over someone's hand.

Talaith, Kyna thought. The woman shifted dark eyes

their way. Her free hand dropped next to her skirt, and she signaled several signs. "I have something for you," Kyna translated mentally. "I'll bring it tonight. *Be careful*." The woman returned her attention to the palm of her client.

Kyna's heart sped up at the warning. Her eyes skimmed along the tent tops, even into the sky. Boldo moved past them. The crowd surged on. Kay sensed her running possible dangers through her mind as she strode forward. She stopped at a candle maker, then a salt seller. Occasionally, her eyes darted around. The hounds pressed tighter sending tendrils of disquiet into her legs.

As she reached the textiles row, Kyna's knowledge told Kay that this was a famous part of the Machynlleth markets. It had been a market town for hundreds of years. Cloth, ribbon, and thread vendors bunched together along this corridor. A vertical banner with a spinning wheel heralded the Weavers Guild. As she approached, a tall woman, hair crisscrossed in braids over her head, called "Kyna!" and waved a blue scarf from inside a booth twice the width of most others.

"Merfyn!" Kyna shouted back. She wove her way between faire-goers and entered the booth. It was richly hung with tapestries and rugs. Kay relished the salty, spicy blend of homespun and exotic fibers as, with kisses and hugs, Kyna was absorbed into a group of fellow weavers who chatted excitedly. Kyna accepted a hot drink and Kay savored it with her.

After a while, she broke away and roamed the booth, hungrily exploring, touching, smelling, and searching for new ideas from other lands. She stopped, transfixed, by a rug. The scene on it—a tall, wooden lodge house with immense doors and ornate iron hinges perched high among sharply peaked mountains—touched something deep within her. At the base were cavernous maws of shadow where a river snaked. A strange and powerful emotion coursed through her as she studied the rug.

Kay longed to know what memory the tapestry evoked in Kyna.

"Merfyn," Kyna called in a throaty voice, as though deeply affected, "Where be this'n from?"

"The Mainland," responded the tall woman stood by her gazing at it as well. "It'll catch a pretty price."

With her strong hands and kindly face, Merfyn reminded Kay of the woman from whom she'd bought the loom. Did these parallels have meaning?

"I mun have it," Kyna said in a near whisper. "What d' ye want fer it?"

Merfyn's eyes widened, but she shook her head. "Y' have credit with us, Kyna, m' love." She took the striking rug down. Kyna watched as the woman rolled it and carried it to the back. "I'll have it brought to your camp, *dewiniaidd iachawr gwehydd*," she said over her shoulder. She had addressed Kyna in terms that meant something like "magical weaver-healer".

Kyna brought several woven bags from deep in her basket. Intricate designs of startling colors—a scene of birds in a wooded glen, another of village dancing and festivity—expertly and intricately stitched. When Merfyn returned from the back, she fingered the bags with admiration. Though she had said no payment was needed, she clearly was not going to resist the bags, and immediately displayed them.

As she left the booth, Kyna called farewells to the weavers. At neighboring stalls, she stocked up on new yarns, packets of dye powders, threads, and needles for which she exchanged sweet-smelling herbal pillows. Her baskets remained heaped, only shifting in content. As she pressed along through the crowd, the hounds suddenly stiffened and growled. Kay glanced up as a hand shot out and pulled Kyna into dense shadows.

Suddenly Kay saw nothing and could no longer hear any aspect of the faire. She smelled sharp, pungent subterranean dankness and heard water rushing against stone. Then she detected the soft sound of breathing.

A painful vice-grip clamped Kyna's arm. She remained perfectly still, overriding her urge to struggle as she took in the surroundings, ears and nose assessing in the blackness as she was forced back against a hard surface. An icy wetness seeped into her dress. Ffyn and Bryn growled, quivering.

"Stay," Kyna murmured, putting her free hand to Ffyn's head. The hounds continued to tremble in a hovering sit.

Suddenly a torch came alive. A tall man with hawkish features stood only inches away. He chuckled, white teeth glimmering.

Fury surged in Kyna. "Unhand me, Galfride. What are you at?" she spat. An electric charge ran through Kyna's heart, hot and nearly unendurable, and shot down her arm.

The man yanked his hand away as though burned.

The current throbbed, then ebbed, and a controlled warmth coursed from arm to heart and back again, slowly dissipating.

Kay was in awe of her abilities.

Arm free, Kyna straightened and stepped from the wet surface.

Galfride's face contorted with rage as he rubbed his arm. "Still have yer powers, I see," a half-sneer forming on his face. His voice rose. "Ye waste 'em in that backwater town. Ye sh'd return with me t' th' courts." His accent was different from Kyna's and Baird's—more fricatives. "Yah never sh'd a left."

"Is that where we are now? Did ye bring me ta court?" Kyna cocked her head to one side, angry and regal.

"I've been waitin' fer ye." A hint of madness gleamed in the man's eyes, struck by a guttering torch that dripped, hissing, on the mossy wall.

Were they below the faire?

"Why, Galfride? Why hayya been waitin' fer me?" Her "r's" had a stronger burr than usual as she spoke with clenched teeth. "I want nothin' to do with ye. Ye ken that?"

"Oh, now, that'd be a mistake, Kyna," he murmurred. He brought his hand up as if to caress her cheek, but thought better of it and pulled away. "Ye shn't make hasty decisions." His lowered voice turned threatening. A terrible energy emanated from him. A predatory wolfish presence scraped at the edges of her mind, sending terror through her.

The hounds continued to shake as if wanting nothing better than to clamp their teeth into him.

"I could turn ye over t' the council fer refusin' to heal Branwyn," he said.

Kyna's stomach tightened with rising anger, intertwined with something else. What was it? Guilt?

Kay caught random thoughts from her:

You would have tainted me, controlled me forever had I entered her mind after you twisted it.

An image of a young girl with long braids and bright skills arose in her mind. This must be Galfride's niece. Then the image changed to a broken young woman tearing at her hair.

"You were no' trained so well, Kyna, only t' waste yer

skills on the common folk of some rustic village. A monastery village, no less," he snarled.

"Ye'd endlessly break innocent young girls and have me fix 'em, w'd ye? Is that your grand plan, Galfride? I stepped aside fer th' court healers to deal with yer mess. Tha's no' my trainin'—the meddlin' with minds. I heal. Ye know that verra well."

"Only you c'd o' helped. Ye knew that," he seethed. Then his demeanor shifted again. He wheedled softly, "Ye c'd still help, Kyna," appealing to the healer in her.

Suddenly, through Kyna's mind, Kay saw Baird in the faire aisle from where she'd been drawn, standing perfectly still as if listening, his eyes slowly searching around him.

Kyna drew up to her full height, imperious. "I'll be goin'. I have no business with y'. Nor will I ever."

Galfride reached for her but she pressed into the blackness with her mind.

"Ye han't seen the last o' me, Kyna. Know that."

The air thickened, then filled with gut-churning nothingness before Kyna turned to smoke. Next thing, Kay sensed the brisk air of the faire and the noisy throng. Baird grabbed Kyna. "What is this? Yer back be wet," he exclaimed, turning her to see the cape soaked through. He drew her between tents. She glanced regretfully at the herbalists' aisle she'd missed as they arrived among the craftsmen and artisans. People waved. Baird offered smiles and nods but pushed on. They skirted between booths, emerging onto a hillside at the back of the faire.

Kyna snatched her arm away and pulled to a stop, facing him. "Stop draggin' me, will ye?"

"Let's walk a bit farther," he spoke low, steel in his tone. He put an arm around her shoulders, moving her firmly to higher ground. At a distance above the faire, he halted and said, "Where were ye just now?" his voice tight with emotion.

Kyna took a breath but did not answer right away. Instead, she strode to a broad stone and sat. Baird joined her.

Kay thought she spotted their encampment below.

"It was Galfride," she said, reluctance in her voice.

Baird's face lost color. "I c'd no' find ye. It was as though y'd left the world." His voice choked, and he cleared his throat.

"He took me somewhere. Like a mountain cavern. Mayhap beneath one o' the castles. I heard a river. Does that sound familiar t' y'?"

Baird pondered silently, then shook his head. "No. It could be... No. I'm not sure." He paused, then continued, "How did he take ye by surprise, Kyna?" He lifted one brow. "I don't imagine y' went willingly." There was an edge of rancor in his voice.

Kyna flicked back a shoulder. "Don't be a fool."

Baird pressed her. "Yer defenses must ha' been down. What's causin' that, d' ye think?" It was rhetorical. He was leading to his point. "Ye be compromised, Kyna. 'Tis tha' spirit in ye." He took Kyna's face in his hands. His thumbs caressed her temples. Desire consumed Kay, though Kyna was clearly irritated. Even so, she submitted as he closed his eyes, a look of deep concentration on his face.

Frozen with anticipation, Kay thought maybe, in that moment, there would be recognition. He had said he kenned her spirit, that night by the oak, in her time. Could he not recognize it now? But he looked younger than at Samhain. They must not have met yet.

He opened his eyes. "I do detect another spirit in y', but still can't tell what it is. We need Aelfwyn's help to get it out o' ye."

My heart sank.

Kyna pressed a hand to her chest with sadness, as though she held tenderness for Kay.

"It be endangerin' ye," Baird said, gruffly.

"I suppose." Kyna sighed. "I saw Talaitha. She...is bringing me something tonight."

Kay noticed she didn't mention the warning of danger.

He sat up straighter, hopeful. "She might be bringin' somethin' from Aelfwyn. A bit late, I might say."

Kay hated the way he looked at her then. He only wanted Kay gone, saw her as a threat to his beloved. What would that mean? What would Aelfwyn do to her spirit?

Movement lower on the hill caught Kyna's attention. A tall figure climbed toward them. Kyna shouted, "Hamelyn!" and ran downhill, arms wide.

Chapter 13

Kyna looped her arm around her son's waist.
Hamelyn squinted up the hill over his shoulder,
into the rays of the lowering sun. "Da' be all
right?"

Baird still sat on the stone, head bowed.

"Aye." Kyna glanced back as well. "Probably contemplatin' some terrible tale o' doom and deceit for tonight's performance."

"Ah." Hamelyn laughed. "I saw him at the faire today. He gave me a length o' wood from a Saxon forest. Almost black, 'tis. I plan to make it into a flute. Or add t' the fiddle I'm workin' on."

"Is that so?" Kyna asked. "The Druid College never let lads your age come to winter faire. How is it ye're here this time?" Kyna peered up at her son.

Hamelyn bore some resemblance to her son, though Rousseau, half-Egyptian, had a light mocha-cream complexion and tighter curls. Nonetheless, Hamelyn was browner than Kyna or Baird, with a deep olive complexion, darker still where facial hair dusted his chin and upper lip. He was close to her son's age and stature. A deep pang closed in on her with distance and inaccessibility, desperate to know she'd be back before Rousseau arrived at her home.

"Some o' th' older students are in the competitions this year and they lacked a fiddler. I'm close t' upper level." He shrugged.

Baird approached, bringing Kyna's baskets. "One o' his songs'll be sung in the competitions," Baird said, pride in his voice as he threw an arm around Hamelyn's shoulders. They were of a height.

The young man's cheeks flushed and he ducked his head with a smile. Kyna gave his waist a last hug, then let go as they reached the edge of camp.

"Next year ye'll be singin' one yerself." Baird squeezed his son's shoulder.

Voices carried from the central fire. One boomed louder than the others. Kay saw a broad back towering above the rest sitting around the fire. The red ponytail and huge guffaw gave him away.

Kyna strode forward and draped her arms over Duff's massive shoulders, pressing her cheek to his. "What lies be y' tellin' now?"

"Kyna. Ye should be ashamed, castin' doubt upon the fine character of yer elder brother." Duff stood and swallowed her in a bear hug. Her feet lifted from the ground.

"Let me go, ye great oaf," Kyna laughed, beating his back. As he set her down, she pushed his mammoth stomach. "Ye donna appear to have fared the winter badly."

Duff patted it in his turn. "I'm fair famished."

"Aren't ye always, uncle," Hamelyn chimed in as he dropped onto the log where Duff had been sitting.

"Th' stew be ready. Help yourselves," a woman said to Kyna before leaving the fire circle.

"What's this on yer chin, lad?" Duff flicked Hamelyn's

beginning growth of beard—a goatee nearly identical to that her son wore the summer before. Kay hadn't seen him since.

Hamelyn pushed away his uncle's hand, then grabbed the end of the great man's red beard. "I'm workin' on one o' these."

"It'll be a while, nephew," Duff teased.

Hamelyn pulled a fiddle from a bag and stroked out notes so sweet they could make one weep. He sang, a pure tenor. The camp hushed to listen.

The song ended as the last orange sunrays struck his hazel eyes.

Duff asked, "Did ye make that fine fiddle?"

"Parts o' it, I did." Hamelyn glanced down at his instrument, its rosewood inlay picking up firelight. "I'm fair fond o' this 'un. Yet I've started work on another. It'll be all my own."

"Speakin' o' charmin' things made wi' th' hands, let's ha' gifts," said Baird, reaching into his cape.

Solstice gifts. Kay's mind returned to her son, who'd be arriving at San Francisco Airport. He'd look around for her, with no idea why she was not there to meet him. He'd try calling her cell phone and get no answer. She fought off a panicked desire to catapult out of this time and back to her own. Helpless, Kay peered out miserably from Kyna's eyes. Kyna shifted on the log and pressed her hand to her stomach.

I've conveyed my anxiety to her, Kay realized.

Baird watched Kyna, frowning. Hamelyn glanced from one to the other. Duff observed this interplay in glances and poked the fire.

"I han't eaten," Kyna mumbled. "Too caught up with m' barterin'. Found a fine rug. They're deliverin' it at th' end o' th' faire." She stood, scooped bowls of the hearty stew, and handed them around. When she sat again, Baird placed a parcel in her lap.

"Fer me?" Kyna untied the ribbon from a silk cloth. Inside, a gold crystal the size of a small egg nestled. It glowed. Kyna rolled it into her palm. It thrummed with power. Kyna gasped. "A verra special stone," she breathed, eyes lifting to Baird's. She held it up between her fingers. The fire shimmered within, making the stone pulse as though it lived and breathed.

The hounds crept closer and tucked their noses at Kyna's sides.

Kay had an ominous sense that the crystal should be hidden. Kyna folded it into its cloth, then tucked it in a cloth bag tied at her waist and rested one hand on it. Protectively? Or still taking in its powerful energy?

"Tha' crystal ha' a story," Baird said, eyes gleaming.

"I'm sure it do." Kyna winked at him.

"A friend o' Duff's," Baird began between bites of stew, "dwarf named Albrik, following the power o' it, crossed the great mountains from his Saxon home t' search fer it. They say he sought it in the depths of tha' range ten years or more until at last he found it in a vein so deep he could barely breathe th' air, so dark no human eye had ever penetrated there before. He had followed a river deep int' the bowels o' th' earth. It's said th' river told him where to go."

"And how did this crystal come into yer hands, perchance?" Kyna asked Duff.

"Ah, well, that be another story entirely." Baird winked.

Duff tucked into a second bowl of stew, dipping hearty bread.

Hamelyn handed Kyna a rolled cloth. She unfurled it, and into her hand dropped a carved flute the size of a piccolo. It was etched with a tiny row of sandpipers. She studied. Glancing at her son, she blinked away a hint of tears, then lifted the flute to her lips and played clear notes on the first try.

"I'nt that a beauty," she breathed. "Thank you, my son." The words were hoarse with emotion.

Hamelyn smiled into his lap. Kyna brushed his cheek with a kiss before she tied the cloth back around the flute and tucked it into one of her baskets. "I mun stitch it its own case. It'll be fair grand to have it in the hills when I walk."

"I just got silver from the Isle of Islay," Duff said. "I plan t' use it for a chalice commissioned by Lord Bawdrip, but I've run out o' knot work patterns, Kyna. D' ye ha' ideas? It's got to be unique, special, fer this chalice."

Kyna picked up a stick and sketched in the dirt by the fire. It reminded Kay of a dragon design of the Sarawak people of Borneo. She'd seen it when she'd traveled to their untouched village for research. A chill ran through Kay, certain Kyna had received the image from her mind. This was the first indication her knowledge might affect Kyna as Kyna's affected her. How might this affect history?

The three men leaned forward, interested.

"I like tha'. Tha' would make a fine etching in silver. Where'd ye see it? Be it from Alba?"

"I dinna ken." Kyna shrugged, baffled and uncomfortable. "I ha' gifts fer all o' ye as well." She reached into one of her baskets and retrieved a vest with iridescent pheasants embroidered on the front. She handed it to Baird.

"You're a wonder," Baird said softly, putting on the vest.

"Has seen births and deaths as I stitched, at bedsides. I've been savin' it for yer Solstice performance." Kyna smiled.

As Baird fingered the design, a shadow darkened his expression. "I wish our daughter c'd be here." He brushed his eyes.

Kyna swallowed over a sudden lump in her throat.

"How she c'd stitch," Duff remarked, barely audible. "She had...*has*," he amended quickly, "...her mother's skills in that, t' be sure."

"More than me," Kyna whispered, then, "A great deal more."

Hamelyn jabbed a stick into the dragon design on the ground, giving the wing a new groove.

A cluster of livid thoughts burst through Kyna's mind: "Foul treacherous trader. Three years now. How could she run off wi' 'im, leavin' us wi'out a word? Or was she forced? Blast! No one able to find a trace o' her in all this time. My own girl. My Gwynnedd."

The spiral of sorrow was the first thought she'd noticed of her daughter. She must bury the memory deep, too painful to contemplate.

Hamelyn picked up his fiddle and began a melancholy tune.

"I didn't forget ye." Kyna set a square package on the log next to him.

He put down his fiddle and opened a book covered in hand-tooled leather.

"Fer writin' yer stories. The pages be blank. I just decorated th' edges a bit."

He flipped through it. Fanciful figures and leafy patterns in colored inks bordered each page.

Will he be a storyteller like his father? Or a historian? Kay caught Kyna wondering. Maybe she'd prefer he not be a wandering minstrel like her mate.

Hamelyn slipped the book into his travel bag. "I'll treasure it, Mum."

"And write many famous tales in it, no doubt," Baird said, with pride. "But y' young fellas 've got to keep yer memories sharp as well." He touched his temple.

Hamelyn nodded with a grin, as if he'd heard this many times.

People gathered around the fire, dressed in their finest. Girls stood adjusting hair ribbons, several eying Hamelyn. Horns blared in the distance. Hamelyn rose, stepped from the fire, and glanced at his mother.

She nodded. "Go on. Join yer young friends." She made a shooing gesture.

Hamelyn laughed and moved off with the other youths.

"We'd best be gettin' ready as well." Baird and Kyna stood up from the logs and hurried to their tent to don warmer clothes and festive capes. Kyna wore a cap with feathers. Baird put on a wonderful bard's hat, the pheasant feather complementing the vest. He stopped at the tent flap and faced Kyna.

"I'm that worried 'bout ye." He touched her cheek.

"Nonsense, my good-lookin' man. Y' mun be thinkin' only o' yer singin' and playin'."

He took her face in his hands and looked into her eyes. "Who's in there?" he asked, his brow furrowed. A mix of emotions vyed for supremacy in her: confusion, protectiveness, and guilt at not sharing least her theories on what was happening within her.

She pulled away and gave him a soft push out of the

tent. Hand in hand, they joined the throng heading toward the fields beyond town. Many carried torches. As they approached the final rise, Kay saw the true Winter Solstice celebration. A sea of people stretched out onto the fields below them. Hundreds of torches lit the edges, and flames from immense bonfires shot into the indigo sky.

With a backward glance at Kyna, Baird left to join the minstrels near a high dais. A patch of dark forest pressed to the side. Galfride's face and iron grip barged into her memory. The trees cast menacing shadows. He could be hiding in there.

Kyna moved quickly into the crowd, as though sharing Kay's worry. Spotting Duff's bright hair above the rest, she made her way toward him. The gold stone banged against her thigh, emitting a powerful energy. It was difficult for Kay to tell if the energy was protective, but it was strong. She was glad for the hounds' warmth on either side.

Kyna stopped next to a massive kettle of steaming apple wassail and held out a tin mug she kept tied at her side. She received a ladleful and walked on, blowing on the spicy liquid, trying not to slosh it on the jostling crowd. The spiced drink burned like brandy as Kyna took a first swallow. It coursed through her veins. She at last reached Duff and relaxed, pressing close to his comforting bulk as they awaited the performances near the stage.

With a thrill she anticipated hearing the bards of the Middle Ages.

A young man on stage belted out a gay midwinter ballad. A white-haired gentleman followed, so bent others had to help him onto the platform. Several musicians, including Baird, accompanied him on their instruments as he poured forth a tale in a surprisingly robust and riveting voice. At last, Baird stood alone on stage, his beautiful harp catching torchlight in lustrous gleams. All hushed as his voice rang with the favorite song of the evening, the tale of Rhiannon and the birth of Pryderi, sacred son of Wales. Applause thundered, and Baird was dragged into the crowd with slaps on the back.

Pride heated Kyna's cheeks. Leaving the field, she moved along with the others. Baird and Hamelyn caught up with her. Hamelyn parted from them at his school's tents, and Duff left for his artisan camp.

Back at their camp, those who remained by the fire called to Baird to come and sing but he declined this time. He and Kyna climbed the short hill to the upper stream and their accommodations. Silence settled like a dark cloud. No wind stirred.

In bed, Baird's breaths came soft and even.

Kyna could not sleep, and instead lay listening.

A whistle, like a bird, caught her attention. It came again. Kyna softly crept from the bed, put on her cape and boots, and slipped out through the tent flaps. Ffyn and Rhyn joined her, moving like Kyna, with silent steps.

A short way up the hill, Kay made out a cloaked figure, grey against grey. Kyna approached, and the two women crouched, knee to knee. Talaitha spoke so low her voice could have been a light breeze in the trees.

Kay paid close attention but didn't recognize the language. Could she be hearing a secret tongue of the Travelers? She forced herself to relax, and the meanings came clear.

"A raven came to my wagons as we traveled south," Talaitha said. "It carried a message from Aelfwyn diverting us to Borth on our way to the faire." Talaitha pressed a bundle into Kyna's hands. "Aelfwyn bids ye wear this at all times."

"What danger does she see then? Did she tell ye, Tay?" Kyna said, her voice almost a whisper.

"Nay," said Talaitha. "But someone's tried to break the protections 'round yer home. And the tower."

She said the word tower with a kind of awe and reverence. Now Kay was dying to look inside that tower when they got back.

Kyna sucked in air. Anger shot through her. "I think I know who t'was. Somethin' happened today."

"I know," Talaitha said.

"I can handle him."

"Dinna be so sure, my sister. Wear th' amulet 'til we know without doubt."

"I will," Kyna responded.

The women rose and kissed, on each cheek, then lightly on the lips. Talaitha melted into the night. Kyna started down the hill. To Kay's surprise, Kyna passed by her tent and descended to the massive one at the center of camp.

Her memories told Kay she was familiar with this great tent from childhood. It had special protections. She knew exactly where the sleep chambers were and turned away from them, slipping silently along a narrow hallway that ran along the outer edge. In a corner space where she'd played as a young girl, hidden by hide walls, she knelt and drew out the gold crystal. Cupping it in her hands, she whispered, "Tell me yer secret."

She waited. Slowly a glow bloomed. She pressed the stone to her lips and blew as though she could push her breath into it. The glow grew brighter. Settling the crystal like a lamp in her lap, she investigated what was in the bundle Talaitha had given her: Three hard, brown balls, tightly wound in seaweed.

Potent herbs, Kyna thought as the pungent scent drifted to her. Sometimes, her thinking was so clear to Kay that she might as well have been speaking. At other times, she caught only fragments or an unreadable storm of ideas mixed with emotions. She wrapped the cloth back around them and settled them in a hidden pocket of her robe. Then, pressing the crystal to her lips, she made the light dim go out. She tucked the stone back into her bag, crept out of the grand tent, and walked back to her own. There she slid into bed next to Baird, melting into his warmth.

He turned to her, his breath tickling her ear. "Thought I heard a wee wood thrush out there."

"Didja now?" Kyna snuggled into his embrace.

"Aye. Soft, it was. Light as a breeze, but I heard it all the same." His warm hands brought her closer. Searching for her eyes in the dark, he perceived the amulet pressed between them and explored it with his fingers.

"I found a trick o' the crystal y' gave me," Kyna said, deftly working it out of its bag and bringing it to her lips. It immediately glowed.

Baird's dark eyes grew wide. "Y' tricky minx," he said, again touching the tiny seaweed spheres in their pocket at her sternum. "This be from Aelfwyn. Am I not right?"

Kyna nodded, breathing the light back out of the stone and returning it to its bag. "I think I'll sleep with this upon my person, though I may be bruised by mornin'."

"T'would be best, my sweet." Baird's tone was serious, his face again concealed by the night's darkness.

The two settled together.

"I'm that glad she came to ye, my love," he said after a while. "That wee wood thrush." His breathing slowed into the steady rhythm of sleep.

Kyna kissed the tip of his nose and lay awake for some

time. "Ye were fair gorgeous tonight, my bard," she whispered, strangely sad, as though she might not get a chance to say those words to him on the morrow, or for a very long time.

Chapter 14

A t first light, Kyna noticed Baird's absence. His side of the bed was cold to the touch. Kay sensed her disappointment and concern. She threw off the covers and quickly dressed.

The camp was deserted as she strode down the hill toward the faire, her baskets again full with handcrafted goods, herbal blends, salves, and tinctures for barter. The hounds trotted ahead then circled back. She wondered if she might see Hamelyn but was fairly certain he would be with his school mates. She pictured the area where the Druid students had always encamped. He would find her, she thought.

She entered directly into the herb and healer aisle from the outer edge. A wise approach, Kay thought.

Kay's mind jumped to the darkness that had engulfed Kyna near the weavers—the sounds of the faire disappearing, the talon-like grip on her arm, the freezing water seeping into her clothing, the smell of earth too deep underground. She wondered what would happen to her—to her spirit—if something lethal befell Kyna. Living in Kyna's spirit and body, the woman's power brought about an internal sovereignty in Kay that she'd never had herself. At the university, she could have used such a fierce, sure core, to fight for her career. She needed a stalwart sense of herself and her work. But she'd never anticipated the animosity her research would engender. She had put her heart into her teaching, her students, into knowledge itself. The controversies had blindsided her. She might have stayed the course if she'd fought back with an inner strength like Kyna's. This woman would be less naïve, perhaps even willing to navigate the politics.

Or would she? After all, she separated herself from what sounded like a high position in the castle.

She wanted to be an example of strength for her children. But what would have been the greatest example? Rigidly staying, even when the environment could have destroyed her soul? Or should she have merely stepped away for a short time to regroup?

She imagined sending a jolt of fiery energy into her former colleague, Sontag. Of course, his attacks were not physical. That was, perhaps, what made them so difficult to confront.

Kyna gave an impatient shake, and a swirl of clean, bright energy filled her. She drew in the essences of trees and birdsong. A prayer permeated her spirit. She started along the healer aisle. Focusing on the fascinating booths surrounding us, she took several deep breaths as she moved on.

Lanterns flickered in dark recesses, along tunnels of wares. Healers and alchemists had created a vertiginous array of displays with all manner of medicinal and magical purposes. Less savory objects—desiccated snakes, lizards, bugs, and unidentifiable shapes floating in murky liquids—took their places along shelves suspended from sturdy ropes. Beautifully carved, translucent marble jars caught sunlight. Herb garlands festooned tent rims. Pyramids of balms and oils rose next to powders in hues of rust and gold, lavender and teal. Kyna bartered for herbs, tallows, and mysterious instruments, refilling her baskets as fast as she emptied them. Earthy and exotic smells blended, both sharp and earthy.

She approached a plump woman, broad-faced with a crown of unruly hair. She stood at the entrance to one of the most intriguing stalls. It was packed with mysterious statues, stone amulets, elaborate tools, and books—the first she'd seen at the faire. The woman held out puffy hands in welcome. "Y' look a tad bit wan, Kyna, m' love. Come, sit a spell."

"Marta, how good to see ye." Kyna took the woman's hands and gave her rounded cheek a kiss.

Marta urged her toward a back corner of the booth. Kyna set down her baskets and sat on a pile of pillows. The hounds lay next to her, their noses on her dusty skirt hem. They rumbled low in their throats.

In a guarded tone, Kyna addressed a wiry woman perched on a stool in the shadows. "Adela. Ye've traveled far."

Adela watched with ferret eyes, her fingers moving over a string of beads. "That I have. Enjoyin' the faire, are ye?" She stared directly at the place where the amulet nestled in a pouch under Kyna's bodice.

The woman, Adela, seemed aware of it. Her scrutiny returned to Kyna's face. She waited. Enjoyment was the last thing she wanted or expected to hear about. Kay did not like her look, and wished the motherly Marta would return, but she heard the kindly woman at the front of the booth, gaily bartering for goods.

"It's been...an eventful time," Kyna answered. "And

fer yerself?"

"I have been noticin' a break in the fabric around us." The woman's frown lines grew even deeper. "I note ye wearin' a great deal o' protection, Kyna. Why would that be?"

Kyna stroked Rhyn, who'd snuggled closer and rested his head on her thigh. He eyed Adela warily.

She's not answering. She doesn't trust this woman.

Marta broke the thick silence by offering a steaming cup and a slice of pie.

Kyna sighed, accepting the fare offered her. "Many thanks, my friend. Just the thing." She took a gulp of hot, milky tea that tasted of roasted grains.

The delicious scent of pastry filled the air. Mushrooms and chunky vegetables in thick sauce oozed out the sides of the crust.

Adela watched Kyna take her first bite. Then she began a long account of recent experimentation with tending to boils.

The topic made Kay queasy, but Kyna had no such qualms. When she finished her food and drink, she dabbed her mouth with a napkin. The two discussed maladies and their treatments at length. Other healers gathered around them, perching on crates and anything else available to sit on. The practitioners' exchange grew lively.

At last, Kyna said, "I must be partin'. We're off today." She tucked items more securely at the edges of her basket before rising.

Adela's eyes followed. "Have a care, Mistress Healer," was all she said.

Kyna bowed slightly to her. "And you." She called her by a variant of the old Welsh word for healer—it related to science and the stars. *Astronomer?*

Kay thought Adela might wish harm upon Kyna, so dark was her look. Did she read her wrong? She thought about Baird's cautions and was, for the first time, unsure. She had begun to think Kyna's strength might be indomitable; she had, after all, sent a bolt into her abductor and then taken them back to Baird in the aisle of the faire. But unease extinguished her blithe trust that Kyna could see them out of any disaster.

What was this world where dangers threatened at every turn? Was it so different from hers or was it merely that here people sensed power, energy, even magic, in ways lost to modern life?

Leaving Marta's booth, Kyna turned toward the weavers' end of the aisle. As she approached the middle of the row where Galfride had snatched her from the faire, Kay wondered why she did not go back the way she'd come, around by the hills.

Kyna stopped, crouched, and searched through her basket. The hounds hovered on their haunches on either side, heads erect like fireplace irons. Kyna pressed her face first to Ffyn's head, then to Rhyn's, breathing in their musky animal scent blended with campfire smoke. Comfort settled.

She rose, hand on the bag that hung at her side, and walked forward, mumbling. As though Kyna's vision had shifted, she saw through tent walls, but not clearly. Figures formed, more like heat and energy than human. When she stopped muttering, the scene returned to normal. Clearly this was another of Kyna's abilities. She drew to her full height and kept walking. Where blackness had engulfed them the day before, and Galfride's hand had shot out to snatch Kyna, there was now a space filled with daylight. A juggler walked through it toward Kyna, tossing bottles into the air. He had the Wanderer look of Boldo, could have been his brother but this man was taller, with a craggy, clean-shaven face. He winked at Kyna as he approached, stepped close, then backed away, juggling on without pause.

Kyna laughed, and said softly, *"Narked jal avree."* The translation was close to "The bad smell has gone away." Kay caught her thought with the words, though it was the language she did not yet understand. She slipped a coin from her belt and flipped it into the air. It spun high and arced toward the Traveler who caught it mid-juggle and tucked it into a pocket.

"Thank you for cleaning the Black Mage's foul taint out o' there," she said, as the juggler backed toward the artisan aisle. She heard metalworkers banging, out of sight. A hearty shout of laughter—maybe Duff's—rose over the others.

Kyna continued to the weavers' line with a lighter step. Kay wondered if Talaitha had sent the Traveler to clear Galfride's dark magic from that space. Kyna arrived under the banner of the spinning wheel, and waved to Merfyn.

The tall, sturdy woman approached. "Yer rug be on its way te yer camp."

Kay again thought of the resemblance to Irene, the weaver of her time, and made a mental note to visit her when she returned, perhaps bring her a length of her own woven cloth. She wished she'd photographed the beginnings of a project that had been on Irene's loom.

"I thank ye," Kyna said. "I have a few more o' the stitched bags that I know ye do well with." She traded for last items—dyes, batting, beeswax—and returned to camp. Tents were already being collapsed and folded, wares were stored in bags and wooden boxes, and wagons loaded. Baird was nowhere in sight.

Hamelyn came to say goodbye. Kyna's deep ache was palpable. "Summer'll be here before we know it," she said, voice straining.

"Aye. You'll check on an apprenticeship with the fiddle maker in Llanbadarn Fawr?" Hamelyn asked.

Kyna's spirits rose. "I will. I'll get word to ye soon as I can 'bout that, son." One more brisk hug, and he left to join his school for their return journey north to Alba—Scotland. The Druid schools were apparently better able to function in those northern reaches.

A crunching on the road heralded their caravan's arrival. Duff rode at the front, leads in hand. His was a sturdy, covered wagon with a smith at his forge painted on the side. He leapt off and helped Kyna haul bags and bedding. Others collapsed the tent and carried it over the bridge toward the stone buildings of town where Kay assumed it must get stored until the next faire. The thick rolled carpet arrived and was stowed in their wagon, tossed upon a heap greater now than when they arrived.

At last, Baird came into view leading a chestnut horse. Kyna raised a questioning brow.

"Th' mare Spurstowe bid me deliver. Fine, be she not?" Baird stroked the creature's nose. Its great soft lips explored for treats. Sweet eyes peered through thick forelock hairs.

"So tha's where ye been. I couldn'a remember what ye said." Kyna ran her hands along the fawn coat.

"Couldn'a remember? Ye were snorin' fit t' wake a bear!"

She slapped his arm. "Were not," she laughed. "Did ye visit our son?"

"I did. Went by the school's tents first thing."

"See any o' our old teachers?" she asked.

"Nay. Too old t' make the trip, I'll warrant."

"Not mine," Kyna snickered.

Baird laughed. "Our teachers were mostly the same. Yours just had better salves for the complexion," he joked, then turned to tie the horse's leads to the back of the wagon.

Kyna put a hand on his arm. "Ride her, why don't ye? She's probably had no running these faire days."

He hesitated, then shook his head. "No, m' love. I'm stayin' close t' you."

The ride back went more quickly, with no stop for lunch. Kyna and Baird joined the lad, Owain, on the wagon buckboard. Baird sang most of the way. Kay saw a different view of the wide vistas, hills, and valleys. The marshlands appeared as they approached the sea, and they again followed the river, then turned onto smaller roads, passing clusters of stone houses, this time riding past the monastery at *Llanbadarn Fawr* before they turned onto the wooded lane that led to Kyna's house. There the caravan slowed.

In front of the house stood several horses and a pony trap. A withered figure perched on the porch bench.

"Aelfwyn!" Kyna climbed off the wagon, hopping to the ground before it came to a stop. She hurried across the bridge and up the steps of her house, and gave the frail old woman with long white hair a fond hug.

Despite her brittle frame, Aelfwyn emanated palpable strength. Her face crinkled in a broad smile as she reached her gnarled hands up and brought Kyna's face close. Her deep-set eyes peered into Kyna's. "That troublesome mage ha' been meddlin', han't he?"

"Aye. It were he who tried to break the protections here,

I'll warrant," Kyna answered.

Baird waved his hat as he led the chestnut mare, loaded with bundles, around the side of the house.

"I imagine so, m' dear. Do ye know what he's after?"

"I do not, *Yw'r Meddyg*." She called her a respectful name for healer, teacher, and doctor all in one. "But he did say he wanted me to return to court life."

Aelfwyn pursed her lips. "There also be a visitor." She tapped Kyna's temple and nodded meaningfully.

I sensed Kyna gathering her thoughts in a momentary silence. "You dinna think she be a danger t' me, do ye? 'Tis a gentle spirit." Kyna's rebellious thought said, *Let me handle this*. Kay wanted to crawl away and hide. But there was nowhere to go.

"Nay. But her presence might make ye more at risk."

"'Tis same as what Baird said." Kyna sighed.

"Yer not safe," the old woman admonished. "And neither be she."

It was a new thought to Kyna.

Kay recalled how Galfride had sensed her, threatened her. But was it her imagination? Was he scraping at Kyna's mind, not hers? It was impossible to tell.

"Mayhap the two spirits c'd reside in one person with great power," the old woman continued, softening, "but until we know more, I sense it compromises you."

Kyna reached for the amulet in her bodice pocket. "Thank ye fer this," she said, patting it.

"Only to gi' ye' help."

Kay shuddered at the word. What did Aelfwyn plan to do?

Kyna rose. "Let's get ye inside by the fire, teacher."

The woman was barely detectable in the layers of clothing, just bones, Kyna thought as she helped her off the bench and into the house. Inside, several figures sat around a blazing fire. Kyna took in the sight. *So, The Thirteen gathers* — the thought came clearly to her.

She settled Aelfwyn close to the warmth at the hearth, draped a blanket over her knees, and exchanged kisses with the guests, greeting each by name. She paused after Brochfael and Anslec and sensed Kyna's thought: They must have set out days ago to be here now. "Rhodri. Fulkh," she said, finishing the circle.

She bustled to the back door and called Baird to bring her the food stores from the trip. Descending into a cellar by the back steps, she collected wrinkled potatoes, onions, beets, and turnips into her skirt and returned to the main room with her load. Shouts and whistling let everyone know the caravan was departing. She rolled the vegetables onto the table and opened the front door, waving and blowing kisses. Horses snorted and shook their heads, jangling their harnesses, and the wheels crunched loudly as the laden wagons moved off.

All but one. Duff broke from the line in his sturdy cart and trundled across the bridge into the yard.

Others arrived, among them, Boldo and Talaitha. Ultimately, thirteen gathered in the main room — women and men ranging in age, about half with Traveler looks and clothing. What they shared was an intensity in their eyes. It varied in degree, but the power was there in each. They helped prepare and then eat fish sautéed in butter and herbs, stew, hearty breads brought back from the faire, and late-harvest wine. Chatting and occasional laughter filled the room. When the meal was finished and darkness fell, everyone rose, with shared glances, and walked to the back hall.

Next to the apothecary, Kyna pushed back a panel that

creaked as it opened, revealing a dark vestibule. Duff carried in a lit torch and settled it in a sconce at the base of a winding staircase.

Kyna took a robe from a hook on the wall and put it on. She told the hounds to stay at the base of the stairs while Aelfwyn started up. The rest climbed single file behind her. At the top, Kyna stepped into a round, flagstone-floored tower room. Wind whistled through narrow slits along the thick, curved, stone walls. To the west, the sea stretched out from the shoreline. Turning, Kyna faced the hills where Baird and Kay had crossed through time. Her heart wanted to cry out as she peered through Kyna's eyes at Baird's serious face. Her spirit did cry, soundlessly, to him, *Can't you take me back to where you found me*? As caught up with the adventure as she'd been, she could not bear to never see her children again, to desert her own century for all eternity. Much as she'd worked to get herself back here, to see Baird again, she could not be imprisoned in this time.

As the robed figures formed a circle in the center, their faces intense, Kay's fears escalated. She imagined her spirit never arriving anywhere once they expelled it from Kyna. Why hadn't she tried to get home before this? She had been selfishly consumed by her own curiosity and now she might lose herself completely. Would she simply disappear? Be extinguished? Snuffed out?

Chapter 15

Torchlights waved like eerie dancers on the curved stone walls of the tower. Light flickered on the hooded faces of those in the circle. Each wore robes similar to Kyna's, black but with different embroidered designs. She'd seen Kyna's briefly as she put it on. It was edged in crimson and gold, of runes and tree branches intertwined. Baird's had shades of green, from pale to nearly black, a tree and moon pattern.

In the center of the tower room hung a copper pan strung between thin metal chains that hung from the dome above them. The pan had a special raised area, like an eggcup designed to hold round objects. It was situated high above the flame in the central brazier. From wooden shelves on one side, Aelfwyn gathered materials, adding musky incense to the fire. It rose, circling the dish.

Kyna glanced from Baird to Aelfwyn on each side of her, then around the circle. Her heart thundered. Desparation rose in Kay, intense as coals burning under ice. She struggled against an overwhelming urge to shout, to be heard, to plead her case.

Kyna's agitation grew. Afraid she might be causing it, Kay forced her thoughts toward hope. Maybe they could send her back to her time. After all, everyone had great faith in Aelfwyn. She prayed to the fates, or whoever might listen, *If you get me back to my time, I will always be grateful. I'll make the most of my education and knowledge and will never take those I cherish for granted. If you could please allow me one more chance.*

But how could they send her to the exact time and place she came from?

Everyone stood still, waiting. Aelfwyn spoke at last. "This past waning' o' the moon, some o' us charged wi' the safety o' this home and our tower perceived an attack on the protections we've woven."

Everyone's focus remained on Aelfwyn. Her expression was unreadable as she glanced toward Kyna. "I suspect they sensed a droppin' o' the strength around Kyna and this dwelling," Aelfwyn continued.

Duff stared at the brazier. Baird looked down. Kyna watched Aelfwyn, eyes hot.

Aelfwyn went on, "Kyna had a visit from...the Dark Mage, the wayward one, at the faire. He made an attack o' sorts."

"What sort o' attack?" a woman of middle years asked. She had fierce dark eyes, and a sharp, hooked nose.

This time Baird answered. "She were drawn t' another place whilst she walked the ways o' the faire in broad daylight," he growled, cheek muscles clenched.

No one wanted to say Galfride's name. Maybe that would draw his energy there. It made sense to Kay. She did not want to hear the name uttered.

Kyna spoke for the first time. "The weakening of my defenses that Aelfwyn suspects..." She looked at Aelfwyn, then at Baird. "I dinna think 'tis the spirit wi' in me. I dinna believe we should be so precipitous as to try to send it out of me quite yet, until I know more."

Kyna's hesitation and discomfort—defensiveness, even—revealed a rising warmth toward Kay's spirit. Her voice dropped to a whisper. "She's like...a sister." Kay loved her for that. "I...think we should wait, secure the defenses 'round the house and tower, take a bi' more time to learn who or what she is." Kyna looked directly at Aelfwyn. "I dunna want her harmed," she declared.

The faces around the circle, stern or sad, appeared unyielding. Aelfwyn spoke then, in a loud, clear voice, ignoring Kyna's words entirely. "Her spirit mun be pulled out from the body of Kyna into an object, then directed back to whence it came. What is the most potent object we have here?"

Baird looked at Kyna. She shook her head. "Kyna," he urged, quietly, "ye know she must go."

"What if she's an ancestor, come to me for a reason?" Kyna whispered over Aelfwyn's head.

"In my experience," Aelfwyn projected with authority, "an ancestor spirit'd speak out strong and clear to ye. No mincin' about who he or she be."

"I thought at first it were an animal spirit," Kyna offered. "Perhaps a doe."

"Could be a deer," a man across the circle weighed in. "Lyin' in the woods, unable t' protect herself, not feedin' her young, waitin' to be released from her hold within ye, Kyna."

"Or a heron needin' to fly south," offered another.

"It's not an animal or bird," Kyna said. "I know that now. She tells me things, human things. She has many words. One time, when I petted Rhyn, the spirit told me seven different names for 'hound'. I think it be she who gave me th' dragon shape I showed ye for yer chalice, Duff.

Many new ideas ha' come to me that are no way possible." She rushed on, eagerly trying to convince them of the value of this knowledge.

Kay looked around and saw only immovable determination.

"All the more dangerous, Kyna," said a woman with red hair like cotton floss escaping her hood.

Kyna looked at Baird, entreating. He looked majestic, dark beard defining his face above the forest green and aqua stitching at his throat. His loving but firm expression defeated her, and her shoulders slumped. She slipped the golden crystal from the bag at her waist. The power in it thrummed in her hand as her eyes welled with tears. She offered it to Aelfwyn.

The old woman reached out, eyes widening as she touched the stone. "A most powerful crystal, indeed," she breathed, her eyes avid.

Dread mounted in Kay. What did they plan? How could she be drawn into this stone?

Aelfwyn signaled to Duff, and they moved to the side to confer. Then Duff ran downstairs.

Baird stepped close to Kyna. He said in a low voice, "Perhaps a message from her will remain in the crystal, some essence we might ken later." He pulled Kyna close and her face pressed to the fine cloth of his draping robe.

Duff returned with a packet of tools. Aelfwyn explained to the group, "Duff'll etch a *sigil* formed o' runes into the Power Stone. *Haegl* to separate the spirits. And through *Nied*, we'll call upon the fates to carry this spirit where she belongs. She just mun know in herself where that may be."

The members of the circle conferred. Squatting in a cluster, they took turns drawing the runes in various overlapping designs with charcoal on the stone flooring. At last, they agreed on what resembled a stylized "H", but with three vertical lines, another slashed across at an angle, that incorporated the two runes. Kay had seen these sigils of combined runes in her research. They carried great power, to the ancients.

Duff laid out his jeweler's case, selected a slender tool, and braced the magnificent, egg-sized stone on a cloth. A gasp went up as he made the first gouge in the flawless surface, but Duff was an artisan of great skill and he made clean, spare lines. When he finished, Aelfwyn gathered the minuscule shavings, pinched them carefully and dropped them into a tiny vial, which she stoppered and tucked into her robe.

Next, she took the crystal and placed it reverently in the copper pan strung above the fire. The stone glowed, sending golden light in all directions. Faces flickered an amber sheen as all clasped hands. Tears filled Kyna's eyes. Kay couldn't tell which of their emotions produced them.

They circled the round walls, one woman carrying smoking incense. She called the gods and goddesses, spirits of the forest and sea, sky and earth, above and below, and to all the directions. She returned to the circle, and they started a chant, low at first, then growing louder until the walls vibrated as if from a single immense voice of many timbers:

> Gods, we invoke thee
> By the power of Haegl
> Draw out the spirit that dwells in Kyna
> By the power of Nied
> Send the spirit into the crystal
> And return it

To where it belongs
Spirits, we invoke thee…

Power built until the air snapped. A howling wind rose and whipped around the tower room. The torch flames waved wildly. The chrystal glowed brighter, pulsing with energy as its intense charge filled the room.

A golden beam solidified in a column from the floor to the peak of the tower, swirled up through the roof, and disappeared. Pain lanced through Kyna. Her knees gave as Kay was brutally pried toward the churning gold pillar. The rune sigil glowed pale yellow as it rose from the stone and into the center of the column of light. Black-gold smoke whirled upward from it. Fierce pressure and unbearable force, beyond endurance, tore at Kay. Then all went black.

Chapter 16

Kay swam through thick muck. Leaden and aching, she sought coherence. Where was she? *What* was she? Something gouged painfully into her chest. She cracked open her eyes, letting in a fraction of light. Everything reeled. She squeezed her eyes shut and pressed her face into her bent arm. Jackhammers pounded inside her skull. Her insides twisted unmercifully. In the shadows beneath her, she made out the pale-yellow Formica of her kitchen table, and writing smeared with her drool. Long slanted marks, now blurred by spit, came into focus. Slowly, knowledge dawned—it was the note she'd written before she ended up in Kyna, and this was her table.

I've returned. I'm in my kitchen!

She heard a knock at the front door. A knock? How could anyone know she'd just returned? She managed a hoarse, "Coming." It was barely more than a whisper. Her throat was sandpaper. Pain slashed through her head as she rose. More knocking. She reached the front hall, slid to the floor, and pressed her face to her knees. *I'm going to vomit.*

"Kay?" Jarl called.

148

Jarl? How often had he been checking? Shakily, she pushed herself to standing and held the wall, stumbling toward the door. It was only ten feet, yet it was fathoms. She tried again to call out and managed, "I'm coming." She hoped Jarl wouldn't give up, although she might be a mess. She ached to connect with a solid being in her time. She croaked again, "Hang on."

Finally reaching the front door, she gave her cheeks a quick swipe for spit tracks, then opened. "Jarl?" Her voice resembled a toad's. Her tongue was dry leather. Her head was splitting apart as she leaned against the door jamb.

Jarl held out a package. "Here. I forgot to give you your present. I was halfway across town when I noticed it on my seat and came back." Sheepish at first, his expression turned to concern as she sagged in the doorway accepting his gift. "You don't look so good, Kay."

Turned around and came back? "How long... You mean...? When did you last see me?" Her voice was a painful sawing of tree branches.

His eyes grew round, and he laughed nervously. "I was just here. Wow, are you feverish?" He laid the back of his hand on her forehead.

Shaky, she wanted to lean into his coolness, his humanness, his solid, friendly there-ness. She glanced past him at her normal, twenty-first century neighborhood, bathed in the light of approaching evening.

"Do you want me to come in and fix you something? Tea or soup?" Jarl asked.

Part of her ached to say with candor, *I've been in another woman's body for several days, in ancient times. They put me in a crystal, though, and sent me back, so I'm just a wee bit tattered.* She wanted to crawl into a dark hole and not explain anything. Despite his willingness to accept her tale of Samhain and meeting Baird, it was too raw to share, and too bizarre. She muttered, "I think you're right. I must be getting the flu. I should probably crawl into bed. Can we get together and open presents when I'm better?"

"Yeah, of course. Are you sure I can't get you something?"

Kay nodded carefully to avoid jostling her pounding head.

"Be better, and have a great time with your son. Hopefully, I'll see you before the new year." He turned to go.

My son. I have to check for calls.

Jarl hesitated. "Take care of yourself, Kay," he said over his shoulder. Then he bounded down the porch steps.

Kay watched until Jarl waved from his car, then closed the door with a sigh and sank to the floor, fingering the present. Oz found her and head-butted her legs. "You're okay." She lifted him into her arms and planted several kisses on his head. He struggled against her grip. "But of course you're okay. I fed you this morning. I must have been gone less than half an hour." She let go of the struggling cat, whereby he flopped to the floor next to her.

Only half an hour? It was unfathomable.

The throbbing in her head continued. She crawled to the bathroom, and started the tap. Hot water gushing into the tub filled her with equal measures of wonder and sorrow. If only she could have studied more, absorbed the intricacies, had the opportunity to sit with Kyna and ask for explanations. What was the seeming magic? Was it illusion? Had any of it been explainable in rational terms?

When the bath was full and covered in a satiny layer of lavender-scented bubbles, she stripped and slid in, sinking gratefully into the foamy heat until only her nose reached above water. Fear and worry melted, along with the terrible ache in her head. For nearly an hour, she topped up the hot water.

At last, clad in long T-shirt and a thick robe, she sat at her laptop and wiggled the mouse. The awakened computer showed the date: December 21. Her son wouldn't arrive for two more days. A sob of relief rose in her throat. She reached for her cell phone. No messages. He hadn't called. Of course not. Almost no time had elapsed. She'd experienced days in ancient Wales, yet it was still the same evening here.

Steadier by the minute, she fed Oz, made herself lemon ginger herb tea, and climbed into bed without dinner but contented. She reached for the Elizabeth George novel on her bedside table, sipped tea, and escaped serious thought via a murder mystery. When the tea was gone, she turned out the light. In the silence, she could no longer keep her mind from those last moments in the tower. She'd had no idea where she'd end up, if she'd make it home, or if her life would be extinguished. The memory of agonizing pressure, the sensation of being torn apart, the sound of Kyna's cry as she collapsed on the floor, froze Kay yet again. She recalled being enveloped in darkness, knowing only terror until she slumped at her kitchen table like she'd gone through a lawnmower.

What about Kyna? Had she been harmed? Kay thought about Baird's look at Samhain—older and sadder. Was he in mourning? Could it be that Kyna had not survived the tearing of Kay's spirit from hers? She shuddered, not wanting to stay with that line of thought. She forced herself to take fast, shallow fire-breaths, then slow, deep ones. The disciplined breathing cleared her mind for the moment, allowing her to focus solely on the exquisite comfort of her modern mattress and sheets. Oz flopped against her middle, and she absently stroked him. His rumbling purr vibrated all the way to her heart. "You're a comforting bumblebee," she whispered and settled her head into her contour pillow.

Thoughts swirled in. She now knew Baird had a wife. She'd stop thinking about him, in fact, put that world out of her head, let them live their tenth-century lives. Starting tomorrow, she'd make down-to-earth plans and be present, here, in her time. She'd keep the promise she'd made to the gods if she survived the return to the twenty-first century.

She hugged Oz tight. She'd purposely not worn the heron fabric that came to her from mysterious hands of long ago. Perhaps she should stop wearing the magical fibers she'd woven. She even considered taking off the silver pendant. It would be the first time since she'd tied it on. The thought brought a terrible pang of sorrow.

Her cell phone played "Rose Tree in the Garden". Her son's name glowed on the tiny screen.

"Rousseau. Sweetie!" Kay said, pressing the phone to her ear. If he only knew *how* sweet it was to see his name on her phone.

"Hey, Mama. Hope it's not too late to call."

"Not at all," she said. Never, never, never could it be too late.

"Good. So, about Saturday. I can take the shuttle to Pomo Bluff if you don't want to drive all the way to San Francisco to get me."

"No, I'll meet you at the airport," Kay said, with a tad too much passion. No way she'd give up the chance to see him four hours sooner.

"You don't need to. But it'll be nice to have you waiting for me."

"You bet, honey. Safe travels. I love you."

"Love you, too."

They hung up. Kay lifted the framed photo of her kids from the bedside table. They were squeezed together on a cable car, ages seven and nine. She kissed it, set it down, and turned off the light.

The next day dawned with exquisite brightness. Kay was made new, like Scrooge after the spirits of Christmas visited. She ground Fairtrade French roast coffee beans and savored the aromatic brew. Each simple task, so assumed and unconscious the day before, she now performed with reverence and circumspection. The toaster, the stove, the light switch—all were marvels.

Still weak, she thought of concocting a blood tonic. She'd have to get herbs and roots from the health food store. Or in the hills. She found herself planning an apothecary. She could convert the closet off the living room, build shelves, get a *tansu* with dozens of drawers. When she stopped to think, she knew this was based on the knowledge of healing plants she'd just acquired by being inside Kyna's mind. She was trying to create an apothecary. She remembered her conviction to no longer obsess on that ancient time. But how could she ignore the knowledge she now had?

She should be able to center herself, meld it all into a normal, healthy life. Shouldn't she? Grabbing a cloth shopping bag, she left the house and ambled downtown. Along the way, she fondly touched stone walls, fences, and gate latches, noticing each detail anew. The air seemed fresher than she'd ever noticed, the colors deeper and richer.

When she returned home with groceries, she readied the house for her son's stay by putting up a few more decorations. She thought of the Solstice Faire in Olde Wales and wished she could wrap some of the unusual carvings and metalwork she'd seen to put under the tree. *My son would love even the simplest of everyday daggers from that time.* She shook her head. She couldn't allow herself to think that way. It was too disorienting to live in two worlds but only share one.

She contemplated the loom, the woven cloths, the yarns, and considered changing everything back to the way it used to be—walls lined with books and *objets d'art* picked up around the world. But she left her weaving area as it was.

The following day, she opened her closet and pondered what to wear. Rifling through drawers, she decided on jeans and a sweater, familiar to her son and unrelated to her recent experiences.

She left the coast well before Rousseau's flight was due to arrive and took her time meandering through country scenes she'd passed hundreds of times. It struck her that she might have never seen the pastoral Anderson Valley again, with its vineyards and hills, the emerald Navarro River, gnarled old oaks with their mossy beards and clusters of mistletoe, pasturelands dotted with sheep and cows that took on a different atmosphere with every shift of light, every passing cloud.

At escalators near the baggage claim, Kay watched passengers milling about, or rushing by with new fascination, taking in their clothing, their luggage, the expressions on their faces. When she spotted Rousseau's curly brown hair above the other travelers at his 6'4" height, riding down the escalator, she nearly hyperventilated with emotion. She might never have seen him again. Now, there he was, gliding toward her, his beloved face beaming as he spotted her waiting. He lock-stepped in pace with the crowd until he reached the cordon holding her back.

They held each other for a long minute, as they'd done in airports so many times after her divorce when he'd flown to visit his father. Now, at his adult height, he kissed the top of her head and rested his cheek on her hair. Her arms cinched around his slender waist.

"Silly old bear," he said. "I'm glad you came."

"Me, too," she answered, voice husky with emotion.

He let go and pulled her along the corridor. "Can we stop at Sonoma Taco?"

Kay laughed. "Of course." Ah, the ease and comfort of familiar ground: providing food for the young male stomach. She thought of Hamelyn speaking of food the instant they settled by the fire. It was hard not to tell Rousseau of the latest happenings in her life. They used to share everything. But she was his mother. How could she explain the risks she'd taken?

"So, how's life in Boston?" she asked, as they moved toward baggage claim.

"Oh. It's fair." He slipped an arm around her shoulder. "Only something pretty strange happened."

"Strange?" she asked, dread creeping into her heart. "In what way?"

"Well, this guy got on the subway at the Fenway stop. He had long, dark hair tied back and these clothes, like...I don't know...like old time. Maybe he was an actor. He had this worn bag, the shape of a musical instrument, I think. He was like someone out of a Robin Hood story. I mean, from the *real* story. Hard to describe. His eyes..."

Kay breathed slowly in and out, trying not to let panic seize her.

He went on. "The second our eyes met, a story popped into my mind. I mean...it was images but the ideas were crystal clear... like I was seeing the visions, real ones. I had to get home and write them down. It wasn't like, 'Oh, here's an idea for a story.' A force pushed me. I was sure it had something to do with that guy on the subway."

There was a harried tone in Kay's son's voice. She watched him intently. The more she listened, the more she dreaded the possibilities of what he was being pulled into. His eyes looked slightly haunted. Her throat constricted as she searched for comforting words.

"Anyway, we arrived at my stop. I got up to leave and then, at the doors, I turned to wave goodbye, 'cause, you know, we'd sort of connected...but he was gone. I swear, I barely took my eyes off him. He's there and the next instant, poof. He's gone."

Chapter 17

They stood silent, watching luggage go by on the belt.

It had to have been Baird. Why? What would he have been doing on a Boston subway? Near her son? The thought of Rousseau being drawn into the same labyrinth of ancient connections that had subsumed her life, and the risk of his not returning, made her stomach tighten with fear.

Kay settled on asking, "So, did you write the story down when you got home?"

"Yeah, I had to."

"What was it about?" Kay held her breath. *Please don't let it include Galfride.*

"Pirates." He grinned. It almost conveyed his old carefree *joie de vivre.*

Pirates, Kay thought with relief. That had nothing to do with Kyna and Baird.

A worn Harvard tag rode a black suitcase around the bend of the belt. "Is that yours?" I pointed.

He nabbed his case and they started toward the tunnel between airport and parking. Somewhere in the tiled hallway, Kay realized Rousseau had been saying something more about the pirates and a kidnapping. She tried to hook into his trail of words, but her thoughts veered away. If she told him—warned him—would it make him any safer? Or would it ignite his curiosity and draw him further in?

"That's as far as I've gotten," he said.

Guilt shot through her. She tried to reestablish their connection without giving away her lapse: "I want to hear more as it evolves. Sounds exciting! Pirates!"

"But it's like something takes over. My hands are typing someone else's story. It seemed like I was being pushed from behind to get home that day. I kept thinking the man on the subway was tied in with it."

Baird had never mentioned pirates to her. "Well, writing fiction is that way, like the story gets channeled through us." What *a jerk I am, pontificating this way when a force I know all too well is moving in him*. She thought maybe if she downplayed it, he wouldn't be drawn. Some say focusing energy on something can draw it to us, she thought. Like once I'd met Baird, I couldn't stop playing with my silver pendant, trying to hear his voice, to identify the language and where it came from.

"I guess," he said, unconvinced.

As they entered the fumy underground parking garage, she battled internally, trying to assure herself there was nothing to worry about. *I'll just keep an eye out and...what? Forbid him to play in ancient Wales?* These were not the simple days—him seven and her concerned about a busy street, or his biking to a park too far from home.

On the long drive home to Pomo Bluffs, Rousseau filled her in on his days as a human rights lawyer: the cases he was working on, his limited social life, his college friends. Luckily, he had plenty to share. Kay could just listen, nod, ask the occasional question, and let her concerns slip into a distant fog.

They stopped for burritos at a favorite place from the past, and drove on. Once he finished his, he slept, leaving her to return to her spiraling worries.

They arrived home after dark. Kay switched on lights. Rousseau took in the added textile elements and turned to her. "Have you gotten rid of your books?" He wore a warm smile, but his brow puckered.

She must have taken too long to form an answer because he said, "Hey, I'm glad you're doing a...hobby, Mom." He studied the cloth emerging from the loom. "Nice...weave? Really... smooth. Are you taking classes or something?"

"Uh..." She hadn't anticipated that question. "Apprenticeship, sort of. I've met people who are teaching me." Somewhat true.

"That's great. How'd you meet 'em?"

She got the sense he was grilling her in his lawyer way. Had he and Sophie spoken? "We met on Samhain. Halloween. Want a Tom 'n Jerry?"

"Yes, please." He squatted to start a fire.

"You want rum in it, right?" She called from the kitchen.

"'Course," he answered. It was an old family tradition, dating from the grandparents and holidays spent in this house with them. "Hey, Oz. Did you miss me?" she heard him ask the cat as she poured eggnog into a pan.

"So, Sophie was here a couple of weeks ago?" he asked. "All the way from Paris, and she couldn't stay for Christmas?"

Maybe they hadn't talked after all. "She was sorry, honey," Kay said, stirring. "She was here for a conference, taking a co-worker's place. It was last minute. But it's a shame she'll be in France without any family for the holidays."

My mind tumbled back to medieval Wales and Kyna's gut-wrenching distress over her missing daughter.

Rousseau's voice broke her reverie. "I'm liking the writing, though. I mean fiction. It's a good switch from what I do all day. Constructing briefs and so on."

"You mean...compelled by it?" She carried their eggnog and rum in mugs, sprinkled with nutmeg, into the living room, her mind cascading back to the scent of spiced hot drinks in medieval Wales. Steadying her hands, she placed the hot cups on the table between the two spacious chairs and sat in one, facing the fire.

Rousseau shoved a log onto crackling flames and joined her, in the other chair. "Well, it is a bit scary," he said, picking up his cup, blowing and carefully sipping. "Yum. But I'd almost forgotten how much I loved making up stories as a kid."

"And those illustrations you used to draw." Kay sipped, savoring the drink as well as a safer conversation.

"Yeah," he said, laughing. "Robotic guys and funny alien creatures."

They planned to search for his old drawings, and reminisced about the past. Finally, as the fire turned to a glow of coals, Kay closed the iron-chain screen, and Rousseau went to bed in the guest room which she'd not yet made into an office.

The next day, they opened presents. It was a quiet affair. Later, they biked to a disc golf circuit overlooking the sea by the local community college. Chained cages on poles poked up here and there across the grassy knolls.

Halfway through the course, Rousseau had hiked ahead after his far-traveling disk. Kay passed through a knot of trees to find him staring at the water where the sea channeled into the Noyo River estuary. Fishing and Coast Guard boats came and went. She looked in the same direction. "Pretty, isn't it?"

"I can picture the pirate ship anchored right there." He pointed. "The river mouth looks similar but the town is right by the water. It has market booths and shanties, like in way olden days, with thatched roofs, a few buildings made of rough stone. Kind of like in my *Age of Empires* computer game. But so real."

It sounded like Llanbadarn Fawr. She had caught thoughts in Kyna's mind about her daughter running off to sea with a merchant who had anchored near their town. Could it be related? She shook her head.

"What's wrong, Mom? Are you worried about how I was compelled to write? Don't be. I'm having fun with the pirate story. I'll send you some of it." He hugged her shoulders, then turned, aimed, and skimmed his Frisbee across a great distance. It floated with ease. "Try to get this next one in less than four tosses," he teased, then loped off, avoiding a fallen log with a neat soccer slice.

Her Frisbee followed with a pathetic spurt. It took her a dozen more tries to get in range of the goal. Her final toss wobbled toward its destination.

All too soon, Rousseau and Kay stood at the airport again. This time rain poured down the giant windows. Her son's eyes were flecked gold-green in the stormy light. She studied them, wanting to keep them clear in her mind until she saw him again. Photos never did them justice.

They checked the departure board for JetBlue Flight 488 to Boston. On time. With a last hug, Rousseau joined the line snaking through security. He waved a final good-bye and disappeared into the bowels of the airport. She stared after him, well aware of her inability to keep him safe.

Back in Pomo Bluffs, the empty house was excessively quiet. In bed, she lay awake, her mind circling. She missed her son. The time with him had been sublime, but it was taxing to avoid telling him about her recent life. This could not go on. No more visits where she suppressed the truth of what she'd experienced, concealing the fact that he might be encountering the same world.

Some of the emptiness, she realized, involved missing Kyna. Living in her thoughts had been like watching a parade of stories pass through her psyche. Hollowed out, bereft, deprived of companionship, she missed the thrill of melding with Kyna, deprived of learning from her tenth-century knowledge. She'd just gained some facility at sorting her thoughts from Kyna's when they brought her into that tower. She loved Kyna's capabilities and being part in her skilled ways.

Granted, she'd had some expertise before she met her. Her research was referenced for having discovered some of women's previously unknown cultural history, based on language morphologies. But when she was in Kyna's mind, she gained a different competence, tied with the essentials of daily life. She loved experiencing the woman's deep connection with the land and the satisfaction she drew from knowing where to pick herbs to cure ailments. It was as though her spirit was intertwined with the saps and gums of trees, the patterns of animals and birds. She longed to continue her tutelage with the medieval healer.

Kyna had learned from her as well. This revelation, at the final hour, had astonished Kay. Maybe that was where the real ethics came in. Had she impacted history?

Kay wondered what essence of her had done the traveling. Her soul? Her spirit? She had her entire mind with her. Yet Kyna experienced her as a deer spirit at first. Clearly not by the time she caught thoughts of the Borneo dragon motif.

Now her singular consciousness was stripped down, unsatisfying. She had promised to stop obsessing with that other time, yet even now, she hungered for more of it. Despite seeing that her son could be drawn in and endangered.

Turmoil overran her. She nosed Oz's fur, breathed deep, and remembered how Kyna had drawn comfort from her hounds. What is it with the calming effect of animal smells? Whatever the cause, humans have known it for at least a thousand years.

Inspired by her attention, Oz stretched, then pulled himself up to her, hooking his claws into the bedspread, legs dragging behind. "You are definitely entertaining," Kay said to him, laughing. As he came into range, Kay wrapped her arms around him. His shoulder worked, bumping her chin as he kneaded, rumbling a purr. "What more can I ask?" she said to the top of his head.

But she could ask for more. She *was* asking for more. She longed for a circle of elders to help her muster her situation into a seemly, livable form. The image of Aelfwyn rose in her mind, as did the rest of The Thirteen. They were a council, but not a warm, fuzzy one. Maybe a council wasn't meant to be warm or fuzzy. She opened her bedside table drawer and drew out the Faeries' Oracle tarot deck. Spreading them out, face up, she studied the images of dryads, nyads, Sidhe, pixies, and gnomes that brought with them the Celtic mythic wisdom, with a splash of Jungian philosophy thrown in.

Sitting cross-legged, she lit a candle and a block of piñon incense. She shuffled, fanned the cards in an arc, and asked, "How am I to adjust to my life now?" Then she picked three, representing past, present, and future.

Turning over the first, the Gnome King gave her his no-nonsense scowl, arms crossed, reminding her time and space are illusions. Well, yes, when this particular principle starts unraveling every aspect of one's life, it's natural to philosophize. Even so, this card represented choosing a path and following it. As the path keeps changing, adjust. That made sense. Whatever had taken root in her life, she had to move forward.

Not a lot of comfort but the only possible way.

Kay turned over the next card, signifying the present. The Chalice. Its message? That fulfillment is transitional; we find one form, then must let it go, allow it to take another shape. *I've learned too much about that recently*. But the Chalice had a point. To experience abundance, we need to let moments of fulfillment be transitory.

The last card, the future, was the Fae Grig or "Mixed Blessings". Now that was not reassuring. "Lighten up. Focus simply. Only in that way will clarity come," said the impish creature.

Pushing the deck of cards into their velvet drawstring

bag, she blew out the candle and slid under the covers, with Oz a warm lump at her back. What could be a simple focus? Kay would soon be due back at work. Did she want to continue there? That was simplicity compared to her old university position but certainly hadn't been bringing her fulfillment.

From nowhere, the plot she'd signed up for at the community gardens came to mind. Planting one seed at a time, one task following the last, unsusceptible to hurry, bringing forth green life. Perfect. What about a winter crop? Each plant has its season. She could grow her own food as she'd been making her clothing. That would be more like Kyna's life, melding the two worlds. More or less.

It was the twenty-eighth of December. She had until January 3 to get a winter garden started. That was the agreed upon time for her return to Luminous Life.

Kay's session with the tarot had reduced the swirling of troubled thoughts down to one simple plan. Comforted, she slept.

Chapter 18

I n the morning, Kay set out with a backpack full of garden tools. She had scarce hope that the plant starts Joaquin and Jarl had given her would be alive. Entering the community gardens at mid-block, she admired the winter growing season as it manifested in the plots she passed. When she arrived at her own, she groaned. Bleak and overgrown, it did not inspire hope of lush crops anytime soon. A few chard starts, albeit gangly, had survived in their six-pack.

For the rest of her winter holiday, she hauled compost, studied the double digging method of preparing garden soil, and planted winter fare. She read about drip systems and water catchment and made sketches and diagrams in a drawing book.

On January 2, the day before she was due back at work, she noticed a board at the community garden office where people often posted things like give-away starts, extra veggies, permaculture workshops, and seed shares. As she examined the notes, an announcement caught her eye: "Need a new garden coordinator." Even though the pay was minimal, she wanted the job.

Don't be ridiculous, she told the part of her that itched

to write down the email address. That is not a step toward returning to teaching, writing, or research. She copied it anyway.

Once home, she emailed inquiring about the position, and included her phone number. The response was almost immediate. Linda wanted to meet her at the garden that afternoon.

"Can I see your plot?" she asked over the phone.

Kay opened her mouth to give a polite apology for wasting the woman's time. "You know, that's okay," she said. "I haven't…"

"Oh, whether you have a winter garden isn't important. Don't worry. Let's meet and discuss what's needed."

Later, in the afternoon, they sat on the benches encircling the firepit at the center of the gardens and discussed hours and responsibilities.

"Which is your plot?" Linda said at last. She was a stocky woman in her late thirties, with a perfectly edged bob-cut. She looked less natural than Kay expected for a garden coordinator, considering the earthy braids and overalls that had populated the workshop.

"Was this your position?" Kay asked.

"No, I'm an accountant. But I'm on the board of directors for the community gardens as well as the farmers market. I'm a local grower fanatic: slow foods, lawns-to-food, all that."

"That's fantastic," Kay said.

"And your plot?"

"This way." Cringing as they passed elaborate displays of gardening aplomb, Kay led her to her nascent attempt at winter growing.

"Oh," she said, studying her area.

Kay's heart sank. She was again about to apologize for dragging her there for nothing when Linda said, "I see you're using permaculture methods, mixed planting."

She squatted and lifted a kale leaf, revealing tiny beet sprigs. "Great start."

"I'm reading the Jeavons methods," Kay replied, tentatively.

"We go on a field trip to his farm every year," Linda told her, standing, knees cracking. She grabbed a fence post to finish straightening up.

"I'd love to go!" Excitement surged in Kay. This was akin to research.

"When can you start? Tomorrow?"

They want me? How could they trust me with this? There were so many seasoned gardeners in the area. "To tell you the truth, I don't have a huge amount of expertise. I'm interested in gaining it, but I've only experimented with home gardens up to now." May as well come clean.

"We'll start you slow. Others will help. It's mainly keeping an eye on the place. Ensuring safe practices with compost. Mediating squabbles like 'she never brought back my trowel' or 'he used my glove and put a hole in it'."

Kay laughed. "I think I can do that. I just hope—"

"We have some books in the office. You can look things up. Of course, there's the internet. You can always call the Master Gardeners at Botanica. They love to help. And as you probably know, we hold regular workshops. You'll be in charge of coordinating those."

"It sounds... I'd really like to do it."

"Fantastic. Let's go fill out forms. The pay's not great but...." She shrugged.

"That's not important." She followed to the office. *Here I go again. Even farther from university professor. How much education does it take to turn soil*? Yet she knew that was the wrong voice to listen to.

At home, Kay called Luminous Life to give notice.

"I'm not surprised," Natalia said, in her breathy voice.

"Should I try to work half time until you—?"

"We've been covering for you. It's not a huge issue, Kay. But we'll miss you." She paused. "Is everything tip-top?" Sometimes, for effect, Natalia tried on a British accent, which was quite interesting when blended with her Chicago upbringing.

"Oh, yes, I just have to...get some things squared away."

"I understand," she said in her airy, understanding voice.

Kay wished her well and hung up, relieved. No more stultifying cubicle in an airless, fluorescent labyrinth. No more coaxing students into overpriced classes or convincing them they'd be staying in a "spa-like atmosphere" if they used the company-owned inn as their accommodation. It wasn't.

She dropped by to sign separation forms and pick up a last paycheck. The queen and king themselves bestowed hugs upon her, along with a signed copy of their new raw food recipe book. She had to admit, her farewell slice of uncooked cheesecake was fabulous.

Pushing her way through the historic building's front doors, Kay looked across the busy main thoroughfare to where the Traveler had brought her the boots. Was she going to turn her back on that world?

She tried to sense what her soul needed by taking the garden job. Did it make any real sense? She crossed the street, reviewing her decision. She could easily live on a part-time salary for a while. She'd inherited the house free and clear, and the property taxes were still based on her parents' 1970s evaluation. In other words, they were minimal in this rural area. She could subsist, in part, by eating from her garden, and save money by walking and riding her bike. She had what clothes she needed, mostly a gardening outfit.

The work at the garden did the trick. Kay got out of the house most days, away from reminders of that other world. As she carefully tended her plot, her seedlings thrived. After a month, she began eating from the garden, harvesting her own and trading with Jarl and Joaquin, who were often there. Sometimes they'd sit together at the central fire pit to share lunch and stories. Helping with the day-to-day workings of a gardening community grounded her.

Ancient Wales and Baird became less and less believable. Kay began to doubt whether the fibers were, in fact, magical. Could she have imagined it all? Maybe the scenes that came when she touched the silver pendant meant she was schizophrenic.

She knew in her heart that Baird had come to her and led her into his world. She was certain she had lived in Kyna's mind. However, after her near extinction in the tower, it was an unwise risk to toy with that other realm. Over time, the pull lessened even more. She would avoid writing the ogham, speaking the ancient language, wearing the magical fibers and the necklace, and focus on tending the gardens. Hopefully that world would slip into a sweet—well, *mostly* sweet—memory.

She couldn't get herself to take off the pendant. It was a natural part of her now yet she had stopped testing its powers.

One day in February, as she worked to remove some particularly stubborn crabgrass, daylight waned, and she realized she was alone in the gardens. Groaning from pro-longed weeding, she straightened her aching back and set-tled against the craggy apple tree. A first star and faint new moon twinkled near the horizon. She sighed and closed her eyes as the strain eased out of her lumbar region.

Kay awakened with a start. She'd drifted to sleep. Im-ages remained from a dream that clung in brilliant detail in her mind. Struggling to hold the picture, she locked the of-fice, checked perimeter gates, and ran most of the way home. There, she tried to sketch the fantastic vision that had bloomed. It had to be painted. She dragged a canvas of her mother's from the backyard shed, quickly set up easel and paints, and started to work. In a near trance, she let the brush lead, not stopping until dawn sent pink light through the glass doors. Then she collapsed, exhausted, and slept.

Hours later, she returned to her painting and stared at the canvas, lit by late morning light. On it, she had captured the scene—the hill, the town, the boats, and the moonlight on the sea—just as she'd seen it at Samhain, only a birds-eye view. It was a sort of topographical map with a surreal quality. The village appeared alive: torches flickered on stone walls and sent bursts of golden light onto cobblestone streets. It was difficult to accept this as the doing of her own hand.

She grabbed a brush and painted one last mark, on the beach north of the town. Why had she done that? She thought of her son's description of his hands being controlled by an unknown force. This might be the same.

Further compelled, she got on her bike and rode north. Once she'd crossed the bridge at the end of town, she followed the old abandoned logging road past sparse woods and across the final trestle. She locked her bike to a signpost and descended a rugged path onto rock outcrops pocked with tidepools. At the base, she jumped to the sand and followed the shoreline. The sea rippled, placid, at low tide. Wavelets lapped with ebbing whispers, then slid back.

She scrambled over a last outcrop before the long stretch of deserted beach that extended toward Ten Mile River and the Lost Coast beyond, disappearing into purple hills. To her right, low cliffs, layered in red and gold, crumbled in slabs. Asphalt remnants of the old logging road dissolved into the sand, returning to the land.

She walked along the edge of the water, scanning the beach ahead. Snowy plovers skittered in unison along the boundaries of lapping waves. When she drew near, the sea birds flew up in sharp, perfect patterns of wings and settled again a short way further on.

She passed a hillock that had been invisible at a distance. Beyond it, a tall driftwood structure formed the rune *Nied*: a cross with a slanted bar, tied to the vertical post with seaweed. It had been part of the sigil that sent her home from medieval Wales. *Here I go, seeing symbols in everything.* But if she were a Celt living in ancient times, she'd notice the forms of runes in nature, and see importance in them. Humankind had become learned and scientific, losing that type of connection to the numinous or sacred. In the process, she thought, we've also lost some forms of knowing that maybe be esoteric but equally valid.

What did *Nied* mean to the ancients? Need. The power of our deepest desires. The friction of such needs provides the fire behind every action, or should. Not yet sure what that need was for her, she retraced her steps to her bike with a sense that she had found what she came for.

At home, Jarl waited on her porch. She remembered belatedly that he said he'd bring by some heirloom herb starts.

"Great day for a bike ride," he said. "Where'd you go?"

"Up to the beach by Ward Avenue. It was very spur of the moment. Sorry I was late." She set her bike at the side of the house and climbed the steps.

Jarl squatted to pet Oz who shamelessly threw himself down for a tummy rub.

Kay laughed. "You're a pleasure glutton, Oz."

They hadn't talked about the strange conversation before she'd slipped away into the tenth century, had just gone on being friends. But she knew there had been elements in that conversation that should be addressed. And she definitely should stop holding a torch for a married man of a thousand years ago.

She unlocked the front door. "Come on in."

He followed her through to the living room. "Where do you want these?" He held out a starts tray.

"How about in here?" She indicated the table spread with newspapers.

Jarl spotted the painting. "Wow. Is this what you saw on Samhain?"

Kay froze, then smiled, cheeks warming. "Yeah, it is."

"This is…" He spoke in a hushed voice, as if he feared chasing the unreal sight away. As phantom as the tale she'd told them, of a bard who led her to a hillside in ancient Wales. Jarl stood still, his eyes moving over the canvas. After a moment he whispered, "That's strange." He sounded excited and beckoned her closer. "Do you see this?"

"What?" She stood next to him, facing the four-foot-square canvas.

"When I turn to the side, something shimmers." He waved his hand, then shrugged. "When I look straight at it, I don't see it so I can't exactly pinpoint it." He stared with such intensity he was almost cross-eyed.

She tried looking slightly away as he'd suggested, then attempted various angles. She saw no shimmer. "Maybe it's the way the colors came out. It's not like anything I've painted before." She didn't say she was in a trance when she produced it. Remembering the mark that sent her on the mission to the beach, she dug a magnifying glass from the side table and brought it close to the upper right corner. "No way," she muttered.

"What?" Jarl approached the corner where she was focused.

She pointed to the mark. "This. It's too tiny to see any shape with the naked eye, right? Just looks like a line."

"True."

"I made that mark, just a quick stroke with the brush, nothing in my mind. Now look."

He brought his eye over the magnifier. "It's a rune," he said. "In Old Norse, it's *Naudr*. *Nied* in Anglo-Saxon."

"Right! I saw that on the beach a half hour ago. A tall driftwood structure in the shape of the *Nied* rune. Exactly where it is in this painting, on the beach north of town."

"What do you make of it?"

She shrugged. "No idea."

"Well, you've seen two of them. The third is a synchronicity or meaningful coincidence, right? Watch for another one."

Sharing with someone, even leaving out facts, was cathartic. "I'll do that." She smiled.

He glanced at his watch. "I have to get to work. Put these in the ground soon." He indicated the multi-colored plants in neat trays on the table. "I think they'll do well."

"Thanks! I'm sure they will."

"We have a lot of compost at our place. Let me know if you want some." He walked toward the front door. "Your plot's looking good. Everyone likes your leadership as garden coordinator, by the way."

"That's great to hear."

Surprisingly uplifted, she saw him out. She missed the compliments she used to get on her teaching and mentoring of students. At least she was being appreciated for something.

Over the following days, Kay rode to the beach several more times to check if the *Nied* structure remained. It did. She tried standing near it while holding onto her pendant, watching for signs, but nothing more happened.

At home, she studied the painting, hoping she would again make an important mark, leading her.

Here I am, obsessing again, she scolded herself, and settled back into working on plans for a drip-system event for later in the month.

Chapter 19

Despite her best intentions, Kay ambled over to her painting for the umpteenth time, hoping to see the shimmer Jarl tried to show her.

Her computer dinged, announcing new email. A friend from her teaching days had sent a YouTube link to a documentary about a blind Turkish painter who produced beautiful art without seeing. Scientists attached electrodes to his brain and detected shifts in activity as he touched parts of his canvas.

Closing her eyes, her hands hovered over her artwork, moving just above the surface, self-conscious even though Oz, sitting in a patch of sun blinking, was her only witness.

Okay, do it like you mean it. She slowed her breathing. Keeping her eyes shut, she again moved her hands over the surface, not quite touching it. She came to a stop, as though a force held her in place, her hand tingling. Kay reached for a paintbrush and dabbed the canvas where her finger had stopped, then opened her eyes. She had painted a mark in the center of the woods. She checked with the magnifying glass. It looked like the *Nied* rune again. *Third time's the charm?*

She tried to judge where the mark would be in her town.

No woods were there, if she based the location on the curve of the river. There should be only streets lined with houses in that spot. Hunting in the kitchen jumble drawer, she found a local map and string and spread it open near the painting. Then she stretched string between the marks on the painting, and triangulated the distance to the river. According to this system, the new mark in the woods landed on South Harold Street. *An unlikely name for a magical place,* she thought. Nevertheless, she pulled on a jacket and rolled her bike to the front walk. Oz got there first. "I know, another madcap adventure," she said, kneeling to pet him. "What's that you say? You thought I was going to get back to normal? Put my life on track?"

He peered at her with lowered lids.

"Nah. I know you. You believe in living for the moment, following your urges."

He stuck out a leg and licked vigorously.

"There. My very point. Living in the moment. 'In this moment, I will lick my inner thigh.' Very tricky, that."

She pushed her bike onto the street and started across town.

South Harold was a single block, broken off from North Harold by a zig in the road. The block widened at the midway point where front yards lengthened and narrowed. She slowed by an ivy-covered house set far back on its lot. In the driveway, a bumper sticker on the old car read, "I may be straight, but I'm not narrow." Well, that fits. A clue maybe. Or she was trying too hard to find signs. Next to it, a rounded trailer with a forest green door stood snug against a petite shed of the same color.

A shimmer caught her eye. She rolled forward, straddling her bike. At the upper corner of the shed, a design glowed golden. Intertwined runes. It was the sigil Duff had etched onto the crystal before she was torn from Kyna. Her heart gripped, then thundered against her ribs.

Movement in the shadow at the front of the shed drew her attention.

Baird stood, insubstantial, leaning against the green double doors. She blinked, afraid to move, even breathe. He straightened, face attentive, and turned toward her. Slowly, carefully, she stepped off the bike, laid it on the ground, and eased closer. He wore his usual tunic and breeches under his cape, along with road-dusty boots. His strong expressive face was lightly bearded. Dark hair fell forward in disarray, wilder than she remembered ever seeing it, the rest tied back. A ubiquitous angular harp bag hung at his back.

He remained still, as if unable to leave the spot. She stepped closer, longing to close the distance and smell the forest and wild winds on him.

"You're here," she whispered. *What else to say*? His image was too faint to detect if his hair had the silver she'd seen at Samhain.

He struggled, concentrating. His eyes grew distant.

She took a breath, fearful he'd disappear. "Before I saw you, last Samhain, I had already been in your time...inside Kyna. Did you know that?"

He nodded.

She stared, angry, betrayed. "*You knew*? At Samhain? That it had been me in Kyna? Why didn't you say? Why didn't you mention it?"

"I did know, by then. I came searchin' fer Kyna, fer her spirit in ye. The crystal must o' held some o' yer spirit from...th' other time."

This wasn't getting any clearer. But something more urgent finally came through to her. "Searching for Kyna?

She's missing?" She pictured her collapsing on the stone floor and dreaded the possibilities.

His head jerked away. She followed his look. A man stood staring from a yard across the street. Could he see Baird, or did she look like a crazy person, talking to a garage door?

She glanced back at Baird. He'd grown mistier.

"Don't go yet," she whispered, pathetic.

"Sorry, Dove. 'Tis difficult t' remain." His voice diminished. "…easier at Samhain… 'r Solstice …"

He faded fast, voice faint. She could no longer see him. Words floated to Kay, as if on a light wind, "*Adfera atat pryd aya, cholomehn.*" I'll return when I can, Dove.

"Baird," she gasped, staring at the place he'd been. She leapt to the garage door, pressed her hand where he'd leaned to see if any warmth remained. How long she stood there, she ddin't know. When she turned, the man across the street was gone.

Reluctantly, she picked up her bike.

She wanted to tell Baird about the painting, to ask him if he'd sent her the vision, if someone had set it all up: The runes on the beach and on her painting, the sigil on the shed. To ask why she hadn't remembered that she'd gone into Kyna's mind at Solstice.

She looked up. No more sigil. Only peeling paint remained. She had a strange thought, that this was like her pendant, the silver strands looping back on themselves; in this case, time had bent backward, then forward. Trying to piece it all together, she slowly walked her bike toward home, wondering if Baird had already been at the shed when she painted the mark, if he drew her, or she drew him. Such an elaborate and diffuse sequence of messages. Could they have been orchestrated? He had said, "*We* searched." Who was we? He and Aelfwyn? Did she cause her to go to sleep against the apple tree and dream the painting? And for everything to depend on matching the marks to the map? Not within the realm of probability. Unless Aelfwyn had manipulated her mind. Could Aelfwyn be behind her receiving the video of the blind painter as well? Come on, now. Internet didn't exist in medieval time.

She thought about the *Nied* rune and its true meaning of calling our needs out to the gods. We attract what we ask for.

She stopped and wrapped her arms around herself, gathering the memory of this recent moment with Baird like a treasure. She longed for a stronger, more sustained, connection with him. And greater control.

Who had she been kidding, believing she could put this out of her mind and get back to a purely present-time focus? She'd failed miserably. Jumping onto her bike, she pumped for home, purposely planning placement of heirloom herb starts.

It would have been nice if the painting marked the beginning of a system for Baird to communicate with her. Of course, it didn't work that way. What had it accomplished? It convinced Kay there was no getting Baird, Kyna, or their world, out of her mind.

She started weaving again. She wore the boots from Boldo and the clothes she'd made from the mysterious yarns. On her way to and from the community gardens, she rode down South Harold though it was several blocks out of the way. For good measure, she also took in Partridge

Street and frequently went past the old oak.

She tried numerous times to turn her head sideways next to the painting to see if it shimmered. She tried closing her eyes and willed the art to precipitate a new rendezvous with Baird. She returned often to the beach north of town to hunt for signs. The *Nied* structure began to slip, slanted sideways, and eventually flopped onto its side in the sand.

In April, the wild purple irises and lupines, and flame-colored Indian paintbrush drew her off the beach and into the dunes. Kay sat in a cleft between carpets of color and gazed down the corridor to the sea. After a while, a lone seagull sailed toward her, circled, and landed on a nearby dune. With a sliding waddle, he descended until he was only a few feet away, his head turned so that one bright, flinty eye peered at her. She had a strong notion Baird was in there, seeing out from the gull's eyes.

"So, you can find me here?" she said.

She heard a response in her head, a birdlike voice saying, "None of it is entirely at my command. I go where I can."

She kept still and said, "I'm helpless. I can't understand what I should be doing, how to control anything."

The gull edged closer. He was mottled grey and brown with ivory specks. He cocked his head. "I'll keep tryin' for a stronger human presence here, Dove."

Funny, a gull calling her Dove. But it warmed her. "At least you're more substantial this time," she said, though it was hard to talk to a bird and be sure she heard answers. "There's so much I want to know." She looked into the bird's beady eyes and willed it to pour more words into her head.

Seagulls do look like they're smiling sometimes. "This is not an ideal form, Dove. I'll keep tryin'."

The bird's thoughts had a Welsh accent. His beak opened. She thought he would give a cry, but instead, something dropped to the sand. He faded, then winked out. Nothing remained but a pair of gull prints in the sand—and in front of them, half of the golden crystal.

She stared. They cut it? There was no mistaking the powerful stone used to separate her spirit from Kyna's in the tower in ancient Wales. The sigil combining *Hagalaz* and *Nied* was etched on its surface. It lay, casting yellow light onto the sand.

She touched it with one fingertip, then withdrew, picturing Kyna, bold and knowing, breathing on it to make it glow brighter. She knew how to handle it. Kay did not. She glanced around, up into the sky. *Are you sure?* Her mind cried out to the clouds and pale blue ethers. Do you really think this is a good idea?

She pulled her sleeve over her palm and scooped up the crystal. Her hand shook as she set it on her thigh. Her leg vibrated with its energy. She considered putting it in her pocket. *Not safe for the bike ride home.* She slipped it into her bra and zipped her sweatshirt to the neck. Her heart raced with the power of it against her chest. Pressing a hand to it, she scanned the landscape. The world appeared different—crisper, more vibrant.

She made her way down the dune corridor to the beach.

Oystercatchers with their bright red beaks were incapable of flying without screaming. The odd godwit left feathery dashes in the wet sand with its long, pointed bill. Near shore, tiny sandpipers dashed in tight formation along the waves' edges. Droves of gulls stood facing the setting sun. Was one Baird? She unzipped enough to slide her hand to the stone snuggled under her shirt. *Are you still here?* she asked silently, wondering if the crystal might show him. None of the gulls glowed or looked otherwise identified as containing a medieval bard's spirit.

She had no idea how to direct the crystal's power, or what it could do, other than to help tear her spirit from Kyna's and send it back to her time. A mighty force to reckon with.

At home, she cupped the egg-sized golden crystal in her palm and meditated, seeking a sense of Baird or Kyna. The swirl of energy went nowhere.

Kay decided to make a special bag to carry the stone. She dyed yarn in shades of blue and green, like deep water, and when it was dry, wound it on a bobbin to weave into cloth.

When she had a narrow strip of gauzy fabric, a single aquamarine strand threading through it, she carefully embroidered the edges with connecting sigils formed from some unconscious knowledge. She hung the bag from her neck with a ribbon. The amulet lay softly on her chest. She wore it night and day. Slowly, she attuned to its properties. Its resonance kept her company.

Chapter 20

The weather grew warmer; even the cloudy coast received spring's onset. Shelley, their midwife friend from Appalachia, took a garden plot adjacent to Kay's. They created a bed of medicinal herbs, some of which she'd learned about from her grandmothers. They had to send away to the South for them. Flowering vines crawled between their plots, intertwined.

One night, Harper in the Glade showed up and serenaded them. The garden crew invited them for fireside feasting. Growing fond of the area, they rented a place in town and started hanging out. They even tried to maintain garden plots but quickly let them go to seed.

Late one morning, all sat shivering in coastal fog, passing thermoses of coffee, tea, and Mexican-spiced hot chocolate to keep warm. The band members straggled over from their house closeby and shared hot drinks.

"We can bet it's warmer east of here," Joaquin said. He described waterfalls he'd visited. "You gotta know someone who lives there and cross private property to get to the river. But they're fantastic. They remind me of back home in the Yucatan."

They decided to trek east and find them, maybe swim.

An hour later, the eight of them set off in two vehicles, with a picnic lunch. Jarl and Shelley rode in Joaquin's truck. He took the lead since he knew the landmarks. The rest jammed into Shane's sedan, with Ian, Candace, and Kay in the back, Sara up with Shane. Kay was glad Ian was on the far side of Candace; the way he looked at her still made her uneasy. Watching.

The band members chattered away in their English and Irish accents, occasionally breaking into song. Kay listened, contentedly watching the countryside slide by as they drove south along the shore, then east. After forty minutes of winding road, they eventually turned down a rutted dirt lane. The truck pulled into a turnout surrounded by oaks and manzanitas—a far different terrain from the coast. They piled out, breathing in sage scent, and reveling in the relaxing warm climate.

Dragging baskets and blankets from the back of the truck, they trouped after Joaquin down a barely trammeled path. A dull roar told them they neared the falls, making the ground vibrate under their feet. They stepped from the trees onto a pebbly shore. Across a dark pool, water thundered from about twenty feet above.

"There's a series of falls," Joaquin said proudly, pointing to the right where the river entered a glade of trees with golden leaves lifting in the soft breeze.

"This is great," Shelley said.

We settled blankets and picnic on the sandy bank.

Already sweaty from the short hike, they stripped down to swimsuits or shorts and waded in. Hoots and hollers testified to the first shock of chill waters.

"No way." Shane, the red-haired fiddler from Dublin, goose-stepped back to shore. The rest joined him, deserting the cold pool and flopping onto blankets. They started in on beers and early lunch.

Kay'd yearned to immerse herself in natural mountain waters for some time, for the sense of cleansing and renewal. She braced herself and dove in, then swam hard to shake off the first shock. Reaching the opposite side, she climbed out and scrambled to the sunny top of an enormous boulder. She had a beautiful view of the lower falls and wooded landscape from the top.

Joaquin spotted her and waved. "Kay, come back. We're starting the feast!"

"You go ahead," she called. "I'll be over in a bit." Gingerly, she stretched out on the hot rock.

Wanting the breeze directly on skin, she stripped, keeping out of sight, and turned onto her stomach. The rock's surface scorched her tender flesh at first, but not for long. She let the heat soak into her. She was reminded of long-past days of skinny-dipping during college summer breaks when she'd worked as a camp counselor.

After a while, she flipped over and looked up at pale, shimmering leaves. The sun re-baked her, and she was one with the heat. Finally, too hot to stand more, she crawled down the shadowed side of the rock and, like a contented, sun-warmed newt, slipped back into the water, naked but for the silver pendant and crystal-half in its bag. The cold pool delicious on her bare skin, she frogged in long strokes, coming up next to the thundering falls. Finding an edge where the force lessened, she plunged through. The thundering water curtained a narrow green cave. Jade and emerald light played in streaks on the wall behind.

Kay paddled beside the verdant corridor to a shelf where she sat submerged to her shoulders. From there she looked through the thick sheet of plummeting falls making her friends on the far shore into patchy Claymation.

"I like this outfit," said a familiar voice, soft and low, next to her bare shoulder. She turned. Baird's eyes were inches away. Water drops jeweled his long, dark lashes. His shoulders were bare. On his chest rested the twin of her golden crystal, glowing yellow at the end of a braided cord. She reached out and touched it. The stone pulsed and glowed brighter.

"It helped me find ye, as I hoped t'would." He spoke with his lips close to her ear. His skin brushed hers and the desire to kiss him ricocheted through her.

"You were a sea gull, last I saw you." She pulled back to see his reaction, compelled to check where they were in his sequence of time.

He nodded, then sat by her, his shoulder against hers, solid and warm.

She edged away slightly. This was Kyna's man. She studied his eyes, purple bruises of worry underneath them.

He put an arm around her.

She pushed against his wet chest, shook her head. "Kyna," she muttered.

His arm loosened. "It's been two years. More. We've had no word." His arm lay loose around her back.

"You're still looking, though."

"Aye. Tha' never stops. But 'tis a long time. I know she's no' dead, nor is she in danger or hurting. I sense she left of her own free will."

"You can tell that?" Kay searched his face. They had to lean close to hear each other with the roar of the waterfall.

"I can, Dove." He brought his lips to hers.

"But Kyna—" she said.

"She left me, Dove." He pulled back and searched her eyes. "Aelfwyn says it as well. There's no sign t'was other-wise."

"But—"

"Not long after ye were parted from her, she disappeared. No struggle. No message."

Kyna had not been permanently injured by Kay's spirit being ripped from her. Kay drew in a relieved breath. "You don't think it was...him? That he managed to take her, as he did at the faire?"

Baird was silent a moment. He slipped his hand along her jaw and brought his mouth to her ear. "I believe he's somehow connected, aye. But if she wanted to, she'd get a message t' me. If she was in trouble, I'd know. Aelfwyn'd ken it."

"Why can you come to me now, so solid?"

"The crystal halves, mayhap," he said.

He pulled her close. The situation was fraught with wrongness, yet in another way, natural. She had, after all, made love to him as his wife, while in his wife's mind. That made it familiar. Yet she was keenly aware that it was just him and her this time.

They made love, entwined in the water like seals, easy, thrilling, as nature intended.

After, they lay in each other's arms on the rockshelf, half submerged.

After a while she asked, "Why are you coming to me, Baird? How is finding me going to help your search for Kyna?"

He flinched. She hated that she'd asked. He rested his head on a stone pillow and brought her to his wet, warm chest. The beat of his heart soothed her.

"What we have, Dove, 'tis somethin' different, and it canno' be explained altogether. I am drawn t' yer spirit. 'Tis part o' me." He kissed her temple, held her close, enfolding her in his warm arms. "That first Samhain... We were celebratin' on the hillside, and yer presence reached out t' me. I followed it and found myself in yer time. I sensed y' coming along the street. I knew where ye would be. I waited for ye. I canno' say why yer my Dove, but y'ar."

She savored his words, and the timber of his voice in his chest where her ear pressed.

Someone shouted from outside the roaring waterfall. "Have you found water spirits back there, Kay?" Through the water curtain, she could see Jarl in the middle of the pool.

She groaned quietly. Baird chuckled, then moved around to give her a lingering kiss. He began to fade.

"Don't go... Don't go...don't go," she begged over the thundering water.

His form dissipated, then he was gone. She rolled to her stomach, tears welling as she watched Jarl making his way toward her through the water, her swimsuit dangling from his finger.

"How long do you think can you stay back there before you turn into a pollywog?" he called.

She made herself grin, ignoring the tightness in her chest. She glanced back one last time at their green, lovers' bower, now empty, then swam out through the thin curtain at the waterfall's edge.

"Thank you, Jarl. You found it. Good man," she said, treading water in the deep pool and reaching out for her swimsuit. She worked her way to where she could feel the shore and pulled on the suit, still submerged. They raced across and stepped, dripping, onto the sandy bank near the others.

"You missed everything, Kay. We ate it all." Shane pulled a hangdog face.

"No, we didn't," Shelley assured her, holding out a

container of olives.

"It must be great to go behind the falls," said Joaquin.

"It is," Kay replied as she accepted Shelley's offering.

They whooped and ran to the pool to try out the be-hind-the-falls effect. Kay helped herself to the last scraps of cheese, crackers, olives and fruits, then lay back on the blanket, savoring the memory of what had occurred.

Squeezed in next to Ian and Candace on the car ride back, Kay watched black trees shoot past the car windows. Ian's voice gradually entered her reverie. She turned to find his face close to her. "Sorry. What was that about Candace's leg?" She tried to edge away but, sitting in the middle this time, he had her pressed against the car door.

"I said a bear tore it off."

She leaned around him. "They look fine to me," she observed, noting the long legs angled into his space.

"You're right! It's amazin'. I could ha' sworn the bear tore it clean off."

Candace rolled her eyes and groaned as he took the opportunity to squeeze one of her knees.

"But seriously, Kay, where were you? Miles away. I was tryin' to bring y' back t' our world, luv." Ian's distinctive Cornish accent, with its rolled "Rs", had charm. The humor didn't reach his eyes. There was a strange intensity in them.

"Sorry. I was daydreaming." *When had it grown dark?* She vaguely remembered the sun hovering over hills as they made their way back to the vehicles. Once they started on the winding road toward home, Kay drifted into memories filled with shifting green light—and Baird.

"What happened behind that waterfall? Did ye find the land of the fey?" Ian glanced toward Shane and Sara in the front seat. "I swear, our Kay here has all the luck." His eyes dropped to her chest.

She thought that rather rude and glanced down to see if she'd forgotten any essential clothing. In the dark backseat, a pale golden glow pulsed to the beat of her heart through her thin shirt. *Crap*.

"I want one of those." His hungry scrutiny unnerved her.

Heat crept into her cheeks.

"There's that tiny French restaurant comin' up." Sara's lilting voice brought warmth and relief as she drew Ian's attention away. "Let's stop and eat. I'm starved. Split somethin' with me, Candace—I'm dead poor." She pulled out her cell phone to call Jarl, Joaquin, and Shelley in the truck.

Ian made an acerbic remark about the questionable contents of French food, and Kay rummaged at her feet for a sweater to cover the telltale glow.

Chapter 21

The next week, Harper in the Glade had a gig at Duck 'n Hen. Jarl called and suggested they walk from Kay's house; Joaquin was bringing a new sweetheart and would meet them there.

They arrived in front of the restaurant. Kay stopped to study the band's poster in the window. She hadn't noticed before the words, "'R *Bloneg Cath*," running across the lower edge. They meant "Harper in the Glade" in Welsh. No one in the band was Welsh. Must be a nod to the numerous bards of that origin? Some Irish bards were best known for the Welsh translations of their songs, she knew.

Eager patrons pressed through the doorway. Inside, the air buzzed with sound and heat. She gave the bald bartender with a tattooed scalp her usual order of eggplant and roasted pepper on focaccia. Shelley, looking Traveler-like in bright draping clothes and crystal-bead jewelry, came to her side. Her dark hair was pinned up, falling in a charming disarray of tendrils.

Jarl leaned over the bar to chat with his work mates.

"Nice job, getting this shift off," one said.

"Yeah, well." He blew on his knuckles and rubbed them on his chest. "Some people think I'm special." He winked at me, eyes lingering.

"Special." Tattoo Scalp made a rude sound. "That's what you call it?"

They laughed in camaraderie.

Joaquin entered. The woman who came in behind him was tiny, even in heeled boots. It was impossible to tell her ancestry—perhaps Filipina. The two looked smashing together. Her thick dark hair was cut at random angles, as was her layered skirt with its deliberate tattered rips showing playful tights, her shirt strategically torn around the shoulders. She had what Kay thought of as an East Bay look: cosmopolitan and dystopian. She smiled and waved them over.

They found a table near the low stage where the band set up. Shelley leaned close to be heard over the general roar. "What's new?"

As always, Kay was tempted to tell her she'd returned to the past, experiencing the life of a medieval healer. As a midwife, Shelley would be fascinated by what she knew from Kyna's mind. Not telling her was tantamount to dishonesty. Yet, she hefted her tall glass of dark beer and chugged. "Nothing much." She told her about a website that sold rare medicinal herbs. "They even have heirloom mandrake root."

Shelley's face lit. "I want some."

"Me, too. Let's order it. We could split the cost."

Strains of Celtic music replaced the canned sounds and quieted the crowd. They sat back to listen, and Kay stepped into memories, fresh, yet seeming eons ago. Baird bathed in the soft green light beneath the roar of the falls. His touch...

The music shifted from ballad to reel. Shelley nudged her. "Want to dance?"

Kay drained her beer, and they pushed their way onto the packed dance floor. Capturing the magic of spring, walls twinkled with white lights woven into bunches of blossoms.

Jarl joined and they danced as a threesome until their food and more ale arrived. They sat and shouted over the music as they ate, then returned to dancing. Joaquin and his date came onto the floor as Shelley tried to teach them jig steps from her Appalachian youth. They laughed, hopping and hooting, tripping over each other.

Finally, flushed and overheated, Kay waved the others to continue and struggled to the hall for a breather. There she leaned and wiped sweat from her face.

"How does it work?" Ian's voice, soft in her ear, made her jump.

Kay realized how shadowed and deserted the hallway was. His face was close to hers, his eyes gleaming as they focused on her chest.

Where had he come from? She'd thought he was playing on stage. She glanced that way. The band had left, and music poured out from a PA system. "How does what work?" Glancing down, she noticed a soft glow in the cleft between her breasts. Edging along the wall, she asked, "What do you mean?"

"Has this to do with your time traveling?" His voice, slurred from alcohol, sounded almost hostile.

Kay didn't understand what was behind the tone. Envy? More like resentment.

In the dim light, his grin reminded her of Galfride's. Before thinking, she asked him, "D' you have Cornish ancestry?" She had to confess she sounded slurred herself.

He gripped her shoulders, desire blazing. "Ye've been there, haven't ye? T' ancient Cornwall."

Not wanting to make a scene, she moved her hands to dislodge his fingers that were digging painfully into her.

"Ye should share the secret, Kay." The "Sh's" of this last sentence sprayed her with dark ale fumes. "Why does a California girl get to go? I was *born* there, dammit!" He had her pinned to the wall, one hand sliding toward the crystal. She tried to twist away but he held her in place, leaning into her.

"What's up?" Jarl's face appeared over Ian's shoulder. Relief gusted through Kay's nerves.

Ian whipped his head around with a snarl, then shifted his expression to a crooked grin, held up his hands in surrender and stepped away. "We were jus' talking about shhharin'." He gave them both a final glare before staggering away.

"It's past midnight. Have you had about enough?" Jarl asked.

Kay nodded. They returned to the table to give a round of hugs and to praise the band. She avoided Ian, who had his arm around Candice.

"Need a lift home, Shelley?" Kay asked. Shelley had ridden her bike from work. "Jarl's car is at my house. You could walk with us, and he could drop you." She glanced at Jarl to make sure it was all right. Did she see a flicker of disappointment? "Is that okay?"

"That's fine. No problem at all," he said, with his usual graciousness.

Outside, the night air revived her. The three of them walked, Shelley rolling her bike. Each step helped clear her head.

At Kay's door, Shelley said "Night-night," and gave her a kiss on the cheek. She turned and walked toward the car.

She knows which car is his, Kay thought.

Jarl lingered. He scanned Kay's face and gave her a sad smile, then trotted down the steps. They fastened Shelley's bike to his roof, waved, and drove off. Kay closed the door, only slightly ambivalent.

In the night Kay woke, sweaty, her throat dry. She sensed she'd been trapped in a frightening dream, but no clear images came to her. She crept to the kitchen, afraid to jostle the dream back into memory. There she fixed calming chamomile tea, then returned to bed with it. Waiting for daybreak, she tried to shake the trepidation that hung like a curtain around her. She didn't think she'd sleep again, but when she next opened her eyes, morning light spilled through the window.

She fixed a tall purple smoothie with huckleberries and kale and settled on the back steps in a patch of sun. With trepidation, she sought the dream that had awakened her; it was important, though she hated to try and bring it back. Reluctantly, she took the gold crystal from its gauzy bag. She had the notion it was related somehow to the dream.

Perhaps she sought comfort. Or answers. Baird said the crystal made it easier for him to come to her. After all, it had glowed with their heartbeats. She pressed the stone to her chest. Her pulse sped with the nearness of the powerful crystal. Its glow brightened. *Can I call Baird to me?* She longed for his presence. Maybe she could reach Kyna, discover her location.

Nothing happened. She stroked Oz, and he flopped on

his side for a tummy rub.

"Just hangin' out through all my turmoil?" she asked.

He glanced up, lids at half-mast, a rumbling purr his only response.

Kay sighed, shook her head, and buried her fingers in the cloud-softness of his tummy fur. An ancient tapestry had woven its way into her life, braiding the strands across dimensions. But it was a loose weave, with frayed edges, and snarls where she searched for clarity. Were there logical threads invisible to her? Did someone else see the layout clearly? Was she a pawn?

She slipped the cord from her silver pendant through the hole in the crystal and let it hang against her skin. Then she went in search of *The Book of Taliesin* and brought it to the back porch. The Dark Age bard called Taliesin had composed his poetry in the Cornish dialect. She turned the beautifully illuminated pages until she located her favorite. "I am the noise of the sea." She read the Cornish: *"Dwi 'r dadwrdd chan 'r aig—"*

The yard grew dark, and a menacing presence crept in with the gloom. Her skin prickled. It was the dream. Heat from the crystal grew uncomfortable. She grabbed it, hearing water dripping. A dark-haired man, outlined in sickly green light laughed, a derisive, malevolent sound.

Kay backed to the French doors as her fingers scrabbled at the crystal. It was now burning hot. She could not grasp it; it had fused to her chest. She smelled charred skin and dug her fingernails at the edges of the searing stone. Finally, she tore it off, taking a layer of flesh with it. She flung it to the ground, then thought better of it, and took it up with the gauze bag before racing into the house. She glanced back. The yard stood empty and bright with sunlight.

In the bathroom mirror, she studied the livid oval of raw, torn flesh on her chest. How had this happened? Was the dark man Galfride? She thought it was his laugh.

She mixed a salve, drawing on Kyna's knowledge, and dabbed it thickly over the sore. Then she began preparation to banish evil from the stone, or at least that was her understanding of a message in her head. It seemed to come from that deep, part-unconscious knowledge she retained from Kyna's mind.

Chapter 22

Wound covered with gauze, Kay returned to the back yard. The stone had drawn Baird once, but also called forth a malignant force. She could not trust it against her skin, nor could she leave it lying around. Where was safe for it?

Her seared flesh burned. She wanted to crawl away from both the stone and the wound, to hide and be comforted. Instead, she forced herself to handle the situation the best she knew how. She opened the door to the closet she'd converted into a tiny apothecary. With sure hands, she selected herbs and roots—agrimony, vervain, fumitory, hyssop, and purslane—from shelves and drawers. Then she rummaged in the kitchen until she found her mother's old iron pot with a lid, shoved to the back of a low cupboard. She dragged it out and set it in the center of the backyard. She took nine of the sacred woods she'd been gathering by the shed which she arranged, three bundles of three, forming a pyramid. She ground a mixture of protective roots and herbs with her marble mortar and pestle. She lit the fire and put in pinches of the powder, along with strands of her hair. She brought out an old white sheet and painted symbols on it that formed a diagram with twelve rays, then lined the pot with it.

The symbols were unfamiliar to her. Kay could only understand a portion of Kyna's knowledge regarding their meanings, but she was sure it was her knowledge in her that guided her actions. When the fire burned down, she spooned ashes into the cloth and chanted, "*Ediuar uyd yr neb ae wnaeth. Ediuar uyd yr neb ae wnaeth. Ediuar uyd yr neb ae wnaeth.*" The symbols all but disappeared under the black soot. She fetched the beautiful golden crystal that she'd loved for its connection to Baird. Reluctantly, she folded it into the ash-covered cloth and closed it into the pot which she stashed in a narrow cupboard that was now her apothecary.

That done, Kay slumped into her fireside chair, exhausted. She tried to remember the words she'd chanted. Something like, "Let whosoever brought ill-will take it back," or maybe "banish the bad, leave the good." Her hand went to the bandage above her heart.

I'd worn that stone with joy. Now, its removal left a profound emptiness, and worse, the knowledge that the attack on her flesh had occurred via the stone. Had its presence on her person drawn Galfride across the millennia? Reading the Cornish translation of Taliesin's poem seemed to have elicited the malevolent being. How was it tied to the dream?

A sob hitched in her throat. She considered a glass of wine but instead swept the house. As she cleaned, positive energy gradually returned. She graduated from broom to mop. Cleaning the floors led to tidying language papers and books that had covered most surfaces of the house. She boxed them, adding the Taliesin book, and carted them to the second bedroom. She lugged the painting, with its birds-eye view of Kyna's town in ancient Wales, to the shed, and stashed the textiles—piles of yarns and fabrics that had crowded the living room—into drawers and closets. Next, she shoved the spinning wheel to one side of the apothecary closet. She found a heavy Guatemalan blanket and draped it over the loom.

A noise from behind made her turn.

Baird stood in the doorway to the kitchen, arms crossed, scowling. He looked furious, which drove any clear sentences from her mind, though a thousand questions begged to be asked. Finally, she stammered, "I never thought I'd see you in my home." She wanted to cry and laugh, and step into his arms.

He continued to glower. She'd never seen him look that way. At last, he said, "It would ha' been easier had the stone no' led me into an iron pot in a wee cupboard." He moved his shoulders and rolled his head as though from a cramped neck.

Her hand went to her mouth. "You didn't arrive... Oh, no...inside the...?"

His scowl deepened. "Not exactly."

She imagined him becoming tiny enough to fit in the pot. A six-inch-tall Baird. Kay's stomach jerked with unbidden giggles. The effort to suppress them made her shake.

Baird said sternly, "Why, Dove? Why did ye put it away from ye? Didje not want me t' find ye?" She could hardly hear the last, he said it so softly. "Did our time at the waterfall displease ye so?"

That was a low blow. She stepped closer and opened the neck of her shirt, lifting the edge of the gauze.

He stared at the torn flesh where the crystal had lain. "The stone did this?" He cupped her elbows, bringing his face close to her cleavage as if he might laser away the raw wound with a close enough examination. His proximity made her heart race. His breath puffed on the exposed flesh. His mussed hair smelled of campfires.

His face came up, eyes drilling into hers. "What happened?" No anger now.

Tears welled in her eyes. He took her in his arms. She pressed her face into his worn jerkin and described the malevolent attack when she'd read the Cornish words. She hoped he would have answers.

When she finished, he was silent. Then he said, "This be somethin' fer the council, Dove. But I'm that sorry it happened t' ye." He stroked her back, and she sighed. That was really what she needed most.

They settled in the chairs facing the cold fireplace. She still couldn't believe he was in her home. "You appear so solid now, yet on Harold Street, you were faint," she said. "How is it you can come here and stay and not fade now?"

"Aelfwyn's helpin' me. I was never the best at this sort o' thing. Song be my strength, no' magic."

"She's watching us? Now?" she asked, self-conscious.

"Oh, aye, she ha' many ways o' seein'. She sees it all." He spread his hands in a circle. "Like a spider's web."

She pictured a grid of luminous threads stretching out from the old woman, her hands working over them.

"When Kyna disappeared, Aelfwyn could no' find her on her web, but she found you," Baird went on.

"She couldn't locate Kyna in your time, but she found me across a thousand years?"

"Aye. Time be no problem for Aelfwyn."

"Why did I forget I'd already been to your time?" The questions tumbled out. "After Samhain, I started having Kyna's memories, of weaving and braiding designs in her hair. If Kyna's been missing for years, then I was in ancient Wales—inside Kyna's mind—years before last Samhain.

Why did I forget?"

"Wait. Wait." Baird chuckled. "I don't have all the answers. But Aelfwyn could ha' taken yer memories t' protect ye."

"To protect me?" She edged away, hugging herself. "You were horrified about Galfride manipulating his niece's mind. How is this any different?"

"'Tis *very* different." He appeared uncomfortable, perplexed.

She backed down. She was not prepared to be someone's marionette, but it was cruel to be sniffy while he worried. She tried to think of the important questions, or some less fraught ones. "When Aelfwyn brought me the yarns, did she bring the whole store to me? Or did she transport me back in time?"

"Dove, I canna say. Ye have to ask her."

When would she have a long enough time to ask Aelfwyn?

"And then Boldo brought the boots," she said, hoping to fit together the pieces that had free-floated in her mind for months.

"Aye." Baird frowned. "He got his bit in there. He just had to come see ye. Everyone was talkin' about ye after Samhain. Some said Kyna'd returned, but we told 'em, 'Nay, 'tis a one who favors Kyna.' Boldo said, 'I want t' see her.' And Aelfwyn answers, 'Fine, Hasty Puddin', take her some o' yer boots.' She adds, 'Go find out how fair a hand she be at weavin'.' And he says, 'Oh, aye, let me go then.' And there ye have it. He be off t' the street where y' work and gettin' a kiss that sh'd ha' been mine." He drooped dramatically.

She laughed as he told the story. When he finished, she stared. "You saw me with Boldo?"

Baird gave a pouty shrug.

"It was only a peck on the cheek," she mumbled. "And it was Kyna really, her memories of him. How did you watch?"

"We were in the tower holdin' th' energy. Boldo's by far the best at this sort o' thing. Though I guess I be gettin' the knack as well. Soon they'll be singin' songs 'bout me and my travels." He winked. "But no' yet."

"Who knows about it? Only The Thirteen?" She thought again about the malevolent laughter and how terrible it would be if Galfride came to modern time.

"Aye. Mostly. Some o' th' other Wanderers. They know how t' keep silent though."

Kay remembered her manners at last. "Would you like something to eat, or drink?" She rose. "I can make dinner. Or tea. Wine?" She held him in her gaze as if he might at any moment slip into the ethers.

"So ye've decided t' store the crystal in a wee black pot." He followed me into the kitchen.

"I'm not sure. Until I know better how to protect myself. It's made of iron." She glanced to where he'd settled on a bench in the table alcove, long legs stretched out, still awed that he was there in her home. "I sensed the iron pot might seal in the stone's energy until I knew what I was doing." She shrugged, a bit defensive and turned to search the fridge for something appealing to offer. "I also chanted, painted symbols, and burned roots and herbs." She decided to treat him to lentil soup with focaccia bread. "I seemed to know what to do." She set leftover soup on the stove, turned it on low, stirred, and grabbed a cutting board. "Kyna's knowledge, I suppose, like the weaving."

Baird watched her. Oz found his ankle and rubbed, purring.

"Traitor," she said to her cat.

Baird petted Oz's head. "A house feline," he mused.

"His name's Oz."

Baird tried the word. "Oss."

She explained, "It's from a popular children's story where someone's taken away in a storm to a magical land with a witch and little people, a scarecrow that talks, a tin man that walks, a lion—"

"I'd like t' hear that story sometime." He paused in silence. "Dove, yer cry reached me."

She stopped slicing focaccia and glanced at him.

"I've tried before to come to ye. I ended up inside creatures. One time I was a rabbit. Ech, he did annoy me. So timid he wouldna go near ye."

She laughed. "One time, I thought you might be a squirrel. It was following me when I went to the university. I wanted to find what ancient language I kept hearing when I touched Duff's silver piece." It was one of the many things she'd longed to talk to him about. "So Aelfwyn is training you to come to this time?"

"Aye. The crystal makes it easier. She thought of it."

"You brought it to me as a gull," she said. "You had no trouble approaching me then."

"Aye," he mused. "A bold bird."

"Was she helping you when we were under the waterfall?" she asked and her cheeks grew hot.

There was no response. She turned from putting bread in the oven. Baird stood inches from her. She sucked in a quick breath.

As he took her face into his hands, his eyes burned into hers. But all he said was, "The old woman sees many things. We can't be worryin' about that."

My heart thundered. There was an awful lot she worried about, whether he thought she should or not.

He gave Kay a sweet kiss, then returned to the alcove.

Adjusting the gas flame, she stirred the soup, heart still hammering. "Tell me about Kyna's disappearance. When did it happen?"

"After your spirit rose out o' her, Kyna collapsed and lay on the floor o' the tower room, as if dead. Pale as ice." His voice grew gravelly. "Her heartbeat were weak. We carried her to her bed and watched over her, takin' turns— me and Duff. Aelfwyn tended t' the village. It took Kyna a month t' regain her strength and start workin' again. Then one day, not long after that, she left."

Kay stopped stirring and leaned against the sink. "The dogs?"

"Still at the house."

It was hard to imagine Kyna without her hounds. "No note?"

"Not a thing. No vision nor whisper."

"Oh, Baird."

"Hamelyn went through items in the loft where he and his sister slept when they were young. He discovered Gwynedd's brooch and other belongin's missin' that ha' been there. It struck us Kyna might ha' taken them with her, seekin' our daughter."

"But why wouldn't she tell you?"

"Perhaps t' protect us." He shook his head, closing his eyes.

She removed the focaccia from the oven. "But it's been so long now." She straightened. "You don't think she's been captured?"

Baird watched her at the stove. "Where's th' fire?" he asked.

"Electricity," Kay answered, moving the focaccia to a cutting board. "Heat is produced by various forms of energy running along wires."

His brow puckered. He let the topic go. "Aelfwyn believes Kyna's alive. I think Aelfwyn may know more, but she's no' tellin' me."

"Are you...? You think she may—be in touch with her?"

Baird raised a hand, shaking his head. "I canna know fer sure." He looked like he didn't want to pursue it further. Maybe he knew the old woman listened to every word. She put the bread in a cloth-lined basket, ladled bowls of soup, and set all on the table.

Baird dug in his spoon, blew, and tasted. "Mm." He tore off steaming bread and dipped it in the soup. "Delicious," he mumbled, mouth full.

She'd grown the carrots, potatoes, and herbs in her garden and was pleased to share the fruits of her labors with Baird.

"I see you han't forsaken the silver piece Duff gave ye." Baird pointed with his spoon at her throat. "I recognize his work. Duff and Kyna learned the patterns from the Wanderers. The designs have magic, ye know. And can be used for messages, like plaitin' the hair, and embroiderin' clothin'."

She dropped a chunk of bread into her soup and spooned it up for a bite. "After Samhain, I had such an urge to plait my hair. That's when Kyna's memories started taking over my thoughts."

"I know. T'was too short at first. Ye got some of it in there now, though." He tilted his head and waved his spoon at her intricate braid, clipped at the back.

She swallowed. "You saw me trying to braid?" She wasn't sure she was comfortable with that.

"Sometimes we've seen ye...me and Aelfwyn...when

we were tryin' t' get me to ye." He carefully chose his next bite, not looking at her.

What might they have seen when she had no idea they were watching?

"It's no' like I watch y'...exactly."

She had to enjoy, just slightly, his discomfort. After all, for Kay, this was an invasion that made her conflicted, torn between pleasure and chagrin.

He made busy work of scraping the bowl for a last bite, set the spoon aside, and pushed it away.

"More?" she asked.

"I'll be fine with the rest o' this tasty bread," he said, taking a bite.

Her thoughts slipped with unruly alacrity toward bed.

He watched with a smile.

She prayed he would not disappear.

Chapter 23

Tea?" she asked. "I could build a fire, and we could sit by it in the living room." With each suggestion, she wondered if they would have the time.

"That would be grand," he said, patting his belly with satisfaction.

She put water on and chose an herb tea she thought resembled a roasted root blend she'd tasted in ancient Wales. "Want it milky?" she asked.

"Ta."

"Honey?"

"Ye spoil a fella."

"I try." She dropped teabags in their cups and waited for the water to boil. Leaning against the sink, she admired the fine man in her kitchen.

He did not belong in these surroundings. She suspected he would soon grow restless, and it saddened her, though his wild edges were part of what drew her.

The pot whistled. Kay took time pouring, ready to address the danger of the gold crystal. "It was when I was reading a Cornish version of Taliesin's song, the one—"

Baird sat up straight and projected, in his warm resonant voice, a well-known poem from the 800s,

I am a hawk on a cliff,
I am a tear of the sun,
I am a turning in a maze,
I am a salmon in a pool..."

Now that's a true bardic delivery, she thought with pleasure, as she stirred honey into their tea.

"Ye think the poem might ha' had something t' do with the stone burnin' ye?"

"I'm not sure. Maybe speaking it in Cornish." Kay thought about Ian and his unsettling hunger for the stone. And her dream. An unsettling thread seemed to tie them. "Do you mind if it's coconut milk?"

"Milk of the coconut. I had that once upon a ship. I'd love t' try it again. It be fair wondrous how ye have these exotic items in yer home." He said it as though she'd conjured them herself. Perhaps he thought she had.

She carried the mugs into the living room. He followed and dropped into a chair. She knelt to make a fire. There was something sublime about sharing these homey activities with him. She knew it could not last long. It would be hard when he left.

She decided to take the story further back and see if answers might emerge. "I got the book of Taleisin's poems from the university where I used to work." She scrunched paper, broke kindling, and started the fire. "I was going crazy trying to track down the language I heard at Samhain." She sat back on her heels and touched the Celtic knot resting on her chest. "I'd see a cottage with herbs hanging, hear voices. I know now it was Kyna's home, but at the time, I didn't. I couldn't hear the words distinctly. I thought by sounding out ancient languages from their extensive collection—"

"Ancient, ye call it." A corner of his mouth quirked as he took a sip of tea. "I know the place. Ye got them from the towerin' temple of learnin'." His eyes gleamed. "A most impressive quantity o' books." He swept his free hand, indicating infinite expanses.

"You were there? Were you the squirrel that followed me down the hill that day?"

"Nay. I only managed a flea that time."

She burst out laughing. "I think I do recall a flea bite right after that trip."

"Ah, my lady, I would never drink your blood." He clutched his heart as if mortally wounded.

"Hmm…" She arched a doubting eyebrow, added a log onto the growing blaze, and sat in the other chair. "I studied the language materials. One day I was trying to write the letters of the ogham, and something took control of my hand. I wrote a note that was incomprehensible to me at the time. That's when I slipped into Kyna's mind. It turned out she was writing that same note at the same time."

Baird stared at me, cup midway to his mouth. He set it down. "That be a mystery t' me. I mun ask Aelfwyn more 'bout it." He got up and knelt by her chair, taking her hands in his. "Dove, I came t' ye at Samhain, searchin' for Kyna. That be true. But what I've found with you is somethin' important. I don't know what it all means. But ye have t' understand. I've known Kyna since we were scrawny whelps runnin' the fields. We have a close bond. She has decided to stay away for two years and more. She does no' think I'll crawl into a hole and die. She be gone. I miss her. I worry about her. But our lives have always been half-separate. I be a free bard, and she, a free healer. She goes where she be needed; I go where I am asked. Most o' th' time." He turned his palms up, willing her to understand. "I loved makin' love to ye behind the great falls. That was one o' the best moments o' my life."

"Mine, too," she whispered. Tears welled, and Baird spangled into several bards through the watery film.

"Aye?" he asked, hoarsely.

"Aye," she answered.

He leaned in, pressing his warm lips to hers.

She woke in the night to a bright moon lighting her bedroom. Baird lay beside her. She moved closer softly, so as not to wake him, pressing to his side. She wanted to affirm his solidity. Lying as still as she could, she breathed him in, playing the previous evening over in her mind.

Languidly, he turned, eyes drifting open, a slow smile spreading. He pulled her against him, kissed her forehead, then her lips. Their bare skin renewed their connection. Again, their bodies merged in that perfect union of wanting and knowing.

After, they lay fitted together, her head on his chest. Outside, the trees moved in a light wind. As if they'd done this a thousand times, they drifted into conversation.

"Aelfwyn has remained living with you?" she asked.

"Aye, we set up a curtained bed for her in th' main room, near th' fire. Hamelyn stays in th' loft, as in childhood."

"I didn't notice a loft." She pictured where a ladder might ascend. "It looks over the main room?"

"Blocked off fer warmth," he said. "Tis no' surprisin' ye missed it. Aelfwyn has been a great help. With th' village healin', o' course. And she be a good cook, like a grandmère to Hamelyn." Baird rearranged the pillow against the headboard, keeping Kay hugged to him. He pressed his lips to her temple. "He's apprenticed to th' luthier in town, ye know. Makin' astoundin' beautiful instruments, if I do say so." He beamed at her.

Oz jumped onto the bed and settled at their feet.

"Th' music they make..." A smile played across Baird's lips, as if he heard sweet notes. "He wants t' learn more about th' fiddles that come up from Umbria. I might have to take him there."

Umbria? Ah, an old name for Italy, she remembered. "So, he has Aelfwyn to keep him company when you travel."

"And Duff. His uncle set up a smithy at our place. Th' two have a regular workshop now. Hamelyn makes instruments, and Duff works wi' silver. Next, they'll be formin' a craft guild." He chuckled, clearly happy with the new developments. "People are startin' to know about 'em. They come from all over. His teacher, Finch, who repairs my harps, comes every day t' see if travelers ha' come wi' new kinds o' instruments."

"It must be fine to have all that happening right at your home." She thought of the solitude when she'd been there in Kyna's spirit. She'd been elated to welcome him home from his travels. She asked, "Has Hamelyn fallen in love?"

"Ah, he falls in and out o' love like changin' boots. Breaks hearts. Gets his broken." Baird leaned his head forward to see her face. "He asked me one day about a Sophie."

She pushed up, and squeaked, "Sophie?" then cleared her throat. "My daughter's name is Sophie." She tried to keep the trepidation out of her voice.

"He must o' got th' image o' her from his mother. He said th' lass be in Paris."

"My daughter's in Paris," she said, quietly. She liked Hamelyn perfectly well, but did not want Sophie pulled into the yo-yo of time travel that was upending her life, or the dangers that lurked around this medieval family. "Can you do that? Share pictures with your mind?"

"Oh, aye. A bit."

"How does it work?"

"Ha' ye a quill an' parchment?"

She grinned. "Something like that." She pulled on a robe and got him a pen and notebook from her desk. "Will these do?" she asked.

Baird touched the spiral binding. "Ye use metal fer hangin' the pages together?"

"Wasteful, isn't it?" she agreed. "That's the tip of the iceberg."

He crinkled his brows. "Ah. A clever metaphor." He turned his attention to the plastic tube he held, pulling it along the page. He watched, fascinated, as a line appeared. "It'll do," he said, maybe overwhelmed by the strangeness. "Now." He set the notebook aside and took her hands. "It's one o' th' simplest lessons we learn from th' teachers."

"What kind of teachers?"

"At th' Bardic school. Well, it's a school o' all forms of…" He searched for words. "What would ye call it? It be th' Druids and healers. We learn about th' stars, a bi' o' magic, and o' course, th' songs, the ballads. Hundreds of 'em. Those be th' real history. Some o' th' students are chosen to go int' the healin' ways. Others might learn t' be historians, I think ye'd say. Storytellers but no' so poetic."

Kay thought that description probably captured the

difference quite well, considering how her stony-faced high school history teacher sounded, droning on about kings and battles.

"We learn t' write and read. And about trees, plants, birds, somethin' about th' world beyond th' Isles though no' much. We learned from th' Wanderers first, as wee ones. That's why we were accepted. We dinna ha' powerful families or wealth." He squeezed her hands. "I k'n teach ye this, though. There's no' much to it."

Not much to it. She almost chuckled as she settled into her pillow next to him.

"Close yer eyes and think o' nothin'."

Not likely, with hot energy surging from his hands into hers. Gradually, she brushed those thoughts aside. A palpable presence entered her inner awareness as he pushed, as through a membrane. She clearly saw a dragon figure carved into the side of a stone.

"Draw what ye saw," he directed.

She sketched the stylized dragon.

He looked at it and nodded. "Good student. Ye can draw as well."

Her cheeks heated in a schoolgirl flurry. The sweet sensation of their intimate mind-sharing stirred her in an inexplicable way.

He pointed at the paper. "I saw it on a dolmen in Northern Alban."

Alban - old word for Scotland. "Do you remember the one Kyna drew in the dirt by the fire at the Solstice Fair?" Kay asked.

"When Duff asked for ideas for his silver chalice for Bawdrip?"

"Exactly. I'm pretty sure she got the image from my mind. It was the design used by a tribe of Borneo, and I'd been thinking about it."

"Born ... Borney?"

"Borneo. A faraway island. I'm not sure it was named yet in your time."

He nodded. She saw his lids drooping and set the book aside.

"You're tired. Shall we sleep some more?" She reached to turn out the light, and they slid back under the covers.

He spooned in behind her and said softly in her ear, "Dove, I don't know what th' grand design is, but I do ken that our destinies are tangled, yours and mine."

She pulled his hand to her lips and kissed it. They slept.

In the morning, she awoke to find Baird still asleep. Again, she marveled that he was there.

He found her in the shower. She'd carefully detached the bandage and kept the spray from the wound. He winced, touching next to the raw oval. Then he examined the shower walls. "Who's pumpin' it? Where are the aqueducts?"

She suppressed a laugh. "People have come up with ways to harness energy for moving the water. The pipes are under the city."

"It be astoundin'," he said with awe. "Magic?"

"Well, not really. It requires extraction of earth's limited resources. Want to join me?"

He stepped in.

"They've found ways to convert nature into energy to power things."

He accepted a washcloth and soap. She glimpsed his backside, then stepped out. "You go ahead. I'll get us some coffee made. Do you need anything else?"

"I'm fine." He began to sing.

"Yes, you are," she murmured. She let him enjoy the hot spray as she applied salve to the sore on her chest, then taped fresh gauze over it. She dressed in her magical clothes in the bedroom, then went to the kitchen.

After a while, he joined her, fully clothed, hair tied neatly back. She handed him a steaming mug of coffee. He breathed in the aroma appreciatively. "Like they drink in the desert lands. Where the people wear cloths wound round their heads."

"Yes indeed," she said, impressed at how much he'd traveled.

He examined gadgets around the room, then took his coffee to the table and settled. "Now, this daughter o' yourn…"

"Yes? Would you like some breakfast?"

"Ye say she be in Paris."

"She is." She started making a tofu-mushroom scramble.

"We sometimes believed our Gwynedd was in France. I travel there, as does Duff, for silver and gemstones. We always ask, but we've ne'er found a trace o' her."

"It must be terrible. Your daughter ran off? With someone on a ship? It wasn't with a pirate, was it?" she asked, thinking of Rousseau's story.

"We know not. She just disappeared one day and there had been traders anchored nearby. The Wanderers search as well. They most oft can find anyone. But they've never found Gwynedd."

"Top up your coffee?" She brought over the pot.

"Aye. That's a fair treat."

"I agree," she said. "It's the darkest roast. Speaking of France, it's called French roast."

"Ver' interestin'." Baird scooped natural sugar and dolloped half and half from a tiny pitcher.

"So how obsessed is your son with Sophie in Paris?" Kay chopped green pepper and onion, sautéing them.

"Smells wondrous," Baird said. "I guess what he saw captivated him. He's writin' songs t' her." Baird's eyes twinkled. "I'm no' surprised if she's yer daughter."

"Thanks, you charmer," she said, tone light though dread crept in as she stirred chopped tofu and spices. *She's in Paris, he in Wales, with a thousand years between them. Nothing to worry about.*

She brought plates.

"What be this?" Baird asked as he scooped a mouthful. Chewing tentatively, he appeared pleased. "Now that's tasty. Ye be a fine cook."

"*Diolch.*" She made a curtsey, saying thanks in Welsh, and for once noticed she was often speaking the other language.

"What be th' texture?" He mulled it over.

"It's bean curd. Tofu."

"It be verra' good, this toe food."

She almost spluttered scramble from her mouth. "I'm glad you like it."

When they'd finished, they washed up, then opened the French doors. The morning air rushed over them.

Baird turned to her, serious. "Get the crystal, Dove."

Chapter 24

Kay's wound still throbbed.

Baird crossed his arms, waiting.

Reluctantly, she hauled the iron pot from the cupboard and set it on her work table. He lifted the lid and pushed the cloth aside, revealing the gold stone. The crystal's glow rose in answer to the proximity of its other half, which shone faintly through the fabric of Baird's shirt.

He examined the cloth, then held out his hand to her. "I want t' show ye how t' protect yerself."

We sat in the sun on the back step. He began by teaching me to sense another's presence in her mind, to shut it out, and to shield her own thoughts. A short while into it, he said sternly, "Ye have t' shut me out when ye sense me."

She squirmed. "But it seems so *mean* to push you away."

He groaned, with a half grin. "Dove, yer practicin' on me. Believe me, I won' be hurt." He took her hands and pulled her toward him. His earnest eyes locked into hers, amusement gone. "Some people may try to get in and use yer thoughts; people who're not kind. Ye were inside Kyna when Galfried, th' swine, grabbed her a' the faire, were ye not?"

She nodded. The sore stung at the near mention of the

man's name. Could he know it was Galfride's laughter she'd heard as the stone burned her?

"Do ye want *him* playin' around inside yer head? I don' think so." He shook her hands to emphasize his point. "These kind o' folk, they can take away memories or make ye do things ye don't want to do. Ye ken? Now, let's try again."

Chastised, she forced herself to push him away as he pressed in and sealed herself after. Tears welled up.

"Tha's better," he said, when she was at a point of exhaustion.

She sighed with relief, but they were not done.

After further practice, he said, "Ye were flogged fer givin' yer friend a wee apple? Poor mite."

He'd retrieved a memory from her childhood. She recalled how her mother had lied, told her father she hadn't asked for permission when she had. She must have been seven or eight.

"Did you see how furious I was after the injustice to my backside?" she said. "How I pulled my mother's sewing cloth off the shelves in the closet and bellowed? I guess I didn't dare protest in earshot of my father." His seeing the scene exposed her. She tried to laugh, make light of it, but couldn't. It was paradoxical, being seen at such a deep level—humiliating and exhilarating, all at once.

"Why did yer mother lie 'bout it?"

"Well, I suppose either she feared his wrath, or she was colluding. My father didn't want me forming the wrong friendships."

"There was a time when I would ha' been a *bachgen* you shouldna play with." He waggled his eyebrows like a melodrama villain.

"I might have run away with you," she said, only half playful.

"Ye'd best not." Baird was surprisingly serious. "Ye were fortunate to have a family." His voice dropped low.

Emotion upwelling, she wondered if someday he'd let her into his mind this way.

He continued gently prodding through her past, finding the sore spots. "Those make ye vulnerable. Ye' have to bring 'em out int' th' light, so someone evil canna snare ye with 'em."

His wisdom resembled modern therapy. By evening, it was as though she'd been through hours of analysis, but with different results.

"You didn't pry too much into my love life." Kay tried to sound light as the core of her dragged with the weight of the past, the embarrassing scenes he might have dredged up, starting in her early teens.

"What a person invadin' yer mind looks for be the things you're not rememberin'. Those're likely to be from yer young life. There's where they can take ye by surprise and get in where ye don't expect 'em. And once they're in—"

"You'd make an incredible psychologist," she said.

"A what?"

She tried to think how to explain. "It's someone who tries to heal our minds. Our thoughts. Despite all the new scientific knowledge, we've lost…well, a lot of abilities of the mind that people of your time have."

He pondered this as if at a loss to understand and finally said, "I must go."

"But the stone…" Reluctant as she was to put it back on her person, she missed its power to lead Baird to her.

"Ah, aye."

They entered the house, leaving behind the twilight of the yard.

Baird took the stone from the ash-blackened cloth. "May

I bring this cloth back t' show Aelfwyn?"

"Yes, of course. I hope one of you can tell me the meaning of what I drew."

"I imagine we can," he said with an enigmatic smile. He folded it carefully and tucked it in a pocket. "Now, do ye have a bag fer the stone?" he asked.

Kay fetched the one she'd made.

"Tha's very nice." He took in the minuscule stitching. Slipping the stone inside, he handed it to her. "Keep it on yer person and practice each day, holdin' it. Shut out any no' good energy." He watched as she tied the bag around her waist. "Ye have to do this," he insisted.

Kay's brow creased, then straightened as she drew determination up her spine.

Baird knelt by his worn pack near the kitchen doorway, and pulled out a bundle. A slender cylindrical object slipped into his hand. He rose and brought it to her.

"The flute Hamelyn made for his mother for Solstice."

She held it, admiring the tiny sandpipers marching along the side, then put it to her mouth. A terrible sound came out. Baird took it and played eight beautiful notes, a haunting tune in a minor key. He put it back in her hands and urged her to try to copy it.

They went back and forth until she could imitate the enchanting song.

"Ye keep it here," he said, as if he had nothing in mind by it.

"I can't. It's Kyna's."

He pushed it gently against her then touched the bag at her side. "Keep it on ye, and practice."

She nodded. They kissed with passion. She wanted to hold him, but he gently held her away and moved to the back door. Lifting his hand in farewell, he stepped into the gloaming and was gone.

She ran into the yard. "Baird?" No answer. "You're gone," she said, quietly to no one. Through prisms of tears, she looked out at the sunset and first evening star.

After a few long moments, exhausted and powerful, she realized the world had taken on new textures. She'd cast off scales and exposed tender new skin. When all rosy tones had faded from the sky and blackness set in, she returned to the house. It was worse than silent, worse than empty. Desolate.

Her cell phone played its tune. She saw it was Sophie and answered.

"You'll never guess where I am," Sophie said.

"Not Paris?" Kay hoped she didn't sound plaintive.

"Wales."

"Wales?" That was the last place Kay wanted to hear.

If she sounded dismayed, Sophie took no notice, just rushed on. "Yeah, have you been here?"

How to best answer? "Not for a long time. How'd you end up there?"

"We got here last night, to do some filming for a client. It's beautiful! So lush."

"Who's we?"

"A couple of coworkers and me. But what I really called you about is this dream I had last night. In it, I was in love. With this Welsh guy. He played music and sang. And his accent—so enchanting. There was something unique about him. Not like the guys I usually meet. I don't know—special."

Baird's revelation of his son's attraction to someone named Sophie sent warning alarms through her. The coincidence was too great. "What did this musician look like?"

"It was a dream," she laughed. "It's not that clear. Wait.

I'm closing my eyes. Yeah, he was about my age, dark curly hair. Tallish. It's more a sense." Sophie chattered on. "The town was ancient. I wish I could paint it or make a film from my mind. It was how you'd imagine a village in the Middle Ages. A river ran through, into the sea. Well, probably lots of towns are like that, but everything was stone and thatched roofs." She took a quick breath. "We're driving up the coast today. Maybe I'll recognize the place of my dream if I see it. I know, that's silly. But it seemed so real. As if the town exists. I'd better go. The others are ready to get breakfast."

"You must report on all of it." Kay tried to sound light, but her heart was heavy. The idea of Sophie being tugged into the past brought unbidden thoughts—the disappearance of young women—Gwynedd, Galfride's niece, Branwyn. She was attracting danger to her daughter. She'd tried to back away, but perhaps not hard enough.

"I will. I'll call you when we get back to Paris."

"That's a deal, sweetie. Have fun."

They hung up. She loved her daughter's youthful excitement. Even so, fear curdled in her stomach. Her daughter, in Wales, dreaming of a young musician in a medieval town, right after Baird told me of his son's interest.

My Sophie, Kay wanted to shout, *stay safe in this world. Forget the fiddler.*

She couldn't stop thinking about Sophie, and Hamelyn's obsession with her. Writing songs to her. Would she hear those next in her dreams? She chafed over it, tried to turn her mind to gardening but was distracted no matter what she did.

A few days later, Sophie called from Paris. "The countryside is so magical. We drove up the coast, and when we came to one town, with a river flowing through to the sea, it was just like my dream. Except, of course, it was way more built up and modern in parts. But there was a pull, as if the lover in my dream called to her. Seriously, Mom, I'm so drawn to move to Wales. I think my true love is there," she laughed.

Kay was not laughing. "Don't be hasty, honey. You have a good situation in Paris, don't you?" She tried to sound casual. "What was the name of the town?"

"Oh. Um. Aber—wait, I wrote it down."

"Aberystwyth," Kay said.

"That's right! Whoa. You've been everywhere."

"Well, there is a university." She wondered desperately how to direct this, change the flow of events. "Anything happening in your *waking* love life?"

"*Nada. Niente. Rien.*" Kay heard her daughter's pout through the phone line.

"It'll come, sweetie. You're beautiful, smart, everything desirable."

"I think I'll stick with dream men. Way more enchanting than the ones I get mixed up with in real life."

She smiled. "Well, that's sometimes true. But it was only a dream."

"Or a vision," she suggested, playfully. "And he's in Wales, waiting for me."

When they ended the call, Kay slid the phone into her pocket and, rolling her bike from the shed, headed for the beach, to listen to the waves and think. Or not think at all.

From the cliffs, Kay saw the tide was high. She locked her bike, descended the path onto the rocks, and faced the horizon. Waves crashed below, spraying on her feet. She'd kept things from the kids to protect them. Was she endangering them? Did she need to tell Sophie about what had been happening or would that make things worse? Just as with Rousseau, she wondered if the story would fascinate Sophie and involve her more. Might Hamelyn draw her across the millennium from an imprint he found in his mother's memory?

Kay didn't think he could purposely put himself into her dream. Could he? She climbed down into the inlet. A crowd of vultures, hunched like shaggy old men, hopped around a desiccated sea lion. Some paused to eye her. Offering no competition for their smelly prize, she crossed the inlet swiftly and leapt onto the next rock outcropping. Navigating around holes in the rock, she imagined herself a giant on a miniature mountain pocked with tiny crater lakes.

On the far side, Kay dropped onto the sand. The beach stretched smoothly toward the Lost Coast, an unbroken vista of shoreline. Marauding seagulls had strewn cracked mussel shells into a crunchy white carpet where the waves swooshed in. The high tide pushed her close to the dunes.

She pictured the gull landing by me in the wildflower corridor, turning out to be Baird, and leaving her the half-crystal.

"Practice," Baird had told her. But she needed much more instruction. She needed more Baird. And there was the conundrum. Were her needs and desires bringing danger to her children? If so, she was a hypocrite.

She picked her way among chunks of pavement that had fallen to the beach as the defunct logging road crumbled—layers of unlikely greens and oranges like a fallen city, rusted pipes jagging out the sides. Even the beach creeped her out in her state of mind.

She returned to her bike and pedaled hard for home. There she found an email from Rousseau:

Mom, it's getting really strange. I keep seeing people wearing Renaissance clothes, like the guy on the subway I told you about. It must be popular. Do you see it a lot where you are? Well, you're not exactly in a trendy hub of civilization, are you? LOL.

But it's not just the clothes. Every time I see them, on the sidewalk or in cafés, if our eyes meet, I get bits of the same story in my mind. About a ship, or ships. I see these two girls. They seem afraid, like they've been captured or something. Oh, and people around them are speaking French. Do you think I'm going nuts? Ha, ha. I'm probably just trying to avoid the work stacking up on my desk. I should have become a novelist instead of a lawyer.

Love, Rousseau.

Kay hit "reply" and started a response, trying to be calm and not overreact. The chat box opened in the corner of her screen.

"Hi."

She chatted back. "Hi! Hey, that sounds strange. Do the girls in the story have names? Just wondering."

"Let me think. One of them is Gwinith or something."

Her heart pummeled her rib cage. She grabbed her cell phone and pressed Rousseau's number.

He picked up. "Hey, Mom."

"So, this is pretty fantastic. What you've been seeing?"

"Yeah. I don't know. It could be actors, but they don't seem like it. Today on the subway, a girl sat across from me. She looked scared. I glanced around. No one else noticed her. There was nothing threatening that I could see—people reading papers, listening to music, the usual. She was both terrified and in a trance. I mean, this is not a crazy person or a druggie. She appears smart, and she's beautiful. But wearing Renaissance clothes. She sat, rigid, staring ahead. No eye contact. It was pretty unnerving."

"That must have worried you," Kay said.

"She seemed...I don't know...not quite there."

"Wow." Kay tried to think how to support him. Again, her mind scrambled through the options and possible consequences of telling the truth.

"It gets weirder. So, that was on my morning commute. Then at lunch, it was sunny so I took my sandwich to the park. When I was throwing crumbs to birds, I glanced up, and there's the same girl, same clothes. She was sitting on the bench across the walkway. I swear."

Dread gripped Kay.

"At one point, she had a pleading expression, so I approached her, but when I got close, her expression didn't change at all. Just intense staring. I lost my nerve and went back to work."

"I don't like this. The same girl?"

"I don't mean to worry you, Mom. It's no sweat. Just kind of weird. Who knows? Maybe she just works around there."

"Yeah, maybe."

"Gotta run, Mom. City basketball tonight."

"I'm glad you're keeping that up."

"Yep. Good fun. Talk to you soon. Bye."

For a long time after they hung up she stared at the phone, heart hammering. She reread her son's email, and a chill jammed through her nerves.

Chapter 25

Sleep did not come easily that night. Kay couldn't stop spinning from Sophie to Rousseau. Their distance and her helplessness ate at her. Eventually, she fell into a restless half-doze. She woke with a start, a shout ringing in her head.

"Mama!"

She sat up, trying to orient herself. It had been so real. Her chest ached. A terrible sense of foreboding consumed her. What had she been dreaming about? The cry still rang in her head. Desperate to help, she wondered, Was it one of my kids? She pressed her hands to her eyes and tried to recreate the scene. A vision came to her of a young woman on a bench formed from a cave wall, staring ahead, terrified but motionless. Rousseau's description sprang to her mind. She knew this was Gwynedd. He had even said the name. Kay had a picture of her looks from Kyna's mind. The girl's mouth opened as if in a silent cry. Misery, deep and enduring, filled her eyes.

Kay had to do something. Sweat broke out around her hairline and beaded in her armpits. This was too real, too immediate, to be only a dream though a dream may have been the vehicle. The girl had shouted into her mind. But what could she do?

Holding the image, she carefully lay back onto her pillow. With her eyes closed, grasping the crystal, she re-entered the dream. Details grew more distinct. Water glistened on cave walls; a torch wavered and flickered across the surfaces. It was a living scene. She stood in a deep mountain cavern and heard the rushing of river water. This was like the cavern Galfride snatched Kyna into from the Solstice Faire. Was this lucid dreaming? Active imagination? A memory?

Gwynedd sat where the cave wall bulged out in a natural seat. The air was filled with dank, earthy smells. Beyond Kay extended a maw of blackness. The ground under her sloped upward in that direction. She heard nothing but water and the occasional hiss as drops hit the torch. Finding herself actually there, she moved slowly into a dark crevice in the wall, shadowed from the torch. Gwynedd was not tied, yet was unable to move. Back rigid, eyes wide and staring, she appeared petrified. Edging from her hiding place, Kay walked into the open, but Gwynedd did not seem to see her. *Am I invisible, or does she see no one*? Kay feared making noise by saying her name. She stepped closer and reached out. As if blocked by some invisible force, her hand stopped midway.

What could she do? She certainly wasn't any match for a spell-casting mage. Was he in the shadows, watching? She imagined his mad, leering grin and malevolent laugh. Peering around, vulnerable, she heard nothing. She had to find out where she was, in order to tell Baird and the others, so they could save Gwynedd. She had to be of some help, now that she was here. But she needed to work swiftly, before Galfride found her.

She crept past Gwynedd, watching to see if the young

woman's eyes followed her. But Gwynedd did not show any sign of seeing her.

Kay left the torch's light, and darkness engulfed her. She trod carefully upward, into the blackness, the sound of the river on her left.

Ahead, she saw a pinprick of light. She approached, listening for any sound, scanning for movement in the layers of shadow. As she walked, the river sound receded, then disappeared.

Kay finally realized her feet did not touch the ground. She must be in spirit form, floating along.

The rough stone became dryer as she ascended. At last, she approached a vertical slash of dim light and stepped through an opening onto a narrow ledge. Pressing against a shielding crag, she surveyed a thick forest carpet. The cave must have been obscured from sight by its angle. How would she tell others where to find it? And how would anyone climb here? How would she climb down, for that matter?

She edged further out and saw a full panorama. Folds of high mountains rose to snow-tipped peaks. The world was cast in pale dawn light, the sky still dark blue above. Everywhere were steep timbered slopes. Her gaze moved across the endless deciduous vista. Nestled halfway up the mountainside across from her was a tiny hamlet with thatched roofs and stone walls. If she were a bird, she could fly to it in moments and explore, find out the name to tell Baird. It would take days to descend into the valley on foot and climb to the village. If only she knew how to enter a bird spirit and cross the gulf.

At her feet, the tip of a rowan tree was broken, the top folded nearly double. She stared at it, trying to decide if this was an important sign. A loud scraping came from behind;

she pressed into the crevice. Was it Galfride? Had he followed from the shadows? Could he destroy her in spirit form, or follow her mind to her resting body and kill her there? Breathing quietly, she listened and heard sounds of the forest: birds chirping, insects buzzing. No more scratching.

Kay concentrated on the broken treetop and it glowed. Only then did the meaning hit her; it formed the rune, *Laguz*, meaning "sorcery". One interpretation was that magic was imagination manifesting into reality. Laguz is associated with water, especially underground rivers and depths of darkness. It represents the deepest knowing we can tap into.

This struck her on some unconscious level. Her hand still gripped the crystal, which may have helped. Like a shaman, she accessed the power of the subterranean river, even though it was no longer in earshot. She knew intuitively that this rune had been used for astral travel. She looked again at the far mountainside and village. As she gripped the stone, the details of the town became more distinct. She focused on a section of grey wall, which protruded at the end of the town's single road, then pictured a glowing Laguz rune on that spot.

Trying to squelch terror, she concentrated on pulling energy from the stone. Please keep me from falling. Almost immediately, she was next to the glowing Laguz, on the other side of the valley and stood on the road leading into the town. A wood sign announced the place: "*L'Argentière-La-Bessée*." Something to do with silver. Must be a mine.

She saw figures moving toward the center of the town. The residents were stirring. She stepped quickly around the wall into shadows. A dark square appeared to be a mineshaft. Duff may know this place, may have come here for silver.

She knew the name. Her mission was complete. She needed to get back. Dawn light grew pearlier on the cobblestone street and buildings. Staying in shadow near the mine's entrance, she examined the mountainside, searching for the cavern, but saw only endless trees. She looked for the bent treetop, her sign. She could not see it. She squeezed the crystal and there was the bent treetop, now outlined in golden light.

Someone screamed. Kay jerked awake in bed, pillow soaked with sweat. She sat up. Had Gwynedd cried out in her mind? She had to tell Baird how to find her.

Kay slipped on a robe and made coffee. Could she call Baird to her? What if she tried writing the ogham again. Would it bring her into Kyna's spirit? What if she were captured and couldn't get out? What if it took her back to when she first entered Kyna's spirit? Could she somehow prevent her disappearance? But that line of thought was futile. Too many elements made up the chain of events. Above all else, the memory of Gwynedd's anguished face remained branded on her mind.

Coffee in-hand, Kay sat down in the living room. Dawn colored the horizon. Her elbow, resting on the side table, bumped the tiny flute Hamelyn had made for Kyna. She picked it up and pressed it to her lips, trying to remember the song Baird taught her. She hadn't played or even thought about the instrument since he'd been there. She blew into it hesitantly, searching for those eight notes. It didn't sound quite right. She closed her eyes and played it again. Baird said Hamelyn wrote the song. She pictured him carving the flute, testing it, trying out the first sounds. Again, she played, putting her heart into the mood of the short melody, hoping to find the accurate notes.

Cold air filled with the sounds of seagulls and crashing surf surrounded her. Mist spattered her face, and the rough rock surface she sat on seeped, wet and cold, into her gown. She opened her eyes and found herself on a rock jetty. A young man crouched nearby. She could tell it was Hamelyn even though his beard had grown thicker. He stared out to sea as waves pounded and spray blew over them. A line of pelicans glided above the waves. A seagull strutted up close, half a crab dangling from its beak.

"Is that your da'?" she asked, partly to test if he could see and hear her.

Hamelyn's head jerked around. His eyes widened, but then, just as quickly, his face fell in disappointment. "I think I know who y'ar," he said. "Me da has thought o' someone very like you. Ye do resemble me ma." He wiped his face with one hand—sea spray? Tears? His glance dropped to the flute in her hand, then up to her face, eyebrows raised in question.

She held the instrument out to him but he didn't take it. "Baird...your father loaned it to me. He taught me a song you composed." Kay rushed to the point, "I know where your sister is." She couldn't be certain if her sighting of Gwynedd was even news in their time.

He leaned toward her. "Where?" He breathed the question, alert, anxious.

So, they hadn't yet found her. Kay described her journey, the cave, the town with the silver mine. "I don't know if she's still there. But if she is, she's frightened."

Hamelyn stood and held out a hand to her. "Let us tell Aelfwyn. She can help get word to Da. He and Duff are in Gaulish land even now."

"I can show them." She stood. Her robe, only the thin silk kimono, sagged with damp weight. She shivered, winding her arms around herself.

"Did she appear...unharmed?" he asked.

She took his hand, grateful for the warmth, and followed him along the jetty toward shore, her bare feet aching from the stone ridges.

"She looked healthy." Though it was hard to imagine anything worse than the misery and fear on her face. Kay's teeth chattered. She stubbed her toes, reddish-purple from cold, and yelped.

Hamelyn turned and checked her over.

Wind whipped at her knee-length gown. "I wanted to tell you what I'd seen in time to help her. I didn't know the flute would bring me here. So, I didn't really get ready," she explained, embarrassed abou her attire.

"The flute brought you?"

She nodded. "I played your song. Your da taught it to me."

"Which song?"

She started to play it for him but thought better of it. "Maybe I'd best wait. I might find myself back in my living room, and I want to tell your da where to find Gwynedd."

From the jetty, they crossed the beach and climbed onto the raised shore road, then rushed past closed market booths. They were passing places she'd seen while in Kyna's mind. She wanted to slow down and take it all in.

The overcast sky made it hard to tell the time. Was it early, or late? A few folks on the road watched them hurry past. Kay avoided eye contact. *What a sight I must be. And do they think I'm Kyna? Even worse.*

They passed warehouses and rustic shacks. She recognized the rough hovel of the wounded fisherman Kyna had visited and wondered how he fared.

By the time they entered Kyna's road, she was out of

breath. "The flute didn't take me anywhere when I practiced the song with Baird." She panted, hugging her gown, trying to keep it from flapping as they ran.

"I imagine it required concentratin' on yer destination, no' just the playin' th' notes," he offered, barely winded as he jogged.

She added to the tale of her time in the cavern—how an unassailable force blocked her when she reached for Gwynedd. She mentioned the ledge and the bent rowan tree near the cave entrance, recounted every sign she could think of to help them find his sister.

"Will we go there, do you think, so I can show Baird and Duff what to look for?" she asked, trying to keep up. "Would we be able to travel quickly?" She meant like she'd done with the flute. Did Hamelyn have means to jump there instantly?

"That I don't know. It'll be up t' Aelfwyn. Perhaps she'll call a council of The Thirteen."

Kay remembered The Thirteen circled, pulling her spirit from Kyna, and grimaced.

Hurrying down Kyna's road, she remembered them striding, singing, anticipating the Solstice Faire. Exaltation laced with fear hit her at the thought that she'd brought herself there purposely. Could she manage to return as well?

Before she became too anxious, Kyna's stone house came into sight. They crossed the bridge over the stream, ran up the steps, and entered the main room. As they passed through, Kay took in the familiar sights she'd seen through Kyna's eyes: the rustic table and fireplace, the kitchen shelves, the loom. At the back wall was the curtained alcove they'd made for Aelfwyn's bed that Baird had mentioned.

Hamelyn strode through to the apothecary, and Kay followed. Aelfwyn turned from grinding herbs by the fire.

Kyna's hounds jumped up and sniffed Kay cautiously, then sat on their haunches, eyebrows turning in apparent consternation. Did they sense Kyna? Think Kay was familiar yet not? "Hey, Fynn. Rhyn." She held out a hand. They were having none of her and held their lightly offended statue stances, heads pulled back. Kay's heart ached for them; she could only imagine how much they must miss Kyna.

Hamelyn knelt by Aelfwyn, and they spoke quietly. Her bright eyes took in the news. She turned and studied Kay, set down her mortar and pestle, and signaled for Kay to sit on a stool.

"So, this be what ye look like, up close," she said, the scrutiny of her owlish eyes unnervingly intense.

Torn, Kay wanted to collapse into her Great Mother strength, while a part of her clanged a warning not to completely submit to her.

"Very like Kyna, y'ar. No' just the way ye look. Somethin' else." Aelfwyn pursed her lips, nodding. She reached, flicked her fingers to say, "Come." When Kay leaned toward her, she put a hand on her cheek, peered deep into her eyes, then released her.

Where her hand had been tingled.

Aelfwyn pushed up using Kay's shoulder, and shuffled slowly toward the door. Hamelyn and Kay followed. In the hallway, Aelfwyn pointed to an unlit torch in a sconce, and Hamelyn pulled it. The wall groaned, moving aside. They started up the spiraling stone stairs, Aelfwyn first, gripping the rail. She was more bent than when Kay last saw her. She stayed close in case the old woman faltered.

At the top, they stepped into the round tower room. The sight made Kay nauseous; the sharp smell of burnt herbs and roots brought back memories of her spirit being torn painfully from Kyna.

At the center, Hamelyn knelt and lit peat under the brazier. Pungent smoke rose as Aelfwyn threw powder into the flames. Kay assumed she would be sent to France. Pleased that the elder took her story seriously, she suggested she put on warm apparel, but Aelfwyn and Hamelyn grasped her hands and pulled her forward.

Her hands shook.

Aelfwyn said, "It's no' hard to send ye back to yer time, not like separatin' spirits."

"Send me back to my time? No, you must send me to France. To Baird and Duff. I have to show them—"

Aelfwyn shook her head and recited words in a low hum.

Hamelyn whispered, "We don't know what ye'd be gettin' into. What dangers there might be. Probably best ye return t' yer home. We'll find the cave. Aelfwynn's got your sight in her mind now."

There was sympathy in his eyes, but that same unmoving, underlying discipline of the Council. The party line. She had no ally here. She fought the urge to take Hamelyn aside and say, "Come on, just you and me. Let's go."

But she didn't dare counter Aelfwyn's fierce hawk stare.

She probably thinks of me as a hazard, with my bumbling, inarticulate mind.

They chanted. Blackness came for Kay. An arctic night grasped her soul and she slipped again into oblivion.

Chapter 26

A soft chair supported her. Kay's living room swirled into view. Her limbs were leaden, and at first, she couldn't move her head. After a wave of dizziness, she experienced only slight nausea and, thankfully, no headache. Her robe, damp from sea spray, rode up her thighs. She still gripped the flute.

She sighed with relief and mopped up coffee that had spilled, then started a shower. Her lips tasted salty from the ancient seashore. Her feet thawed in prickles as she stepped under the hot water and washed away ocean residue from a thousand years ago. If only she could preserve the salty traces, it might be of great interest to scientists, potentially informative for sustainability.

Soaking, she tried to take in what had happened. Had it been worth it dashing across millennia. Did it take a toll on the body, all this coming and going between centuries? She had delivered the message. Most likely, Aelfwyn would send Hamelyn to his father with it. Could they possibly spot the cave, though? Had she told them everything they needed to know? Why had Aelfwyn been so anxious to get rid of her?

Exiting the shower, she spotted the flute on the sink.

Could she play it now, think of Baird, and take herself to him? And go against Aelfwyn's plans? Probably not a good idea. She couldn't keep looping this in her mind, or she'd drive herself mad. Besides, she was exhausted.

Oz entered. With his look, he demanded she sit somewhere and make a warm lap for him.

Kay dried off and bundled up in a warm robe and socks. He sniffed the damp gown on the floor.

"Guess where those scents are from, Ozzy? Better yet, guess what time they're from?" She knelt and put her face against his fur. Then she picked him up and held him in her arms until he started a rumbling purr.

She had to admit, it was a let down. She was the one who'd seen Gwynedd in the cavern, frightened and alone. Maybe it was a vision, but it was her vision. She deserved to be the one to take the information to the men in France. If Hamelyn told them all that she said, they could probably manage the same trick with the rune and bent treetop. She did wonder how she could have gathered any information unknown to Aelfwyn.

"Okay, sweet cat. I'm going to make more coffee." She set him down. He tried to get back up into her arms. "Lots of snuggles later, buddy," she promised.

She put a coffee thermos into her backpack and dressed for the gardens, eager to dig into soil, plant seeds, and perform earthy tasks. She longed to anchor herself in a furrow of land, root deep, and let the nutrient-rich loam hold her tightly to just one plane. On the way out, she snagged a few pieces of fruit and munched an apple as she walked. She noticed how wobbly she was. But the fresh morning air and normalcy settled her nerves.

Over the next few days, Kay pushed thoughts of Olde Wales and the Alpes Anciennes out of her mind. She could do nothing more for Gwynedd. It was up to them now.

Back in the garden, she was thinning carrot starts when Jarl's face appeared above her plot's fenceline which was patched together out of driftwood, willow reeds, and an old baker's rack. "Want to get lunch?" he asked.

She thought he looked quite appealing, surrounded by flowering vines, backlit by the late morning sun, his shiny brown curls dusted with silver-grey, the top buttons of his thermal shirt open to reveal a spray of dark hair. *Too bad I'm in love with a bard living a millennium ago*, she thought. "Okay. I'm starved." Her stomach rumbled, proof that the fruit had not been enough. The walk in the Alps might not have required actual body energy, but the run-in Aberystwyth—what they called *Llanbadarn Fawr*—had.

"Good." Jarl entered the plot and gave her a hand up. "I want to show you something, as well as eat." He brushed garden dirt onto his pants, which already had a good share.

"Do you think they'll let us in?" She looked down at her smudgy-kneed overalls.

"They let anything into Headlands Café." He grinned.

"I guess that's some comfort." She chuckled and grabbed her backpack. "You have something to show me? Very mysterious."

They strolled toward the central shed where she stored her tools, and scrubbed dirt from her nails at the deep outside sink. She checked messages before she locked the office and put a note on the door: "Be back one-ish. Call if you need me."

As they walked the six blocks to Headlands Café, they chatted about their gardens. Kay described the Old-World kitchen garden she wanted to design. He was excited to see her plans, and they delved headlong into dizzying topics like chive borders and heirloom bee attractors.

The usual young denizens, with dreadlocks all shades and lengths, juggled and smoked outside the café. A skateboarder nearly bisected her as they crossed to the restaurant door. Inside, old coastal hippies mingled with professionals and everything in between. She gave Jarl her order, handed him some cash, and claimed a table for two near shelves overflowing with board games and newspapers. Soon, Jarl brought order numbers on stands, set them on the table, and fit his long legs, with some trouble, under.

"So, what's this you want to show me? Is it portable?" She glanced at his backpack. "Bigger than a breadbox?" She drum-rolled.

Jarl rummaged in his pack, pulled out a notebook, and removed a paper from between the pages. Checking that the table was clean and dry, he laid a dramatic charcoal drawing in front of her.

The sight jolted her heart. She stared, unable to understand. Clearly, she had drawn it, yet had no memory of it. She knew the scene, and it terrified her. Galfride's cruel grin and intense eyes reached for her from the detailed, lifelike picture. She glanced up at Jarl. "Where did you get this?"

"In Ian's apartment." He sounded as if he wished he hadn't shown it to her, probably based on her reaction, which she could only assume included a significant drop of color from her face.

"Ian's…?" She stared, puzzled.

"Ian and Candice invited me over for music the other

night," Jarl explained. "I saw this on his desk. I knew it was your style from the sketches I've seen at your place." He checked her expression for confirmation.

She nodded. "I don't remember drawing it."

"That is strange." He studied her. "Well, I thought I'd take it and show you. I had a hard time imagining you giving it to Ian so…" He looked like he seriously hoped he was right.

She thought of the night at the Duck 'n Hen when Ian had come on strong with his interest in her crystal. "No, I can't imagine that either. I've never given him anything." Though she'd wanted to give him a slap, she almost added.

"Who is it? In the drawing?" Jarl asked. The question stuck, heavy, in the air.

She'd hoped he wouldn't ask. She took a deep breath, playing for time. "It must be... uh... sometimes I draw my dreams." That was the truth, yet it was a lie by omission.

"Some dream." Jarl's eyes dropped back to the drawing. "But it's great. I mean, it's vibrant. You captured something menacing." He trailed off.

The drawing held a powerful magnetism, all in dark shades with a touch of deep purplish-red under Galfride's eyes. The cavern glistened. Eerie green light reflecting off dripping moss tinted his hollowed cheeks. A trick of the drawing brought it alive, as if torchlight flickered in the café.

Their soup arrived, along with artisan bread. Kay picked up the drawing to save it from soup sloshings. Hesitating, she held it in the air. Part of her did not want to take it, never wanted to see it again. She feared even having it in her possession. What if it attracted the mage to her? Still, she asked, "Do you mind if I keep it?"

"Of course not. It's yours."

She slipped it inside her sketchbook where she'd been designing her medieval, walled garden.

They ate their soup—hers a thick lentil, his, taco.

She knew nothing of this drawing. Jarl's concerned glances indicated he awaited a response. She swallowed and asked cheerily, "What have you been up to? Other than gardening."

He told her behind-the-scene stories of Duck 'n Hen, and they shared garden woes. He asked for advice on an infestation of flying insects harassing his Brussels sprouts.

"Oh, I do have news," he said, after a while. "Joaquin took your suggestion about getting himself out there as a sculptor, not just doing odd jobs and yard work. And he's getting orders."

"That's great!" She thought of the sea lion bench, so creative and unusual. "He's got too much talent to waste." She knew the same could be said about Jarl. He spoke several languages and was a trained engineer, yet he worked as a night chef. Not one of them lived the life they'd prepared for, or so it appeared. Who really knew the underlying web of their life tapestries?

She forced herself to relax and enjoy the rest of their meal. But as they parted, the drawing thundered from inside her bag. She turned back. "See you at the garden," she called, needing to make one last healthy connection.

Jarl called, "Rain or shine, fellow earth digger."

She smiled and reluctantly walked in the other direction. The sunshine should have given her cheer, but was out of tune with the darkness enveloping her as she gambolled toward home. Galfride's portrait burned at her side, palpable and discomforting. She switched her pack away from the gold crystal, surrounded by overcharged energy.

In the house, she put her backpack in the closet. She

hated the idea of looking at Galfride, so real on the page. Yet, as she changed out of her grungy garden clothes, she was drawn to study the portrait. She'd only seen him once, through Kyna's eyes, when she'd thrown him away with a fire bolt that had gathered in her heart and charged down her arm. Kay sure hadn't been able to do that when he burned her. She heard his laughter in her head. The sore on her chest still hurt at times. It did now as she slipped on a soft tunic and linen pants.

Like testing a sore tooth, she kept bringing back that scene in the cavern. Was she fascinated? No, it was just…what? She wasn't used to having an enemy, or being part of a plot with an evil wizard. Now, her kids might be endangered. She owed it to them to help them understand. But therein lay the conundrum. Should she give their involvement more attention or less?

In the living room, she dropped into the cushioned chair. What was it Kyna and Galfride had spoken of when he captured her? They'd referred to his niece and how he'd twisted her mind. He'd goaded Kyna to return to court life. She recalled the painful grip he'd had on her arm.

The crystal's energy pulsed against her leg. The air crackled around her. She tried to calm herself and reduce the rising force before it got out of hand. But how? She thought of weaving. The steady rhythm always put her into a calm trance. She was walking toward the loom when the image of Gwynedd in the cave invaded her mind. She heard her calling again. She stopped. Baird and Duff might be searching for the cave. The entrance was so cunningly hidden in that flap of granite. Perhaps she should go and try to help.

A rising tide of power seemed to want to swallow her. Swaying, she put her hand to the wall and tried to take control of the energy, wishing she didn't have to deal with this alone. Was she inadequate? A deep place in her was aware of new capacities.

A cloud must have passed over the sun, for the house darkened. Something called to her. She found herself moving toward the closet. Not the drawing! With effort, she slowed her feet, then stopped. She fought the pull. She needed to do something. Maybe weaving wasn't it. She padded to the glassed-in back porch and settled on her puffy meditation pillow. Surrounded by houseplants, she lit a thick, longburning candle and piñon incense. The scent of high-mountain chaparral filled the air. Its smoky fragrance shifted her mood, cleared inner chatter, and smoothed the jangling atmosphere that had surrounded her. Through the long row of windows, the back yard looked reassuringly domestic. In the past year, she'd encouraged a few mature fruit trees in the wilder areas of the yard. Legs crossed, she dropped into slow, rhythmic breathing. The afternoon sun once again warmed the room.

Oz flopped next to her, and she stroked him, glad for his presence against her leg. He rose, stalked away, and dropped on the other end of the porch in a puddle of sunlight.

"Fine. Even you desert me," she said, with a pout. Could he sense the energy building inside her? Was her power unnerving, or did he just want the sun on his fur?

The backpack pressed against her other side. She didn't remember taking it from the closet. Panic rose. She worked to slow her breathing again. *Okay, it's here. I'm not going to be afraid of my own drawing.*

Slowly she slipped the crystal from its bag. She laid it in the hammock formed by her long shirt and cupped hands. Then Kay reestablished the safe wall she'd built with Baird, carefully easing negative energy out, creating a solid sanctuary.

At last, only slightly shaky, she pulled the portrait from her bag and laid it before her. She studied the perplexing drawing: the striking boldness, the drama of deep shadow, just enough highlight to render the eyes piercing, the smile dark—or was it merely power that he bore on his face?

Galfride's eyes shifted in her direction. She jumped, letting go of the picture. Sweat trickled down her back. Had his eyes moved, or was it a trick of the drawing? She looked away, stared at the candle flame, breathed in the chaparral smoke that curled from the incense burner. Again, her eyes strayed to the drawing. This time, she brought her focus to the folds of the cavern surrounding the face. She spotted a dark ledge that she had not noticed before.

"Laguz," she whispered. The rowan tree with the bent top seemed present.

"Friend to all who work magic." She heard the voice of a shaman she'd visited in the Finnish outlands a decade before. "Laguz connects us with wisdom from the depths of darkness and mystery. It is the entrance to the Underworld Passages and allows us to move through dream states."

Underworld passages. Underground river. She heard a quiet rustle of water and shook herself. *Not now. I don't want to go there now.* Why was she doing this anyway? But her fingers traced the rune on the floorboards. Her eyelids drooped and she descended further and further.

Chapter 27

K ay lay on her belly in blackness, hearing a steady whisper of water sliding on stone from below. She edged forward. Gritty stone grazed her arms. At the edge, she peeked over. Gwynedd sat on the low shelf of cave wall, a single torch flickering nearby. Kay was in the mountain caverns again, but this time the subterranean river ran between her and the girl. Clasping her hands together, her fingers discovered a deep groove at the base of her left thumb. She recognized the scar, and knew whose it was. Not hers.

"Hello, friend," Kyna whispered in Kay's mind. "I hope ye dinna mind me bringin' ye here?"

Again, Kyna had drawn her spirit. Kay wondered how to speak to her. Maybe she already reads her mind. With that idea, she searched for a thread of control, sorting memories, tucking some behind the ice wall as Baird had taught her, then realized she was starting to panic. She told herself to calm as she watched Kyna's daughter, far below, motionless and afraid. She was the real issue, Kay told herself. *I'll focus on her.*

"I need yer help," Kyna thought, as though she had waited patiently for Kay to emerge from her anxiety.

"You do?" Kay asked with surprise and trepidation. How could these skillful magic-workers need her help?

"Aye. We, The Thirteen, noticed a tremendous power when ye were in my spirit. Well, most especially as ye were extracted, ye might say. It was dangerous, at the time, for we dinna yet understand how t' work with it. Aelfwyn and I have been experimentin' since then."

A thought of hers flickered, but she quickly suppressed it and went on. "We've made a plan to get Gwynedd."

Since Kay was not there physically, she hoped their plan didn't rely on the use of the golden crystal. "What was this power you sensed when we were together?" she asked.

"It's no' somethin' easily defined." Kay perceived her shuffling through memories as she searched for evidence. "Just the fact that ye were able to go into the crystal and return whole to your time. That requires strength of character on your part. Perhaps a certain...mm…" She dug for a word. "...imagining power. Do ye ken?"

Kay searched for a reference point. She'd done some work with active imagination, trying to discover meanings in ancient writing systems. She thought it might be similar.

"Mm-hm, I ken that," Kyna thought.

It was frightening, yet exhilarating, to share a mind. Gently, subtly, Kay checked the sovereignty of her own mind and memories. A mental finger probed the edges. The effort made her brain hurt. It was something to be practiced in bits. But here she was, thrown into full exposure.

We looked down at the frightened young woman. "She called to me in my sleep," Kay said. "She cried out 'Mama!' And then, she'd come here. She'd walked through here the other night."

Did Kyna already know? Kay could tell she did.

"I can't understand why she called *me*. You were right here. And now, I know you and Aelfwyn already had this under control. I traveled to tell Hamelyn. I didn't mean to. I played your flute, and it took me to him. But Aelfwyn sent me right back to my time." No wonder.

"I've heard that cry ever since yer spirit was pulled from mine. But I am unable t' respond," she said, with anguish. "Galfride ha' sealed her int' isolation. She can call to me. I imagine that be his purpose. T' draw me. But she canno' receive my call t' her, or Aelfwyn's, or I could ha' got her away by now, like we did w' Branwyn."

How awful! Kay thought. The man was abhorrent. "So, the night she came into my dreams, and I came here in spirit form, you knew? Could you see me walk through here?"

"Yes," she said. "T'was only after ye were inside o' my mind, and we were torn apart, that I began t' hear my daughter calling. Somethin' opened, or changed."

That's why Kyna disappeared from home. She was following Gwynedd's cries.

She went on, "The connection between you and me...somethin' o' it remained — remains. Aelfwyn also perceived a residue o' our combined spirits in th' gold crystal."

"So Aelfwyn has known from the start where you were, what happened to you?" Kay couldn't help a souring, thinking of Baird and Hamelyn kept in the dark, not knowing if Kyna was alive or dead.

Kyna continued, "Once I came in search of Gwynedd, I could no' communicate with Baird."

She sensed her accusation, Kay was sure.

"Any attempt and Galfride'd discover it. He ha' set snares b'tween Baird and me. But Aelfwyn can obscure my connection wi' her. Galfride kens naught."

That was pretty much what Baird had told her.

"If the others knew where I was, it would endanger us all," Kyna said.

"But you got Branwyn away from here?"

"Aye."

They said Galfride twisted his niece's mind, damaged her—perhaps beyond repair. Kay remembered his accusation that Kyna had refused to heal her. "How did you get her away? And why not Gwynedd as well?"

Kyna related her travels as she tried to follow her daughter's thought-cries. With mind-spirit connection, Aelfwyn and Kyna found the mountain cavern in Les Hautes-Alpes. "We c'd reach Branwyn because Galfride had less protection on her, most like presumin' we'd go after Gwynedd, and he would sense me comin'. He had traps around her."

"What is his purpose with all this? To draw you?"

"All three of us—Gwynedd, Branwyn, me—we have powers he'd love t' exploit. I don' know all his plans, but he must want all thray o' us together. We've been bait for each other. Gwynedd and Branwyn were mates as girls. Met in the Druid school. They both ha' great talent." She tapered off as a dark shadow of despair crept into their shared psyche.

"So, your daughter didn't run off with a handsome trader?"

"Nay." Kyna added, with acid thoughts, "Gods curse his vital organs. This lout must o' kidnapped her. We still don' know all o' it."

"So, Branwyn is now safe from him?" Kay asked.

"Aye."

Kay thought of the drawing and the mysterious way the backpack had come to be lying against her when she had purposely avoided getting it. "Just before you pulled me here, I concentrated on a charcoal picture I drew but don't understand. It appeared in a friend's apartment, and I don't know how it got there, don't even remembering drawing it." Kay thought back to the yarns and boots Aelfwyn orchestrated into her life. "Do you think Aelfwyn might have...I don't know...been involved with the drawing?"

Kyna was silent.

"Anyway, as I meditated on the portrait of Galfride, I slipped into a sort of trance, and then maybe I was susceptible to your call, and that made it possible for you to bring me here." She tried to work logic into the equation.

"I suppose Aelfwyn could o' helped. I know nothin' o' this drawing." The image floated clearly on the shared palate of their minds. "Perhaps ye drew it sometime in the future, and she brought it to ye in yer past. She donna depend upon th' order o' things the way others do."

That was an understatement.

Kyna grew suddenly still, as if on alert. "Aelfwyn calls me. They're gathering."

A new level of tension rose in the air and the stones under them, like a growing storm. Power surged, petrifying Kay as Kyna reached for reserves of energy. Kay tried to remain open, to help if she could. Hopefully she would know how to draw what she needed. A monumental force continued to build. Shaky, she thought she might lose control. At the edges of her awareness, she sensed Aelfwyn's presence, a vein of ancient strength shoring her up.

Below, Aelfwyn and the rest of The Thirteen manifested, their dark, hooded robes filling the chamber. Gwynedd continued to stare, as if unaware of the group gathered before her. Some faces Kay recognized: Baird, standing closest to Gwynnedd, his head turned to her, staring with a father's love and anguish. He reached out to her, and stopped abruptly; an invisible shield separated her from him.

Hamelyn, beside him, stood tall and sturdy, emanating the strength of a man much older than his years. The Traveler brother and sister, Boldo and Talaith, stood on each side of frail Aelfwyn. Duff towered over all, his bullish chest straining his immense robe.

Tense, Kay struggled to see Baird's features. Suddenly, his eyes flicked toward the shelf where Kyna lay, his focus aimed directly at her, confusion in his expression. Clearly, he processed something but was not sure what. Angry on his behalf, Kay saw hollows under his eyes. The fact that he could not know of Kyna's presence, even that she was alive, made Kay ache for him.

His focus returned to the circle, face registering no sign he had discovered Kyna's presence.

With a scraping sound that screeched in the silence, the wall behind Gwynedd moved incrementally. A dark crack appeared and grew wider. Out stepped Galfride. He looked deranged, eyes red-rimmed in the wavering light from the torch.

The Circle of Thirteen drew in tighter, hands clasped. Galfride laughed derisively but said nothing, only stepped so close to Gwynedd his thigh touched her shoulder. Her expression remained unchanged. The barrier separating them from The Thirteen now shimmered, a translucent gauze, visible for the first time. Tense silence filled the chamber.

Something twanged, as though a cord grew taut from groin to heart.

Aelfwyn, tiny amid the others in the circle of long robes, kept her eyes on Gwynedd. A surge of voltage swing up—solid as an iron cable—forming a bridge between Kyna and Aelfwyn. As Kay struggled to maintain her mental stability in the throbbing power pulsing between them, she heard a throaty chanting rising from the priestly circle. She steeled herself, trying to let her spirit be a tool while she battled to hold her sanity. The power increased until she doubted whether her heart could handle it—though in truth it was Kyna's heart.

An immense triangle, perhaps thirty feet long, formed in the air. It narrowed to a point at one end and was covered in jagged tongues of flame. Was it visible only to them? Kay stared through Kyna's eyes as suddenly it shot forward, slicing through the curtain.

In that instant, Gwynedd snapped out of her trance, turned to Galfride, and shouted. Her hands flew up, shaped a symbol, and threw it at him. Gold sparks formed a ribbon that circled the mage. His head yanked back, eyes wide. Amazement and fury tore across his face just before a blasting crack shook the walls. A shouting chant thundered from the Circle of Thirteen. Galfride flew backward, lifted, and flung, arms splayed. He hit the wall with stunning force and crashed to the stone floor where he lay still.

With the barrier vanished, Baird swept Gwynedd into his arms.

Instantly, she disappeared. His arms closed, empty against his chest. His look of anguish tore at Kay's heart. All eyes watched as Galfride moved, struggled to rise, a growing lightning storm suffusing his face.

Chapter 28

Floorboards pressed against Kay as she lay on her side watching leaves wave outside the glassed-in porch. Clouds drifted by. Oz still stretched in the warm afternoon sunrays. She must have slipped from the wall to the floor while inside Kyna's mind. It couldn't have taken long; the chunky candle had barely burned down.

She shook from the impact of having carried that massive charge in the caves of the Ancient Alps. She had brought some of the energy back with her spirit; it vibrated in her. Kyna had been able to send her back without having to tear her spirit out and shove it into a golden crystal, hurling her, nauseous, back into her time. Kyna and Aelfwyn had apparently figured out that part.

Gingerly, she pushed herself up. What happened after she left? She reached for Kyna's presence in her mind, but found no trace of her. Then again, she did not always know when she was there. Desolate, distanced from that other world, loneliness swept through her.

Oz came over and flopped where Kay could reach his belly. It was hard to say whether it was more for her or him. She stroked his underside. Kyna said Kay's spirit made her more powerful. Had she really made a difference in building that huge charge that sheered through the barrier? She had to believe so. Kyna would never leave her daughter in that misery longer than necessary. If she and Aelfwyn could have done it without her, they would have.

But where was Gwynedd now? Kay pictured Baird's look of dismay, and her heart ached. He knew even less than she did. She longed to comfort him, at least give him hope. Should she try to get to him? She could concentrate on him as she played Hamelyn's flute. But what if she showed up in the middle of a wizard's duel?

She wished she knew all the powers of the crystal. Could it give her sight across space as well as time? Perhaps she had to try to work with it on her own. In the caverns, Kyna told her that she, Kay, had found magic they knew nothing about. She slipped the crystal from its pouch, held it on her palm, and reached for inner strength. Her burnt skin ached. She thought of the scarring shamans sometimes must endure as part of their initiation. What doesn't kill you makes you stronger, right? She blew out the candle and watched the crystal's glow increase. "What can you do?" she asked it.

Oz turned green-gold eyes toward her. His tail twitched. Normally, that was his way of accusing her of withholding expected petting. "Not now, saucer eyes," she told him. Could she look into the caves without showing up there. She didn't want to interfere with Aelfwyn's plans. They were clearly working on intricate strategies.

But, if she could get to Baird somehow… She pictured sitting by a fire with him. She'd tell him Kyna was alive, no matter what Aelfwyn was keeping from him. She'd let him know Branwyn was safe, and probably Gwynedd, too. Oh, to see the happy look on his face.

Yet Kyna and Aelfwyn had accomplished much by

keeping their doings secret.

Maybe he knew by now. Perhaps they were gathered in the woods beyond the caverns, sharing everything, ready to stop Galfride for good.

If only she knew what was happening.

For now, she'd better restrict her exploring with the crystal to her own neighborhood. She would experiment with its shifts in energy so she could at least learn to draw on it for protection. Maybe it would tell her how to use it. Kyna mentioned their shared residue in it. Could she tap into that to guide her?

Oz gave her a back-foot bunny kick, with claws. "Ow. You beast. You affection glutton." She tweaked his nose. "Maybe you're hungry." She got up to feed him. "But then I'm taking my crystal for a walk," she declared as she filled his bowl.

With an hour of daylight left, she pulled on her boots. This sort of energy work needed the great outdoors. In addition, her cupboards were bare. She grabbed a cloth bag. As she walked toward Down Home Foods—the town's only natural food store—she noted changes in energy when she squeezed the crystal, or pressed her lips to it, blowing. She watched for it to glow. These physical actions did not affect it as much as focused energy.

After a few blocks of this attention, the crystal began to thrum with a steady, low vibration. She focused her energy. *I'm just experimenting,* she told herself. *If I happen to be transported, I must stay hidden and try to bring Baird to me.*

No, no. She jumped back to her plan to try to see what was happening. She thought she might chant to keep her focus on the one objective. "Let me see what's happening at the caves."

Nearing the commercial district, she passed an alley

bordered by tufts of dry weeds, trash caught in them, fluttering in the breeze. The crystal pulsed. She peered down the alley, trying to figure what had wakened it. The afternoon had darkened with a thick cloud cover. On one side of the alley were overgrown back yards, on the other, roll-down metal doors for deliveries to stores that faced the next street.

Kay held the stone in front of her and took a step into the alley. The glow brightened and throbbed with her heartbeat. She knew a church served free meals to the needy at the far end. At the middle, someone crouched. She started to turn away, but the crystal grew hotter, almost burning her hand. Maybe that was even more reason to leave. She sealed the inner chambers of her mind by wrapping a wall around her core and turned, hovering, undecided. "Could you be clearer?" she whispered to the stone. Experimentally, she stepped back into the alley. The crystal pulsed harder and sent a spray of golden light between her fingers. She cupped it. "All right, all right. I'm walking. See?"

She stepped over muddy potholes, the alley seeming interminable. At last, she drew near the huddled man and edged wide to skirt past him. He raised his head.

It was Baird, crouched among trash-littered weeds, face streaked with tears and dirt.

She stopped mid-stride. "Baird?" She knelt by him, resting her hand on his shoulder.

He stared at her. "I had her in m' arms," he whispered hoarsely. He brushed a sleeve across his eyes. "She disappeared, taken away from me again, just when we got t' her."

"I know." She put a knee on the pavement and edged closer.

"Ye know?" he said. "What d' ye mean, y' know?" Suspicion crept into his expression. She saw realization flickering in his eyes. Was he thinking of the moment when he glanced up at the rock shelf to where Kyna lay hidden with Kay in her spirit?

Herpalm stung. The heat from the stone must have risen while she concentrated. She slipped it into its pouch, wincing. Baird took her hand and pressed it to his cool wet cheek, bringing instant relief.

"I don't know everything," she said, "but I know a bit." Though back at the house she'd thought fiercely that she'd be the one to tell him Kyna was alive, now doubt made her waver, and she tucked that knowledge behind the ice wall. Who was she to ruin plans, maybe endanger lives?

Baird's lips were cracked, his clothes covered with dust. She had to wonder how long he and Duff had trekked in the Alps in search of the cave. He still carried his underlying strength and beauty that no amount of dirt could obscure. A breeze stirred his hair. The alley had grown otherwise eerily still, almost stultifying in after-rain mugginess. Yet the scent around them was of forest, with none of the taint of old garbage she'd experienced at the other end. Baird carried his own aura, untouched by detritus.

"Were ye in the caves just now? Someone were above us and a great power came from there." His eyes scanned her, as if to say, "Did you do all that?"

"There's so much that's still a mystery." She hated herself. How could she be disgusted with Aelfwyn when she carried on the same subterfuge? "I kind of helped Aelfwyn."

"What are ye sayin'?" he said, softly. His eyes darted around her face. Did he sense her inner conflict? "I know

Kyna's alive," he said then. "I've never told ye different, have I? I told ye she was stayin' away for her own reasons."

"Yes, you did." Relief cascaded through her; she wouldn't have to give anything away. Her throat ached from the strain.

"But ye were there, helpin' Aelfwyn?" He shook his head, eyes wide with admiration.

I'm a cheat. I wasn't there alone. I can't claim the credit.

But, his tears had dried. That gave Kay a glimmer of joy.

"I was only there until Gwynedd slipped from your arms. What happened after that? What did Galfride do?"

"Ah, he slithered away like the snake he be," Baird said.

She settled next to him against the warehouse roll-up door. "So, the rest left? Just walked out of the caves, unharmed?"

Baird rested his head back. He looked exhausted. "Nay," he said, eyes closed. "They be in th' tower at Llandadarn Fawr. They never left."

She sat forward. "That can't be." She edged her knee away from glass shards on the pavement. "They helped bring down the barrier. She heard their chanting. It reverberated on the walls." Her voice rose in disbelief as she stared at him. "Wait, none were there? Not even Aelfwyn?" She thought of the tiny, old woman holding that cable of electric energy stretching down from their shelf, breaking the invisible barrier Galfride had held strong for years.

A couple of men in long, filthy coats entered the alley, digging in worn paper bags. They eyed them as they approached.

She lowered her voice. "Are you telling me none of you were there in the caves?"

The men slowed. Their leathery faces had the reddish-brown tone of daily exposure to the elements. Did they see Baird, or did they think she was talking to herself? They passed on by.

Baird watched them. Then he said, "Just Duff and I were there in our bodies. Duff's gone on t' th' silver mine." He looked thoughtful as she processed this. Then he asked, "Aelfwyn drew y' there? How did that come about? Did ye jest find yerself there?"

"I found a drawing I'd made of Galfride."

A sour look passed over Baird's face. "Ye drew *him*?"

She shrugged, defensive. "I don't know why. I don't even remember doing it." *An artist can draw whatever she wants*. Still, her heart sped up. Was it jealousy? Or just pure hatred?

"And then?" he asked.

Telling the story without going into forbidden territory exhausted her. "Then I found myself on the shelf."

Baird leaned his head back again, eyes unfocused. "Mayhap Kyna sent her power through ye, connectin' with Aelfwyn from wherever she be." He brought his head forward, turned to her. "Tha's it, most like." He looked satisfied with his idea.

She was, too.

He watched her face, and then said, "It's all right." Now she was sure he read her inner turmoil. "If ye know ought else, it's best ye don't tell me. I'll know when I need t' know." He sprang up and held out a hand to her. She took it and pulled herself to standing. The sun chose that instant to send a ray through the clouds on its way toward the horizon and sunset. It glowed on his beautiful face, his golden-brown eyes. Wind lifted strands of his hair and tossed them. He gave Kay one of his dawn-breaking smiles.

The crystal vibrated against her leg.

He kept her hand, and they walked out of the alley onto Alder and away from town. She did not want to bring up the topic they'd left, now that late-day sun hit sweetly landscaped yards, and Baird's hand, strong in hers, warmed her. They strode on a while before he spoke. "Will ye' come back with me?"

This took her off guard. She wanted to be with him whenever possible. Her mind scanned over prospects, wondering how many times she could pop back and forth in one week without damage.

"When ye came t' our time with news o' Gwynedd, ye reminded Hamelyn greatly o' his ma, and he liked it, seein' ye there. He's been playin' that tune, travelin' down t' th' jetty where y' appeared."

This touched Kay. She recalled Sophie, drawn by a handsome young Welsh musician. "Are you sure he didn't start doing that before I came?"

"I'm certain. Come with me." His eyes bore into hers with incandescent allure.

"Kyna might be back now," she forced herself to say.

"If she be there, she'll want t' thank ye."

She thought of the awkwardness. It was one thing for Kay to slip inside Kyna's psyche, at her invitation, quite another for her to come into Kyna's home with Baird, after all that had happened. Granted, she'd been missing for years. But now?

Baird studied her. "I donna think she be there. She'll need t' hide until we figure out a plan t' deal with...him. And besides, you're part o' this now." He tugged at her hand. "Come."

Kay looked around at the waning daylight. Intermittent pedestrians and a few cars passed.

Baird stepped into a shaded archway formed between a fruit tree and a parked van. He pulled her to him. She rested her head on his chest and gave in.

Chapter 29

Baird and Kay held hands facing Kyna's house, backed by night sky. Smoke rose from the stone chimney, sending the aroma of burning peat. Slivers of golden light glowed along the edges of hide-covered windows. The house's energy seemed to permeate the very ground under their feet.

A light mist touched her face. Then thunder cracked and rain pelted down. They ran for the stairs, laughing. Before they entered, Baird let go of her hand. Hesitating only an instant, he unlatched the front door. It swung open on leather hinges and they entered. Hidden behind Baird, Kay pressed the door shut against the weather.

The scene inside was peaceful: Hamelyn wrote in a leatherbound book—she thought it was the one Kyna gave him at the Solstic Faire. Duff whittled, and Aelfwyn spun. The hounds' chins rested on Hamelyn's boots. All eyes turned their way. None looked surprised to see Baird. He pulled Kay from behind him and all eyes widened. Hamelyn sprang up, expression shifting, as on the jetty. His elation at the thought of his mother faded, but, recognizing her, he swiftly schooled his features into a polite, welcoming smile. He greeted his father, "Da," then to me, more shyly, "Greetin's, Mistress."

Aelfwyn glanced up with misted eyes, then returned to the yarn forming in her fingers as it stretched onto the whirring spindle, her feet pumping, her lips moving. She seemed only partially aware of her surroundings.

Baird threw off his cape, shook it, and hung it on a peg. "Evenin', son. Duff." He clapped Hamelyn's shoulder. "*Gwrachod*, Aelfwyn." He gave the honorific for a magic-working elder woman and nodded to her.

Kay stood, wet tunic clinging. He urged her toward the fire.

Duff pushed his bulk out of the chair and approached them, glowering.

"We had her, di'n't we? We had Gwynedd, and then...wha' happened to m' niece?" he yelled, his eyes never leaving her. "And who be she?"

By his look, he blamed me for her disappearance. His massive shoulders towered over Baird who was tall himself for that era. Duff's brows, thick red tufts, bunched over penetrating blue eyes that glared at her.

"Duff, meet Dove," Baird said.

"She be familiar. Why do she appear like Kyna?"

"Y' met her at Samhain. Wi' me." Baird faced the giant calmly.

Duff's brows rose. He appeared to ponder. Then he recalled. "I thought ye be Kyna," he said, accusingly. "I thought Kyna had returned t' us. I was that happy on Samhain." He turned away, disgusted.

"She also be the spirit we sent out o' Kyna," Baird added. He bent to add a log to the fire.

Kay glanced at Aelfwyn who watched the scene with hooded eyes as she worked.

Like a bull deciding which way to attack, Duff huffed

a few times. "She be that spirit, be she?"

Kay supposed he needed someone to aim his fury at. Yet anger kindled in her breast at the injustice. After all, she had been called by his sister and helped break the barrier to free Gwynedd. She stood taller, ready to set the record straight with all her five-foot-seven.

Baird squeezed her shoulders. "Peace, Duff," he said. "Dove brings news ye'll be wantin' t' hear. Sit and we'll tell ye."

"Da', her name be Kay," Hamelyn said, quietly.

Baird looked at his son, then at her.

"I know it from me ma," Hamelyn said.

"'Course y' do, lad," Baird said. "Kay." He tried the name awkwardly.

"Why do she favor Kyna in her look?" Duff asked again, reluctantly returning to his chair, his furious steam waning.

"Let's all sit and hear her story. 'Tis no' much but 'tis somethin'." Baird's eyes strayed to Aelfwyn as if for permission to tell it. She bent over her task.

Kay guessed Aelfwyn would stop her if she said too much.

Baird dragged a chair from a corner and set it close to the fire for her. Then he settled on the bench by Hamelyn.

Uneasy that she'd brought tension to a calm, familial scene, Kay sat.

Baird began the tale, filling them in on what he guessed about Kyna, that she must have helped from a distance.

"Ye deserted us outside the caves. I was fearful fer ye," Duff said.

"This witch pulled me away." Baird looked at me proudly.

So, I did draw him with the stone, she thought with excitement. At the same time, she registered the responsibility of such a power and how it could have compromised the situation.

"I was stayin' close, tryin' to watch for Galfride," Baird went on. "To get a sense of Gwynedd, if she be still in the caverns. I dared not enter the cave and risk bein' found by him. In fact, I thought Galfride might detect my spirit, even outside." He slammed a fist into his hand. "Gods, how I hate skulkin' about and not confrontin' the *dyhiryn*." Though the Welsh word was unfamiliar to her, he said it with such venom, Kay could easily guess its meaning. Lout or the like.

Aelfwyn's eyes came up. She watched him intently.

"I did no' find anyone there," said Baird. "Not anyone. Curse him." His voice caught. He sat seething, glaring into the fire. Then he took a deep breath and continued. "I though' he must ha' gone somewhere with m' girl. There're many ways through the Hautes-Alpes. He might ha' gone toward Saxony land. But he might ha' just had a shield 'round her." He paused, said, "I was drawn then, t' Dove's time."

Reddening, Kay looked down. Here were Kyna's son, her brother, and her teacher in the healing ways. She had drawn Kyna's mate to her. Aelfwyn's eyes rested on me now. Hamelyn appeared unsure where to look and kept his eyes mostly on his book, though clearly he listened. Duff was on the edge of exploding.

"I found myself in a most uncouth byway," Baird went on, "lined with dyin' plants. The only denizens were an odd pair o' men, lookin' like they'd come off the desert and a three-turn fast. Place smelled like Machynllydd after the faire."

Hamelyn smiled appreciatively.

Baird grew serious again. "Dove found me there, and she—" he looked from Hamelyn to Duff— "told me Kyna were in the caves, helpin' Aelfwyn."

"She were there?" Duff burst out. "Helpin'?"

"And she called Dove to her to help as well. With The Thirteen, they broke the barrier."

Hamelyn's eyebrows shot up, and he leaned forward with interest.

Baird turned to her.

Kay nodded and looked over to the old woman. Her eyes had taken on a predatory sharpness, her expression clouded and dimmed, as though she turned inward. She must have been doing her spiderweb thing in order to see into Galfride's caverns. She closed her eyes a moment, then opened them. "It's all right. They're all three safe. Kyna. Branwyn. Gwynedd."

A massive sigh went around the room.

"Will someone jus' tell me what's goin' on?" Duff demanded, flinging the knife he'd been whittling with to the floor by his immense boots, where it stuck.

"I still don' know everythin'," Baird said, his voice timbred to placate the overwrought giant. "We mustn't know where they be. Is that not right, *Gwrachod*? Ye be keepin' it secret, t' help her."

"T' help her? What be wrong with us helpin' 'er?" Duff shouted. "What be wrong with me knowin' if my sister be dead or alive?"

"Peace, Duff," Aelfwyn said. "Y' know we tried—The Thirteen—t' find Gwynedd. Ye recall The Thirteen decided the two women—Kyna and her twin here—ha' a unique shared power. Kyna only heard Gwynedd callin' after Kay been in her spirit, then were pulled from 'er. I'm no' clear on which was the decidin' factor, the bein', or the pullin'. In any case, Kyna worked out how t' take Galfride by surprise. If we c'd reach Gwynedd, we c'd break the barrier. We tried on our own, ye recall?" Her piercing eyes glared at Duff.

Reluctantly, he nodded.

"So, Kyna drew Kay's spirit to 'er and, together, we broke the barrier. She sent Gwynedd a mental message the instant she could, the words t' shout, the sign t' make."

"The girl did well," Duff said. Heaving forward with a grunt, he rescued his knife from the floorboard. "I was that proud when she flung him t' the wall." He obviously savored that memory.

"Aye," Hamelyn jumped in, sitting forward. "Galfride was thinkin' she were still under the spell and the barrier up and all." He was clearly excited to be putting the pieces together. "But it drops, like that." He clapped his hands, throwing book and pen to the floor, then retrieving them. His face flushed, but his pleasure was not to be quelled. "Then bah!" He flung himself back in his chair, reenacting how Galfride's head smacked the cave wall. He pretended to drop to his side and pass out, as Galfride had.

"Aye, t'was just so, lad." Duff guffawed, appreciating his nephew's antics. "I c'n see now how the plans ha' come together." He returned to carving. "Kyna been in the caves, then, wi' us? Or some ought else? I dinna see her. Nor sense her."

"They ben on a high shelf above us, hidden from view," Baird answered.

He'd figured out Kyna was there when he glanced up. Not good enough yet at the mind-breaching to enter his thoughts, Kay watched to see if signs of accusation appeared on his face since she hadn't told him that part. But none did.

"Kyna kept herself shielded," Aelfwyn put in. "I helped her, had been helpin' her for months, as she spied on the accursed mage and tried to reach her daughter."

"Hidden from me even?" Duff sounded hurt.

"Galfride could ha' discovered Kyna. He could a' found out from us if we knew," Baird reasoned with the man.

"Tha's how we took him by surprise." Aelfwyn stated what she clearly thought should be obvious.

Duff stared at her, then dropped his eyes to his huge hands which clasped wood and carving tool. Pale shavings curled and fell into a neat heap on the plank floor between his tree-trunk legs. "So, where be they now?" he asked quietly.

"Safe," said Baird firmly, willing the other man to be satisfied.

Duff heaved a sigh. "When can we see 'em?"

There was silence, broken after a moment by Aelfwyn. "We need t' make sure 'tis truly safe. In time, Duff, lad. Ye mun be patient."

Duff struggled to quell his frustrated energy, but could not remain subdued for long. "Y' knew all along, woman." He glared at Aelfwyn, who had returned to her spinning. "Ye' sat in this house wi' us, shared our meals, watched us grievin', and all th' time, ye knew m' sister be alive. Ye said nothin'." His voice broke. His face had turned a dangerous shade of red.

"*Dawelu i lawr, Ab*," the old woman said sharply, her commanding regard forcing him to silence. "Y' would ha' had to keep th' knowledge t' yerself, ye great lummox, or endanger us all. Y' think y' could ha' done that, shielded yerself against *him*?" No longer did she appear a frail old woman, benignly spinning. She sat forward, the force of a

270

molten furnace pouring from her eyes. She added, "Yer magic be in yer hands, son, no' in mind-shieldin', though ye provide a powerful strength when we work together."

The huge man collapsed back in his chair, one great hand wiping across his miserable face. He glared at the fire. His coloring, which had reached a shade of purple, slowly returned to normal.

Aelfwyn pushed up out of her chair, hobbled to the shelves, and brought herbs to throw into a pot hanging by the fire. She edged the kettle closer to the flames with an iron hook, then busied herself poking and stirring the coals. After a bit, she brought Duff a steaming cup. He accepted it with a "ta" and drank.

"The main thing be they're alive and someplace safe. Is that no' righ', *Ddewines*?" Baird checked with Aelfwyn.

She shuffled back to her seat, resettled, and took up her work. Then she said, "Safe for the moment."

"But ye canna' tell us where," Duff grumbled.

"That I canno'. And I think y' do not wan' to carry the burden o' that knowledge, *ab*," she said, using the term for "lad" despite his graying hair.

"Well, we do know we ha' a power among us t' counter Galfride's, when Dove's is combined with Kyna's," Baird said. All three men looked at me with admiration.

It was wrong to take credit, she thought. She'd squatted like a toad inside Kyna, trying to hold onto whatever she could of her sanity. Kay glanced at Aelfwyn, hoping she might offer more explanation. When she didn't, Kay confessed softly, "I'm not sure I was that much help." She had to say it. "I couldn't have built that triangle myself. I nearly panicked that my heart might rip apart."

Baird winced at the image.

Kay gave a sheepish smile. As the others mulled it over,

Kay imagined Aelfwyn and the Thirteen holding the power in the French Alps caves from hundreds of miles away in Wales.

The storm had abated, both in the mood and the weather. Duff heaved himself to standing and announced that he must be off to home and bed. Then he squatted and carefully combed the heap of wood curls from the floor by his chair. He took one long stride and flung the shavings into the fire. He started to collect the dust but Aelfwyn said, "Leave it, son. It'll help t' pick up dirt when I sweep."

We joined Duff near the door. Baird pulled it open and peeked out. Kay heard a light patter of rain. Duff donned his voluminous cape, then, to her surprise, put his great, hot hands on her shoulders. His eyes skimmed over her face with something like affection. He kissed her forehead. Her throat swelled with emotion.

He clapped Hamelyn and Baird on the arms, nodded to Aelfwyn, said, "G'night, Mother," and strode out into the night.

Hamelyn then said good night and left with his book and lantern. Kay heard his footsteps climbing to the loft overhead.

Aelfwyn got up and disappeared behind the draped rugs in the corner of the room where Kay heard her moving around.

Baird turned to her. "Wait here." He went out the back and soon returned with a pile of fresh rushes. He made Kay a bed in the corner opposite Aelfwyn's. Kay helped him cover it with down-filled quilts. Then he brought a soft nightgown, which must have been Kyna's. He left with the lantern, and the room was dark except for the deep red glow smoldering where the fire had been banked. She sat on the edge of the bed, waiting. After a while, when Baird did not return, she put on the nightgown and, surprisingly tired, climbed between the covers, trying to remember the last time she'd eaten. Oh yes, lentil soup at Headlands Café with Jarl.

Kay breathed in the scent of sweet, fresh grasses mingled with the pleasant aroma of burning peat, overwhelmed by the way the evening had ended, with the men's admiration. The only sounds were coals cracking intermittently and light snuffles as the hounds settled into sleep. She pulled the down pillow under her head. As her lids fluttered shut, she made out Baird's figure padding across the room. He perched next to her, leaned close, and whispered in her ear, "I hope this is no' too disagreeable for ye. It's no' as soft as your sleepin' arrangement."

"I'm happy to be here," she whispered back. "And the bed's lovely."

Baird slipped a hand under her hair, cupped her neck, and gave her a tender kiss, barely brushing her lips. "May yer dreams be sweet," he said, barely audible.

She was aware of the old woman in the corner. Her breathing had grown louder, as though she slept but who knew what a witch could hear in her sleep or seeming slumber?

Baird hesitated, then left. The touch of his hand tingled on her neck.

She lay awake until the coals stopped crackling and beyond, alone, very far from her world.

Chapter 30

Next day, Baird and Kay followed a rutted track across the road. They passed Duff's neat stone house, snuggled into the hills. When they came over a rise, Kay recognized the rounded hill we'd climbed at Samhain. The standing stones stood out against the sky.

"Can we go up there?" She wanted to see the view she'd seen that night, the scene of her painting.

She was surprised by the vehemence with which he said, "'Tis no' th' time t' be there."

She studied his face. "What time would that be?"

"'Tis near Beltaine, lass! Fae spirits be about. Come."

He pulled her with him down a narrow path. Woods opened out into open countryside enchanted with spring. Streams burbled and baby lambs cavorted in meadows sprinkled with wildflowers. Baird showed her where Kyna and Aelfwyn picked medicinal plants. He pointed out some Aelfwyn would appreciate and demonstrated which parts to harvest. They returned to the house, arms full. Aelfwyn accepted the freshly picked herbs with a pleased crinkle around her eyes. Kay imagined she didn't make the steep climb much anymore.

In the evening, they gathered for supper. After, they

sat by the fire. Kay asked Aelfwyn if she might study one of the books from the apothecary, and Aelwyn willingly agreed. She selected a volume and laid it carefully on her lap, admiring the drawings as she tried to comprehend the spidery strokes of the ogham that labeled them. She made notes on scraps of homemade paper Aelfwyn provided, while Baird and Duff talked quietly. Hamelyn went to work in his bound book.

After a while, Baird brought out his harp and played for them, singing sweet songs. When no one was looking, his eyes lingered on Kay. At those moments, she imagined his arms around her. An hour or so after sunset, Duff left for home. Hamelyn and Aelfwyn retired. Baird repeated his tender goodnight at her bedside, but this time he donned his cape and left the house.

Next morning, Baird paced, restless. Kay wondered if it was her or if he just couldn't bear the indoors for long. At mid-day, a messenger rode up and asked for him. When he eagerly gathered his harp, it was a relief. He gave her a cursory peck on the cheek and left with the young rider without explanation, the door clattering shut after him, and the horses' hooves receding down the road. She wished she could be with him on his travels, see him sitting by a fire in the woods, laying out his bedroll. She wanted to watch him play his harp at court. She also thought she'd see his true nature revealed in the wilds on a journey away from houses and towns.

Deserted and unsure how to spend her time, Kay went in search of Aelfwyn. Soon, the healer woman had her making herb blends. She sat at the long apothecary table, surrounded by measuring and cutting tools, mortars and pestles, ground powders, and instruments whose uses she did not yet fathom. She watched her, fascinated, as she consulted the many books on the shelves. She seemed to read Roman letters along with the ogham and runes with equal ease.

She fulfilled the role of apprentice the best she could, hoping some of Kyna's knowledge would give her at least a modicum of adeptness. For her part, Aelfwyn accepted Kay as her assistant as if it were the natural order of things. She gave explanations in a rasping drone, her sharp eyes watching closely.

"Then ye place only the slightest bi' o' burdock int'... No, not that much, girl. Only a pinch." She handed over a dried branch and told Kay to drop the tiny leaves into the mortar until the mixture was a knuckle high.

She helped label the herbs and roots that added to the shelves crammed with containers of every description: covered pots sealed with wax, wood boxes, thick blown-glass jars, and carved stone urns with stoppers. Aelfwyn praised her hand as she learned how to form the ogham. The elder's gnarled fingers had trouble holding the quill pen, which made her lines shaky. Kay longed to learn more from her about the ogham. She knew the lettering—like twigs growing off tree branches—was based on the Druids' respect for plants and all things in nature, which they held sacred. The letter associated with the rowan tree was two downward-slanted marks. The letter also designated a goddess, a bird, and a way of being, similar to the runes, with complex symbolism.

But her questions met with an impatient "Ge' on with it, girl. Tha' be *cherw*." She showed her the strokes for the label and held her hand as she ciphered it. A fire blazed on the north side of the room. She settled among pots and baskets, filled with healer supplies. More hung from hooks on the walls and ceiling. They watered the plants that twined along the shelves and around high windows. Soon, she had learned many of their names.

One of the plants she and Baird had brought back was purslane. He explained that he'd brought it from Gaulish lands for Kyna to plant. He'd kept it in wet leathers all the way. "It be special. See the color? No' common in our part o' the land. She's been cultivatin' it, tryin' it here and there. Seems t' be takin'."

"What's it good for?"

"Good for? Ah, that be one magical plant. It ha' many uses. Aelfwyn'll tell you."

Later, Aelfwyn explained that it could be used for protection against unwanted magick. The herb was also used for cleansing and purifying, to keep away nightmares, and to help in trance work. "M' dear, let's jest pull off one bit fer the garden." At the back of the house, she pointed out where to plant it. She had difficulty bending, so Kay knelt and burrowed the young shoot, with its rich red stems, into soft wet soil.

Back in the apothecary, she took up a bar of dark-red chalk and colored in her sketch of the plant, then labeled it, and indicated its position in the garden. At mid-afternoon, Aelfwyn prepared to make her rounds, caring for patients in the village. Loaded down with packets they'd made together, she handed Kay a list of tasks to accomplish while she was gone, brief missives in her shaky writing. She eyed it skeptically.

"Do you want me to come and help?" Kay asked. "At least carry your baskets?"

"Nay. I'll do a bit o' visitin' along the way. Yer time'd be better spent here," she responded from the doorway.

She watched Aelfwyn amble down the front walk and imagined her stopping off for secret meetings with other witches in town. Then she studied her list. Inadequate to pursue any of the tasks alone and unguided, she returned to the apothecary. Instead of starting in on the assigned duties, she turned to the bookshelves to peruse the bindings.

Kay calculated about ten minutes had gone by in her time, based on her first visit, though perhaps it made a difference being in her own body rather than living in Kyna's. Oz would not even notice her absence, as long as she did get home. She should give Jarl a key next time, just in case... She shook off that line of thinking. Of course, she would always return. And Oz had a cat door. He could hunt if need be.

She chose a thick volume with a leather casing that smelled of pine resin. Tassels hung from several silky place markers, and the cover had bright, ornamental writing. She ran her fingers over the tooling. It must have come from travels on the mainland. Inside the front cover was a legend with archaic forms of French, Gaulish, Latin, Frankish, Roman and Cyrillic letters. This strange combination ignited her curiosity, and she carried it to the desk under the single low window that faced the out buildings. She longed to know more about the enigmatic woman with this impressive ancient library.

She sat and held the heavy book, trying to imagine where Kyna, Gwynedd, and Branwyn were, and how they spent their time in hiding. She wondered if Kyna had Aelfwyn's gift of sight, her scrying abilities, allowing her to watch the house. Surely, as the old woman's student, she must. She might be watching Kay at that very moment.

She shrugged and carefully laid the book on the desk. Taking a deep breath, she exhaled, and opened it. Past the legend, with its stiffer leaves, came creamy pages. She suspected vellum by the delicate animal pungency, a pleasant muskiness. Something slipped from the center. It was an insubstantial set of onionskin sheets stitched together with embroidery thread as fine as a spider's skein. Concerned they might disintegrate at her touch, she lifted the golden-brown sheets. Light came through them. With utmost care, she turned the top paper. Inside were beautifully rendered drawings of hands—open palms with individual ogham letters marking each segment of the fingers and around the palm in inks of varied hues, color-coded to match entries along the sides. As she turned the pages, she came upon other symbols entirely unfamiliar to her, but she had the sense that they were of the Wanderers or Romani.

Thrilled, she made herself stop and gaze out the window. She knew the Romani had ancient history in Wales. They had developed at least one unique tongue there—Welsh Romani—as well as secret dialects. Could these sheets contain the hand signs she'd seen Kyna and Talaitha exchange?

She heard sounds of lutes and mandolins drifting through the open window and saw Hamelyn in his workshop fitting together pieces of a fiddle at a high bench. Duff's laughter bellowed from inside the shop. Visiting musicians passed back and forth from their camps in the wildflower-sprinkled fields that stretched toward the sea. Gulls circled and cried. The scent of honeysuckle vines wafted in. She brought her attention back to the delicate pages, which she held lightly at the edges for fear of her fingers transferring corrosive oils onto detailed etchings that decorated the borders.

A presence behind her made her jump. She slid the volume forward to cover the translucent pages, and turned, saying, "Kyna?" She scanned the room, saw nothing. She listened, holding her breath.

Hoof beats sounded at the side of the house. Kay waited, carefully sliding the thin pages back to the center of the book. Baird rode into view, smiling and singing. He was in far better spirits than when he'd left, giving her a pang, that her being there had not created that mood in him. Whistling, he jumped from his horse, then turned toward the apothecary window, as though aware of her watching. He grinned and, lifting a hand to his lips, blew her a kiss. "Dove! How be you?"

She blew a kiss back. Sawing and sanding stopped at the sound of his shout. The others came out to greet him. They stood chatting, so she pulled the book toward her and opened to the first vellum pages. She tried to call upon knowledge of the languages, and longed for reference volumes from her university office, now boxed up. Glancing out, she saw Baird lead his horse into the stable. The rest returned to their activities.

Duff passed through the yard, wood piled in his arms. The sun moved toward the horizon. Time for setting up the bonfire. The *coelcerth*, bonfire of May Eve. The great redhaired man dumped his load in the clearing to the side of the house. He crouched and rubbed two sticks together over wood shavings—a sacred ritual. People all over the Isles would put out the fires from the past year and light new ones built from nine sacred woods. The night before, she'd tried to guess the nine, wondering if they'd be the same as she collected at home. Hamelyn laughed and helped her recite them, as from a children's nursery rhyme: "Oak, hawthorn, and birch. Elder, ash, and rowan. Holly, willow, and yew."

A spark flew out and took. Duff blew to coax it further. A truly new fire. Every family would keep a piece of it, taking home a coal in a brazier.

Villagers arrived carrying baskets of breads and other foods, casks swinging from wood handles. Hamelyn and the other musicians came out to join those already playing. If she leaned forward, she could see it all through the narrow window.

The hairs on her neck prickled. Again, she sensed a malevolent presence. A light breeze, almost like a breath, moved across her skin. Kay jerked around but saw nothing.

Maybe she wouldn't wait for Baird to come get her. She'd hoped for a moment alone with him, had imagined he might at last take her in his arms, savored the thought of some brief intimacy. But the apothecary was making her edgy. She started to stand and return the book to its high shelf. Shock ran through her arm and she froze. She could not move a muscle. Galfride's face appeared at the corner of her vision, grinning. His malicious eyes gleamed. Never in her wildest imaginings had she thought to see him in this house, in this apothecary, at the base of the tower. Where were the protections?

She remained petrified. Galfride knelt by her chair. Activity bustled outside, but she could not cry out. Only her heart moved, in a wild, trapped hammering.

Chapter 31

Galfride's face hovered inches from Kay's. His hand touched her arm, and an enervating charge again shot through her. Baird was so close, just across the yard. She wanted desperately to shout. But she could not. Paralyzed, she could only sit still. Galfride forced her to turn toward him by the will he imposed with his grip on her arm.

She'd seen him when she'd been inside Kyna's spirit and he'd snatched her from the faire, as well as in his caverns with Gwynedd, and he'd looked like a madman, eyes bloodshot and crazed. Now, with his face close to hers in daylight, he appeared beautiful: fierce and terrifying, yes, yet also dynamic and intensely sensual. Was this a glamour? His skin, almost Mediterranean, purpled lightly at the edges of his eyelids. Shadows from a day's growth hollowed his cheeks. His crimson lips stretched in a smile over teeth that overlapped slightly at the front—somehow sexy, and strangely familiar. Like Ian's, she realized. There was a slight resemblance, though their coloring was different, Ian's hair light brown, eyes pale blue, Galfride's hair dark, curled into his neck. His eyes were shapely, a lustrous chocolate-brown.

Only in her deepest reaches did she protest, her gut churning with anger and helplessness as Galfride took her mind where he wanted. He poured in a steady stream of vivid images, of him standing close to Kyna, nearly touching, in a richly furnished library. A torch in a wall sconce pooled light on them as on elegantly bound books that stretched in rows. Was this a real memory? In their late teens, they gazed into each other's eyes, intensity snapping, longing vibrating through them.

They were lovers. She watched, astounded.

Then she was in Kyna. She smelled leather, old parchments, and aromatic smoke from a fire popping nearby. Its heat warmed her legs. Her boots pinched, making her shift position to find comfort. Galfride drew her closer. Her chest burned with desire. His lips approached. She was breathless, giddy. She wanted his kiss.

"Come, Kyna." His mouth nearly touched hers. "Ye know I love ye." His dark, almond shaped eyes shone through curving lashes. His face, taut with passion, looked carved, a perfection of lines. He was something to behold, irresistible.

"I belong to Baird." Her voice was low and husky. "Ye know that." Her conviction was lacking.

"Baird's no' comin' back," Galfride said, through clenched teeth.

Kyna took a startled breath and stepped back, but he pressed her to him, his hot hand spread into her back.

More sweetly, he wheedled, "Ye ken it, Kyna, don't ye? He's been gone t' the mainland—how many moons is it? That be where he wants t' be. No' here. He'll never want to stay here. But us? We're different."

"Then I'll go to him there," Kyna whispered, her strength dissolving.

Galfride perceived it, too. "You and I have a future here, Kyna. A great one."

Hadn't he said the same words to her at the Solstice Faire? No wonder her emotions held paradox. Kay had wondered why she wasn't entirely livid even though she'd fought Galfride off. She understood now the mixture contained old passion.

His voice was strong and confident. His hands at her back drew her tight to his chest, and his lips hovered tantalizingly over hers.

Kay's heart pounded. Yet a force, playing beneath her consciousness, pulled at her. In some distant place, she fought it. She knew if she gave in, something terrible, irreversible, would happen. But the thought was so murky, hidden under the blanket of his spell.

Suddenly the vision broke. She was again at the desk in the apothecary. Galfride's face struggled, as if battling an invisible force. His fingers clenched tighter. It hurt, and she cried out, trying to free herself.

He disappeared, evaporating from where he'd knelt.

She clutched her chest, gasping for air. Then she heard a hoarse breath from across the room. Aelfwyn sagged against the doorjamb, her cape's hood still up as if she'd rushed back from her errands.

Kay exhaled with profound relief and stood shakily, then hurried to Aelfwyn. "Are you all right?"

The old woman nodded, brow furrowed.

Ashamed over the recent tryst with their arch nemesis, Kay wondered how much Aelfwyn had seen. Did she know she'd gone along, been giving in to him? A maelstrom of emotions tumbled in her gut. She held out her hands to Aelfwyn. "Thank you," she said, and grimaced at the dampness between her legs, result of being a party to

Galfride and Kyna's heady connection in the library of...where? A castle perhaps? There had been wealth in the wall sconce and rug, the quality books and polished wood.

He'd left her partly under his spell. Her mind was not completely clear. Terror and confusion remained, the guilt of the abused.

Aelfwyn looked pale and worn.

"You should sit," Kay urged.

"Let us join th' others. They're gatherin' now. I believe we need fresh air. Don't you?" Her eyes, tired, yet still filled with potent energy, peered into Kay's, studying her fiercely. She urged her out of the room and down the hall toward the outer door.

Tainted, as though Galfride's influence remained her, she wondered how she could be trusted around good people? She allowed Aelfwyn to coerce her along. Pushing the back door, she heard cheery sounds. Across the yard, the workshop doors stood open, exposing a shadowed interior.

To the side of the house, Duff fanned the growing bonfire. Village folk dragged logs to sit on, and settled in with blankets and baskets of food. The spring breeze had settled down with the deepening twilight.

Baird was nowhere in sight. She drew back inside. She needed answers, assurance, an idea of what danger they might all be in.

"*Iachawr*," she said to Aelfwyn, using the polite term for healer. "I thought the house was defended."

"T'was. And t'will be again." She pointed to torches moving at intervals along the edges of the property, slowly and steadily. "See them movin' sunwise 'round the house? They re-make the protections. Nothin' has gotten through for a very long while. But 'tis Beltaine, and that be a testy time." She reached up and patted Kay's cheek.

Light illuminated Boldo's face as he passed between the stable and the workshop. He glanced their way and nodded.

"Galfride thought I was Kyna." Kay wore the other woman's skirt, her bodice and muslin blouse, her shawl. Her hair was plaited like Kyna's and was a similar shade of auburn with a few silver streaks at the front.

"He might ha' been too busy forcin' his thoughts int' ye t' take heed o' who ye really are. Just like a man." Aelfwyn cackled, then sobered. "Even powerful mages can be careless." She took Kay's hand in hers. "What did he say to ye?"

At her touch, Kay quickly pushed the attraction to the mage behind the ice wall. But an embarrassed flush warmed her cheeks. "He reminded her of their love." She wondered if Aelfwyn had known about it.

She nodded.

"Do you think he planted something in my mind? Something permanent?"

Aelfwyn tugged her down so that she knelt before her. Then she closed her eyes and pressed her hands to Kay's temples. Kay tried to open her mind to her, but feared she'd discover her own part in the heated seduction.

"Let me go deeper." Aelfwyn lifted Kay's chin so she could look into her eyes. "Close yer eyes and go out o' focus. Let yer thoughts drift. Remember someplace ye loved as a child. Go there with yer mind and see it clearly." Her voice was a hypnotic singsong.

Kay gave up trying to hold thoughts behind barriers as the old woman's voice reached so deep she could not follow. Eyes closed, Kay did as she was told. She was under the weeping willow with her sister. Sunlight dappled through a curtain of bright green leaves. She smelled the earth and tree bark. They were setting up a campsite for their dolls. They had food for them: tiny oyster crackers as hamburger buns, pennies for burgers, toy vegetables and fruits. In a forest made of fruit tree branches her father had trimmed, they set miniature dishes on a doll house table and sleeping bags made of eyeglass covers. They stacked twigs for a campfire.

Aelfwyn's voice brought me back. "Galfride was tryin' t' take ye away. That much our barrier stopped. He could no' draw ye with him. And somethin'...ye were fightin' him. Good fer you, my lamb." She patted Kay's face and encouraged her to rise. "He's left nothin' o' danger in ye. Only attraction. Ye may be vulnerable to him in that way. But that's to be expected. He's always been a compellin' man." She nodded. There was compassion in her expression.

"My thanks, *Iachawr*," Kay said, slightly less filthy inside.

She pointed to a heavy cape hanging on a hook and Kay put it on. Then they descended the steps together, Kay's hand under Aelwyn's arm, crossed the yard and joined the gathering. Rows of local folk surrounded the bonfire, situated well back from the bright glow. They made room for Aelfwyn and Kay on a front log.

The night swiftly grew cold. Kay pulled the cape close and accepted a rug over her lap, grateful to be surrounded by people and not next to the woods crouching at the side of the clearing. Kay searched for Baird. Part of her did not want to be near him. He was sure to sense something. Not spotting him, she studied the country folk in their bulky clothing, ready for the evening's festivities. The faces of the adults looked care-worn, with reddened, chafed skin. The younger ones wore bright clothing, girls with blossoms in their hair, boys sporting cocked hats. Clearly excited, they chattered in clusters.

The Travelers continued to reinforce the protections around the property. They would be safely cocooned again.

Baird appeared and sat next to Kay. She took in his craggy face and gleaming eyes, and turned away. Would they sparkle like that if he knew the sensations she'd recently experienced with Galfride? Even though they weren't her desire, per se.

She had to close off those thoughts. She mustered a smile and turned back to him. Her eyes smarted with unshed tears. Her heart hurt, wanting to wipe the taint from her spirit. Aelfwyn had assured her it was gone but she knew something remained.

"What's happened?" Baird whispered, close to her ear.

His voice, so near, sent a tingling rush through her. But she could not enjoy it, with guilt smothering any pleasure. His dear face, his smell from the road, so good, so familiar, only hurt now.

"How was your trip?" she asked.

Someone handed them mugs of spring wine. She gulped, grateful for the interruption though it was slightly tart. Giddiness dulled her turmoil, and she took another long draught.

"'Oo's this, then?" said a crusty middle-aged man with a mottled red nose, standing near, cocking his head in her direction.

"Cousin o' Kyna," Baird explained easily, as though he'd planned this moment. Not a careless man, she realized, for all his charm and apparent ease.

"Sure do look like 'er," the man said, suspiciously.

Kay thought he might always look that way though,

his features pulled downward; a smile might be an effort.

Baird studied her out of the corner of his eye. The look said, "We're not through. I'll be askin' ye again, later."

"Favors 'er, t' be sure. 'Tis uncanny," said another man, reaching a calloused hand to her. "Finch, I be."

"Glad to meet you." Kay gave him her hand, and he bowed over it decorously.

Duff approached and bellowed, "Ha, Finch, playin' the gen'leman wi' the ladies tonight, are ye'?" Beer sloshed from his mug as he clapped the man on the shoulder.

Relief trickled in. Introductions would soon be over.

"What be yer name?" Finch wasn't finished.

"Ceirwen," Baird answered for her.

Kay glanced at him. The name meant "shining or beautiful deer". She checked his expression to see if he teased, but his look was utterly sober. Was he remembering when Kyna thought she was a deer spirit?

Players struck up a tune. Baird stood. He squeezed her arm, then nodded to Aelfwyn before he strode to the opposite side of the fire to join the musicians. A space had cleared for dancing.

"Ceirwen, be it?" Aelfwyn said, so low only Kay could hear. She offered a bowl of soup that had been passed down the line. "Good choice of name." The elder's eyes held hers a long second with a twinkle in them.

Kay agreed, and hoped she'd remember the name if asked. It was hard to keep her cheeks from flaming when Baird called her Dove. Maybe this would be better.

She accepted a bannock and blackened fish, and devoured it with grateful bites. The food settled her stomach. She stared at the high flames that licked into the now dark sky. Sparks leapt upward toward blazing stars. Kay drew an oat cake from a basket passed down the row. A treat made from spring ewe milk, cubes of freshly made cheese, followed. She savored the flavors with the yeasty coarse-grained bread. The strains of mandolin, harp, and flute filled the air and dancers moved to the tunes. Other elders joined Aelfwyn along the front log, and they prattled away. She was left to her own thoughts. The tension of explaining herself had passed, and she could sink into this flurry of lively celebration.

Boisterous laughter broke out. She turned to see a young man performing handsprings and other acrobatics across the dance area.

A bent, aging man stood and began the singsong of storytelling, "May Eve be a spirit-night"—projecting his voice strong and clear.

Another High Day, or "spirit night" in ancient Wales: Samhain, Winter Solstice, now Beltaine. Just as ancestor spirits cross the veils more easily at those times, she seemed to be drawn by the power of these seasons.

A singer told the tale of *Gwyn*, king of the Otherworld, battling *Gwythr*, another god-king, over the hand of *Creiddylad*. Symbolically, of course, they battled to rule the other half of the year, winter fighting summer for dominance. Two strapping young men played out a battle scene. By the look on some of the children's faces, the fighters' fierceness was convincing.

A wholesome-looking maiden, breasts straining her laced bodice, played the part of the majestic Creiddylad. She wrung her hands at the sidelines until Gwythr, Summer King, won and knocked Gwyn playfully out of the circle. All cheered. The reigning couple broke bread, drank berry wine, and fed each other. They shared bread and wine as well, then formed a long spiral dance that wound around the yard.

Kay watched the line swing close to the dark woods that bordered the land. Those trees were beyond the protections. Was he there? When hands reached to include her in the spiral, she declined. A chill ran through her.

"Ye be safe now, child," Aelfwyn said, leaning close. She encouraged her, and Kay joined the line for a circuit, actually enjoying it, getting caught up in the spirit of the night. After one round, she settled back on the log bench.

Once the moon had set, Aelfwyn stood up. Kay started to follow but she pressed her shoulder. "Stay. Greet the spring in proper." She kissed Kay's forehead.

Kay watched her, accompanied by other elders, head to the back door. On the top step, Aelwyn signaled out into the dark. A Traveler returned Aelfwyn's hand signal, torch held high. They must be conveying that the job was done. Aelfwyn entered the house. Those with the torches left their posts, moving off into the fields dotted with Traveler wagons, lanterns hanging from their roof corners.

Parents carried away their sleeping children. Dancers grew sparse, and Kay realized young couples were leaving. They giggled as they strolled arm-in-arm into the fields or across the road into the hills.

She sat alone as the last song drifted to an end and the players moved to sit by the fire. Baird settled next to her. Someone asked him for news.

"Tryin' t' keep th' Angles from takin' any more o' the Cymry," Baird began and described recent skirmishes over land and castles near the border. Conversations sprang up around them, along with some heated debates.

She whispered, "I'd love to see you sing in a royal hall."

"Would ye, now?" Baird looked at her speculatively.

"Oh...well..." Kay shrugged. "Hardly realistic, is it?"

"Perhaps 'tis," he said, picking bark from a twig. He gave her a quick glance.

A giddy shudder coursed through her. *Would I know how to behave with medieval royalty? I might get my head cut off.* She laughed at herself, until she realized it was a possibility, and exiled the thought immediately.

Conversation dwindled. A final toast went around for abundant harvests. Then the last of the revellers rose. Those leaving for their homes took pieces of the fire, holding them like torches, or pushing coals into braziers. Finally, the fire was dampened. Kay and Baird made for the house. At the back steps, Baird reached for her hand and stopped her.

"What happened earlier?" he asked.

She considered lying but decided on truth. "Galfride came. Into the apothecary. Well, he wasn't exactly there." Kay hesitated. How much to tell? "He thought I was Kyna."

Baird grabbed her shoulders roughly. "Galfride? Here? What happened?"

"He just...showed me things."

He pushed me ahead of him up the stairs and into the house. "Showed ye what, exactly?" he asked as they stood in the dark back hall.

"He wanted to remind Kyna of their past times together. The worst was that he froze her. I couldn't move or call out." She shook with the horror of retelling it.

He wrapped his arms around her. "Poor Dove." He kissed her hair. "We should ha' been keepin' ye safe. I never thought I'd be bringing ye int' harm's way here." He put me away from him. "I mun ride t' Aberffraw in the morn'. Would ye want t' come with me? 'Tis a castle, after all."

The name jolted her. "Is there a library at Aberffraw?" she asked.

"Aye. Quite a lavish one. Why d'ye ask?"

"Does Galfride ever reside there?" she pursued.

"As a matter o' fact, he has. Often. But not for while, I think."

Fate wrapped itself around her and she shivered.

Chapter 32

I n the morning, they ate hot porridge in the front
room with Duff, Hamelyn, and Aelwyn.

"Go with Baird t' the castle?" Aelfwyn looked skeptical. "Do y' know what a castle be? 'Tis a nest of alliances, loyalties, unseen doin's, and duplicitous plannin's."

Baird laughed. "Aren't ye paintin' the picture a might bleak, old woman?" But he turned to Kay. "She be right. Ye sure ye want t' go?"

"On the other hand," Aelfwyn interjected, "there be a lot ye can find out at a castle. If ye must go, keep yer eyes and ears open."

Baird's horse pranced forward as they started into the hills. He jigged sideways, waiting for Kay to catch up. "Now ye be happy, *Aderyn Du*, lad." His horse's name meant blackbird, which fit its color. The horse was not the only happy one. Baird was clearly most joyous on the road.

She wished she could find the excitement when they'd sat by the fire talking of her accompanying him to a castle.

Since she heard the name of the edifice they were going to, she could not shake a sense of doom. Galfride's visit to Kyna's apothecary had left its mark. Seeking comfort, she stroked under the mare's rough mane as she would her cat.

The horse's name, *Niwl y Bore*, meant "Morning Mist", apropos to the fog that rolled over them as they traveled. It briefly obscured Baird. She kicked her steed's sides to catch up.

We descended from the hills into pastures and more woodlands. Soon they could see the flats of the River Dywi.

Baird pointed to the left at a cluster of seaside buildings. "That be Borth, Aelfwyn's town."

Kay pulled on the reins, scrutinizing the place. She might see the very shop that had appeared at the back of Dragon's Lair in Yakota.

"Can we go there?" she asked.

"Aelfwyn's not there." He looked amused. "But we can stop. We be some way from Aberffraw. I wasn't plannin' to get there tonight."

Borth's frontage stretched along a straight shoreline with a low stone wall protecting it from the sea. The main road of the town was lined with May Day booths and a street celebration. Entertainers passed by, including an organ grinder and monkey. The man wore Middle Eastern garb of red and gold. An acrobat did daring feats on a pop-up stage. A Punch-N-Judy-type puppet show inside a curtained wood box drew a crowd of laughing children.

Kay watched for Aelfwyn's yarn shop. She had no idea what it would look like from the outside. When they reached the more crowded part of the frontage road, they stopped and climbed off their horses. Kay unclasped the heavy cape and threw it over *Niwl y Bore's* back as morning sun finally sent warm rays.

"Baird," she called over the noise. "Where's Aelfwyn's shop?"

He pointed to a low, thatched, stone structure. "That be it."

"Can we go in?" she asked, excited. At least one puzzle piece might fall into place.

"They're most-like out at the festivities," he said. But he strode in the direction of the shop.

Sure enough, the gaily painted door was locked. She sagged in disappointment.

"Mayhap on the return. Would ye care fer a currant bun?" Baird suggested.

She nodded. They made their way to a baked goods seller.

The rounded glossy rolls steamed as they broke them open. They bought hot spiced cider from a vendor and perched on overturned crates against a shop wall, watching the May celebration and enjoying soft yeasty pastries. Soon, she stripped off another layer of clothing, down to her shirt. Such a sunny morning was not to be taken for granted in Wales at any season, and she soaked it in.

When finished, they rinsed their mugs at a water stand, tied them to their waists, and climbed back onto their mounts. Kay was disappointed but let it go.

They traversed mud flats dotted with sea birds, and crossed a bridge over the Dywi. From there, the coastal road hugged the shore for some time. As the sun approached the horizon, she asked if they were going to look for a place to camp.

"I thought we'd stay at an inn tonight," Baird said.

"Are you sure? I don't mind roughing it." Kay had for so long pictured Baird sitting alone by a campfire. She still wanted to sit next to him by the fire and quietly talk, the two of them, staring into the coals. On the other hand, a medieval inn might be fascinating.

They stayed at a rustic place. No one asked questions when she and Baird took a room together. Her inner thighs stung from prolonged horseback riding; despite the layers of clothing, and she was glad to stop.

Their room at the top of a narrow stairway had the smell of old cabbage, but at least she noticed no bed bugs.

The next morning's ride brought them to an isle, viewed across a channel. Barges lined the mainland shore.

"We take one o' these to 'The Dark Isle', *Ynys Môn*," Baird explained.

"Sounds mysterious." It looked bright and sunny now, but uneasiness returned at the thought of the castle where Galfride sometimes dwelt. "Aberffraw is up there?" Kay studied the land across the water, shading her eyes.

"That's where it be." Baird stopped by a raft.

The burly bargeman dickered over prices for delivering parcels—chickens in carriers made of sticks lashed with reeds—and the like. When he came to them, he waved Baird aboard.

"Telynor, what be the news?" he asked Baird, addressing him as "harper" as he pushed off. His red nose dripped, and he wore his dark cap pulled low.

Baird leaned his back to the rail and shared stories with the bargeman. Kay recognized names from frequent conflicts between Wales and neighboring England. She faced out and watched the approaching landmass, only half-listening.

Sea birds circled, and spray from the channel waters salted her face. They skirted along the shoreline to the west until they pulled into a sheltered cove with a stretch of beach. A thin river ran into the sea. A scattering of shanties and a rough dock crouched at the base of the hill next to a stretch of beach. They led the horses off. The ferryman again refused fare. Baird chuckled and tucked the coin bag back under his belt. He had bartered with news. They climbed a tiny road that was barely more than a path. A rivulet appeared and disappeared in foliage along the steep incline.

Topping the hill, they mounted their horses and rode the short distance into Abyrffraw, next to the River Ffraw. There, they stopped for savory pie and elderberry wine. Then they started up the hill road. The castle came into sight, looming high above. It was set in hill folds that obscured it from the mainland. They proceeded upward as the sky darkened toward dusk, sending long shadows toward them.

Baird paused for Kay to come up next to him. "Want to go ahead o' me?" he offered.

She glanced back down the road. "Why? Did you see something?"

"Nay, I just want t' watch ye from behind." He wagged his eyebrows as she started forward.

"That can't be all that exciting."

"Ah, ye'd be surprised," he said.

She quirked a brow and kicked forward.

Rounding a final curve, they encountered a guardhouse topped with elaborate stone carvings of gargoyles. The lower walls rose, sheer. She stared upward. A helmeted head appeared in a tiny window. Apparently, they recognized Baird, for the gate lifted. They clattered through. The gate clanged behind them, metal spikes into stone. They coaxed their horses over a series of timber bridges that crossed deep ravines. The fortress now dominated their view. A last steep slope took them to an inner gate in a stone wall that wrapped around out of sight.

They rode side-by-side through a high arch, between immense wood doors that opened into a bustling courtyard: the inner bailey. As they slid from their horses, her knees buckled, unaccustomed to days of riding. She grabbed hold of straps on the mare's back to stop from falling as she observed the lively scene. Compared with the silent road in the hills, the courtyard exuded life. Young and old folk in rough country clothing hurried past, pushing carts, carrying sacks, and shouting. Animals bellowed and bleated as they walked their horses into the melee.

Two young lads ran up to them. One took hold of their horses' reins and Baird ruffled his hair. "Torf, lad, ye've grown half a hand since I last saw ye."

The boy, probably twelve, ducked his head, cheeks flaming, as he eyed the bard with awe. The other, slightly older, helped Baird pull their bags from the horses before Torf led them away.

"What's yer name, boy?" Baird asked the older one who remained to help carry their bags.

"Leof, Sire Bard."

"Have ye just come t' the castle, Leof?"

"Aye, sir. M' da has been recent called t' th' guard. Will ye follow me?"

They passed through a number of courtyards and climbed slowly until the boy opened a door in a row of narrow cottages built against a wall on the outer side of the cobbled road. He set Kay's bags inside and offered her an enormous key.

"Thank ye, son." Baird handed him a coin.

The solemn boy took it with a bow and left us, though he grinned as he ran to join friends who peeked around the corner of a building.

Baird stepped through the doorway and looked around. "Rest, Dove. I'll come fer ye in a while."

"Where are you going? You're not leaving me alone?" Kay followed him in and examined a cold, stone-walled room with sparse furnishings. Narrow windows, cut into the thick walls, faced bulwarks and barren hills under a russet sky.

"They'll expect me to stay close t' th' great hall, where entertainers lodge," he explained. "Believe me, this be better for ye."

"It's all right. I'd just like to know where to find you." She sounded whiny to her own ears.

He shut the door part way and touched her cheek. "Use the crystal if ye need me. I'll go settle my things and be back to take ye t' dinner. They'll want me t' play this evenin', the May Day feast." He glanced out the narrow slits in the wall. "Shall I pull th' curtains shut?"

"No, they're fine. You go ahead. I'll be okay."

He nodded. Outside, he hefted his bags. She stood in the doorway and watched him climb the castle road until, with a wave, he walked out of sight past a square tower.

She closed the thick door and sighed, alone for the first time in days. Though strange, she had to admit, she could use a moment to herself. She sat on the bed, a cot of woven leather straps covered in a mattress stuffed with fresh grasses. Green heather, by the scent. She was learning to discern.

Through the windows, she heard sounds from below. She stepped to a narrow opening and leaned out. She had to lie across the sill to peer downward to the street. It was like watching a play from a balcony. For a while, Kay observed the comings and goings. She could see the roofs of the buildings and animals pulling loads. She wedged herself, sitting, legs pulled up, and took in the vista. Wings of the outer walls extended onto the humped shoulders of the closest hills, with ramparts wide enough for archers to run and perch at slits. Stone structures marked the intersections. Beyond, forest spread down the river valley. The next higher wall to the right was curved, with dark arches. Furtive movement in one of the openings caught her eye.

Aelfwyn's warning about castles came to her. Kay jerked her head back in. Had the movement really been furtive? Or had Aelfwyn made her paranoid?

She went in search of means for lighting before night fell in earnest. Beside the bed, on a side table, sat a lantern. In her travel bags, she'd stashed a fire-starting kit of Kyna's. She fumbled until she lit the wick of the lantern and studied the room. There was a pitcher of water and a bowl on a side table where she could wash up.

Unsure why Baird thought the evening would require rest, she lay on the bed's scratchy wool blanket and tried to relax. She pulled her cloak over her against a growing chill. There was a fireplace with scrappy wood stacked near it, but she didn't know how soon she'd be summoned for supper. She turned on one side, then tried the other. Her mind was too active, full of questions. What if people asked about Kyna? Or thought she *was* Kyna? She wouldn't know what to answer.

What was the worst that could happen? Strange expressions? Executed at dawn?

She knew Galfride could appear at any moment. *Was he here in the castle?*

Maybe tomorrow I can try to find the library. But why? Just curiosity?

Giving up on a nap, she decided to prepare for dinner, first washing off road dirt using the pitcher of water and basin. Then she dragged the travel bags to the bed and spread dresses. Up to now, she'd worn Kyna's plain, serviceable clothing: linen blouses, vests, dark skirts, and unadorned bodices. For this occasion, Baird had selected Kyna's finest. One in particular caught her eye: a velvety dress of deep burgundy with satin panels of a darker red, almost black. Pearl-like beads were stitched along each pleat. The dress cried out to be tried on. She immediately indulged. The neckline scooped to show the tops of her breasts, more than she was used to. She moved Kyna's hand-held mirror around to check the effect and blushed.

It was beautiful. And revealing.

Now, she would stand alone as Ceirwen. "Kyna," she mumbled. "I wish you were here. I'd rather be doing this with you." In medieval clothing, at an old-time court, she would act on her own behalf, without the other woman's wit, poise, or knowledge fit for the times.

Kyna, if you're there, I wouldn't object to you advising me. Help yourself to my mind, my sight, whatever you want. Just make sure I don't make a fool of myself at this dinner. She sent the thoughts into the mirror and wished Kyna's face would look back. Then, propping the reflective glass by the lantern, she applied moisturizer, a lovely scented salve Kyna must have made, and did her best to enhance her eyes with round cakes of indigo and violet clay mixed with oils.

There was a powder of herbs in ground clay fine as porcelain that smelled like rosemary and fennel. She thought it might be a sort of deodorant, though it might also be a deterrent to mites and fleas. That couldn't hurt.

She put some under her arms to gather sweat. Last, she fastened a snood studded with tiny crystals over her plaited hair and added similar crystal earrings and necklace.

She was satisfied with her appearance—at least, what she could ascertain by a final round with the hand mirror.

A knock sounded.

She jumped. "Who is it?" she called.

"'Tis yer escort, m' lady," Baird said, through the door.

She opened, holding the lantern.

He checked her up and down. "Ye look quite fine," he said at last. "Quite fine, indeed." His hair was pulled back neatly. He wore dark, elegant clothing in black and gold. A hat with panels of matching fabric flopped jauntily to one side; a pheasant feather arced to the back.

"Why, thank you," she said, with a brief curtsy. "Will you come in a moment?" She re-entered the room and picked up one of Kyna's stitched handbags. "Do you think it'd be all right to carry this?" she asked Baird.

"Yes," he said soberly, though she thought there was a glint of amusement in his eyes.

She picked up the room key. The golden crystal was in its usual pouch, obscured among the folds of her skirt. She pulled on a forest green cloak with silken lining. "Okay, I suppose I'm ready."

"Ye sound like yer goin' t' the guillotine," he said, brows lifting in question.

She thought the possibility was not entirely remote.

Chapter 33

I 'm worried about people asking me questions," Kay said, as they stepped onto the cobblestone street. She turned and fumbled with the key in the lock. A faint clunk left her uncertain of the results, though the door held when she tried the handle.

"Ye'll be fine. Ceirwen." Baird touched her cheek. He stroked his hand through the air near the door. "That ought to hold it."

She raised a brow.

"I never trust keys," he said, making her feel no more secure. He held out his elbow, and she took his arm. He winked at her as they joined others climbing the hill toward the main hall.

She asked in a hushed voice, "Have you found out if he's here?"

"He's no been to his lodgin's for some time." Baird squeezed her hand reassuringly.

Torches were all that lit the now dark street. She stumbled only a few times as she climbed the uneven cobblestones in Kyna's formal boots.

They approached a tall wall with cornices, towers, and turrets. Horns blared. The assemblage poured in through wide doorways. Carried with the rest, they entered a foyer. Kay caught a glimpse of the great hall, but before she could study the opulent scene, Baird pulled her to one side, letting the tide of guests pass them.

"I mun sit with th' other players. Will ye' be all right on yer own?"

She looked at him sideways. Did she have a choice? She mustered a cheery expression. "Of course." She would not be a pain after she worked so hard to get there. But she had not envisioned navigating the social niceties alone. Aelfwyn had hinted she might hear things not said near a bard. This was all fitting her plan.

The last of the guests filed in, and Baird urged her forward. Putting his head close to mine, he indicated a back corner. "See the redhaired femme with feathers in her green cap?"

"I see her," she said, though her heart sank as she took in the distance from where Baird would be seated near the royal dais and minstrels.

Baird patted her shoulder and slipped into the shadowy corridor. He strode around a corner and out of sight with the harp on his back. This instrument's bag was far less road-worn than the one he usually carried. She contemplated the table she was intended to join and considered bolting back to her room, but she became entranced with the scene before her.

Rows of elegantly dressed aristocrats conversed, their jewels catching the light from hundreds of flames in massive candelabras hanging from heavy beams over the tables. Servants in dark purple and midnight-blue livery scurried back and forth, carrying massive platters heaped with glistening meats and vegetables, pies, and great mounds of twisted breads. The smells intoxicated, and the din nearly overwhelmed her. At the far end, by King An-rawd's high table, great hounds stretched out near temple-sized fireplaces, adding Beowulfian drama to the scene.

Immense tapestries covered the stone walls. Torches waved in intermittent drafts. Higher still, at regular intervals, curtained alcoves with curved railings had the vantage of the entire hall. In the closest one, heavy fabric twitched aside and for a quick instant, eyes peered down at her.

Locating the woman with the feathered cap, she edged away along the wall, not daring to look back. *Ah, Kyna, where are you when I need you?* She made her way past strangers. No one noticed her since servers also traveled back and forth. Arriving at the designated woman's side, Kay was about to touch her shoulder when the woman's head turned toward her. Taking her arm, she pulled her down onto the seat.

"I be Aline. You must be Kyna's cousin. Ye do favor her."

Kay straddled the bench and scrunched her skirt to get her second knee past a short-sighted elderly man who squinted vaguely at her. She gave him a weak smile as she jostled him and landed in place. His bony frame dug into her side, and he shot her a sour, pinched look.

The crowd's elegant clothes held a multitude of pungent body smells. Aline slipped into conversation with her neighbors. Kay listened to a hundred voices. Bursts of laughter rang off the high walls. Soon enough, she would need to make connection. It would be odd to stay silent the whole evening. She decided to tackle Sour Face.

"Hello," she said to him in her best ancient Welsh. Of course, Kyna being the source of her knowing the language, she could not go wrong with the accent. It was having all the vocabulary at hand that posed difficulties on occasion. What Kyna had put in her mind left gaps.

She thought the unpleasant man might not answer but then he spoke. "There's someone been watchin' ye."

Her eyes widened. He'd seen. His attention darted, swift as a tiny bird's flight, to that alcove high above, then back to her. "I know ye not be Kyna, but ye c'd be her twin."

He was full of surprises. Would he keep throwing me curve balls all evening? "Do you know her?" she asked. She needed a friend. She would tread lightly and hope for the best with him.

"Oh aye. I be th' tutor here when she and Baird used t' come t' visit. And that other fella. Won't mention his name. But I know 'bout her disappearance, too." He spoke so low no one else could hear. "So, what be yer story?"

She studied him, a mix of emotions crawling through her. On the one hand, she'd love an ally, and he appeared to be a solid man, a teacher. But who could tell? She didn't want to let down her guard. It seemed a good sign that he didn't like Galfride.

A server set a glass of dark red wine before her. Kay took it up with both hands, eager for a softening of her jangling nerves. She sniffed the bouquet, then let some puddle on her tongue. It hadn't aged quite long enough for her taste, yet it had complexity—smoky, woody. She swallowed and let it take soothe her jitters. She also hoped it might pickle any plague-ridden parasites in the food. She took that time to decide how to answer. "My name is Ceirwen," she said at last. "I'm Kyna's cousin."

"I see." He shot another glance at the wall above them, and dropped his voice even lower. "There'll be trouble fer ye, lookin' like her."

It had already! But she wouldn't share that. "What did

you teach?" she asked. "Or do you still?" She hoped to move all the attention onto him.

He willingly told about the history of Wales—*Cymru* in the native tongue—until steaming platters were set before them. She breathed in over the plate then prodded a slice of savory pie and guessed at the ingredients: mostly potatoes and root vegetables in a rich leek and onion sauce. She started to eat, then checked to see how forks were being held. Matching the overhand grip she saw others use, she tucked in her first bite and explored the flavors.

When she'd taken a few more bites, followed by swallows of wine, she found herself more at ease. Intrigued, she listened to a conversation about a fabric that had recently arrived—the texture never encountered before. People guessed its origin. Kyna would have liked to hear about this. She would have contributed well to the exchange. She pushed aside worry of being less than Kyna and relished a garnish of candied pears, then moved on to a neat pile of baby potatoes and beets, browned and lightly glazed. The tutor tackled his fare with concentration.

Minstrels struck up a tune, and the roar of conversation died down. After a few songs, a true hush fell over the crowd. She craned her neck to see Baird stand, harp poised. He struck a chord, and his voice carried easily. Melodious tones filled the hall. He went from soft ballad to bawdy humor. People called out comments or jokes, and he responded quickly, greeted with uproarious laughter. He was obviously a favorite. There was such an ease and elegance about him, one foot on a stool, as he played and sang, stopping to tell stories.

Movement above his head caught her eye. A curtain twitched in one of the high arches. Was someone watching Baird as well? She studied the crowd to see if others noticed but all listened, enthralled, or chatted with neighbors. She glanced back at the drape, but it hung in place.

Rustling and murmuring traveled through the room. Those sitting further down her table whispered and nudged each other. She realized many focused their eyes on her. She surveyed the hall and tried to figure out what caused the disturbance. On the royal dais, someone leaned and whispered to the prince. He straightened and peered around, calling, "Kyna? Be she here?"

"Kyna!" A shout traveled through the room.

Might there be another Kyna? She could only hope. She looked around to see if someone stood.

"Come gi' us a song. Join Baird like ye used to," said the man from the raised dais. He was young—perhaps in his thirties. His voice and demeanor had the hauteur of royalty. He turned to the minstrels. "Bring Kyna t' join ye fer a song," he commanded Baird. "It be too long since I heard her songbird voice."

Baird started toward her. Now everyone faced her way.

Couldn't he just explain that she was a cousin? She shook her head ever so slightly, eyes beseeching. He continued toward her. As he drew near, he reached out his hand to her. What was he doing? She couldn't sing like Kyna. People liked her voice, but it wasn't strong, not for singing to an entire hall. Slowly, she rose, her cheeks hot from the attention. She climbed from the table as gracefully as she could and followed Baird toward the front, trying her best not to trip on unseen crags in the rough stone floor.

They drew near the raised dais, covered in embroidered cloths shot through with gold threads, draped with flower chains. Silver goblets gleamed with the light from a dozen candles in elaborate filigreed holders. She turned to face the staring throng. To her chagrin, Baird picked up his harp. She'd held some slight hope that he'd explain she wasn't Kyna, though why he'd bring her up there to do that, she hadn't yet guessed. She considered running for the closest exit. Her dinner and wine went sour in her stomach. Kay searched her mind madly for a sense of Kyna—thoughts, memories, anything to draw on—as Baird strummed out a set of beautiful resonating notes.

She didn't know the song. He smiled and brushed his fingers across his harp. His thoughts entered her mind. She willingly let him settle in. His presence immediately calmed her as he began to sing. Without hesitation, she harmonized. The words of the old Welsh song about a mockingbird that turned into a maiden poured forth from them. It was her voice but stronger, carrying across to the farthest reaches of the long hall. She took the lead on the second verse, and at the chorus, Baird harmonized with her. Their voices blended to perfection.

At the end of the song, applause erupted, along with calls for another. She glowed from the admiring expressions and shouts, the enjoyment on the faces of the audience. Baird grinned and started another tune. She did not pause before joining him this time.

At last, the evening's festivities wound down. Deflation ensued as they moved with the crowd out of the great hall and down the cobbled castle road. They called good nights to others who shouted praise of their singing.

She turned to Baird, giddy. "I liked that!"

He grinned. "Didja now? Ye see how it can be?"

She did, indeed. How had it been for Kyna, she wondered, at home raising children while Baird was on the road, performing to admiring audiences like this?

"Kyna has sung like this with you?" It was rhetorical

since the prince had said she had. She wondered why she had not joined him singing at the pub that night in Aberystwyth.

"When I c'd talk her into it."

"She didn't like to?"

"'Tis no' that. Just she'd say she be a healer, no' a bard. That's not her callin'."

"Ah. Do I sound at all like her?"

"Very like," Baird answered, somber. "Now everyone's goin' t' be requestin' ye. I won't be able to let ye go back." He gave me a sidelong glance, with an unreadable expression.

I laughed. "Oh, I think you'll manage without me, with that silver tongue of yours."

"Have I that? A tongue of silver?"

"You do. But you know that."

They reached her lodgings. With a few stragglers still passing by, Baird stood back a decent distance while she unlocked the door.

She realized that he'd be leaving her for the night. The memory of spies flooded back, and the inflated hubris of their singing vanished. "A couple of times tonight it seemed like I was watched," she told him. "The man next to me—who said he'd been your teacher—he saw it too, in the archways above us."

"That were Brochfael. I mun speak with him."

Hardly the response she had expected. She fumbled again with the key. Loose in the hole, it had no effect on the door. Baird put his hand over hers. The handle pressed down, and the thick door swung inward. He glanced back. The street now empty, he followed her in, moved across the room with ease despite the dark, and stood in one of the narrow archways. She pressed against the door, heard a bolt fall into place.

"Ye said ye were bein' watched?" he asked, side pressed against her.

Comforted by Baird's warmth, she was glad he was taking her misgivings seriously. "Yes, in the great hall and from that next tower over." She leaned into the alcove and pointed.

"Where? Up there?" he asked.

His scent, and the pressure of him, sped up her heart.

He pulled her into his arms, and they stood looking out at the night together. No moon was visible. She could barely make out the arches that earlier had appeared menacing. "Someone in one of those archways moved and disappeared when I looked that way." She shrugged. "It might have been coincidence, but it was creepy." She'd used the word *ymgripiol.*

"Creeping? Like a cat?" he asked, amused.

"Sort of."

"Give me yer crystal." He slipped his half from around his neck and took hers. When he pressed the two united, energy snapped in the air. They put their hands together over the crystal. Whole, it emanated far greater power.

Baird pulled the bed from the wall, and they walked the perimeter of the room. They spoke a chant. She knew what to say, the words' power. They vibrated, resonant, from deep within her. They finished the circuit.

"Keep th' door bolted. That's a sheer wall below th' window. No one's goin' t' climb up here."

We both knew Galfride hardly needed to climb the wall to get into her room.

"I'll do somethin' extra outside th' door as well."

Before he left, he again held her. He reached into her mind. Kay thought she'd never had such an all-encompassing hug, as if he held her in a high, safe nest. She lost herself in it.

Finally, he let go. She lit the lantern on the table by the bed.

"Remember. Ye have yer crystal. Ye can call me." He gave me one of his beautiful smiles and went out.

Kay's heart sagged with the emptiness he left behind. It was not until she lay alone in her narrow bed that a thought struck her. Had he allowed them to think she was Kyna in order to bait Galfride? Perhaps under Aelfwyn's orders? She tried to banish the thought.

Chapter 34

The night was interminable. The tiniest sounds had Kay sitting scanning the dark. At one point, she got up and went to the open arches in the outside wall. Better to look out than keep imagining what might be peering at her. She thought she might watch the dawn come up across the island. She tried to scramble onto the deep shelf under the arch but came up against a barrier. She thought she should have been comforted that their work with the crystal had been effective. If she could not get through, then most likely no one would get in. But instead, claustrophobia set in. She might have helped create the protection, but she did not know how to break it.

She walked around the dark room, testing. Near the outside door, she discovered the same seal. She could not get to Baird even if she knew where to find him. She remembered what he'd said about calling him with the crystal.

Wrapped in the heavy travel cloak, she knelt at the center of the room and held the crystal-half in her palm. She concentrated. It lacked its usual glow. She detected no connection with Baird.

Perhaps she could reach beyond the castle, to Aelfwyn. But should she wake her? It wasn't an emergency.

She slowed her breathing and defined her purpose: to sense someone's presence, and know she could make contact across the barrier. The crystal warmed in her hand. A spark of gold light bloomed at the center. A frisson of energy ran through her, carrying a picture of Baird into her mind. Happy with this response, she let the light go out, returned to bed, and nestled the stone under her chin. It was still warm. She had the odd sensation of Baird stirring, his heart beating in the stone. Fanciful, she thought, but it comforted her, a form of connection.

Eventually Kay drifted to sleep. Next time she opened her eyes, the grey of dawn etched the chamber outline. The residue of a dream lingered. In the dream, she needed to stand in a circle to receive a book from her daughter. It was essential, a matter of life and death, but when *they*—some ominous presence in the dream—came to the circle, no one could see or hear her. She was left with a forlorn sense of her invisibility.

Despite the uncomfortable dream, she was relieved that she'd gotten through the night. Morning sounds of castle life drifted up from below the arches. She was overjoyed to hear human voices. Again, wrapped in the cape, she hurried to an arched window and lay across the stone sill to look down. Wagons passed on the narrow road that hugged the base of the wall, forty feet below. She looked over the hills. Only a scrap of dawn light touched the night sky, still full of stars. Guards carried torches on the hillocks.

Someone tapped on the door. Hearing hooves clopping slowly on the cobblestones outside and the footsteps of someone running by, Kay scrambled back into the room.

Baird's voice called quietly, "Dove."

She crammed her feet into boots, saying, "Just a sec."

"Open up, sleepyhead," he called, louder.

She tested the air by the door. Her hand slipped right through to the handle. She unbolted the lock and dragged open the heavy door. "Guess you took off the protections," she said. "They really held." Only then did she wonder what her hair might look like. She touched it. Too late to do anything with it. "Sometime in the early hours, the barrier disappeared from the room," she said. "I was able to go to the window at first dawn, but I couldn't in the night."

"I dropped it when I was headin' this way t' come see ye," he said. He stood in the street, his long dark cloak draping, Robin Hood hat cocked to one side. In his tall boots and breeches, he was as captivating as ever. He slouched with ease, head cocked to the side, mouth quirked, eyes brimming with mirth.

She probably looked worse for wear. It wasn't fair— him dashing and fully dressed. Behind him, a tired-looking woman led a donkey, piled high with breads, up the hill. Torches along the curving wall lit her way on the still dark street. She nodded a greeting to them. A boy in a leather apron ran downhill on some errand.

"How was yer night?" Baird asked.

"Not too bad." She opened the door further. "Did you have to hold the barriers all night?" She searched to see if he had dark circles from lack of sleep.

"I sleep like a cat. Always, part o' me's awake." He shrugged as if this revelation were nothing.

She leaned against the doorjamb. "What will you do the rest of the day?"

"I've come t' ask ye, would ye like a bath? They ha' some o' th' Roman type in the main castle."

"Truly?" She breathed it out, as if he'd offered me the crown jewels.

"Only good thing they brought."

"The Romans?" She nodded, understanding. Though they'd left in the fifth century, she knew they'd trammeled the Isles in every possible way.

"Some might say."

A hot bath sounded heavenly. She hadn't properly bathed for days. Her head buzzed from lack of sleep, and being away from home too long. She wasn't sure she could take another night like the last one.

Baird read some hesitation. "I've promised t' perform again t'night. Ye don't mind, do ye?"

"You mean me as well?"

"They're sure to ask for ye. Ye were quite spellbindin'."

Heat crawled up her cheeks as a mixture of anticipation and nervousness prickled through her. What if she couldn't do it again? "I don't mind," Kay said. "I'm nervous about everyone thinking I'm Kyna, though."

"They don' think ye're Kyna."

She stared at him. "They don't? But they called out last night for Kyna to sing."

"I told 'em ye're her cousin. The way news travels, the whole castle knows by now."

"Oh." She might have slept better had she known. "Did they ask more about me? We'd better get together on our stories."

"I told 'em ye're from the south and a widow, that ye're visitin' me and Hamelyn for a time, t' help out." He switched subject. "I thought we might take lunch out o' doors. There be a garden I think ye'd like. I c'n ask th' kitchen staff for a basket o' vittles." He paused. "So, what about th' bath? Shall I ask if ye can have a soak in the ladies' pools?"

Taking a deep breath, she detected a hint of body odor. "Please," she said, pulling the cape tighter around her.

"I'll see about it then." He turned and, with long strides, was already up the cobbled way.

By the time he returned, she'd dressed in a clean blouse tucked into the serviceable skirt she'd worn for travel. She held the cloth bag with Kyna's toiletries, including a bumpy bar of soap smelling of lavender and mint. She locked the door, and they climbed the hill, passing the main hall where they'd dined. As they skirted the great buildings, the sun cast wan early rays.

This was the first time she'd seen the castle up close, in daylight. "It does have Roman influence, doesn't it?"

"Not entirely," he said firmly. "It's still a *llys*."

She dredged the term from memory; it meant a Welsh princely court. "Which parts reflect Welsh architecture?" she asked.

Turning a corner, he pointed at two sculpted heads. "Ye can see th' *Cymru* flavor there." He obviously relished the name of his land and emphasized it. "The inner buildin's were raised seven, eight hundred years nigh. Ye see th' central tower be round? Not Roman a'tall. Look at how th' walls emanate outward, like rays round th' sun, with th' inner walls higher than th' outer. That's no' Roman neither. There's th' thatchin', too." Baird indicated roofs nestled farther back. "And tiles made from the hill slate. Some o' it might be built Roman, but it's dug from *these* hills, *this* land." Baird indicated the stones at their feet, passion thickening his voice, as though they walked on his ancestors. "Ha ye been t' Rome?"

She nodded. "Though I don't know if we've seen much of the same city. I mean, some things have crumbled." It was terrible to say, as though his era was only bones now.

"Some 're bound t' be gone, aye. Fallen t' th' ground in

yer time. Covered over."

"But there are still many historical places that hold the lives that have gone before. You sense the time that's passed. It's almost like they hold human spirits in them."

"Aye," he nodded, peering speculatively up at the walls. "I know about that. I suppose this castle may no longer stand, in yer time."

She made a mental note to research it when she got back. Then thought she might not want to know.

They walked on. Baird stopped before a shadowed portico. "And here be the bath house for dames."

A beautifully tiled archway stood beyond rows of columns intertwined with vines. She thanked him and started for it, then glanced back. Baird remained watching her. He waved, then turned down the columned walk.

She entered the dark, steamy bathhouse, wishing she weren't alone. It would have been more pleasurable with a friend. Of course, Baird could not accompany her into this area. But still...

Inside, dim light shafted from high windows, penetrating steamy mist and forming shifting patterns on the stone floor.

Through the steam, she made out a young woman in a long dark dress and apron seated by one wall. "Mornin' Miss," she said, rising and curtsying. She showed Kay to a deserted pool, handed her a chunk of brown soap, and returned to her station by the door.

Kay took the soap and a towel and walked by a row of columns. Past a low wall that might double as a bench, she found the first pool, steam billowing from it. She sat, smelled the rough, strong-smelling bar and set it aside, then worked off her boots. Too exposed, despite the dim, shadowy lighting, Kay squeezed between a wide column and the sidewall to finish undressing.

She heard women's voices. They echoed off the tiles, sounding far off yet near at the same time. She peered through the warm fog, down the long, narrow bathhouse. Over more low barriers, she could make out a second pool and maybe a third. Dark forms moved. At least she wasn't alone.

She brought her bag to the edge of the water and slipped her feet in, finding a first step. The temperature scalded. Anticipation for soaking the layers of dust and sweat off her skin gave her increasing fortitude. Slowly, she lowered herself into a crouch on the wide first step, eying the dark unknown center of the pool with unease. Of course, how long could anyone hold their breath under there? No one could be under there. She sank down until she sat, legs stretched out. Submerged to her neck, her feet touched nothing, just trod water. At last, head resting on the rim, she floated until the heat penetrated, relaxing away the tension of the night.

Sluggish as a sloth, Kay rolled over and reached for the bag with Kyna's herbal soap. Finding its smooth buttery surface, she rubbed it all over, even into her hair, then slipped under to rinse. Reaching out to set the soap on the side, she heard rustling and scraping. She pushed wet hair from her eyes, listening. She no longer heard women's voices in other pools. She stared, trying to penetrate through the thick mist rising from the pool. Footsteps stopped then started again. She thought she saw a dark shape move between columns but the thick mist shifted so confusingly, she couldn't be sure. She slid down under the lip of the pool, only her nose above the water. Vulnerable, naked among strangers, with nothing to defend herself, she snaked her arm over the edge to find the crystal, but it was not there.

She remembered then that she'd left it folded into the clothes by the stone bench.

The young attendant appeared between columns. Relief flooded through her, and then chagrin. It must have been her all along. She moved out from her hiding place and sat on a step. As the young woman walked toward her, a figure darted between the columns behind her.

The woman did not notice. She held out a towel. "Would ye like to move on to the next pool?" She pointed.

By now, Kay longed for sunshine, to have everything clear and solid around her, not this shifting mist that could hold furtive, darting shapes.

"*Diolch*," she thanked her. Red with heat, she rose out of the water. "I believe I'll finish up now."

A short time later, dressed in a fresh change of underthings and another simple daytime outfit, she exited the bathhouse to find Baird lounging against a column.

"Yer bringin' flamin' good weather to our Cymru," he said, glancing at the bright blue sky as he approached with a basket draped in festive cloth. An earthenware flask poked up from one corner.

Hair tied back in a leather thong and beard trimmed close, he looked fresh. "How was yer bath?" He touched her flushed cheek lightly.

"Delicious," she said. *Mostly*. Now, in the growing light of day, she wondered if she should tell him about the shadowy figures. She hated to darken the festive mood his basket promised.

He must have seen something in her eyes, for he said, "Ye can always use yer crystal, like ye did last night."

"Last night? But I didn't." She hadn't called him. She'd held back.

"Oh, aye, ye did. That were good magic. Sent me t' sleep like a babe curled up in yer hand."

She stared realizing he referred to how she'd held the crystal to her chin.

Tenderness resting between them, he slid his hand under her arm and they moved companionably along the road. Sunlight had never appeared brighter or more sparkling. They skirted an ivy-covered wall and arrived at a gate arched over with tiny pink roses. The scent of honeysuckle hung in the air as Baird held the gate open and swept his arm broadly, with a bow, for her to enter.

Chapter 35

Kay passed through the archway and stopped, taking in the view. A long-walled garden sloped downward. Beyond, the island stretched to an indigo and turquoise sea. Baird nudged her back with one hand, and they started down the path, passing tiny gardens with flowered arbors. They approached a light forest of silver birches and alders, pale leaves fluttering in the breeze. The sounds of the castle dimmed inside the high garden walls, and the enchanted quiet of whispering trees surrounded them.

We walked among dappled white tree trunks under a green-gold canopy, moving between streaks of shadow and light.

"Is that a stream I hear?" she asked.

"This way." Baird stepped off the path, and they followed the sound into a fresh green meadow. A creek cut through high grasses. At the center, falls splashed into a pool.

She high-stepped through the grass toward the water.

"Would it please ye here?" Baird set the basket on the grassy knoll above the playing waters. From there they viewed the countryside over the tops of trees on the slope below them.

"Perfect."

He spread his cape and sat, indicating the space next to him for her. She added her cloak and lay on her back, arms stretched above her head. Early May sunshine bathed her as she watched the cloud shapes drift slowly overhead. Bees hummed. The breeze carried the scent of sage and wild thyme while the waterfall splashed soft rhythms.

Baird, perched on one elbow, said, "Waterfalls bring me good memories." He looked sideways at her.

Though there had been the rare embrace, these were the first intimate words of this trip. She gave him a hint of a smile and wondered what was next. She couldn't help but notice dark hollows under his eyes. Concern about Kyna always lurked there, she was sure.

"Ye know," he said after a long moment. "Even if they did think we were...that you and I... With Kyna gone this long, they'd expect me t' take a new wife." He fell silent. Then added, "But we both know that Kyna…"

She squinted at him from under her arm and finished his sentence, "Is trying to come back."

"Be alive." He emphasized the distinction.

She rose to one elbow and searched his face. "You don't think she's trying to come back?"

He shrugged. "Could be yes, could be no."

She protested. "She's trying to keep herself and the girls safe." She sat up and studied him, waiting for him to agree, but he remained silent.

Softly, she asked, "Are you angry that she hasn't tried harder to contact you?"

He hesitated, sitting and resting his arms on bent knees. "Ye should understand that I was gone for long times. Always."

"Did you take other lovers?" She'd wondered this but part of her didn't want to know.

"Occasionally."

She groaned silently, ridiculously disappointed.

"Not often, and that were long ago," he added quickly. "Kyna was not exactly…" He looked directly at her. "Kyna be a handsome woman. Well known for her extraordinary talents and charms. She be her own mistress, doin' what she cares to do."

Kay had a new sense of Kyna. She must have had lovers other than Galfride.

"What about you?" he asked. "Ye have two children and no husband. Be that not true?"

At the mention of her children, alarm bells went off. "I do have two offspring. We've spoken of my daughter, Sophie, in Paris." She watched to see if he would mention his son's interest in her. He only nodded. "And my son. You sat across from him on the subway in Boston." She'd longed to find out if he knew it was Rousseau or if he'd merely been drawn to a spirit similar to mine.

"On the what?"

"You were riding with a number of other people on an underground train? Do you remember it? In a dirty city with tall buildings?" She reached her arms up, parallel, like skyscrapers.

"I recall findin' myself in an enclosed movin' conveyance under the ground. Most unnervin'. But I were there only briefly. How did ye know?"

"You appeared in front of my son."

"Did I now? He told ye that? How did he know t'was me?" He sat up straighter now.

"Rousseau described a man who appeared on the seat across from him. He sounded very much like you—the hair, the harp. He said your clothing was from a different time. When he turned to wave goodbye, you were gone. That sounded more like you than anyone else I know." The thought reminded her of the distance from her kids, in a time she wasn't sure she'd get back to. She ached at this thought, yet had to believe she'd make it back, as before. "I had a husband, yes. We parted ways."

"Ah. And before ye parted, were ye loyal?"

"I was. Yes. Not that the lout deserved it."

"Mm... What was he like? Yer husband?"

She thought about her former partner—Ari, somber Egyptian engineer, a professor at Berkeley. "He was serious. Without a lot of imagination." She peeked sideways at Baird. "And he couldn't sing at all."

"Pity." Baird gave me a grin. "But he must have had some qualities you liked."

"Indeed. I liked his seriousness, at the start. His way of focusing intently." She didn't want to go too deeply into that minefield of thoughts. "Why did you stay away so much from Kyna and your home?"

Baird stared off into the distance as if looking for answers there. "I no be like Kyna," he said at last. "After her childhood of wanderin', always movin', she craved attachment to a place. I feared losin' th' road, gettin' held inside four walls." He turned to her. "If it weren't for th' few free bards remainin'..." His voice heated up, pride in his role clear. "Where would people get real news? Th' regular people, simple folk in th' villages? Those in power'd have that much more control o' their lives. I tell 'em things that won't be told by official criers. Sometimes I can put them on alert to danger, make it harder for those who plot and manipulate. Like Gal-fride." He bit off the syllables with venom.

"What kind of influence does he have?"

"Controls people's minds, even from afar. Over time, he gets better and better at it."

She quickly tested the barrier around memories of Galfride with her in the apothecary.

"He influences rulers t' keep himself in demand and in luxury. He takes enjoyment in stirrin' up trouble, but he may ha' a bigger aim. I dinna know." His voice was bitter.

"Living in those caverns in France doesn't appear to be the height of luxury," she mused.

"Did ye e'er see his chambers in the castle?"

He knew Galfride had given me the memory with Kyna in the library. Was he trying to find out if they'd been in his chambers, too? Maybe guilt brought that thought. "No," she said, firmly.

"Nor I. But I imagine they're quite well furnished. Even when we were young, studyin' together, he collected fine things. He had a taste for 'em."

Kay's stomach, just then, gave an enormous rumble.

Baird reared away. "Gods, woman, did that atrocious noise come from you?" He reached for the basket. "Let's get ye fed before ye eat *me*."

So alluring. She punched his arm, embarrassed, and watched as he drew hearty bread, cheese, smoked fish, wine, and fruit from the basket.

She learned no more of Galfride's intentions, content to depart from the topic as they divvied up the lunch fare and discussed its finer points and probable origins. When they'd eaten their fill, they tucked what was left into cloth parcels and stowed them neatly back in the basket. Baird took up his harp and sang a song he said he'd composed for her.

BRAIDED DIMENSIONS

Back in her room, alone with sweet memories of their time together and mounting fear of a second dinner, Kay pondered Baird's remark. Kyna not trying to come back? He had mentioned taking another wife. Her hands shook as she fumbled her dress buttons into place.

Baird arrived later in the afternoon clothed in forest green and indigo, with a cap of midnight blue draped to one side with a cluster of arching indigo-dyed owl feathers.

She beckoned him into the room, saying, "Good thing we're here for just one more night, since we only packed two special dresses. You look handsome, by the way. How about me?" She swished the skirt.

He shoved the door shut and pulled her to the windows, intent on something as he stared down at her dress. This one was of soft lavender muslin. Patterns embroidered in dark purple, turquoise, and deepest green coruscated down the skirt panels and scalloped over her breasts on a low-scooped neckline.

He knelt and lifted the skirt to inspect the stitching closer in the natural light from the tall, arched openings in the stone wall.

"That's right, Knave. On your knees," she said, playfully.

"Any time of any day, m' lady." He pressed his lips to her palm, sending excitement through her. Then he rose. "This be m' daughter Gwynedd's stitchery."

That explained his strange behavior. The dress he'd selected for Kay had been crafted by the daughter he'd hardly seen in years. "How do you know?"

"'Tis her design. Helpful in spirit travel, should ye decide to do any."

Not bloody likely, she thought, as she raised her brows for further explanation. "I think I'll try to stay put this evening, thank you very much."

"Or other travel. That's *Ing*, woven in t' th' stitchery."

She tried to think what the rune had to do with spirit. "Ing is associated with Frey and Freyja, isn't it?" Would he know the Nordic associations? Male and female joined. The rune, when placed in a chain, indicated an ancient understanding of DNA. She'd written about that.

"Very good." Baird nodded approval. "Ye've studied well. Th' seed that holds life and so on." He added, "Ye see th' wee shape, like a bee, in th' center o' each o' th' diamond-shaped runes?"

Kay lifted the fabric to look closer, her long underskirts remaining modestly in place, and spotted the tiny insect figure in the diamond's center. She nodded.

"'Tis a symbol fer spirit."

Alchemical symbol, she thought, longing for a research notebook, and made a mental note to sketch it when she had paper. She dropped her dress back into place.

"Come then. Mustn't be late," he said.

She pulled a cloak of midnight blue around her shoulders. "Let's have at it."

Before they exited, Baird paused. "And t' answer yer earlier question, yes. I think this dress will do nicely. That's why I chose it." He winked.

Smart aleck. "Well, it's exquisite stitchery. Your daughter outdid herself. I'm privileged to wear it." She locked the door and dropped the key into its bag.

"Ye fit it well, madam." Baird took her arm. She enjoyed a heated flush at the compliment. They joined others in their finery, ascending the cobbles in the deepening twilight. Noticing the women covered their heads, she pulled up her hood.

"And you, sir," she returned the praise, leaving the exact nature of it vague. Everything he wore dazzled her, even the dusty worn clothes used for travel. After their discussion at lunch, he fascinated her even more—his heroism, devotion to truth and justice, as a free bard.

"Ah." He doffed his cap and bowed low. "Ye do me honor."

Noticing the flourish, some around them smiled and called greetings. They flowed with the tide up to the great hall and in through the wide-standing doors. The interior was festooned with chains of fresh flowers and greenery. Once more, candelabras along tables heightened the opulence of satiny clothes and bright jewels. The scene was even more elegant this night—clothing of plush velvets and lustrous silks created a rich panoply of color and texture.

Again, servants rushed to meet the gentry's needs. But something was different. The men sat mostly separate from the women. She asked Baird about it. He bent close to her ear to whisper, "Some dignitaries arrived today for counsel." He was clearly anxious to take his place.

"I'll sit where I was last night. You go ahead." She waved him off, trying for confidence.

He patted her arm and started toward the front tables.

She turned to the corner she sat in the night before. As she approached, though, she realized no one looked familiar. Skirting the back wall, she found a separation between two women and asked in her best ancient Welsh, if they minded her joining them. For a moment, all conversation at that table died as the women scrutinized her, then looked at each other.

Finally, one asked, "Ye're Kyna's cousin, are ye?"

She bunched her skirts, stepped over the bench and sat. "Yes, I am."

Then questions and comments poured forth as if a dam had broken.

"Beautiful dress."

"Yer family has such ability with dyes."

"The purples—I've never seen quite those shades. Did ye do th' dyin' yerself?"

"Do ye weave, like Kyna?"

Relief that the moment of explanations had arrived surprised her; she could break that ice and be done with it. "I borrowed the dress from my cousin. Her daughter did the stitching." Lucky that Baird had made that observation. "Kyna may have dyed the threads, though." Kay wanted to accommodate their ideas and make friends. Besides, she somehow knew it to be true as she touched the fabric. She recalled Kyna picking out dye powders at the Solstice Faire.

"Yer niece, Gwynedd? Isn't she the one who's missin'?" said a woman with a pinched face, hair pinned so tightly it pulled her skin upward in tiny eddies, like water-shaped sand.

Kay started to answer but before she could, her neighbor said in a hushed voice, "They both be missin'. Gwynedd and Kyna. Strange business." She clucked her tongue.

"Missin'? What do ye mean, missin'?" said the woman next to her.

"I heard it be a spell gone wrong. Ye know, *The Thirteen*." She said this with a mixture of awe and disapproval.

All eyes turned to Kay for explanation. She opened her mouth, then shut it, like a fish, as she tried to decide what to say. Finally, she offered, "Well, we don't know for sure." She distrusted some of the faces, as if they thought she might be planning to spirit someone away.

Thankfully, food arrived. When conversation began again, it was about court intrigues and a new fruit that came over from France.

A young performer struck a chord on his mandolin, and all grew quiet.

She took a gulp of a rich fruit wine, then held it up to the candlelight. Its amber color caught with inner sparks. To distract from unease, she peered through the golden liquid and thick blown glass, examining the room, seeing it distort. The young musician's hat stretched up, his chin pulled down.

A second singer rose, an exotic woman, her skin dark, her dress of a desert culture—Bedouin, she thought—ornately embroidered, with flashing mirrors down the panels, cut low over ample breasts. She walked onto the platform carrying a rustic instrument carved in a long tubular shape with rugged gut strings. Her voice, low and husky, vibrated through the air. Kay sat mesmerized, along with the rest of the crowd. The first song was melancholy. Then she shifted to a tune with strange dissonance. Kay craned to see if Baird watched but he faced away, conversing intently with a man too short to see.

Dinner plates were removed and dessert set down. Fruit piled high on dense cake. She started on a second glass of wine—or was it her third? A need to relieve her bladder caused her to whisper to the woman next to her, "Could you possibly direct me to the latrines?" She hoped she had the right word. The woman pointed toward a curtained archway, then turned back to her neighbor.

That was vague. Kay looked around, wishing someone might accompany her, loath to be the only one rising. Did she have to wait for the prince to stand?

Unable to wait, she scrambled to sort her skirts from her neighbors. Somehow, she made it over the bench without tripping. Apologizing as she bumped elbows, she scooted along the wall to the first curtained exit. She shoved the heavy fabric aside and peeked into the dim hallway, then glanced back toward Baird. He was still immersed, facing away.

She slipped through. As soon as she dropped the thick drape, noise from the feast dimmed. Her footsteps echoed in the stone tunnel as she aimed for the single torch guttering at the far end. It wavered as in a draft, a good sign. It must lead out of the castle.

At the end of the hall, Kay took the direction that tilted downward. One more turn and she approached an archway nearly filled with a guard's silhouette. She skirted him, hurrying now, concerned about leaving a substantial puddle on ancient Welsh flagging. The immense guard barked at me in a strange accent and pointed the other way. She about-faced quickly. she could only imagine stumbling upon the men's ditches. Good call!

Stars packed every inch of visible sky as she hurried along wood planking. She came upon a long ditch by the outer castle wall, hidden by a barricade of lashed stakes. With boards for squatting, this was the extent of the facilities. The stench was appalling. Breathing through her mouth, she hurried to do her business then rearranged her clothes and scurried back toward the castle. Torches set high above in turrets gave wavering light. She arrived at the low entrance. The guard no longer filled the archway.

She slipped in, trying to repeat the turns of her original journey in reverse. But the floors kept slanting downward where they should have ascended.

Torches set deep in indentations looked unfamiliar. She took one out of its holder and moved on, determined not to be caught in blackness as she searched for the way back to the great hall. She'd gone some distance, making decisions at several branchings, when her torch sputtered and went out as if doused. At the same time, all the torches along the hall extinguished. She crouched and backed to the wall, gripping the dead torch as a possible weapon.

Chapter 36

Kay was no longer in the castle hallway. She heard the familiar sound of water sluicing against stone behind her and pressed herself tighter to the wall. Wet seeped into the beautiful dress, and a cold draft chilled me to shivering.

The draft also clued her to an opening not far from where she crouched. She slid toward it, still in a squat but poised to run. Light bloomed, revealing the room she was in, formed by tall cave walls. Galfride lay on a bed draped in rich coverings, a fur-lined robe thrown carelessly over his legs. His attention was on a massive book lying open in front of him. He was unaware of her presence, or affected to be so. Watching him, she scooted further toward the archway, trying not to make noise.

He had snatched her from the castle and brought her here. This had to be a room behind the cavern where she'd seen Gwynedd sitting, under his spell. The river sounded the same.

Languidly, his eyes lifted. He looked startled to see her. She tried to rise and dart toward the river, but it was too late. Her muscles no longer answered to her will. She sank, feet held in place. Galfride closed the heavy book and stood. As he approached, he flicked his hand, and she stood as though her body answered his command. Silently, she sent urgent messages to her legs to run. A water drop hit her cheek. She tried to wipe it but could not. Another splatted her face and ran down her neck.

As Galfride came closer, his energy invaded in waves until her insides quaked. He took her arm, pulled her from the wall, and loomed over her. His force pushed against her.

"Kyna's cousin, are ye?" he said, leering. As if moved by invisible hands, her head tilted up to him. Face close, Galfride's lip curled. "Didn't know she had one."

His dark gaze penetrated into hers, and her thoughts scattered. *Kyna? Cousin? What story had they told?* He must have heard conversations at court. Had those been his spies watching her—at the great hall, in her room, in the Roman baths? Or could he listen from here? She imagined someone creeping behind her through the fortress passageways, silent as a ghost.

She grew dizzy, her breath shallow, as she became aware of her cleavage, exposed and swelling with each breath. The dress was drenched and heavy, constricting. Anger bubbled within her. She chafed at being this vulnerable.

Stroking his neatly trimmed beard, Galfride circled her. "Who are ye really, I wonder?" He stopped and studied her. The power in his eyes battered her insides. With difficulty, Kay pulled her attention away and stared past his shoulder. Her teeth chattered.

With a sound of disgust, he swept his arm, and a fire blazed from a hollow in one wall. Another wave and two torches along the walls flared. A final flick sent a flame up through a tall iron lantern in one corner, shaped as a dramatic tower of twining black dragons. Light seeped through gaps in the dark metal. The cavern grew instantly warmer. She glanced around. How did he keep the damp from ruining the elegantly bound books lining rough-cut shelves, the wood of a polished writing desk, and several luxuriant, woven tapestries? Perhaps he put a spell of dryness on them, she thought, inconsequently. She craved distraction from her terrible predicament.

This would be a fine time for a cleverly plotted escape. She thought of the crystal hidden in the folds of her skirt and almost reached for it but what might this man do with such a potent stone, one that had held her entire spirit? She shoved the thoughts behind her ice wall, determined to get herself away before she needed to use the stone.

Should she lull him into perceiving her as Kyna's simple cousin, a rural bumpkin?

He continued to stare, arms folded and head tilted as though he expected something. As though he anticipated—what?

She awaited his next move. He dropped his arms and stepped closer. His face softened. He picked up her hand and looked into her eyes. "Ye must help me," he pleaded, deep voice vibrant, persuasive.

She tried to snatch her hand away, but then schooled herself. Maybe she should go along, appear charmed. "Help you?" she asked, feigning guilelessness. "How could I do that?"

Though she wanted to not respond, his appeal was magnetic, reminding her of Kyna's attraction to him in the apothecary and library. Kay was no more immune to him now. She had wanted to fool him into thinking she was enchanted, but she was not in league with his control—nowhere close. Lust rose.

He moved closer, caressed the back of her hand with his thumb. "Hamelyn be my son," he said. He dropped this bomb with ease, eyes on hers, shapely lips close, tilted in the barest smile.

This was unexpected. Shocking. As he had surely planned. She stared at him, thrown off-balance as she tried to tug her hand away. The circling thumb sent unbidden sensations into her abdomen. Do not give him the power of an emotional reaction, she told herself. He scraped at the edges of her mind. She deliberately slowed her breath and heart rate, drawing on the discipline she'd learned with meditation.

Calmer, she sorted her thoughts and tested the ice barrier. She had to believe her memories were protected. Therein lay the power. "What does that have to do with my help?" she said, almost evenly.

He brought his nose close to her neck and breathed. "Ye look like her," he whispered. "Ye even have her scent."

Her groin reacted, disgusting her. He and Kyna had appeared to be lovers when he'd put the spell on her in the apothecary. Now he was saying their trysts had produced Hamelyn. She tried again to push him away, desperate for space to gather her wits.

He grinned, held her without even straining. He kept her face toward him by the power of his will. She saw in his expression—or did he send the thought into her mind?—that he knew exactly what sensations he produced. She cringed, anger mixing with his allure, his attractiveness. She admired his strength, his ability, his mastery, and hated herself for it.

"We have powers, the men of my line," he said, his lips close to mine. She could not move away. She breathed in dark chocolate and musky incense. "Hamelyn has 'em as well." He backed away slightly, head tilted, to read her re-action. His focus moved from one eye to the other, drilling down. He hissed, "Hamelyn needs to know about 'em."

For diversion, she tried to analyze his accent, slightly different from Baird's or Kyna's, but his lips, so shapely, brushed hers. His piercing eyes were spellbinding. "He deserves t' know," he said.

"He's happy where he is," she said, her voice faltering. She pushed words out more firmly. "He's content with his life." Picturing the activities across from the apothecary: visiting musicians, Hamelyn's joyous expression as he stepped outside and tried a new instrument, made her un-accountably protective, as though he were her own son.

"He's no' content." Galfride backed his face from hers and glowered, teeth clenched. His hands bit into her shoul-ders like a steel vise. She gasped. "I know what it's like at his age, what he must ha' been experiencin', since he came into manhood."

"And what would that be?" Rage coursed through her. She almost flinched with its force. Again, she made herself stay in control. It wouldn't do to incite violence. Perhaps it would not do for him to sense weakness.

Despite his effort to appear candid and needy, he clearly seethed. She attempted to shield against the force of his fury and access the lessons she'd learned from Baird of how to protect herself. But Galfride's energy pummeled her in mental waves.

Taking a breath, he mustered patience and returned to the alluring, reasonable man. "I'm sayin' his powers must be growin', different from those around him. He must wonder about them." His voice shook slightly.

He planned that for effect, she thought. "I haven't no-ticed any such angst about him."

"At his age, it nearly drove me mad."

"Well, he isn't you, whether or not he has your blood." She was amazed at her audacity. It gave Kay hope, confidence, yet she was not sure it was wise.

His temper flickered, but he dropped his voice into a quiet plead. "I know what he's goin' through. He needs t' at least ha' a chance t' know what's in him." He schooled his striking features into a vulnerable, pleading expression.

Drawing on her protective anger, she finally yanked her hand from his and spat out, "So he can twist people's minds, like you? Hold them captive?" Having abandoned the simple country cousin act, she glared, disgusted. "Anyway, why would I be the one to tell him?" She stood rigid, shaking, trying to remain steadfast.

He drew to his full height and stared down his perfectly formed nose. "They won't let me near him," he said through pearlescent teeth, maddeningly attractive. "Ye must know they keep a thousand shields around th' place."

"Hmm...I wonder why." She was doing well with sarcasm and pulled in a breath of righteous wrath. "You merely stole their daughter, held her captive. And god knows *what* all you did to your niece." She glanced around and tried for feisty and bold. "Where are we, anyway? Is this your hideout in the Alps where you kept them bound and helpless year after year?"

She realized too late that she should not get his mind onto them. Her hands now loose, she tried to back away, but his energy held her, increasing until it drained her again. Her fierceness waned. Even the ice wall around her memories was fading.

Like a hunter, he sensed this, and a feral expression sprang to his face. Suddenly, a ghastly green light filled the centers of his eyes, a toxic glow that had no place in his mahogany irises. She'd seen that light before. It was the green in the cavern when he'd stolen Kyna from the Solstice Faire. She tried to piece this together.

He jerked and shifted as though something were trying to control him.

The poisonous light receded. He faced away, then slouched on one hip and turned back to her, waving a casual hand. "They stayed in another chamber. Equally comfortable, I assure you." His smile, slightly less sure, dared Kay to accuse him of any wrongdoing.

"They were prisoners, nonetheless." She wanted to be appalled at his audacity but, to her astonishment, sympathy rose in her. He'd been tormented by some outside force. She searched for the thread of censure. "I don't know why I would help you." She almost managed to get the nastiness back in her voice, though it sounded thin now.

He stepped close again, and his hands snaked out, grasping her arms. He pulled Kay to him, his face so near she smelled his breath, like fancy confectionary. "I want t' tell ye everything," he said. His voice was constricted with emotion. His iron grip pressed her to him until her head bent back. His lips skimmed a path from the corner of her mouth to her ear, sending sensations through her belly. "Gods, I need to trust someone." His breath touched her ear sending more cascades to her groin.

What trick now? said a voice in some distant chamber of her mind.

He released her arms, but before she could back away, he had her by the waist. She shoved her palms against his chest, and he laughed.

"Tell me what?" she hissed, struggling, although she wanted him at the same time. It was useless. He had her crushed to him. She couldn't even squirm. His musky scent increased her desire. He recruited a new wave of magnetism from his endless well of power and sent it through her until she hardly knew who she was.

She was losing the battle. Kay heard him speaking softly in her ear but this time, could not follow the sense of his words. Waves of torrid sensation reverberated through her. Shallow breathing made her dizzy, disoriented.

He moved one slender but powerful hand to her back and pressed her as the other turned her face to him. His was almost purple with rage, his expression transformed beyond reason. His fingers gripped her cheeks. "I need to know where Kyna and the girls are," he said, through gritted teeth. He shook her. The green light again flickered in his eyes. Beads of sweat appeared on his brow. Something drove him. He appeared feverish, mad. There was far more to this than greed. But what?

She thought her neck might crack. The women? Wasn't he talking about Hamelyn?

He dropped all finesse and buffeted her insides with the force of his thoughts until she was nearly cramping. His thumbs dug cruelly into her ribs. He could play her so easily. In the next moment, he might elicit sympathy, or have ger swooning. It appalled Kay that he could hold her in the grip of fear, pain, anger, and lust, all at once.

"So that were you in Kyna's workroom? I should ha' known."

He read that memory! She panicked. *I'm not good enough at this. Why did Baird ever bring me to the castle? Why did we not spent more time on training?*

"I could put ye in that spell again and take every memory ye've ever had, dig through every thought in that simple brain o' yours." His hands slid an inch up her ribcage, sending off alarms as they moved toward her breasts.

The ghastly green light gleamed again. She could not pull her attention away. His energy sucked life from her. Inside, molten terror turned her bones to gelatin.

I am simple, she told herself, as her insides quaked and her defenses crumbled. *So simple that I have no thoughts at all, no memories whatever.* Sweat dripped down her ribs. She tried to imagine his intent. With that look in his eyes, she thought he'd do just about anything—crush her ribs, rape her. *But I don't know. I don't know where the women are.* She rasped, "I don't know."

Seeking a place to put her hands, Kay slid them along her sides and pressed against her thighs, trying to galvanize strength. Her palms, slick against the skirt, found an anchor to reality in her flesh underneath. *He can't know my memories.* Her mind scuttled around for thoughts that did not involve those she loved. She rubbed the fabric. *Think of something simple, basic, safe.* Her fingers touched the stitching on the skirt panel. Yes, something intricate to focus on. She traced the pattern in the threads. *Ing.* Diamond shape, repeated in a chain. In her mind, she recited the meaning Baird had told her. "Seeds, germination, becoming," she chanted to herself, as she traced the crisscrossing lines, like a DNA helix. Inside the diamond-shaped rune, her fingers found the spirit symbol. Alchemical symbol of becoming, she recited to herself as she traced the figure of the bee within a crosshatched circle. Down to the next Ing and repeat the pattern.

Something new stirred within her mind. She knew the source. Kyna. And someone else. At least one other. "Ye can say goodbye now," Kyna told Kay. A thread of electricity, taut as wire, ascended through her, reminding her of the rock shelf, when her spirit had been inside Kyna's, and they broke Galfride's barrier holding Gwynedd. She pulled on that electricity and, drawing tall, announced firmly, "I must go."

Surprise, then fury, bloomed in Galfride's face as she turned to smoke in his hands. Just as his grip collapsed, though, he raked her mind.

Slipping into oblivion, agony coursed through her.

Chapter 37

She floated. All was pain, with no anchor, only a toxic cloud of darkness. Shards of nightmare pierced Kay's core. She had no sense of life or a reason to take air in and out of her lungs. Was she breathing? She hovered, without physical reality, only pools of fetid waters, smelling of reeking rot.

Then she heard women's voices, softly murmuring. They blended into the painful morass. She begged them to go. Leave her be. *If I die, the ugly visions, the hateful phantoms, the wraiths in the shadows will be gone.*

A touch to her brow threatened to pull her back. Please, let it all end!

"Try. You mun try to come back t' us." A woman's voice was quite close to her.

It was a trick. It had to be. She sounded sincere, but Kay was certain there were only enemies. And she had nobody. No body!

She tried to see. The voice seemed familiar but that was only another of Galfride's deceptions. She managed to open her eyes a mere slit. Pale light blasted her nerves. She squeezed them shut again. A ringing in her head drowned out sounds.

She now knew she still had a body. Her heart sank. She could not slip away from this. The weight of her head lay on something soft. Fingers rubbed her temple.

Horror tore through her. She jerked away. Pain lanced. Nausea welled. She hugged herself, curling onto her side, then lurched, vomited. Eyes squeezed shut, she crouched.

Strong hands held her. A cool wet cloth wiped her face. Her body shook uncontrollably.

The woman's voice came again. "Take a sip, love."

Something pressed her lips. She moaned and pushed it away.

"It'll make ye better. Drink," Kyna said.

What is she to me? She knew nothing, not even her own soul. More than anything else, hope scared her. It allowed all the rest to flood her. She did not want to open those gates. Yet a swelling of hope penetrated. She sent signals to her mouth, which opened slightly.

Bitterness soaked her tongue. She pushed it out like a child. Liquid oozed down her chin.

A low chuckle. "None o' that, now. I know it be fierce unpleasant, but ye mun drink it all." Kyna's voice took on a stern, healer tone.

She sipped and this time swallowed. "Oh god, oh god," Kay heard herself repeating as she shoved it away, curled on her side and rocked, fists pressed into her abdomen. The nightmare returned—fetid waters, beast forms in the shadows—a fog of terror filled her mind, and she screamed.

A knee wedged into her back. "Drink it *now*." Hands took her shoulders firmly, held her neck, gripped her chin, and wedged the cup between her lips. Another hand forced her chin down. "Every drop. Ye drink. Ye finish it."

A sob hitched in her throat. Tears welled and ran down

the front of her dress. At least this new attack of the healing hands forced away the nightmare scene for the moment. Nasty liquid filled her mouth. She gagged, swallowed compulsively. Finally, the hands let her lie down again. The fire's warmth and rug's thick softness comforted her and despair faded.

She heard women's soft conversation. The gripping of her stomach muscles gradually eased. Someone tucked a sweet mint lozenge between her lips. She pulled it onto her tongue and gratefully sucked, sniffling. Tears slipped into her ear and she shook uncontrollably. Someone laid a blanket over her.

At last, she opened her eyes. The pain had dulled to a low throb. Through her film of tears, Kyna's face floated into view.

"I wasn't sure we'd bring ye back," Kyna said.

Somewhere in her, the shadowland still lurked—an oily, smelly tar seemed like it would never wash away.

Kyna said, "The taint o' him be gone. No lastin' damage, my friend."

She wanted to believe her. "You could see all that happened?" she rasped.

"I saw some o' it. Galfride's caves."

Heat welled. Had she seen the seduction? She tried to sit up and gingerly tested her head's reaction.

Kyna and Gwynedd helped her into a chair. Her head lolled to the back, eyes closed. "He raked my mind as I left. I hope he didn't hurt you as well," she said.

"I ken how t' shut out the worst o' it while still knowin'," she answered.

"That must be a helpful skill when midwifing," Kay said. Opening her eyes a crack, she at last looked around and recognized Kyna's living room. The same walls, same leather hide door at the back, loom next to baskets of fibers.

How could this be? Had they returned home? "This is your house, isn't it, Kyna? Have you returned? Where are Aelfwyn and Hamelyn?"

"The same house," Kyna said. "Two hundred years hence."

Kay took in more details. The loom had some refinements. There was a treadle underneath, not just the hanging weights. The chair she sat in was softer, more cushioned, than the ones they had before. A wood stove with a cooking surface stood in the alcove by the food shelves. Windows with panes of thick glass let in moonlight, which silvered the edges of a crude sink and pump.

"Two hundred years ahead. But if the house still stood all this time, weren't there people living here?"

"Aelfwyn laid a spell that preserved it. Village folk thought it haunted and stayed away," Kyna explained.

Kay heard the two girls snicker. Gwynedd, she recognized. Her auburn hair, plaited similarly to her mother's, had red and purple ribbons woven in. She pulled a needle through an embroidery hoop. The other Kay thought must be Branwyn. Her fiery red hair formed a halo round her head, a thick braid dropping over her shoulder. She held a quill pen poised above a bound book, and smiled at her. She gave her a tentative smile in return and pain jabbed her. Laying her head back, she closed her eyes again. Tremors took hold and drenched her anew with sweat. Pressing her hands into her lap, she sucked on the mint lozenge and begged the shaking to diminish.

After a moment, she asked, "The villagers have accepted you?"

"Aye. They have. There were some talk o' witchery at the start. But a town can always use healers. We've made friends." Kyna winked at Branwyn, who flushed. "There be a lad."

Kay smiled at the quiet young woman. "You like to write?" she asked, pointing at the book.

Branwyn nodded. "Especially drawing."

"That's wonderful," she said.

"I believe I may ha' found some o' your work, Kay," Kyna said. "All my books were wrapped in oiled hides and placed in the cellar, well preserved. Among them, I found some interestin' writin'." Her eyes sparkled. "No' mine. Nor Aelfwyn's."

My notes! She wondered how far she'd gotten. When was the last time she'd been in this house?

"Would ye like t' see? T' take them with ye?"

Kay was torn. Maybe she should leave them for further work in the past. Unsure about getting them back safely to her home, she said, "I'm not certain. Hopefully, I can come back here. I'm weak right now. I think I've stayed in the past longer than I should." A thought occurred to her. "How do you stay in this time indefinitely?"

"I anchor us t' the standin' stones," Kyna answered. "Aelfwyn keeps experimentin'. If we're weak, we try somethin' new. Also, Gwynedd embroiders spells." She pointed to new tapestries on the walls, scenes surrounded by symbols.

Kay would have gotten up to study them but was too feeble. Two days before, she'd sat in this same room, with another set of residents. "It must be very odd to know the others live here, in the same space, two centuries back," she remarked.

"'Tis strange, t' be sure," Gwynedd said. "I can almost sense Da and Hamelyn here some ought." She sounded wistful. Such a young woman to endure so much. The long captivity in Galfride's caverns, and now, exile. "Thank you for helping t' save me," she added, quietly.

Kay sought words as Gwynedd gazed at her earnestly. "You've certainly repaid me by freeing me from Galfride's hold."

Gwynedd's luminous eyes dropped to the dress Kay wore.

Kay glanced at the muddy hem. "I'm so sorry. It got soaked in the cave," she said.

"I knew it be that one," Gwynedd said, looking pleased.

"You knew?" Kay stared at her, questioning. "How?"

"That be the spell what alerted me to yer trouble."

"When I rubbed the pattern? I didn't know a spell. I just repeated to myself what Baird said about the symbols on the panels." She lifted the skirt to reexamine the design. "He'd told me, right before the dinner in the castle about the alchemical sign for spirit. I tried to concentrate on it and the Ing rune to keep Galfride from getting into my thoughts and stealing my memories. I chanted the meanings in my mind, tracing the stitchery under my fingertips."

"Ye must ha' invoked it with intent, just what it be designed for," Gwynedd said.

All three women's eyes shone with pleasure as they shared a congratulatory glance all 'round.

Kay turned to Kyna. "At first Galfride spoke mainly of Hamelyn."

Kyna rose abruptly. "Ye still be wan. I'll prepare ye somethin' else."

"Oh, no thanks. I'm fine." Kay raised a protesting hand.

Kyna laughed softly. "This one'll not be bitter. I promise."

"Oh, okay. Thanks. Galfride claimed..." Kay quirked a

half smile, anticipating a disbelieving denial.

As Kyna crumbled herbs into water, she interrupted, "I may know. Did he claim t' be Hamelyn's father?"

"Yes, he did," Kay responded, startled. Surely, she would deny it. Of course, it was a lie.

"It be true," Kyna said.

Kay stared at her.

Kyna heaved a sigh. "Baird had been gone a very long while," she explained as she stood over the pot by the fire. "I dinna know if he'd return. There were rumors he'd gone east, past Saxony. Others that he'd taken a likin' to court life in Tuscany. Galfride came often t' visit. He brought new learnin'. Books. Instruments, amulets, all manner o' objects from his travels." She carried cups of tea to each of them and sat.

"Books from Aberffraw?" Kay asked.

Kyna looked up mid-sip.

Kay explained, "Galfride came to me in spirit, in your apothecary, and put pictures in my mind, of you and him in a library, very plush."

"Into my home?" She looked stunned. "He's never done that uninvited. Not since we put protections around the property."

"It was on May Eve. He thought I was you and tried to remind you..." Kay's cheeks warmed as she recalled the intimacy she'd experienced that was really theirs.

Kyna watched her, brows raised.

" —of a romantic tryst you and he—"

"He were powerful attractive. *Could* be." Kyna glanced an apology at the girls, who both shrugged.

"I could see that," Kay said, still flushed, remembering the lust he had raised, against her will, but still very effective.

"He were different then," Kyna said. "He showed ye

the library at Aberffraw?"

"I think so. I've been to the castle but not to its library."

"The three of us were there t'gether often—me, him, Baird. That castle had a collection o' books from all around the world. Our teachers, the Druids, dinna like it that we went, but Galfride had boundless curiosity. I followed him t' see the books. Baird followed me. He hated palace life. The walls. The politics and games of power. Often he left and ventured across the water." She gulped her tea. "Galfride were a year older than us. He had a way about 'im. Commandin' and fierce, sometimes, aye, but his passion fer knowledge were appealin'. And he could be kind."

She paused, stared into the fire and drank her tea. Then went on. "Baird and I were like brother and sister, ye know. We grew up wi' the Wanderers. They took us all in— me, Duff, Baird. When we met Galfride at the Druid school, well, he was somethin' like she'd never known—new and excitin'. He had such skills." Her eyes grew dreamy, then sharpened. "Not always twisted and power-hungry, like he's grown to be."

"I wish I had more skills," Kay said. "I might have kept him from taking me."

"That'd be some tremendous magery, t' resist the snares Galfride's set in the bowels o' Aberffraw," said Kyna. "Few c'd fight such a trap."

"You saw him take me?" Kay stared at her.

Kyna shook her head. "I sensed what happened to ye when I took his taint away," she explained as she finished her tea and set the cup aside. She switched track. "Hamelyn knows Galfride sired him. Baird, as well, kens it. It never mattered. Baird raised Hamelyn as his own, with never a moment o' hesitation."

"Galfride tried to convince me that Hamelyn needs to

know the magical lineage he inherited. That he must be suffering not to know."

"Hamelyn be well protected," Kyna said firmly, but a shadow edged her eyes.

Kay gulped the last of her tea. "I'm sure he is." She tried to comfort her. Her head swam. She leaned forward. "I'm...fading. I suppose I'd better return to the castle. They'll be searching for me."

"I fear puttin' ye back where ye were," Kyna said.

"You're right. Galfride might retake me," Kay agreed, shivering as fear returned.

"I think I know what t' do," said Kyna. "D' ye ha' the stone?"

"The gold crystal?" Kay searched among the skirt folds for the bag and removed the golden crystal half.

Kyna's shoulders relaxed. She rose and came toward Kay. "I'm surpassin' glad Galfride dinna take it from ye." She held out her hand, eyes gleaming.

Chapter 38

She be wakin'." A grizzled middle-aged man hovered over Kay, holding up a candle. He wore the rustic clothes of a woodsman.

I made it, Kay thought. But where was she? Who was this man?

Baird's face appeared past the man's shoulder. Kay's heart swelled to see him. She glanced past the two men, expecting the hallway under the castle where Galfride had snatched her. Instead, she took in her bed chamber in the castle keep. "Where did you find me?" Her voice croaked.

"Dove." Baird dropped to his knees beside me and took her hands. "You're alright!" He studied her.

In truth, she was queasy and dark in spirit. The additional travel had weakened her almost to extinction. "How did you know where to look for me?"

Baird stood abruptly. "Thank ye, Tobias. I never could ha' done i' wi' out ye."

The man shrugged. "T'was you carried 'er."

"Tha's no' the part I'm meanin'," Baird said.

Exhaustion gripped her, dragging her downward toward oblivion.

Tobias pointed at the bedside table. "Gi' 'er tonic, s'much

as she needs fer a night's rest."

Kay followed his gesture and spotted a dark flask next to Kyna's mirror. The room whirled with the movement of her head. It frightened her to be so frail, so insubstantial.

Tobias lifted a lantern from a wall hook. He squinted back at her. "She don' look good. Take care o' her, Baird, 'til Beli come." He strode out, rocking on bowlegs.

Baird again knelt by her. This time, he took her in his arms and held her to him. She pushed back to see his face, then kissed his beard-shadowed cheek. The effort cost her and her head dropped back to the pillow.

"Thought we might' o' lost ye," he said, voice husky.

Kay wanted to pull his face back close to hers but couldn't lift her arms.

He settled in a crouch, arm around one knee. "T'was Galfride. Am I right?" His cheek muscles clenched.

Kay nodded, just a hitch of her chin to avoid further dizziness.

He leaned in so that his eyes penetrated hers. "Did he take ye somewhere in the castle?"

"No." She spoke with effort.

He moved his ear closer.

"Same caverns where he held Gwynedd," she croaked, throat raw. Had she screamed in the darkness before she arrived?

Baird reached for the tonic.

She grimaced, thinking of Kyna's drink. "That's okay."

His mouth creased at one corner. "It's no' bad." He poured and helped Kay up for a sip. It tasted like syrupy whiskey. Warmth moved down her throat and through her. Like a baby bird, she opened her mouth for more.

Baird chuckled. "A smidgin'. Ye need t' eat and sleep.

Beli 'll be bringin' ye dinner." He allowed her another gulp, then set the glass aside. He fetched her cloak from a hook by the door and rolled it to tuck behind her. Then he settled on the edge of the bed. "What happened, Dove?"

She wished she could nestle into him and doze off. "Well, I left the dinner to…relieve myself." Her voice came stronger with the tonic bolstering her. "I made it out there okay, but then, returning, I reentered the castle at the only lit archway, thinking it was where I'd exited." She stopped to think. "Someone must have moved the torch to a different entrance. This passage sloped downward. I kept trying to find my way back up to the dinner hall. Then, in a long corridor, all the torches went out. Next I knew, I was in Galfride's caves."

"And then, you got away, back here?"

"With a detour. I had help getting away."

"Ye did?" He frowned. "From whom?"

"Kyna." She watched his face.

His expression only gave away a flicker of surprise.

"And Gwynedd and Branwyn," I added.

Slowly, astonishment arrived on his face. "Yer not sayin' they're back in his caverns?"

"No." She wanted so much to describe to him the new things in their house and all that they'd told her. But she wasn't sure if she should give away their location. "I don't know if I'm to tell you." She checked to make sure some thoughts were safely hidden behind the ice wall.

"Nay." He shook his head. "I'll find out when I'm meant to. But they helped ye. They got ye away. And they be safe. That be enough fer me t' know, fer now."

"Where did you find me?" she asked again.

"Right outside the dinner hall," he answered.

So that was Kyna's solution, to return her to a different

place, away from Galfride's snares, where people walked often. "You were right about the dress," she added with a weak smile. She held out her hand for more of the sweet tonic but he shook his head.

"Was I now?" He studied her.

"It *was* good for travel."

He guffawed, but with a creased brow.

"It saved me in the end," she said.

"Saved ye?" he asked, just as a knock came at the door.

"That'll be Beli." Baird went to the door and opened to a squat woman who waddled in lugging an overflowing basket as wide as she was. A young boy followed, burdened with a pile of bedding that nearly obscured him.

Beli bustled past Baird, and thumped the basket to the floor. The boy dropped the bedding next to it. Beli handed him a bread roll before sending him away. Then she turned to Baird. "Ye be needed with the fine folk in the great hall, Master Bard."

He bowed. "Good evenin' t' ye, Mistress Beli."

Her cheeks dimpled, breaking her stern frown. "Go on with ye. I'll be takin' care o' this-un."

Baird threw on his midnight blue cape. As he pulled the heavy wood door open, she heard thunder roll, followed by heavy downpour. She thought of the boy caught in the storm and hoped he wasn't going far. Baird yanked up his hood and stepped out. After a few moments, he returned with an armload of scraggly wood.

"That's a good lad. Build up the fire," said the round woman who was busy laying out bedding. "I'll be here all night so make it toasty." She dug in her basket and pulled a dark bottle from its depths.

"She be needin' food, not more tonic," Baird said from the doorway.

"Ah, be she tipsy on Tobias' healin' brew?" Beli chuckled.

"I'm not hungry," Kay said. "I just need to sleep." She burrowed into the covers.

Baird said. "She's all but snorin'. She better ha' a might o' vittles in her."

"Tellin' me my job, are ye, youngster?" Beli gave him a terrifying scowl.

Baird winked at her. "I'll check by after I make an appearance at the festivities."

Beli watched his attention on her. "She'll be right enough. Go on."

Baird appeared torn but pulled the door shut behind him.

An owl hooted as it sailed past the windows. Its call filled the room. The old woman turned to the sound, and Kay could have sworn she hooted back. A hawk screeched as it swept over the hills, sounding like a mad woman shrieking. The predatory bird sounds, combined with the old woman's intense stare, unnerved Kay so much that, when the woman touched her arm, she jumped. Was a shock her imagination? Or was she just overwrought?

Beli laid her palm on Kay's brow and energy ran through her.

The owl hooted again, closer by. Was it on the sill? She tried to lift her head to see. The energy emanating from Beli's hands was too much. She wanted to pull away. Yet she was strengthening. "Did you talk to the owl?" she mumbled.

Beli chortled but did not answer. "Th' bard's a charmer," she said. "Always has been." She dragged the low stool and her basket to the bedside and sat.

Much as Kay appreciated the woman's ability to strengthen her, she longed for someone familiar, someone soft and easy. Without appetite moments before, now, suddenly, she was ravenous.

As if reading her thoughts, Beli reached into her capacious basket and drew out a covered pot from which she scooped thick stew. The rich scent of onion and seasoning reached Kay and her hollow stomach growled. Beli set the bowl in her hands, and Kay shoveled in a bite.

Next, she pulled out a stack of cards. Pushing lantern and tonic aside, she spread the deck on the bedside table. "Can never do a true healin' wi' out knowin' the source o' what ails ye." She drew a card, turned it over, and glared at Kay. "This be no man t' meddle wi'."

Kay stopped chewing. The card showed a figure in a black robe holding a strange contraption. A beam of light shot from it, lighting a scene of tortured souls.

"Do you mean Galfride?" No fooling. She hadn't intended to meddle with him. She needn't act like Kay went looking for him.

Beli pulled another card. An acrobatic figure cavorted by a fire in a cave, his face red in the glow. She tapped the image with a broken fingernail. "There be another, far worse, behind Galfride's foul games," she said, with certainty.

Kay knew that. "What can you tell me about him? Where he is?"

"Far away, he be." Her voice grew faint. "Gazin' at the past." She drew her finger along a river at the base of the card that snaked through a dark ravine. She swayed, took a startled breath, and gathered the cards, jamming them back into her bag. "Ye be needin' sleep. Eat up," she grunted then pushed herself from the stool and stood over her.

Kay scraped the last bite. It was tasty. She was sure there was meat but had given up asking.

"Let's get yer nightdress on," Beli said, taking the bowl. She rummaged through Kay's bags, found her gown, and wrestled her out of her dress and into it.

The owl hooted again. How could it sound so close? There was no tree near that window.

Beli arranged her covers over her and placed a cup of water on the table nearby.

"Is the owl on the windowsill?" Kay asked. It was obscured by the long heavy curtain.

"Lie back and I'll tell ye a story."

Kay had to smile. It'd been a while since anyone told her a bedtime story.

Beli poured a draught of tonic and held it to Kay's lips. This one had an earthy flavor, more herbs, less sweetened liquor.

"Is Tobias a healer, too?" Kay asked.

"O' sorts." Beli removed the rolled cloak and helped her settle, scratchy blankets, softened by a heavy flannel sheet, pulled to her chin. The healer woman sat back on her stool and began a story about a girl who lived near a river. Each day, the girl called out to the spirits in the water. Her village needed the answers she brought to them.

"Is the girl Kyna?" Kay mumbled, almost asleep. She caught a sort of grunt from Beli.

The last thing she heard was the owl hooting. She was sure it was in the room now.

Chapter 39

Pale morning light revealed Beli, a rounded shape in the chair next to Kay's bed.

"My mouth tastes like something died in it," she mumbled.

Beli burst out laughing. "That foul, be it, lass?"

A knock came at the door. Kay rubbed her eyes and shoved back tangled hair as the old woman opened to Baird. He stepped in, accompanied by the aromas of baked goodies and sweet spice.

"Brought somethin' for ye," he said, crossing the room.

"Your good smells precede you," Kay croaked.

He grinned and lifted a cloth to show warm rolls still steaming, next to a ceramic pot promising a hot drink.

"Mmm..." she said.

"Ye been charmin' the kitchen ladies, no doubt." Beli grabbed a muffin as Baird poured hot, dark liquid from the cask and added fresh cream.

"You amazing man," she rasped, accepting a full mug and hot roll eagerly in her weak hands.

He made a slight bow and stepped away to pull open the curtains, letting in wan morning light. An owl perched on the sill.

"*Noson Dywill*," the woman called. The owl launched into the air and glided to her shoulder.

"Its name is 'Dark night'?" she asked. "That's lovely. I was sure I heard an owl in the room last night. It *is* your friend."

"Not so sure he be a friend." Beli squinted at the medium-sized bird on her stout shoulder. It swiveled its head to peer into her face.

Kay wanted to laugh but was still weak and insubstantial.

Baird stood. "Are ye ready t' ride?" He opened the outer door. "I'll get th' horses." With that, he was gone.

"Just like a man. Ask a question, no need fer an answer," Beli muttered. "Ye still look feeble." She busied herself gathering her belongings into her basket, shaking her head all the while. "Looks like ye be leavin' whether ye will it or not." Standing, she said, "I mun tend t' a child in the village who's poorly."

Jostled, the owl winged back to the window alcove.

"I suppose Baird's right. I do need to get back." Kay wasn't sure what the woman knew about her. Getting back, for her, meant a bigger leap than a horse ride down the coast. "Of course, you must go tend to others." She made to rise but fell back on her pillows.

Beli tsk'ed, shaking her head. "Yer sure 'bout travelin'? Ye can say no, lass."

"I'll be fine. Just got dizzy."

Beli pulled on a thick wool cloak. "I'll help ye dress and then be off."

"No, no. Don't worry," Kay forced herself out of the covers.

"Ye're quite certain?" she said as she crossed the room.

Kay nodded.

Beli hefted her baskets and bedding. When she opened the door, morning light streamed in. Hooves clattered and wagon wheels crunched in the street outside. With a noisy beat of wings, the owl landed on her substantial shoulder, then turned its lantern eyes toward Kay. "Hoo-hoo!"

"*Dawel, fy aderyn mawr*," Beli cooed to him fondly. "Quiet, ya big ol' bird." To Kay, she said, "Take good care of yerself, Kyna's cousin."

"Thank you, Beli." She suspected it might be due to her magic that Kay could even stand.

When Beli had gone, Kay worked her way across the room to her clothing and pulled on riding layers.

Baird called from outside the door, "'Tis yer royal escort."

She opened to him. Sunrays reflected off wet cobblestones, making her wince from the brightness. She'd been in the dark too long.

Their two horses stood behind Baird blowing steam and nickering, stomping hooves restlessly. Baird strapped her bags onto *Niwl y Bore*. Kay had to marvel that they were loading baggage onto horses at the door of her accommodations on a cobbled castle road.

Returning into the dim room, she checked for anything she might have missed. After all, these were Kyna's belongings. It wouldn't do to leave any behind.

Finding nothing, she set the key on the table and pulled the thick wooden door shut behind her.

Baird gave her a hand up onto the mare, and she settled her travel cape in a tent covering legs and horse. Their hoofbeats echoed off high stone walls as they descended the roads of the keep, tilt throwing her toward the horse's head. She gripped its mane to hold herself up.

Lower down was a busy morning bustle. At the final gate, they moved with a throng clustered to exit. Baird maneuvered his black stallion, *Aderyn Du*, through, and she followed. They navigated planking across deep ravines until reaching the road.

The hills were peachy with the vestiges of dawn. She spotted Beli astride a wide pony rounding a curve below them. From their vantage, they saw across the island to the narrow strip of sea between Wales and Ireland.

Baird slowed, then stopped. Kay came up beside him.

He pointed down into forest. "That be where we studied wi' the Druids."

She followed his finger, scanning for a sign. "You never mentioned."

"Well, it be a secret, now, i'n it? The Romans tried hard to get 'em out, not wantin' their troublin' influence." He said it lightly but there was flint in his voice, hinting at a dark history.

She scanned the endless view of trees.

"Ye won't see it. The Druids' temples be sacred oak groves."

"I'd love to see those," she said.

"Another time, mayhap, I'll show ye." Baird clucked at his horse and gave a gentle kick to prod him forward.

At last, they came to the cliff above the cove where they'd first arrived. Across the narrow channel, through wisps of morning mist, she caught glimpses of Wale's mainland. They descended the narrow twisting path to the beach, walking the horses, and waited for the ferryman.

Back on the mainland, towns along the coast road had

finished celebrating May Day; folk in everyday clothing were back to their usual business.

After some hours, Kay wearied and clung to the horse's neck to keep her seat.

Baird glanced at her. "Almost t' Borth. We sh'd stop fer shepherd's pie and cider."

"Can we see the yarn shop this time?" Kay had to satisfy her curiosity, to see if it looked like the one she'd gotten her first magical yarn from, behind Dragon's Lair in the 21st Century.

"We can try." Baird glanced quizzically at her.

After a time, they left the marshlands and entered the fishing village hugging the shoreline. They made their way to the squat building with slate walls and thatched roof.

The door jangled as Kay pushed it open. She stepped into the shadowed interior, holding her breath. It was identical to the low beamed shop that had magically revealed itself to her in the twenty-first century. Instead of the wizened Aelfwyn by the fire, though, a younger woman sat knitting. Was that the same gold cat, curled on the rug at her feet?

She drew in the salty scent of natural dyes from yarns of earthy hues—rust and gold and moss green—filling shelves built into all four walls.

"Hello," she said.

"Good day." The woman hurried to set her needlework aside and rise. "How can I help you?"

Baird stepped in after her. "*Ddiwrnod da*, Malit."

"Baird?" She hurried forward.

He kissed her cheek.

"Is ought wrong with Aunt?" She looked anxious.

"Nay. Ceirwyn—Kyna's cousin—be visitin' from the south. She wanted t' see Aelfwyn's shop."

Emboldened, Kay stepped to the yarns and touched them. They did not tingle with magic. So Aelfwyn had enchanted hers specially.

"I'm that glad t' be meetin' ye, Mistress Ceirwyn." Malit curtsied.

"And I you," Kay responded, pulling her hand away from a luscious mauve yarn and extending it to the woman who was, perhaps, in her thirties.

"All's well wi' Hamelyn? Duff?" Malit asked.

"All are well, gods be praised," Baird answered. He turned to Kay. "Well, is your curiosity satisfied, Dov—Ceirwyn?"

"Won't ye stop fer tea?" Malit offered.

"We won't trouble ye," Baird said, warmly.

Kay thought he had his mind on a certain pie shop.

"Give Aunt my love then," Malit said from the doorway and watched them go.

They waved back at her, then led their horses along the boardwalk. To their right, a low wall protected the town from the sea, while on their left stood a line of inns and shops.

"Aelfwyn drew me to that shop," Kay told Baird, "from my time. Or brought the shop to me."

"Did she now?" He did not seem particularly surprised.

"Yes. That's when I first obtained magical yarns for weaving. She somehow made a tunnel at the back of a fantasy shop, where no tunnel exists." She watched him, hoping he had explanations.

He reached out and stroked a strand of her hair back. "She be a bloody great spider. I don't pretend t' understand everythin' she can do, but I wouldna want t' face some o' the trickery in this world without her."

She pondered that as they continued to the far end of the frontage road. There they came to the tavern with the promised savory pie and cider.

It was late afternoon when they rode up the hills that separated Borth from Aberystwyth.

Past the abbey, *Llanbadarn Fawr*, they rode through the forest edging Kyna's road. At the house, Baird led the horses to the back while Kay climbed the front steps.

In the front room, Aelfwyn sat stitching by the fire, chatting with a friend of a similar age.

"Afternoon," Kay greeted them.

"And to you," Aelfwyn answered. She set down her handwork and introduced Seren.

She made a polite response, barely hearing the name as Kay gave Aelfwyn a kiss on the cheek and excused herself, saying she wanted to wash off road dirt. She wasn't sure how much Aelfwyn knew but when she squinted, studying Kay's face critically, Kay guessed she was aware of the abduction.

In the back hall, she started toward the bedroom but turned toward the apothecary instead. Kyna might be in there this very instant, two centuries in the future. She shivered with mixed emotions. Just in case, she sent her a mental greeting, but heard nothing back.

Through the window she watched Baird lead the horses toward their stable. He glanced over and smiled. Afraid to remain alone in the apothecary, she hurried out to help him. Taking in the distinctive smells of hay, animals and wood in the outbuilding, she watched Baird remove saddles and blankets, brush the horses, and give them hay and oats, speaking softly to them.

Together they lugged Kyna's bags to the bedroom. Her outfit lay neatly washed and folded on the bed. Tears suddenly pricked her eyes. She would soon be gone. She had only to change her clothes.

Baird saw her focus but not the emotion. "I'll let ye change," he said and left.

With some struggle, she undid the many buttons of the travel-dusted dress, then pulled off sweaty layers of under-clothing. After scrubbing her body as best she could from the basin and pitcher on the dresser, she donned her hand-woven tunic, vest, and leggings, then pulled on her boots.

In the hall, Baird waited. Slipping his arms around her, he pressed his face into the crook of her neck, and breathed. She closed her eyes. He smelled of the road—salty sea air, wood fires, horse musk. She probably smelled the same this time. He pulled back and studied her face, then put his mouth against hers, hard, lingering, hungry.

Aelfwyn's voice came through the wall, moving closer. "She needs to get back."

They broke apart guiltily as she pushed the rug divider aside and stood, hands on hips. "Come." She signaled.

Was she annoyed? It was hard to tell with the many creases in her old face and the enigmatic expression they formed.

She glanced at Baird, her heart still pounding.

His eyes met hers, heated.

"Ye're goin' to need a strengthenin' tonic for travel," the old woman said, walking ahead of her into the apothecary. "I'm goin' t' renew yer shields, now Galfride has had a taste o' yer spirit."

So, she probably did know he'd grabbed me from the castle, and more. Maybe a lot more. She perched on a stool and watched her prepare a drink that took on a strange coppery hue.

"Drink up," Aelfwyn commanded, holding it out to Kay.

She'd steeled herself for bitterness, but it was just tart, a bit citrusy.

The old woman reached her gnarled fingers and touched the silver piece with the Celtic knot that always hung around Kay's neck. She lifted and rubbed it with her finger and thumb. "This be a verra magical piece," she said. "I had Duff forge it from Welsh silver."

The story reminded her of the crystal half that Kyna had kept. A pang of loss hit her.

"This—" Aelfwyn unfolded a cloth on the workbench, "—ha' a different power." She picked up a smooth, shiny ring and held it to the light. A tiny circlet of Ing runes running around its outer edge seemed to glow. Aelfwyn took Kay's hand. The silver band fit to perfection, squeezing just enough to hug the base of her right ring finger. It frightened her, as unfamiliar energy trickled into her, up her arm and disseminated throughout her body. But a sweetness soon filled her.

Aelwyn appeared satisfied. "Aye, it be charged. Ing appears t' work well for ye—based on the dress." She gave me a meaningful look. "So, I had Duff inlay the rune 'round this."

As many times before, Kay tried to imagine Duff's great hands achieving such delicacy. If she ever returned, she must watch him work, she told herself.

"Now concentrate," Aelwyn said, briskly.

Chapter 40

In the apothecary, the tiny healer, Aelfwynn, taught Kay to draw light from the new ring and make it climb in a column that surrounded them. "Buildin' yer tree," she called it. The trunk formed, sparkling with fairy-dust-like swirling particles. As they worked, the apothecary grew pitch black around them, despite it being only dusk. The column of light that was the tree shot upward toward a star-spattered sky, as though the ceiling opened onto night.

They repeated this process over and over. Each time she challenged Kay to create the tree, a vibration started low in her belly and moved up her spine. She stood taller, held by a cord that pulled her toward the heavens, taut, at once both hot and cold. A power Kay had never known tingled in her cells.

At last, she stopped, and it was again late twilight in the herbal workroom. They hadn't lit any lamps, so she could make out only the gray shapes of tabletop and iron pots.

Aelfwynn looked her over carefully and nodded. "I think ye're ready."

"To travel to my time without Galfride snatching me?" Kay asked. She could not tell if this new power entailed a strong enough shielding to prevent that.

"Aye. And we'll build protection about ye as ye leave us."

Kay followed her into the hall. Running her hands over her clothes, she sensed the subtle patterns in the weave, more magical than ever. She walked with a spring. In the main room, she stood, alive with energy, not knowing what to do with herself.

Aelfwyn slid a savory pie into the oven built into the stones by the fireplace.

In a short while, Hamelyn, Baird, and Duff filed in from the work sheds and they dined, squeezed in at the square table. Kyna and the girls might be sitting there at that very moment.

Still overwhelmed by new sensations, she found it hard to eat as they chattered, but nibbled to keep up strength.

When the meal was over, the five of them climbed to the tower room. She ran her hand along the curved wall, trying to ground her swirling, runaway energy, combined with a sad sense of finality—like they were sending her away for good.

Baird laid a hand on her shoulder and said quietly in her ear, "Ye'll return t' yer time, get yer strength up."

"But I don't have the crystal half. It will be harder for you to find me."

"Where be it?"

"Kyna has it."

"I'll find ye, Dove. I'll always find ye."

And in that moment, their fates seemed sealed together, no matter what.

They circled round the brazier. Heavy scented smoke from roots and resins billowed. Through the narrow window slits, Kay saw the first stars twinkling, and heard the sea, a distant rumble. Turning the other direction, she made out the standing stones, black against dark sky like spaced teeth.

Aelfwyn reached. Baird dug his golden crystal half from a pouch. Aelfwyn laid it in the iron bowl attached to chains above the brazier, and shouted a bone-chilling cry. Yellow light excaped from the center of the stone in a burst. The sound lunged into Kay's stomach with a sharp snap. The air crackled. Her emerging powers zinged and the ring tied to her spirit as one fine whole.

Confusion, protest, and acceptance warred in her. She glanced across the circle at Hamelyn—Galfride's biological son—and searched his face for any trace of the treacherous mage. She did see similarities, in their coloring and features—a dark cast and aquiline nose—yet Hamelyn exuded a gentle strength. She hoped she would always see that in him.

Duff towered on her right, his immense hand grasping hers. Aelfwyn's bird-like claw took her other and a surge of power thrummed up her arm. The elder tilted her head to Kay, her all-seeing eyes set into her dried-apple face, and intoned, "Bring forth yer oak, *Derwydd*."

The word meant "oak-seer". She nearly shook with the honor and momentous responsibility of being called a seer.

The other four trained their eyes on her. Even in their midst, Kay stood alone drawing the column. Electricity shot through her veins, starting in her toes and climbing, the strength of a mighty oak growing within her. Her ring glowed. Rays of light shot from each tiny Ing rune. As she drew the power into a column, she heard chanting as if from a distance.

She needed no chant. She *was* the chant. She was the fire, the light, the tree, the pillar that filled the tower and grew, then shot into the night sky, iridescent, incandescent, seeming to make the tower roof disappear. She thrilled, rising up the column, indomitable, ecstatic in the light that was her.

The chanting continued somewhere far below as she rose above the tower and shot up into the night sky. There was a brief instant when she hung weightless in blackness, the column of light gone from around her.

Abruptly, elation left as she struggled for oxygen. She could not find herself, only pitch-darkness among the stars. Her arms were pinned to her sides. All around, pressure pushed in. She could draw no breath.

This was worse than outer space. Not only could Kay not breathe, but her limbs could not move. She fought panic, grasping for answers. Finally, she forced herself to calm by concentrating on details.

Cool wetness pressed against her skin. Even without breathing, She took in the scent of green living surfaces. Knowing came in her cells. She did not need to breathe. *I am receiving oxygen*. The scent of oak filled her. *I'm inside a tree*. With this realization, anxiety rose, but swiftly abated. *I am one with the tree*. She detected the veins carrying sap, the sinews of the trunk striating around her. I *breathe as tree*. Then, with a new sense of creating the truth she needed, she thought, *I am a moving mist. I am neither* of *the tree nor foreign to it*.

Like a cloud, Kay drifted.

Cool air struck her skin, slipped up her sleeves, ruffled her pants. Her eyelids stuck, with sap. She tugged them open, rubbing, to reveal the yard where she'd first met Baird. Standing outside the sturdy oak, she knew the tree's presence as she'd never sensed it before, as partner, ensouled.

Slowly she made the transition from tree-sense to human. Gravity arrived under her feet. Mundane thoughts asserted themselves.

Kay looked around. The yard appeared unchanged. The dilapidated old house still stood in shambles, shadowed at the back of the lot, dark windows obscured by cobwebs. The weedy lawn, however, glimmered now, as if coated in glass. Tiny rainbows shivered over its surface.

Why had Aelfwyn sent her into a tree? Perhaps to avoid Galfride's grasp. Had it provided safety? Still, she might have warned her.

She entertained resentment briefly, but that was not worthy of her new powers. Every living thing spoke to her as she stood under the oak's leafy canopy, breathing deep, utterly new. Taut as a deer poised to leap, she rose onto the balls of her feet, animal-strength coursing through her. The magic in the stitches of her boots had its own decipherable spirit that told her Boldo had made the boots himself. Boldo's spirit seemed present in them. *Hello*, she thought to him.

Greetings, Oak Traveler, he thought back.

She held her breath, stunned. Had she contacted the Traveler across the millennia? Hearing no more thoughts from him, she sent him a mental kiss on the cheek and stepped toward the street, her boots crunching dry grass. She looked left and right, taking in the neighborhood, which was bathed in a pink glow. Sunset or sunrise?

Sunset, she thought, as a car pulled up in front of a house across the street and a weary-looking woman tugged out groceries. She bumped the door shut with her hip and strode up her front walk.

A hummingbird darted over Kay's head. She captured a fleeting communication from it, of its destination, what it smelled, how it tasted the air.

With an awed sigh, she started down the sidewalk, knowing her boots were carrying her toward the community gardens instead of home.

In several blocks, she arrived at the lush plots and skirted the northeast quadrant.

"Kay!" someone shouted.

Searching the tops of corn stalks and bean teepees, she spotted Jarl waving.

"Hey," she shouted and turned in at the closest path.

"Checking to see what's grown since noon?" Jarl teased as she drew near.

She stopped and stared at him. *Since noon? Could that be?* She had to quickly account for her day in this time, while her five days in the ancient world seemed far more clear and vivid. She'd been here at the gardens at noon, then had lunch with Jarl at Headlands.

Who could fathom it?

"Are you okay?" Jarl set down his rake and moved toward the entrance to his garden.

She searched for her voice. "Yes. I was...astounded by the size of your corn stalks."

Jarl seemed to search for a response, ducking his head with an amused smile.

She entered their garden. The scent of honeysuckle met her. Extra sensory awareness clung to her. Jarl exuded health. She detected miniscule clumps of soil adhering to his aquamarine thermal shirt. His presence, so solid, made her want to hug him, to experience the grounding contact of another human being. But she'd seen him at noon, in this time. He had no idea how far she'd traveled, how much she'd been through.

Instead, she looked around, breathing deep, taking in the aliveness of the garden. Tiki lamps glowed and wavered in the corners of the plot so that her friends could work past twilight.

Each stem and leaf appeared articulated, vibrant with verdant hues.

Joaquin greeted her from where he knelt, tying up a tomato branch.

She grinned. "Hey, there."

"Hi, Kay," Joaquin said, concentrating.

The electricity in her dissipated, cascading toward jittery nerves. She grasped the entrance frame. Jarl laid a warm hand on her shoulder, head tilted, brow lifted.

She gave him a crooked smile and patted him reassuringly. "You guys take community gardening to a whole new level." With a slow inbreath, she took in the scents of abundant growth.

"We harvested extra chard and arugula. Want some?" Joaquin crossed the plot, holding out a pile of immense leaves, thick and shiny.

"Gorgeous." She pressed them to her face.

"Hope we got all the earwigs off." Joaquin shot Jarl a glance, mischief in his dark, almond eyes.

She brushed her cheeks, laughing, and sat on the bench Joaquin had crafted in the shape of a seal, to examine the thick leaves for bugs.

Jarl dropped beside her. "You seem different, Kay." He rested one elbow on his leg, head cocked to study her.

"How?" she asked, truly curious.

"Mm." He glanced to Joaquin for help.

Joaquin thought, then said, "Kind of...glowing?"

"Have you taken up marathon running? Or had an incredible massage?" Jarl suggested.

"You do kind of have that endorphin-rush look." Joaquin nodded sagely.

"Maybe more ethereal than that, though. Kind of...I'm not quite here."

Jarl still squinted at her.

It was hard to tell if he liked her new appearance or feared it. "Well, I have been practicing a type of active imagination, actually." She came up with the answer on the fly. It seemed to fit her creation of a tree that could bring her all the way from a thousand years ago to now, and float through the tree when she got here. "Sort of...shamanic. Maybe that's it." It surprised her to be able to tell the exact truth, while telling none of it.

"Wow, you have to teach us!" Joaquin said.

"It appears...gratifying," Jarl agreed. "Need a lift home? We're going to finish here soon."

Not all the electricity had left her. She bounded to her feet. "Oh, no thanks. I'm going to check my plot and grab a few things to go with your magnificent chard, for stew, I think." Exiting their plot, she held the bunch up high and fanned a goodbye.

"See ya," Jarl called, watching her leave.

She glided along the garden path, sensing pure oneness with movement with the currents of air, with the life growing around her. Suddenly she knew an infinite intertwining beyond her time, connecting the dimensions of the millennia. It seemed tied to the stitches in her boots as she walked, in her ring, and in the woven fabrics she wore. She thought she might sense a tentative tendril of mind-speak with Baird across time. Powers were growing in her. She would protect her children, if it took learning to see the web of time as Aelfwyn saw it.

What else might she see?

Marie Judson is an avid fantasy and sci-fi reader. She's been an editor, coffee roaster, and college professor. She lives on the wild coast of Northern California.

Visit her blog and sign up for her newsletter:
www.mariejudson.com

www.ingramcontent.com/pod-product-compliance
Lightning Source LLC
Chambersburg PA
CBHW030223120726
47903CB00005B/1340